FORBIDDEN

A Novel Set in Medieval England

C. DE MELO

Copyright 2003 C. De Melo
www.cdemelo.com
All Rights Reserved
ISBN-13: 978-1544065083
ISBN-10: 1544065086

DEDICATION

Thank you, D.

To those who have fallen in battle...

To those who have fought in battle...

To the spouses and families of these brave warriors...

This book was written for you.

Chapter 1
Kent, England
1127

"Whoa, girl, easy now," Lady Beatrice Fitzwilliam cooed in her horse's ear.

The white mare halted in a cloud of dust outside the imposing Romanesque cathedral. Despite her anxiety, Beatrice admired the elongated figures of Jesus, Mary, and Joseph carved into the stone lintel.

Leading the horse toward a sprawling elm tree, she dismounted and tethered the animal. The hot breath of the mare merged with her own in the cold night air, forming a delicate swirl of white vapor.

It was unwise to travel alone at night, especially in her condition, but her husband's reputation—and ultimately her family's safety—depended on this encounter. Placing both hands on her swollen belly, she took a deep breath and slowly ascended the stairs. Her heartbeat was so fierce that her temples throbbed with each step.

The heavy oak door creaked open slowly, mimicking the sound of an old woman's tired sigh. It took her eyes a moment to adjust to the dimness of the church's interior. Toward the eastern end of the building, several candles burned on the high altar.

Clutching her expensive wool cloak around her shoulders, Beatrice nuzzled her chin into the warm fur lining and walked down the long nave toward the chancel. Moonlight illuminated a small chapel, affording her a brief glimpse of a Byzantine mosaic depicting the *Ascension of Christ*. She crossed herself when she finally entered the pool of candlelight and sank to her knees before the altar. Tilting her head back, she raised her eyes to the crucified Christ figure hanging above the communion table. Blood poured from the crown of thorns on his head, and flowed onto his hollow cheeks. Christ's mouth was set in a grim line, his sad eyes reflecting the terrible suffering of humanity.

Beatrice shuddered and tore her gaze away. After a few moments she felt the heat of Edward's stare; she knew he watched silently from the shadows. She was reminded of her cat and the manner in which it stalked its prey. There was always that tense moment before it pounced and killed an unsuspecting mouse with feline precision. She imagined Edward's body coiled and rigid, his gray eyes with their sharply defined pupils narrowed into two slits, waiting...

Closing her eyes, she fought the urge to run out of the church and waited for him to show himself.

Satisfied that he had tortured Beatrice enough, Edward emerged from the darkness to stand before her in a finely cut robe of black brocade lined with costly miniver. Holy men were strongly urged to avoid such worldly luxuries, but her brother-in-law thought himself immune to monastic rules. As the second son of a powerful noble family, the strict laws of primogeniture had forced him to procure a living by means of the Church. Although he was only the Prior of Canterbury, his clothing and lifestyle were as luxuriant as the bishop's. Beatrice focused her gaze on the gold embroidery adorning the hem of his garment and wondered if Jesus had ever owned anything so fine.

"Beatrice, dear *sister*," he whispered into the silence.

Edward used the term 'sister' as a mere formality, for what he felt for her was far from fraternal. He stared down at her golden hair, which was parted in the center and fell in two long braids, before dropping his gaze to the bodice of her azure silk gown. The fullness of her young breasts, accentuated by the low neckline, caused a stirring in his loins. Despite being heavy with child, Beatrice was desirable. How he envied his older brother, Richard.

Resisting the temptation to ravage her right then and there, he cleared his throat and put out his hand. "Rise, my child."

She accepted his hand and stood, facing him. "My lord.

Thank you for seeing me, Edward."

He studied her face, taking in the sharp, delicate features. "How fares my brother?"

"He is the very reason why I asked to see you."

"It's cold here. My private chamber is warm and comfortable. Come."

She obediently followed him around the altar and down a narrow passageway lit by torches. They went outside through a side door that led to the cloister garden, then through another door. Nothing stirred in the quiet night as they headed toward a private wing reserved for the prior's cell.

Edward stopped. "Here we are." After opening the door, he stood aside for Beatrice to enter. When she hesitated, he placed his hand on the small of her back and gave her a slight push.

His living quarters were not only spacious, but richly furnished with exquisite tapestries, several warm fur skins, and a sturdy desk containing a pile of expensive manuscripts, inkwells, and goose quills. The high-backed chair by the desk boasted two red velvet cushions, and a stylus lay across a hornbook exposing a few Latin verses of the Paternoster. A patterned velvet curtain separated the two rooms. The luxuriant fabric was slightly pulled to one side by a golden rope, allowing a glimpse of a silk-canopied bed.

"I know it's not as grand as what you or I are accustomed to, but my father's death put an end to *that*," Edward commented derisively.

"On the contrary, my lord. Your rooms are quite grand." No expense was spared to furnish the rooms, and she wondered what the other monks thought of their prior's flagrant hypocrisy.

He walked to a table containing a silver decanter of wine and proceeded to pour the garnet liquid into two silver chalices. "Here, this will warm you."

She accepted the chalice. "Thank you."

Edward stirred the embers within the hearth, then motioned for her to sit by the small fire. "Why did you request to meet with me?"

Beatrice had rehearsed her speech all afternoon, but now she was at a loss for words. How could she ask for his help without her husband's knowledge?

Edward found her discomfort amusing and had to stifle the urge to smile.

"I came to ask for your help," she finally admitted.

He regarded her for a moment as he ran his index finger along the rim of his chalice. "In what way do you require my help?"

She hesitated, unsure of how to proceed. He took a long sip of wine and watched with anticipation as she, too, placed the chalice to her lips. Her full mouth was sensuous and he suddenly wanted to kiss and bite her lips. Beatrice caught his lustful stare and averted her eyes. He and Richard were so alike in appearance and stature that it was unnerving—especially their steely, gray eyes. The only difference between the two men was that Richard's hair and complexion were dark, whereas Edward was fair to the point of appearing angelic.

"Well?" he prompted.

"Richard is in trouble," she replied breathlessly.

"In *trouble*? How so?" Rather than answer the question, her face turned pale, prompting him to inquire, "Are you feeling unwell, Beatrice?"

"Forgive me, my lord. As you can see, I'm so close to my time…"

Edward sat on the edge of his seat. He was neither prepared nor inclined to help his sister-in-law give birth at such an ungodly hour. He was relieved when she took a long sip of wine and the color returned to her cheeks.

Beatrice cleared her throat and said, "Richard has enemies who wish to destroy him."

"My lady, we *all* have enemies who wish to destroy us. The richer and more powerful the noble, the greater the chance of envy and strife. The feudal lords of Europe are constantly in battle."

"It's more than that, Edward. There's talk of Richard being guilty of treason. If this kind of malicious gossip reaches the king's ears, there's no telling what can happen."

"This is indeed serious, my lady. I hope for Richard's sake that these accusations are untrue."

"Of course they're untrue! These envious and greedy lords are spreading lies."

"What can I do? I can't stop wagging tongues."

"You're powerful," she replied, leaning forward and placing a hand on his forearm.

Edward glanced down at her hand, relishing the warmth of her touch. "Go on."

She retracted her hand and blushed. "You can silence the mouths of those seeking to ruin your brother's reputation. The Bible openly condemns crooked speech and deceitfulness."

He rubbed his chin pensively. "Do you suppose Richard would help me if I were in his predicament?"

"Despite the rivalry between you two, I know he would help his own flesh and blood." In reality, she was unsure.

"Humph," he snorted, crossing his arms.

"Edward—"

He raised his hand to silence her. "You and your husband do not speak to me for months…"

"Please—"

"And now you seek me out in the middle of the night to ask for my help?"

"He's your *brother*. Please, my lord, I'm begging you. I'll do anything for the safety and well-being of my husband—even at a great risk to myself."

He looked at her pointedly. "Richard doesn't know you're here."

"No."

"He would be furious if he knew." He smiled but the gesture lacked mirth. "He would probably have you flogged." When Beatrice's eyes filled with tears, he added, "I know very well how stubborn and proud he is."

"And jealous," she added.

"Ah, yes, perhaps the most jealous man in England. You must love him a great deal to risk so much."

"I do."

Her honest proclamation of love annoyed him.

"Say that you'll help me," she pleaded.

"And keep your meeting with me a secret?"

"That, too."

Edward stared at her for a long time. "If the rumors are indeed lies, I'll dispel them. If not, be warned—I don't condone acts of treason against our monarch."

"You can rest assured that Richard is innocent. I give you my word."

"I believe you, Beatrice." He stood from his chair, indicating that their meeting was over. "Richard would be wise to tread cautiously."

Beatrice rose to her feet and pulled the hood of her cloak over her head. She looked so young and fragile in that moment that he couldn't resist touching her face.

Caressing her soft cheek, he whispered, "May the Lord watch over you."

They exchanged a brief look before she lowered her eyes and left the room. He stood in the doorway watching her retreating form until she turned the corner and was out of sight. He closed the door, refilled his chalice, and paced the floor.

A satisfied grin spread across Edward's face for he knew that Richard lurked outside. After having received Beatrice's message that morning, he had dispatched an anonymous message of his own to his brother.

The stage is set perfectly, he mused.

It had been easy to plant the seeds of doubt into the minds of a few greedy lords. Those seeds were now giving fruit as the doubts turned to suspicion, which encouraged dangerous gossip that could lead to damning accusations. The fact that Beatrice had come directly and unwittingly to the source of her woes was an extra delight he had not anticipated.

Edward caught his reflection in the polished looking glass. Was he evil for behaving so despicably? *No*, his reflection silently replied. It wasn't fair that his older brother had everything handed to him: lands, money, title, castles, and the prestige that came with being firstborn. Richard even got Beatrice, too—the only woman Edward had ever loved. The laws of primogeniture were cruel, and the resentment he fostered toward his brother resided within him like a malignancy.

***

Lord Richard Fitzwilliam, Earl of Kent, crept from behind the elm's massive trunk to witness his wife's hasty retreat. Had he not seen Beatrice with his own eyes, he would never have believed the anonymous message slipped under his door stating that his wife would betray him that night.

"Damn you to hell, Edward," Richard cursed under his breath. "And damn her, too."

A door within the cloister wall opened and he receded into the leafy shadows just as Edward walked out and stretched lazily. Richard's eyes narrowed in loathing as his vivid imagination conjured lustful images of his wife and his brother tangled in bedsheets. A low growl lay at the base of his throat as his hand involuntarily wrapped itself around the hilt of his sword.

Richard debated whether to confront his brother, but then decided against it. His experience in battle taught him that it was always better to wait for the right moment to strike.

You shall pay dearly, brother…and so shall she.

Chapter 2

"Push!"

"*Sweet Jesus…*"

A moment elapsed before the order came again, this time with urgency. "Push, my lady! Push *hard*!"

Beatrice's face turned crimson as she followed the old midwife's instructions and pushed with all her might. A cool, wet cloth was immediately applied to her brow by one of the servants. The stifling heat inside the bedchamber made it difficult to breathe.

"Gretta…water," Beatrice whispered to her maid.

The girl pushed back a limp strand of flaxen hair that had fallen across her mistress's cheek before going to the brown earthenware pitcher on the table. One of the older female servants added feverfew to the raging fire in the hearth. Within minutes, a heady scent permeated the room, making Beatrice nauseous. The herb was often used in aiding childbirth, but she disliked its strong scent. She prayed silently to the Virgin Mary as she gasped for air and prepared for the next push.

Gretta returned with the water and placed the cup to Beatrice's dry lips. It was cool and offered small comfort.

"I see the head, my lady! Push!" cried the ancient crone while reaching down with both hands to help the infant out. "Quick, girl, fetch me a clean cloth!"

Gretta obeyed the command as Beatrice struggled to lift herself up onto her elbows. If the baby didn't come out soon, she would surely die from exhaustion. The birth of her first son, Robert, wasn't half as difficult as this one was proving to be. Her thoughts were slowly ebbing into darkness and she began to feel drowsy.

"My lady, 'tis no time for rest!" cried the midwife.

Beatrice pushed until she could push no more, then fell back hard upon the bed. There was a brief silence, then one of the servants gasped in delight. A moment later, the infant's cry filled the room.

The brown, wrinkled face of the midwife appeared within Beatrice's line of vision. "Another boy, my lady!"

A warm little bundle wrapped in clean linen was placed in Beatrice's arms. She looked at her son for the first time and a smile lit her face. "How precious you are," she whispered before kissing his soft, pink cheek.

Unlike her other son, who had inherited her husband's dark hair, the baby's silky hair was as fair as her own. He had Richard's gray eyes, however.

"Congratulations, my lady," Gretta said, sporting an ear-to-ear grin. "He's a fine boy."

It wasn't long before all the female servants were gathered around the bed fussing over the child. The longer Beatrice gazed upon him, the more her heart swelled with love. She never wanted to let him go—not even when the wet nurse came to feed him. After reluctantly handing her son over to the buxom woman, she reclined and watched him suckle hungrily upon the woman's breast.

"A healthy appetite for such a wee babe," exclaimed the surprised wet nurse.

The woman looked at her mistress and smiled. Beatrice politely returned the gesture then closed her eyes. Spent from exhaustion, she soon fell asleep.

***

"Felicitations, my lord," Gretta said.

Richard stopped pacing and turned at the sound of Gretta's voice. "Is it over?"

"Yes. You have a fine and healthy son."

"My wife?"

"Her ladyship is resting."

"Where is the boy?"

Gretta eyed him warily. "With the wet nurse, feeding."

Richard mumbled something incoherent and waived the woman away. *A fine and healthy son…*

He sought the privacy of his bedchamber and poured himself

some wine. It wouldn't be easy to carry out his plan, and he prayed to God for courage.

***

Beatrice was awakened by the shrill cries of her newborn son. She opened her eyes to see Richard attempting to pry the infant from the wet nurse's arms. Mustering her strength, Beatrice threw off the covers and crossed the cold stone floor in her bare feet.

Taking her son from the wet nurse, she inquired, "What's wrong with you, Richard? You'll frighten the poor child."

Richard's face darkened with rage as he stared at the baby's downy blonde hair. It was the same color as Edward's. "Give him to me."

"What?"

He sighed impatiently. "I don't wish to make this more difficult than it already is. Give me the child now."

Confused, she backed away from him. "My darling, of course you can see your son. Why are you so angry?"

Eyeing her coldly, he sneered. "My son, eh?"

A cold chill settled upon her bones. Something wasn't right. "What's this all about?"

"Hand him over, Beatrice."

"I will not!"

"You'll do as you're told this instant."

Smelling the wine on his breath, she shielded the baby from him. "Not until you tell me what madness has taken possession of you."

Richard took a step forward and smacked his wife across the face. More offended than hurt, she sank to her knees, still clutching the infant to her chest. A crimson colored welt in the shape of her husband's fingers bloomed on her cheek.

"I will raise no bastards under my roof," he said icily.

"*Bastard*?" she repeated, stunned. "This is your son!"

"Liar!"

"I swear to you, this is your flesh and blood," she whispered softly. "I have *never* been unfaithful to you."

The love Richard bore for his wife was so great, it verged on hatred. He deeply resented the fact that Beatrice possessed such tremendous influence over his emotions. Even now, as she knelt on the floor clutching the infant bastard, his heart ached with longing. Her big blue eyes flooded with tears and her long, golden hair fell loosely over her shoulders. The low neckline of her dressing gown exposed the fullness of her breasts, which were heaving gently with every breath she took...

God damn the woman.

Richard averted his eyes in order to harden his resolve and resist temptation. He snatched the child out of her arms and quickly backed away.

Scrambling to her feet, she demanded, "Dear God, Richard! What do you intend to do?"

When he said nothing, she sprang to her feet and lunged at him. Beating him with her fists, she cursed him. Richard called out to his knights and two men ran in to restrain their lady by force.

Beatrice's female servants were scattered about the room, appalled, watching the scene in silence. They had witnessed many an argument between their lord and lady—especially Gretta, who was never far from her mistress's side. This outburst, however, was uglier than anything they had ever seen before. They knew their lord was a jealous and possessive man, but the last few months had been particularly grievous for his wife.

Richard held the infant at arm's length, regarding him with a look of distaste before meeting his wife's desperate stare. "As punishment for your unfaithfulness, you'll never again set eyes upon this child."

His words drew shocked reactions from everyone in the room. Accusing a noble wife of adultery before witnesses was no trivial matter.

"No!" Beatrice cried. "I'm innocent!"

The sheer agony in her voice was so great that one of her captor's winced. Her body went limp, forcing the two knights to hold Beatrice upright in order to prevent her from falling to the ground.

She knew her husband well enough to believe he would carry out this cruel punishment. Hanging her head, she wept aloud. "I beg you, Richard, don't do this!"

Richard's heart twitched slightly, but he wasn't about to let himself be manipulated. "I won't be a cuckold who houses and feeds the fruit of his wife's adultery. I do this for the affection I still bear for you, and for the sake of our son, Robert. Another man would have you beaten before divorcing you and placing you into a convent."

The thought of spending her life in a dreary convent away from her son terrified her. Despite this, she said, "Surely Lucifer or one of his demons has taken possession of your mind, husband."

Richard raised his hand as if to strike her again, then stopped. Rumors of heresy were already circulating throughout the kingdom, and the last thing he needed was to be accused of being possessed by the Devil.

"Don't ever utter such a vile thing in my presence, woman," he warned. "You're fortunate they don't burn adulteresses on the stake."

"How can you accuse your own wife of such treachery? *Look* at the baby," she implored. "Any fool can see he's yours. He even has your eyes."

Unimpressed by her words, he turned on his heel and walked toward the door.

Beatrice's mind raced frantically as she tried to find reasons to stall him. "Stop! Please…at least allow me to give him something. A gift from his mother. After all, he is innocent of sin."

Richard stared at her for a moment, contemplating her request. He nodded to the knights, who in turn slackened their hold on Beatrice. Reaching up behind her neck, she undid the clasp of the heavy gold chain she always wore. Attached to it was a large gold crucifix adorned with rubies of great value. The heirloom had been passed down from mother to daughter for generations.

"Here," she said, extending her hand toward him. "Promise

me that wherever you take him, he shall have this as a reminder of me." Richard said nothing. "Please," she urged, taking a step closer.

He snatched the crucifix. "I promise."

Beatrice took advantage of the knights' slackened hold and lurched forward in a desperate, futile attempt to reclaim her son.

Frustrated by her thwarted effort, she stopped crying and gave her husband a look so venomous it surprised him. "God will punish you someday for what you're doing, Richard. And if He doesn't, *I* will."

The words reverberated throughout the room and hung heavily in the air as though she had uttered a powerful curse. All eyes turned to Richard in anticipation of what he would do.

Never before had Beatrice dared to speak to him with such blatant disrespect, let alone threaten him before several witnesses. He found her words unnerving, and for the first time since their marriage, he saw something in her eyes that actually frightened him. "God has already punished me, my lady, by making me love you the way I do," he said quietly before placing the chain around the infant's neck and stalking out of the room.

Chapter 3
Lewes, England

Every time the infant shifted within the crude basket, the rough burlap binding scratched his tender skin. Outside, the birth of dawn brought forth the first fragile rays of sunlight from behind the distant hills. Meanwhile, a thick fog wound its way throughout the empty courtyard of the monastery like a stealthy serpent. The church doors loomed high above the basket, and the monks attending Lauds within the sacred walls were completely oblivious to the tiny intruder outside. The infant grew restless with each passing minute, and as the hunger pangs began to gnaw at his tiny stomach, he let out a thin wail that was swallowed by the fog.

***

"Careful not to spill the water, Gwen."

Agnes McFay handed her three-year-old daughter a rough wooden bucket half filled with water, making sure it wasn't too heavy for the child to carry. The ancient well stood on a grassy knoll east of the monastery, allowing her a clear view of the horizon and spectacular sunrise. She pulled the fresh morning air into her lungs and closed her eyes for a brief moment.

"*Tom…*"

"What did you say, Mama?"

Not a day passed that Agnes didn't think of her late husband, Thomas. Pushing a lock of curly auburn hair from her eyes, she forced herself to appear cheerful. "Nothing. Go on and tell Simon I'll be along shortly."

"Yes, Mama," she said, running down the hill.

"Slow down child, lest you fall and hurt yourself!"

The little girl slowed her pace to a skip. Gwen had inherited Tom's black hair and vivid blue eyes; both were a constant reminder of the man she had loved and lost.

Destitute and with a small child to raise, Agnes was grateful when Tom's cousin, Simon, arranged for her to work alongside him at the St. John's Cluniac monastery in Lewes. Prior to her arrival six months ago, the only thing she knew about the Cluniac Order was that it was founded in Cluny. She was surprised to learn that, unlike the original Benedictine monks who believed in hard labor through agriculture, the Cluniac monks paid people to toil their land. Since their liturgical regime was one of the strictest in Europe, the monks spent several hours of their day in church. Hiring lay servants to cook, clean, and care for their needs allowed these holy men more time for education, devotion, and meditation.

Simon had worked as the monastery's kitchen knave for years. His direct supervisor was the cellarer, an educated monk named Linus who preferred to spend his time in the library. The cellarer agreed to hire Agnes under the condition that the official consent be obtained from the prior, Bartholomew.

The prior was an easygoing and compassionate man who respected his vow of chastity and avoided women, but he didn't hate the female sex. It was thanks to his balanced view of the Scriptures that Agnes and Gwen found their place at St. John's.

A raven swooped down and landed on the edge of the well, interrupting her thoughts. The service of Lauds was held at five o'clock each morning, which was followed by Prime about an hour later. The time in between was when the monks broke their fasts. She would have to hurry if she was going to help Simon prepare the morning pottage.

***

When Gwen reached the priory gates leading into the courtyard, she headed for the brick buildings behind the monastery where the kitchen was located. Hearing a strange sound, she stopped and squinted, but the remains of the morning fog made it difficult to see clearly. Her mother had told her several times to stay away from the monks and from the church, so she usually remained within the confines of the kitchen, the garden, and the dairy. She turned away and continued toward the kitchen when she heard the sound again.

Filled with curiosity, she placed the bucket on the ground

and ran toward the church. She could hear the monks chanting inside as she climbed the steps toward the basket. Something inside moved and mewled, and she imagined a furry little kitten. When she pulled back the burlap, she was surprised to see a baby.

Carefully, she dragged the basket down the stairs and through the courtyard. The church doors opened and the monks headed to the refectory for their morning meal, except for Prior Bartholomew, who walked in the opposite direction toward his chamber. She followed him into the forbidden cloister garden, then down a stone hallway before stopping at a withered door.

Gwen pounded on the faded wooden door. "Prior Bartholomew, I have something to show you!"

Bartholomew opened the door and peered down at her with a puzzled expression. "What are you doing here, Gwen? You know you're not supposed to enter the cloister garden."

She pointed to the basket. "I found a baby!"

The prior's eyes were a mixture of surprise and softness as he took the baby out of the basket and held him. The infant prattled and reached out to pull on Bartholomew's ear.

"Ho, now!" he said with a chuckle while easing the infant's hand away. "That's quite a strong grip for one so tiny." He looked to Gwen. "Where's your mother?"

"At the well."

"Where was he?"

"On the church steps. Can the baby be my brother since I don't have one?"

The prior hesitated. *What harm could come of it?* "I suppose so, at least until his mother returns."

Gwen scrunched up her little face. "Do you think she'll come back?"

"I think so."

Throughout the years a few ruined maids from the village had left the evidence of their sin on the monastery's doorstep, but the combination of maternal instinct and guilt always compelled them to return.

Just once, he wished they wouldn't…

He chastised himself for the selfish thought. The possibility of ever being a fleshly father was sacrificed forever when he swore an oath of allegiance to the Abbey of Cluny. For almost thirty years he had faithfully kept his vow of celibacy, but the strong paternal desire had always been present.

"Does the baby have a name?" Gwen inquired, cutting into his thoughts.

"I don't know."

Her little brow creased as she contemplated various names. "I want to name him Nicodemus!"

"Nicodemus?"

"Like the *farsay* in the Bible."

"*Pharisee*," he corrected with a smile.

Gwen's intelligence and memory never ceased to amaze him. He had told the girl the Biblical account of the Jewish Pharisee, Nicodemus, several weeks ago when he came across her playing outside by the dairy.

"Very well, our little friend will be named after a wise and faithful man. Nicodemus is a rather long name for one so small, don't you think? Perhaps Nick would be a better choice." As an afterthought, the prior added, "Nick St. John, since he was found on our steps."

The baby let out a loud cry.

"There, there, now," the prior said as he held the child and patted his back. "He's hungry."

Nick kicked his legs and, as the fabric around him shifted, something fell to the floor. Bartholomew was shocked to see a ruby and gold crucifix attached to a heavy gold chain. Gwen picked up the exquisite piece of jewelry and held it out to him.

Bartholomew took the crucifix, then studied Nick with renewed interest. Obviously, he was no son of a peasant girl to be in possession of something so valuable.

Who are you, little one?

Bewildered, he gently placed the child back in the basket. Extracting a key from the pocket of his simple habit, he unlocked the top drawer of a nearby writing desk littered with quills, and hid the crucifix inside of it.

"Come along, Gwen," he said, picking up the basket.

Simon was busily spooning pottage into wooden bowls when Agnes entered the kitchen. "Where's Gwen?" she inquired, placing the two buckets of water she was carrying on the table.

"I thought she was with you," he replied.

"I sent her in here ahead of me. What could that girl have gotten into now?"

"You know Gwen. She probably stopped to catch a butterfly or to pick flowers."

Agnes nodded as she took her place beside Simon and helped him with the pottage. Bartholomew and Gwen entered the kitchen a moment later.

"Good morning, Prior Bartholomew," Agnes said. "I'm sorry if my child is bothering you again. Gwen, what does the Bible say about obedience to one's parents?"

"Mama, I found a baby! See?"

Surprise registered on Agnes's face when she saw the basket. She picked up the child and tenderly cradled him with maternal ease. "Where did you find him?"

"Gwen found him on the stairs of the church," Bartholomew replied. "Then she brought him to me."

Simon scratched his head. "Another foolish girl from the village, no doubt."

Bartholomew decided to keep silent about the crucifix. "After the monks have broken their fasts, I need you to go into town and find a wet nurse for Nick."

Simon and Agnes asked in unison, *"Nick?"*

"Nick St. John," Gwen said proudly.

Nick cried loudly so Agnes procured a clean piece of linen and dipped it into a ceramic cup filled with warm goat's milk. Placing the sodden fabric in the infant's mouth, she watched as he suckled hungrily.

Simon looked to Agnes and said, "We can be back before Vespers if we hurry."

"Take the babe with you, but bring him back here along with the wet nurse," Bartholomew instructed.

Simon looked askance at the prior. "Wouldn't it be better to leave the infant in the village?"

"I think it's best if we keep Nick here at St. John's. I have my reasons. Agnes, would you mind helping to care for the child?"

"It would be a pleasure," she replied, kissing the baby's cheek.

***

The Lewes Priory was not actually in Lewes itself, but in Southover by the River Ouse. The town center of Lewes was less than a mile away, and since the day was fair they set off on foot. Accompanying them was an old mule in order to bring back the wet nurse's belongings. Gwen sat atop the mule and pretended she was riding a pony. They sang songs as they walked along the path from the lush, green valley where St. John's was located to the thriving town center.

Simon eventually came to a halt by a small, dilapidated dwelling where one of the town elders lived. Knocking on the door, he called out, "Greetings, Abraham. It's me, Simon."

A gaunt old man opened the door and peered at them. "What's all this ruckus?"

Simon reached into his leather satchel and extracted a small round of cheese wrapped in a large green leaf. "For you."

"The famous goat cheese of St. John's," the old man said as he patted Simon's shoulder in appreciation of the small gift. "What can I do for you, Simon?"

"We seek a wet nurse for the child."

Abraham's eyes slid to Agnes, then the baby.

Gwen said, "Nick is my new brother!"

Abraham grunted and frowned in thought. "Sarah Gunther. Has a child about the same age. Husband abandoned her."

Simon obtained the address, then bade Abraham farewell. It didn't take long to arrive at the neat cottage where Sarah resided. Several chickens scratched and pecked outside. As they approached, a black dog ran out from behind the cottage and barked, sending the chickens scurrying in a cloud of dust and feathers.

The commotion brought a matronly woman to the door. "Who are you and what brings you to my home?"

"We come in peace from St. John's," Simon replied. "We'd like to speak with your daughter, Sarah."

The woman exited the house followed by a plump young woman toting an infant. Simon told Sarah of their plight and their need for a wet nurse.

"You should go with them," the woman said to her daughter. "This is God's doing."

Sarah quietly agreed, then handed her son to her mother while she went about the cottage gathering her few belongings.

"My name is Anne," the woman said. "Please, come in and sit while you wait for my daughter."

Simon, Agnes, and Gwen entered the cottage and settled on wooden stools.

"This will be good for Sarah," Anne said. "Ever since my good-for-nothing son-in-law left her, all she does is cry and mope around the house." She kissed the top of her grandson's head. "I'll miss my little Jeremy."

"You can visit him whenever you wish," Simon said. "And Sarah is free to visit you whenever she wishes."

Sarah came out of an antechamber with a threadbare cloak over her shoulders and a burlap sack filled with her few earthly possessions. "I'm ready."

***

Beatrice turned her head in order to achieve a better view of the hairstyle Gretta had created with her golden locks. Her lady's maid held up a polished looking glass, anxious for a reaction.

"It pleases me," Beatrice said. "Now, please fetch the essence of rose."

Gretta obeyed and applied the sweet perfume to her mistress's temples, throat, and the tops of each breast.

"How do I look?" Beatrice asked nervously.

"A vision of loveliness, my lady."

The brocade tunic worn over her fine linen chemise was deep crimson, which flaunted the creaminess of her porcelain complexion. The low-cut neckline was trimmed with gold braid and exposed a generous amount of cleavage. Gretta fastened a black leather girdle studded with gold around Beatrice's slim waist and allowed one end to dangle down the front of her skirt, in accordance with the latest fashion. Beatrice walked to the small silver chest that housed her jewels, and selected a garnet necklace.

"Perfect," said Gretta. "You're sure to bewitch him."

"Hopefully, I'll convince him, too."

Four months had passed since the birth of her son. Richard had barely spoken to her since the terrible incident, and had avoided her bed. It was a big surprise when he summoned her to sup with him tonight. Beatrice planned to use the opportunity to win back his favor. Not a day passed that she didn't think of the beautiful gray-eyed boy.

She descended the stairs and walked toward the main hall. The torches caused eerie shadows to flicker across the walls of the fortress, which was known throughout England as *Kent Castle*. The Fitzwilliam family had lived in the mighty Norman fortress for many generations; the original structure itself dated back to the days of the Holy Roman Emperor, Charlemagne.

She shivered and longed for the comfort and warmth of her cozy bedchamber. Turning down a long corridor, she heard the fire crackling in the great hearth. Feeling the blood rush from her face due to anxiety, she quickly pinched her cheeks before entering the room.

Richard sat at the head of a table laden with delicacies. Clad in a black leather tunic with matching boots, he gave off a dark, menacing air. The elaborate silver stitching on the front of the tunic was in the form of a lion on its hind legs—the Fitzwilliam family crest. Around his muscular neck was a heavy gold chain boasting a large medallion carved into the likeness of a lion's head. Her husband normally reserved such finery for meetings with other noblemen in order to flaunt his family's noble lineage, wealth, and power. Was he attempting to send her the same message?

His black hair and goatee were both clipped and neatly

groomed. The heavy steel sword, which he almost always carried on his person, was propped up against the leg of the chair in which he sat.

"My lord," Beatrice said quietly.

After staring at his wife for a long moment, Richard stood. "My lady," he said, walking toward her with the stealth of a predator.

His eyes devoured her hungrily from foot to head, and Beatrice wondered who had warmed his bed these last four months. A young maid? A hired prostitute from the town? If there were other women, Gretta had neither seen nor heard anything.

He gallantly bent over her hand, his thumb gently caressing her fingers as his lips brushed against her knuckles. Beatrice wondered why he was being overly formal as he led her to the table. A silent servant stepped from the shadows to pull out a seat for her at Richard's right hand. After his lord and lady had taken their seats, the servant proceeded to pour the wine.

Beatrice avoided her husband's smoldering gaze. With a trembling hand, she reached for her chalice and took a long sip. The deep red liquid burned in her empty stomach, but it made her relax.

Richard sensed his wife's nervousness and decided to keep her in that anxious state a bit longer. Edward was plotting against him, and he had to know if his wife was in league with his brother. Up until now, Richard's jealousy and pride had kept Beatrice at a distance, but he couldn't afford any more enemies. He needed to know the truth. *Tonight.*

Beatrice finished drinking her wine and Richard motioned to the servant in the shadows. "More wine," he said, indicating her chalice.

The servant obeyed and Beatrice realized she had better eat something quickly before she lost her wits. Richard's expression was a mixture of suspicion and desire, causing her to blush.

"You look quite fetching tonight," he said. Were it not for his pride, he would have sought her bed months ago. The last words she uttered to him on that fateful day still rang in his ears, however.

She swallowed the wine with difficulty. "Thank you."

The servant stepped forward once again at Richard's urging and filled their plates. Beatrice noticed that the meal consisted of her favorite foods—stewed hare, capons stuffed with chestnuts, and poached quail eggs. Various pies and fruits were also displayed elegantly on polished silver trays.

Finally, Richard said to the servant, "Leave us." When they were alone, he continued, "You must be curious as to why I invited you to dine with me this evening."

"I am," Beatrice replied.

"I wish to propose a truce between us."

"A truce?"

"Aye, but first I need to know something." He paused. "Are you in league with Edward?"

How many times had she sworn her faithfulness to this man? "No, my lord, I have never betrayed you."

He pounded his fist on the table's surface so hard that she jumped in her seat. "I want the truth!"

Her eyelids prickled with unshed tears. "I *am* telling you the truth. You know of my whereabouts every hour of every day. When any male enters our home, you have twice as many servants spy on me. You don't afford me any opportunity to betray you."

He frowned. "Are you implying that you would do so should the opportunity arise?"

"No! I'm only pointing out that you always know where I am and what I'm doing."

"I didn't know your whereabouts when Lord Dunn's wife summoned you in the middle of the night. You simply took flight without my permission!"

"Be reasonable, husband. Lady Anabel was in labor with her first child. The poor girl was terrified and had no female relatives to assist her during the birth. How could I refuse her plea for help? Besides, I couldn't ask your permission because you were away at Court!"

"May I remind you that you spent an entire fortnight in Lord Dunn's castle? I've seen how he looks at you."

"Lady Anabel almost died during the delivery. She was so weak. God's teeth, Richard, Lord Dunn is a valuable ally and your friend."

"I sincerely doubt you spent *all* of that time at Lady Anabel's bedside."

"Actually, you're correct. I also tended to the infant and made sure the household ran smoothly while Lady Anabel convalesced."

Richard crossed his arms and glared at her. "You always have an excuse…"

Beatrice rose so suddenly that she almost knocked over her chair. "Is this why you summoned me? To interrogate me and accuse me yet again?"

Richard also stood. "I want the truth from you. My brother is plotting against me as we speak. In fact, he's been plotting for months. The last thing I need right now is a scheming, adulterous wife!"

"How can you say such a thing?"

"Do you take me for a fool? Do you think I haven't noticed the way Edward looks at you? How his lustful eyes follow you wherever you go?"

Beatrice felt a hot tear writhe its way down her cheek. "You make it sound as if I seek his attention."

"It's not only my brother—there are other men as well. I see it happen every time you and I attend Court."

"Shall I gouge out their eyes with a dagger as I pass? I don't believe the king would appreciate such behavior."

"Don't take such a tone with me, wife."

"I'm merely attempting to reason with you. I have no control over what any man does, including your brother."

"Am I to believe you had no control when you met with him in secret? Were you forced to go out in the middle of the night?"

She gasped in surprise. "How do you know about…?"

"I know *everything*," he retorted icily.

The full weight of his words crushed down upon her like a

pile of stones. Her head began to spin as the pieces of the puzzle fell into place.

"Is that why you took my son from me? Because you thought that…that Edward and I…that we..?" she trailed off, placing her hands on the table for support.

Fearing that she was about to faint, Richard took a step closer to his wife. "I received a message during the afternoon stating that you were going to betray me that night, so I followed you."

"*You*? How?"

His mouth hardened. "*How*, you ask? With the same cunning I would follow an enemy in battle. Unseen and unheard." He paused, his eyes glittering with anger. "I saw you exiting the church with my own eyes. You met with Edward *alone*, in the middle of the night, knowing how much he desires you and despises me."

"Richard—"

"What am I supposed to think, Beatrice? How can I believe that you're telling me the truth when you say you have always been a faithful wife?"

"It's true that I met with your brother in secret." At the sight of Richard's pained, yet oddly triumphant, expression, she added, "But I did it for *you*."

He grabbed hold of her shoulders, forcing her to look up at him. "Explain yourself, woman."

"I thought Edward could stop the dangerous gossip being spread about you. He's the prior of Canterbury, after all, and you're his brother. I remember the days when you two were close."

"That was a long time ago."

"Forgive me for being hopeful."

"Naïve is more like it," he snapped. "The thought of my wife crawling to my brother and begging for his help turns my stomach."

"I fear for you and for the future of our son—*sons*," she said. "If the king pays heed to these vicious rumors, it will destroy you and our family."

Richard laughed aloud, but the sound lacked mirth. "And you believe my brother would help prevent such a tragedy from happening?" When she didn't respond, he shook his head in disgust. "Stupid woman! Edward would be thrilled to see me fall from grace."

"Do you honestly believe that?"

"He's ready to step into my shoes and take my title, my properties—and my wife."

"He can't. There is Robert—"

"Robert is still a boy and no match for my brother's cunning. If something happened to me, Robert would not stand a chance against his uncle."

"We have allies. Don't forget that you have several men in your debt."

He balled his hands into fists. "If the king ever accused me of treason, none of our allies would help us. No one would stand against the king."

She sighed, defeated. "I was only trying to help you."

"Instead, you made matters worse for me and for yourself."

She knew he was referring to the child he believed to be a bastard. "Where is my child, Richard? *Our* child?"

Richard walked toward the fire burning in the hearth. The red light and deep shadow across his face gave his profile a sinister appearance.

"Richard," she prompted.

"The boy is safe and alive."

Beatrice sobbed in relief. "Oh, thank God…"

"I'm not the monster you believe me to be," he said defensively. "I wouldn't harm a helpless baby."

"Please, my lord, let me have my son. It's been a living hell for me not knowing where he is or how he fares," she pleaded. "I've told you the truth about my meeting with Edward."

Richard's mouth hardened as he stared at the leaping orange flames. A few days after having followed his wife to her secret rendezvous with Edward, he had been summoned to Court. Edward was also present. Knowing Beatrice would soon give birth, Edward had approached Richard and indicated another pregnant noblewoman at Court. *'Look! Lady Heddington, is as big as a house! It's rumored that her husband is a cuckold. In fact, they say Lord Heddington's nephew is the father.'* At this point Edward stared directly into Richard's eyes with a smug expression, and said, *'These days a man must be absolutely certain that the seed growing inside his wife's womb comes directly from his loins. Adultery can take place so close to home—even with a family member—right under an unsuspecting husband's nose. It's bad enough being a cuckold, but to raise a bastard...'* He trailed off, laughing. Then, with a knowing smile he inquired, *'How is Beatrice, by the way?'*

Richard could still see the mockery and insinuation in Edward's eyes. He regretted not striking his brother then and there. For days afterward, Richard conjured painful images of Edward and Beatrice intimately entwined in bed. It was a scene that played itself over and over in his head—even now.

Then a new thought occurred to him. *What if his brother's tactic was to divide and conquer?* What if the gray-eyed child was truly his and Beatrice was indeed telling the truth?

He stole a glance at Beatrice, whose gaze was also directed at the flames. She was so beautiful, so sensuous; a temptation to any man—especially to Edward, who had lusted after her since they were boys. Richard could never be sure of the infant's paternity. For Robert's sake as well as his own, the child couldn't be raised under his roof.

Suddenly, he demanded, "Did you suspect that Edward was attempting to ruin me when you went to meet with him?"

Her face paled. "No."

"No?"

"I know the relationship between you and Edward has deteriorated since…"

"*Since you chose to marry me*," Richard said, finishing her sentence.

She looked away. It was true. She had never intended to come between a man and his brother.

"Do you regret the fact that he was not firstborn?" Richard demanded bitterly. "Your father would have arranged your marriage to him instead of me if that had been the case."

Sometimes her husband's jealousy offended her deeply, but she never stopped loving him. "No, Richard. I've never regretted you being the firstborn."

"Edward loved you," he pointed out. "He still does."

"I know."

"If I ever discover that you're helping him to plot against me—"

"I would never do such a thing! Edward once loved you, too. He looked up to you as his older brother."

"I've already told you. Those days are long gone."

"I met Edward in secret because I knew how angry you'd be if you knew I was seeking his help. I had no idea he was behind anything…I didn't think him capable of such treachery. I would never betray you like that."

"Oh? How would you betray me, then?"

"How you love to twist my words, Richard. I would not betray you at all."

"The thought has never crossed your mind?"

"Never." When he cocked his eyebrow slightly, she added, "I swear on my mother's soul."

Richard stared long and hard at his wife. He was still uncertain of her marital fidelity, but he was certain that she was not plotting with Edward. His instincts would have warned him otherwise, and his spies would already have reported any suspicious behavior.

"I believe that you're not in league with Edward," he finally conceded.

"Thank the Virgin," she said, crossing herself.

"As for the other matter…I'm willing to overlook your indiscretion for the sake of our son, Robert, and my fondness for you."

"Richard, I—"

He cut her off, his face stern. "Don't push me. Many a noblewoman in your predicament has found herself out in the cold or forced to spend the rest of her days in a convent. Do I make myself clear?"

"Yes."

After a moment he stepped away from the hearth and reached for her hand. "I miss you, Beatrice," he confessed. "My bed is cold."

"As is mine, my lord," she replied dutifully.

Taking hold of her chin, he greedily plundered her mouth. Her body naturally responded to the kiss as his hand caressed her face and slid down to take gentle possession of her throat. In spite of his suspicion, he could not deny the passion he felt for this woman.

"Please let me see my son, Richard," she whispered between his kisses.

Turning his face away, he cursed under his breath and slackened his hold on her at once.

Undeterred, she prompted, "What can I do to prove to you that he's yours?"

"You ignore my threat and try my patience, Beatrice," he said before striding out of the main hall.

Filled with unsatisfied lust and rage, Richard stormed into the kitchen. His eyes fell on a flaxen-haired girl, and with a toss of his head, he indicated that she should follow him. The girl quickly wiped her hands with a cloth and rushed out of the kitchen with the eyes of the older women burning into her back.

The young scullery maid practically ran to keep up with Richard's long strides as he headed for the privacy of his study. His desire and love for Beatrice had prevented him from satisfying his lust with whores, but every man had a limit and today he had surpassed his. Opening the door, he waited for the girl to step inside before locking it behind her. She stood in the center of the room as he took in her pale skin, full mouth, and freckles. Her eyes were the color of honey and fringed with blonde lashes.

"Come here," he ordered. "How old are you?"

"Fifteen, my lord."

Without another word, he picked her up and set her down on a sturdy desk before untying the laces that kept the top of her linen shirt modestly closed. Unsure of what to do or where to look, the girl kept her eyes focused on the tapestry behind him. He pushed the shirt open, revealing a pair of plump breasts with tiny pink nipples. She gasped when he cupped one of milky orbs with his hand.

"Have you ever been with a man?" he demanded.

The girl nodded. Had she been a virgin, would he have stopped? Instead of pondering this question, Richard's other hand slipped under the girl's skirt and he hardened with lust. Grasping her thigh, he buried his face in the warmth of her neck. Her hair smelled of smoke and freshly baked bread; comforting scents.

Beatrice's face crept into his thoughts and he froze.

"God's teeth!" he cried.

"My lord?"

He turned his face away. "Cover yourself."

As the girl slid off the desk and quickly began to lace up her shirt, Richard reached into his purse and procured a coin. "Tell no one what has happened here, do you hear me? Not a soul." The girl nodded, her eyes wide. He continued, "If anyone asks, tell them I sent you on an errand to buy cherries—or whatever bloody berries you can find at the market—for my wife. Keep the remainder as payment for your troubles."

The girl's fingers curled around the money. "Now I believe the rumors, my lord."

Richard frowned. "What rumors?"

"Forgive me, I—"

"What rumors?" he demanded impatiently.

"That you're hopelessly in love with your beautiful lady wife," she replied sheepishly.

He grimaced. "Well, for once the rumors are true." The girl wrung her hands, watching him. "What are you looking at? Go!"

She scurried off and he sighed tiredly. Beatrice had cast a spell on him—he was sure of it.

***

In the safety and comfort of her bedchamber, Beatrice poured her heart out to the only person she was allowed to befriend—her lady's maid. "He threatened me, Gretta. I fear he'll soon banish me or force me into a convent if I continue badgering him."

Gretta slowly ran a comb through her mistress's hair in an attempt to soothe her. "May I speak freely?"

"Please do."

"Why not try to find the boy?" she suggested, picking the loose hair out of the ivory comb's teeth. "You're the wife of one of England's most powerful men. That alone gives you a certain amount of power as well."

Beatrice spun around in the chair and took hold of Gretta's hand. "How right you are! All this time I've been grieving over my loss rather than taking action."

Suddenly, she ran to the door to check if any of Richard's spies were lurking about. Convinced that none of his knights were eavesdropping, Beatrice whispered, "I've been living in fear of my husband rather than worrying about the well-being of my son. My mother—God rest her soul—would never have allowed my father to treat her the way that Richard treats me. Unlike me, she was a strong woman." She looked heavenward. "God, I wish I had her courage."

"You're very strong, my lady! Take this evening, for example. You left this room with your head high, even though you had no idea what to expect."

Beatrice nodded. "I must find my son, but how? Richard has every servant bribed—even you."

"Aye, 'tis true that Lord Richard asks me questions and tosses me a coin now and then, but I swear to you, my lady, that I would never tell him anything that would cause you harm. Besides, he only asks about mundane things."

"Such as?"

"Where you go when we leave the castle, who you speak to, if you correspond with anyone, and so on."

"What do you tell him?"

The girl shrugged. "I tell him the truth, my lady. That you're a good wife who never entertains the attention of other men. I tell him that you give alms to the poor and hand out bread to the beggars who come to the door, as every good Christian woman should. Lord Richard smiled when I informed him that you read from your Bible each night before retiring."

"I see, and what about the correspondence?"

"Oh, I told him that you received word from your cousin a few weeks ago and that her children are growing up fine and strong." Gretta stopped speaking and appeared uncomfortable.

"And?"

"Well, your husband left me with instructions…"

"Instructions?"

"Lord Richard is to be notified at once if any letters arrive from his brother.

"I expect you to continue obeying Lord Richard's instructions. I do, however, expect your primary loyalty to be to *me*."

"Of course, my lady. It has always been so."

"Good. I'm going to need your help and your sworn silence in order to find my son."

Someone knocked and opened the door. Only one person had the right to enter without awaiting the lady's reply—her husband. Gretta curtsied and vacated the room, leaving the couple alone. Beatrice noticed that he had a small basket of cherries in his hands.

"I got these for you," he said. "A small peace offering."

She smiled faintly. "It's been a long time since you've offered me such love tokens."

"Things were so much easier back when we were younger, were they not?" He took a deep breath and eyed her doubtfully. "Our courtship was sweet."

"Aye," she agreed, glimpsing the little boy residing within her powerful husband.

"My father's death, my brother's rivalry, the birth of my first son. All of these things change a man." He paused, his eyes sad. "I miss you, Beatrice. I miss how things were…before."

"As do I, my lord."

He placed the basket on a nearby table. "Make love to me the way you used to…like you mean it in your heart."

She took his face in her hands and gazed deeply into his eyes. "I always mean it in my heart, Richard."

They made love for the remainder of the afternoon. Afterward, Beatrice cradled him in her arms, stroking his hair. Richard was a combination of power and vulnerability. The stark contrast never ceased to amaze her, and it never fooled her into believing that he was weak—or easily manipulated.

Chapter 4

Gwen loved the two little boys, and was always willing to help Agnes and Sarah as much as possible. Although she was only three years older than her adoptive brothers, Gwen imagined herself a miniature adult. Since Agnes and Sarah were close to the same age, and both were without husbands, the two women quickly bonded. Each day after they had completed their chores, the women would retire to the room they shared behind the kitchen and sit by the fire.

Simon often watched with longing as Agnes and Sarah whispered together or exchanged knowing glances before bursting into laughter. Sarah had attained a level of intimacy with Agnes that he desired but would probably never achieve.

One morning, while Agnes was bent over a bowl shelling peas, the ties of her bodice came undone, exposing her cleavage. Simon, who had come in from the garden, couldn't resist the urge to gaze upon the exposed skin. Out of the corner of his eye he saw movement in the doorway. To his mortification, it was Sarah. She had been watching him the entire time, and the knowing expression on her face made his cheeks burn with shame. He hastily exited the kitchen and went back into the garden without a single word.

Agnes heard the receding footsteps and raised her head in time to see Simon's retreating back through the doorway. She smiled when she saw Sarah. "I didn't realize Simon was in the kitchen."

Sarah raised an eyebrow. "He was watching you."

"Why on earth would he do that?"

"Because he's fond of you." When Agnes rolled her eyes, she added, "You're very pretty, you know."

Agnes laughed as she pulled her hands out of the bowl and held them up for inspection. "Look at these hands so rough and red." She sighed and added, "Far from pretty, my friend."

"He wasn't staring at your hands."

Agnes shook her head dismissively. "Are the boys asleep?"

Sarah bent to help Agnes with the peas. "Like two little angels." She paused. "I'm serious, Agnes, you *are* pretty. When was the last time you saw your reflection?"

"Yesterday morning I caught my image when I peered down into the well."

"And?"

"My disheveled hair made me step back in fright."

They both laughed. Sarah found it amusing that Simon secretly pined for her friend. She had noticed it within the first few days of her arrival at the monastery. Simon was a few years older than Agnes, but he was still an attractive, virile man. His nose was a bit large and his mouth was slightly crooked when he smiled, but he was kind, which was by far the most appealing asset any man could possess.

Sarah eventually came to the conclusion that Simon was intimidated by Agnes. In the village, male eyes followed her as she wandered through the market stalls. Her hazel eyes were almond shaped and her fair skin was unblemished, but what drew the most attention was the thick mane of auburn curls.

Later that night, when both women were sitting by the fire, Agnes offered Sarah a shy smile. "What you said earlier today…I think you're mistaken about Simon."

Sarah shrugged. "I may be a simple country girl, but I'm far from blind."

It was the first time Agnes had ever considered Simon's attentions as more than just those of a kind relative. "Do you really believe he fancies me?"

"Aye."

"But…he is my cousin."

"I thought he was *Tom's* cousin."

"He's never indicated any interest in me."

"Well, perhaps you should pay closer attention. If a man like Simon fancied me, I wouldn't hesitate for a moment." Sarah stood and stretched. "We have to get up early, so I'm off to bed. Goodnight."

"Goodnight."

"Aren't you coming?"

Agnes nodded distractedly. "In a moment."

In the days that followed, Agnes paid close attention to Simon and was convinced that Sarah was mistaken in regards to his feelings. The man revealed nothing, and treated her as he always did, with kindness and respect. She chose to dismiss the matter and reprimanded herself for behaving like a silly girl.

Chapter 5

"What do you mean Richard is confiscating my grain mills?!" Edward fumed.

Bertrand, the lanky solicitor who had served the Fitzwilliam family for almost two decades, stood before the prior with a document bearing Richard's official seal. "He wants them back, my lord," he replied, knowing that Richard wanted to keep his plotting younger brother under control.

"My brother is taking everything from me bit by bit!" Edward roared. "How shall I be compensated for the loss of income?"

"As I have already explained to you, my lord, the grain mills are in your brother's name. He has the right to do with his property as he sees fit." Bertrand paused to give Edward a sidelong glance. "Be thankful that he hasn't confiscated your land."

Edward lurched forward and struck the solicitor across the face. Bertrand was caught off guard as his green felt cap flew off his head to the floor. "How dare you tell me to be thankful to that swine?"

"I meant no disrespect," the solicitor said as he bent to retrieve his cap. "I was merely pointing out—"

"I don't pay you to point things out, Bertrand."

"Forgive my impudence, my lord."

Edward Fitzwilliam's temper was far worse than that of his older brother. From now on, Bertrand would prudently keep his opinions to himself.

Edward had been unsuccessful in his past attempts to destroy his brother, but he was hopeful that his luck would soon change. The gossip he had sparked against Richard evoked jealousy in a land hungry nobleman—John of Hallamshire. It was only a matter of time before he took action against the Lord of Kent.

Edward's eyes narrowed. "When was the last time you paid my brother a visit?"

"I was there last month."

"Did you see his wife?"

"Aye, my lord."

"How is the lovely Lady Beatrice doing these days?"

Bertrand shifted uncomfortably. "She is well."

Edward chuckled as if he was thinking of a private joke. "Go now, and don't return unless you have good news to share with me."

***

Richard confiscated Edward's grain mills to teach his younger brother an expensive lesson. Beatrice had been in a constant state of agitation ever since, fearful of Edward's retaliation. Whether her brother-in-law had actually started the gossip or not, she couldn't be sure, but she was certain he had done nothing to stop it. Perhaps he had even fanned the flames.

It was a bright May morning when Richard approached his wife in the garden with a letter in his hand. Recognizing the royal seal, she set aside her embroidery and stood.

"Henry wishes to see me at once," Richard said.

"What are you going to do?" she asked, trying to stay calm for her husband's sake.

Richard glanced at Gretta, who was seated a few feet away, then urged his wife to walk with him a bit. "I'm going to tell the king the truth about Edward's treachery. This morning, I received word from one of my spies that John of Hallamshire is ready to declare war on me."

"War?" she repeated, horrified.

"How very convenient to accuse the rich of treason then steal their lands. I pray that Henry is clever enough to see through their ploy."

She never suspected Edward of being so base. "Don't underestimate him. Besides, you've always supported every law Henry has implemented."

"I want you to accompany me to London. The king likes you, and your presence will soften the situation."

"I shall pack my things at once." Richard's eyes revealed anxiety, so she stroked his cheek. "Everything will work itself out in the end."

Placing his hand over hers, he closed his eyes and indulged in a rare moment of tenderness. When he opened his eyes again they were hard. "Be ready within the hour."

Richard rode at the head of the retinue, which consisted of a dozen heavily armed men, two pages, his valet, Beatrice, and Gretta. Despite their insistence on riding with the men, the women rode inside a small wooden carriage. Richard felt it would be safer for them in case of an attack. With Edward scheming behind his back, he would take no chances.

Several royal guards lined the battlements as they arrived in the castle's courtyard. Grooms and servants came out to tend to the horses and greet the noble guests. A well-dressed page led Richard and Beatrice to their chamber, informing them that the king wished to see them first thing in the morning.

The next day, Richard and Beatrice donned their finest clothing and jewels after hastily breaking their fast.

"Lord Richard Fitzwilliam of Kent and his wife, the Lady Beatrice," the herald announced as they entered the large hall where King Henry I sat on a fine throne.

The young and attractive Empress Matilda stood beside her father, her bejeweled hand resting upon his slumped shoulder. After the death of Henry's son, William, seven years ago, she was named sole heir to the throne. Although many nobles disapproved of a female heir, they reluctantly swore fealty to Matilda at the king's insistence.

To make matters worse, Matilda's husband, the Holy Roman Emperor, Henry V, had recently died. The old man's body had been barely cold in the grave when the king procured another husband for the childless widow—the non-English Plantagenet, Count Geoffrey of Anjou, who was several years her junior. While this strategic alliance would secure the southern borders, Geoffrey was a foreigner and disliked by many.

Richard thanked God for Beatrice's shrewdness in encouraging him to swear fealty to Matilda of his own initiative.

The spontaneous gesture had impressed both the king and his daughter.

"Ah, Lord Richard," Henry said. "It's good to see you and your lovely wife here at court."

"Likewise, Your Majesty. It's an honor to be here."

The king coughed a few times and rubbed his chest, instantly drawing furtive glances from nearby courtiers. Henry didn't look well at all, and Richard wondered if he'd been eating stewed lampreys again. Despite the advice of royal physicians to abstain from the creatures, Henry continued to eat them on a regular basis.

"I've known you too long to waste time with trivialities," Henry said tiredly. "Distressing news has reached my ears, which is why I've summoned you. The rumor is that you're plotting against me. Is it true?"

Richard calmly stared the king in the eye. "Sire, I've never plotted against you, nor do I have any intention of doing so. My wife and I are loyal subjects."

"I'm inclined to believe you, especially since you seem as disturbed as I am over this news. Tell me, why do you think these rumors are infiltrating my kingdom?"

"The plain and simple truth is that my brother wishes to destroy me."

Several noblemen overheard the exchange and shuffled closer to eavesdrop on the conversation.

"I'm aware of the bad blood between you two—there usually is with firstborns and their male siblings—but to spread *treasonous* lies? Edward couldn't have been the source. He's a holy man."

"With all due respect, trust me when I say this is my brother's doing. I even have proof."

Henry waved his hand. "Go on."

"Edward has joined forces with John of Hallamshire in order to seize some of my most profitable lands."

"These northerners are always starting trouble. How do you know this to be true?"

"I employ the best spies, sire."

"Since you've never given me reason to doubt your word, and there's no evidence of treason, I'll put an end to these vicious rumors at once." Matilda bent to whisper in her father's ear again. "Ah, of course," the king said. "My daughter has just reminded me that you led my army on my last military venture, and that you swore fealty to her of your own accord."

Richard gave Matilda a look of gratitude.

"All the more reason to forget this silly gossip," Henry stated loudly enough for everyone to hear—a direct proclamation from the king's own lips.

"Thank you," Richard said, barely able to disguise the relief in his voice.

"How do you intend to handle your brother? And John of Hallamshire, for that matter?"

"I was hoping you could aid me in this matter, Your Majesty. In exchange, I'll give you half of the lands that he and my brother intended to conquer for themselves. The fertile soil is tended by loyal serfs who faithfully pay their taxes when due."

"That's a generous offer, and one that I can't refuse." Henry motioned for Richard to come closer and whispered, "As for your brother, I'm sure we can figure out a way to keep him in check without inciting opposition from him or his supporters. We'll discuss the possibilities another time."

"I look forward to that day."

Richard and Beatrice thanked the king as they backed away from him, as was custom in order to not show their backsides. Richard was soon surrounded by his allies, many of whom were enemies of Edward.

***

Edward led the solicitor to his private quarters and poured some wine. "What brings you here, Bertrand?"

"I have news from Kent."

"You've come to tell me that Richard is confiscating my last plot of land."

"There's nothing I can do," Bertrand confirmed.

Edward fixed him with an accusatory glare. "Did you even

try to reason against this action?"

"Yes," Bertrand lied.

"Richard has taken everything from me these last few months—bit by bit—as if to torture me," Edward said through clenched teeth as he set down the chalice and paced the room. "Are you certain there's absolutely nothing I can do?"

Bertrand chose his words carefully in order to not incite Edward's violent temper. "As the eldest son, Lord Richard has legal right to all properties and land. If you remember, my lord, Richard allotted those properties out of familial generosity, not obligation. It's unfortunate that you two are no longer on civil terms."

"True, but don't you agree that a man should stand by his word through good times and bad?"

Bertrand shrugged in the face of Edward's hypocrisy.

Edward continued, "Damn it, Bertrand! As second son I was forced into this clerical role, but I found some consolation in those lucrative properties. Now, I have nothing! The last thing I wanted in life was to be a son of the Church!"

"Be careful, my lord, some could interpret your words as heresy," the solicitor warned in a bland tone.

"Heresy, indeed! I've proved my faith and loyalty to the Church. Didn't I contribute handsomely to the king's latest project? That monstrous cathedral."

"True, but—"

"But, what?"

"You have no choice in this matter, my lord." Bertrand paused. "There's something else…"

Edward's eyes narrowed. "Something else?"

"The king has offered you the See of Rochester."

"Rochester?" Edward repeated, confused. "That would mean a promotion for me."

"It seems that the election for the bishopric was held and you won."

"That's preposterous! I didn't even volunteer myself as a candidate!"

"No, you didn't," Bertrand agreed with glittering eyes.

Realization lit up Edward's face. "How convenient that Rochester is located between London and Kent. I'm sure Richard's spies, as well as those of His Majesty, will be aware of my every move. I'll have a dozen puppet strings tied to me and pulled in all directions by the barons and nobles who support Richard and Henry. Is that it, Bertrand?"

"I don't know," Bertrand lied.

"And if I refuse the bishopric?"

"It would be an offense to the king."

Edward balled his hands into fists and paced the room like a caged animal. Bertrand quietly took his leave just before Edward violently struck the chalice on the table. The red wine ran down the white walls like blood.

Chapter 6

One of the two knights tickled Gretta under the chin as she passed him. "Come now, my pretty."

"Get your hands off me, you filthy beast," she spat, eyes flashing. "Look! You've made me drop my basket."

The knight laughed as he grabbed Gretta's shoulders and attempted to kiss her. She kicked him in the shin.

He cursed. "Go on, you little shrew!"

"I'm no shrew, you ill-mannered oaf," Gretta snarled as she picked up the basket full of items from the market. "I'll be sure to tell Lady Beatrice of your impertinence."

Both of the knights repeated her words in a mocking tone, like unruly children.

"Just you wait," Gretta warned as she checked the items in the basket for damage.

She knew he troublesome knights would never cause her any real harm, but they were coarse and a nuisance nonetheless.

"Go on and tell your mistress, see what good it will do you," he taunted.

His friend snickered as Gretta turned her back and headed for the castle gates. "Lord Richard doesn't give a fig what his wife says."

"Aye, he made the little bastard a monk, didn't he?"

Hearing this, Gretta ran upstairs to her mistress's chamber.

"He said *what*?" Beatrice demanded once she had heard Gretta's story.

Almost two years had passed since Richard's victory over Edward. Even though her relationship with her husband had improved during that time, being reunited with her lost son was still an impossibility. Despite the risk, she had attempted countless times to reason with Richard only to be met with disappointment. She and Gretta would often ride out under the pretense of going to the market or visiting the poor, then ask everyone they came into contact with about the missing gray-eyed child. So far, they hadn't met with any success.

Until perhaps today.

Beatrice paced the solarium. "*Made the little bastard a monk*," she whispered, staring out the window. "The night Richard summoned me to dine with him, he assured me that the baby was safe. We've been searching in the towns and villages, questioning every wet nurse, every servant. All this time I've assumed Richard was paying someone within the local vicinity to care for the child."

Gretta wrung her hands nervously, knowing they had stumbled upon something significant. "Do you think it's possible...?"

"My son is in a monastery," Beatrice concluded as she spun around to face Gretta. "It's the only reasonable explanation. Why else would the knight call my boy a monk?" Knowing Richard's distrustful nature, he would have left the baby with those who would certainly care for the child.

"Aye, but which monastery?" Gretta inquired. "There are several in England."

"I don't know, but this is at least a start in the right direction."

"How will we ever find him?"

Beatrice's sigh was heavy, but her eyes were fierce. "I swear to you before God, I will find my son."

The women stood in pensive silence for several seconds. An idea slithered into Gretta's mind like a garden snake. Glancing at her mistress, she thought: *do I dare?*

Beatrice caught Gretta's look. "What is it?"

"The Bishop of Rochester could find out."

Beatrice stared at Gretta in disbelief. "I can't go to my brother-in-law after what he's done to my husband."

"Forgive me, my lady."

Gretta was right, however. Edward could gain access to information pertaining to every monastery in England. As much as she loathed the prospect of seeking his help again, he was the only person who would keep her secret out of sheer spite for

Richard.

"The king wishes to meet with his nobles in order to propose a new tax," Beatrice said. "Richard leaves for court on the morrow, and I will go to Rochester."

Gretta made a face. "That would be unwise. What if you get caught? I should go in your place."

"It would be an affront to Edward's pride. He would never negotiate with a servant."

***

Beatrice's heart pounded fiercely as Gretta helped her fasten the clasp of a black cloak. The moon was almost full and would offer sufficient light on her short journey to Rochester. "Is my horse ready?"

"Yes, my lady."

Beatrice patted the full leather pouch that hung from her belt—*bribery money*. "I'm off. Wish me luck, Gretta."

"Godspeed and good luck."

Beatrice crept along a stone hall, and past a pair of knights who were snoozing at their posts. She slid quietly into the main hall and clung to the shadows as she made her way to the stables.

The night air felt damp against her cheeks as she led the mare on foot away from the castle. Upon entering the edge of the forest, she mounted the animal.

"Don't fail me, girl," she whispered before the horse took off into the night.

It was well after midnight when she arrived in the Saxon village of Rochester. The ancient Norman cathedral boasted one of the finest façades in England. The bishop's residence was located off to the side. She tethered her horse and swiftly ascended the stairs to the front door.

An old female servant with sleepy eyes opened the door a crack. "Who knocks at such a late hour?"

"I need to see the bishop at once."

"His Excellency is asleep."

"This is a most urgent matter."

The old woman eyed Beatrice's fine clothing and jewels.

"Come in, my lady."

The old woman urged Beatrice into a chair before shuffling off to fetch the bishop. Fine rugs and fur throws, ornately carved furniture, and several pieces of highly polished silver glinted in the dimness of two lit candles.

Edward eventually appeared in the doorway arrayed in a mahogany velvet robe trimmed with glossy mink.

Beatrice rose from the chair. "Your Excellency."

Wearing the title of *Bishop* like a king, Edward extended his hand and waited for her to address him properly.

She dutifully bowed and kissed the holy ring on his finger. "You look well, my lord."

Edward's eyes ran slowly up and down her body with unabashed admiration. "As do you, Beatrice. Yet I'm sure you didn't travel all this way in the middle of the night to comment on my appearance."

"No."

His eyes lingered at the base of her throat, and she suddenly felt like a lamb exposed to a wolf. "What's the reason for your nocturnal visit *this* time?"

"I've come to ask for your help."

"Why am I not surprised? What kind of help are you seeking now?"

"I want to find my son."

He circled her slowly, his body so near that she could feel his breath upon her face.

"What does that have to do with me?" he demanded.

"I've reason to believe that he's being raised in a monastery. I need to know which one. As a bishop, you have the power to obtain this information."

"Assuming that I can obtain the information you seek, *why* should I help you?"

"You're a man of the Church, and it would be the Christian thing to do—the *right* thing to do."

"Helping my sister-in-law locate her bastard son behind my brother's back is far from a holy endeavor."

"Your nephew is *not* a bastard."

He waved his hand dismissively. "Richard will throw you in the dungeon if he discovers that you came to me for help. *Again*."

"I'll endure it if it means finding my son."

"A mother's love—how touching. If I help you, what's in it for me?"

Beatrice handed him the pouch full of coins. "This."

He took out one of the gold coins and examined it before tossing it back in the pouch. "This is a generous sum."

"I want my son. Please help me, Edward."

Beatrice was impossibly lovely. Her face was flushed, her blue eyes bright, and her parted lips were ruby red. Oh, how he wanted to slip his tongue into her mouth and taste its sweetness.

"As you can see, my dear, I don't need your money," he pointed out with a sweep of his hand, indicating the material wealth around him. "I suspect Richard didn't realize how profitable being the Bishop of Rochester would be for me."

"If you won't help me for money, then do it for friendship," she implored.

"Friendship?" he repeated incredulously.

"We were friends once, just as our fathers were friends when they were alive. Help me for their sake."

"We were indeed friends *once*—you and I." His expression turned nostalgic as he recalled happier times. Suddenly, his eyes turned cold. "Until you spurned my affection in order to marry Richard."

She winced. "I had no choice in the matter."

"Would you have chosen me if you could?"

"Let's not discuss this now."

"Perhaps we should discuss how your husband confiscated my properties without any resistance from you—my supposed friend."

"Richard would never have taken anything from you had you not plotted against him. For God's sake, Edward, you tried to get him accused of *treason*! How did you think he would react to that? There was nothing I could do to stop him even if I had tried."

"But you didn't try!" he bellowed, eyes blazing.

She regarded him levelly. "Did you honestly expect a reward for betraying him?"

"Unlike my brother, nothing has ever been handed to me on a tray of gold."

"*Your Excellency*, may I remind you that Richard convinced the king to give you this bishopric?" She paused to let her point sink in before continuing in a soft tone, "Let the past die and help me now in this noble cause. I'm coming to you in great need as an old friend. *Please*, Edward. I plan to pay you well, regardless of whether you need the money or not, so what have you got to lose?"

"Very well." Beatrice sighed in relief and he continued, "I shall send word to all the monasteries in the surrounding area. What did the child look like?"

"His hair is fair, like ours, and his eyes are gray, like Richard's...and *yours*."

Edward's eyes turned soft and Beatrice witnessed a rare glimpse of vulnerability. "He could have been our child, Beatrice."

She lowered her eyes and her cheeks burned. "The Fitzwilliam resemblance is strong."

"I'll help you find your son."

She took his hand in a surge of emotion and kissed it. "Thank you."

"I assume you wish to keep this matter secret," Edward said, taking a step closer.

"No one must know."

Edward placed his finger under her chin and forced her to meet his lustful gaze. "My lips are sealed. Perhaps someday I may need a favor from you."

Beatrice remained perfectly still as his finger moved from her chin down her throat and slowly traced the delicate line of her clavicle.

She averted her eyes. "Edward...please."

He leaned forward, placing his mouth to her ear. The hot breath on her skin caused her to shiver. "If I were you, I would water my horse and make haste back to your home before I do something you'll regret."

Beatrice understood the threat, but refused to believe that he would stoop so low as to take her by force. "Farewell," she whispered before darting out the door.

Edward remained rooted to the spot long after her departure. The smell of her skin was still in his nostrils, and he wanted to relish the moment for as long as he could. For the hundredth time, he wondered what life would have been like if he had been the firstborn son.

***

Gwen picked parsley from the herb garden when a tiny speck in the distance captured her attention. Shading her eyes against the glare of the morning sun, she stood and squinted.

Agnes busily prepared the midday meal for the monks inside the kitchen. She missed the days when Sarah was at the monastery. It had been a long time since her services were no longer needed. Sarah and Jeremy still came to visit on occasion, but those visits were not as frequent as Agnes would have liked.

Gwen ran into the room. "Someone is coming!"

Agnes set the knife on the table and followed Gwen out into the garden. She spotted a man on horseback coming toward them. The comely rider wore leather boots with silver spurs and his dark green cloak was fastened by an ornate silver clasp.

"Good day," he called out.

Conscious of his station, Agnes politely gave the stranger a deep curtsy. "Good day to you, my lord."

"I'm searching for the prior, a man by the name of Bartholomew."

Simon appeared and, having overheard the exchange, said, "The prior is in his cell at this hour. I can tether your horse and take you to him."

Agnes watched in admiration as the man gracefully dismounted and handed Simon the reins. She noticed that his eyes matched the green of his cloak.

A moment later, the man stood face to face with Bartholomew inside a simply furnished cell. "My name is

Martin Sinclair, and I'm here because of a certain boy."

The prior knew this day would come.

"Please sit," said Bartholomew, indicating a simple wooden chair. He picked up a ceramic pitcher from a nearby table and filled a cup with watered wine. "May I offer you some refreshment?"

"Thank you," said Martin, accepting the cup. "My master has sent me here to ask you a few questions."

Bartholomew was surprised that the articulate, neatly dressed man sitting before him was a mere servant. "I imagine you have many. For my own peace of mind, can you describe the boy you seek?"

"An infant with fair hair and gray eyes. A gold and ruby crucifix should have been in his possession."

The prior fetched the crucifix from its hiding place and handed it to Martin, who examined it carefully. Satisfied that it matched the description he had been given, he handed it back to the prior.

"Who is Nick's father?" Bartholomew asked as he locked away the crucifix.

"*Nick?*"

"The young daughter of one of our servants found the baby on the church steps. She insisted we name him Nicodemus after—"

"The Jewish Pharisee," Martin interjected. "I'm familiar with the story. I saw the girl when I rode in."

"I thought that Nick was abandoned by a ruined maid until I saw the crucifix. No one in the village is rich enough to possess something so fine, let alone part with it. I'm surprised it's has taken this long for someone to come and collect him."

Martin extracted a leather pouch from his belt and handed it to the prior. "I was instructed to give you this to cover the expenses you've incurred in caring for him.

Bartholomew was shocked to see several gold coins. "There's enough money here to raise many children!"

"I'll bring more on my next visit."

The prior's brow creased in confusion. "I don't understand.

You're not taking Nick with you?"

"No."

"Why? Who are his parents?"

"I can neither reveal the identity of Nick's parents nor why he must remain here. The boy is to have the best possible education that money can buy. My master was very clear on this. You must spare the boy nothing."

"Well, you have no need to worry on that score. As prior of this Cluniac Order, I make certain that all of the brethren are educated above and beyond theological doctrine," Bartholomew assured with an air of authority.

"You are much like the Benedictines, are you not?"

"The Benedictines take four basic vows—obedience, chastity, poverty, and manual labor. We believe in the first three vows and exchange the fourth for secular and theological learning. Be thankful Nick wasn't dropped off on the steps of the Augustinians, who spend most of their time preaching, or the Carthusians, who live their lives in isolation in the wild northern wastelands and take the vow of silence."

Martin shuddered at the thought of the latter. "I'm sure my master will be grateful. May I see the boy now?"

"Wait here while I fetch him."

Martin waited no more than five minutes while Bartholomew went into an antechamber where Nick was receiving instruction from one of the monks. The charming boy was holding the prior's hand tightly as he entered the room. His golden curls bounced with each step and his eyes were clear and intelligent.

"Hello, Nick," said Martin.

"Hello," the boy said in a small voice.

"Can you tell me how old you are?"

Nick held up three chubby fingers.

"You're a fine looking lad for three."

Nick put up a fourth finger. "I will be this old very soon. Prior Bartholomew said so."

Martin smiled. "Do you know your alphabet?"

Nick recited his letters without error and gradually lost his shyness when Martin praised him. They talked for a few more minutes before Nick returned to his lessons.

"You have cared for him very well," Martin said. "My master will be relieved and happy to know this."

"I'm glad to hear it." Bartholomew paused, troubled. "It's difficult to imagine a set of parents that wouldn't be proud and joyful to have Nick as a child. It pains me that your master does not want him."

"I never said *that*."

"If I understand correctly, your master wants the boy, but for reasons you cannot divulge—"

Martin cut him off. "Forgive me, but as I've said before, I'm sworn to secrecy on this matter. For the sake of Nick's safety, please don't ask me again."

Bartholomew paled at the thought of Nick being in danger. "Will you be spending the night here in Lewes?"

"I have instructions to return once I've seen the boy."

"It's almost time for the midday meal. I usually eat here alone while the monks dine at the refectory, but if you want to meet the people who are most influential in Nick's life, we could eat together. I'm afraid that we have no luxurious feast to offer you."

"I accept your hospitality," Martin said, deciding it was a good idea to meet everyone. "It's obvious to me that you love Nick."

"Aye, I do. I look upon him as my own."

"That's a good thing. I have to ask something of you."

"What is it?"

"You must make sure that my identity and my reason for being here remain within the walls of this monastery. No one on the outside must know."

"Very well."

"Can the others be trusted?"

"They are fine people and have Nick's best interests at heart, so, yes." Bartholomew hesitated. "What shall I tell Nick when he's old enough to ask questions?"

"I don't expect a man of your position to lie. Tell him that he has a generous benefactor."

"That's true enough, I suppose."

"It will have to suffice."

Bartholomew led Martin into the kitchen where the table was set with ceramic earthenware cups and trenchers of hard bread. Simon, Agnes, and Gwen were surprised, but pleased to share their simple meal of stewed peas and onions with Martin. Luckily, Agnes had baked some small pies filled with apples and berries the day before. There was freshly churned butter, brown bread, and plenty of ale.

"Gwen, don't play with your peas," Agnes whispered to her daughter, who was placing the peas in her trencher in various designs.

Martin smiled in amusement as the little girl sulked. He caught Agnes's eye and confessed, "My mother used to reprimand me for the very same thing."

"Is that so? I hope you've learned your lesson since then, my lord."

"I'm no lord," he corrected. "Please call me Martin—and yes, I did learn my lesson."

Agnes blushed. "Do you live far from the monastery?"

"Quite far."

"But you can't tell us where?"

Martin leaned back in his chair and slowly sipped his ale. "I'm under oath to divulge nothing except what I've already told you—and not even that can leave this room."

Gwen peered up at him. "Do you live in a castle?"

Martin leaned close to the girl and whispered, "A great big one."

She clapped her hands. "You're a prince!"

Martin shook his head, laughing. "Far from it."

"But you live in a castle," she said, confused.

"I am a servant."

"Oh," she said. "What's it like living in a castle?"

Martin described in vivid detail the banquets held in his master's house. Gwen sat motionless, listening in awe to tales about musicians, dancers, troubadours, and poets. When Martin went on to describe the pretty clothing and jewels worn by the noble ladies, she barely blinked.

At one point she turned to Agnes and inquired, "Mama, can I have a dress like that, too?"

Agnes smiled sadly. "Someday, perhaps."

Everyone was somehow changed by Martin's visit and sad to see him go. After that day, Nick was viewed in a very different light. He was not just some abandoned village child, but the son of someone wealthy and powerful.

***

When Martin arrived at Kent Castle, he was ushered immediately to his "master's" chamber.

"I am desperate for good news, Martin."

"I bear *only* good news, my lady."

Richard was out hunting and wouldn't return until nightfall, allowing Beatrice plenty of time to speak with Martin in private. "Sit," she said, indicating a chair. "Tell me everything."

Edward had sent Beatrice a secret message a few months after their meeting stating that her son was in a Cluniac monastery in Lewes. Richard had sent him far enough away to keep Beatrice from finding him, but now that she had, she planned to track the boy's progress. Of all Richard's knights, Martin Sinclair was the brightest and the most trustworthy, which is why she had chosen him to act as a liaison. More importantly, he was her distant cousin, a poor relation she had aided soon after her marriage. Martin owed Beatrice his knighthood and his loyalty.

Beatrice listened with delight as Martin recounted everything that had taken place during his visit to Lewes. She was immensely pleased and relieved by how well "Nick" was being treated and cared for by the good people at St. John's.

Martin visited Nick at the monastery whenever it was safe to do so. Sometimes he went laden with gifts, such as books, ink, quills, vellum, and clothing. At other times Beatrice sent him to Lewes with money.

Any attempt to see her son would put him at risk, so Beatrice resisted the urge. Richard would surely move the boy to another hiding place if he knew she was employing Martin to look after him. Unwilling to take such a risk, she had no choice but to witness her son's progress through Martin's eyes.

Beatrice found solace in her other son, Robert, and tried to live a happy life—or at least as happy as the circumstances allowed.

One morning, as she and Robert walked hand in hand through the castle garden, he asked, "Mama, when will I be allowed to go to court?"

Beatrice stopped to examine a tree laden with unripe apples. "When you're old enough, I suppose."

"I'm getting very tall—everyone tells me so," the boy pointed out, standing beside his mother to demonstrate how his shoulder almost touched her own.

"Yes, you are indeed getting quite tall, but your height has naught to do with your age. Your father and I feel that you're still too young."

"But—"

"Try to enjoy what's left of your childhood, my son. These carefree days will end before you know it."

Robert pouted slightly. "I'm *not* a baby."

"No one is suggesting that, my love. Now run along and see to your lessons. The king dislikes ignorance."

He took three steps toward the castle and stopped. "When can I have a real sword?"

Robert was considerably skillful in the art of swordplay, but like most boys his age, he practiced with a wooden sword. "That's up to your father, but I suspect it will be soon."

Robert grinned before running off.

Gretta approached her mistress. "I have a letter for you, my lady. It's from the bishop," she said, slipping a folded piece of parchment into Beatrice's hand.

Beatrice tucked it up her sleeve and proceeded through the garden, mindful of the knights who were staring down at her from the battlements. Richard was enjoying a bit of falconry with the Earl of Sussex while trying to convince him to buy their land in Westfordshire. Located on the outskirts of London, the fertile plots would yield a high profit if sold to the right person.

Later, in the privacy of her bedchamber, Beatrice broke the holy seal. Edward's message was clear and brief: *It is time to repay the favor.*

Beatrice dared not dally in Kent for too long. She and Gretta would have to devise a plan that would allow her to sneak away soon.

Richard approached Beatrice in the solarium prior to sunset. His outing with the earl was cut short due to rain, but had produced desirable results.

"The Earl of Sussex is interested in the land and wishes to meet in Westfordshire two days from now."

"That's good news, Richard."

"I've been trying to get rid of those plots for a long time, and he's the only man rich enough to buy them. This calls for celebration. Let's enjoy some sweet wine."

They partook of wine in the main hall, toasting his shrewd business sense. Richard then proceeded to talk about the various ways the money from the sale could be invested. This was most unusual since he rarely discussed such matters in her presence. She attributed the lapse to high spirits.

Two days later, after Richard had departed for Westfordshire, Beatrice met with Edward. Like last time, she crept out at night when the castle was quiet and reached Rochester undetected.

"I take it your son is doing well," Edward said after they had exchanged greetings.

"Your nephew is a fine, healthy boy."

"Ah, good. It wasn't easy to find him, but I managed."

"I can't begin to describe how grateful I am, Edward."

"Oh, I know you're grateful, Beatrice. So much so that you wouldn't think twice about returning the favor." His honeyed tone was laced with venom.

"What kind of favor?" she inquired warily.

Edward's eyes dropped to the neckline of her green velvet gown, which was trimmed with ermine. The soft fur caressed the tops of her breasts in the most sensuous manner. "Richard has been rather friendly with the Earl of Sussex as of late, has he not?" he asked in a tone that implied he already knew the answer.

Beatrice was shocked. Were Edward's spies scattered *everywhere*? She feigned ignorance. "My husband doesn't include me in his affairs."

"Don't play the fool with me, Beatrice—it's most unbecoming." He took a firm hold of her chin and forced her to meet his steely gaze. "Well?"

"Yes," she reluctantly confirmed.

"Good," he snapped, releasing her chin. "I want you to notify me immediately if the earl agrees to buy Richard's land."

"Edward—"

"My brother and the earl are in Westfordshire now."

"What if Richard doesn't share that information with me? How will I know?"

Edward smiled without humor. "I'm sure you can figure out a way to pry it from him." His eyes ran up and down her body. "A woman like you should have no trouble getting what she wants from a man."

She felt her cheeks burn at his insinuation. "Why do you want to know?"

"That doesn't concern you, Beatrice. Women shouldn't meddle in the affairs of men."

"Is there anything else?" she demanded, eager to return to Kent.

"If I need anything else, I'll summon you," he said in a dismissive tone.

Beatrice turned to go and Edward placed a hand on her arm. She recoiled involuntarily and he gripped both of her shoulders. He stared at her solemnly before tenderly kissing her cheek.

"Go now, Beatrice," he said hoarsely.

***

Richard arrived from Westfordshire and Beatrice went out into the courtyard to meet him.

"The earl has agreed to buy the land," he said while

dismounting. "Tell the servants to prepare something special. I'm famished."

Beatrice felt sick, but managed to smile. "You bear good tidings, husband."

"I'm going to clean the dust from my journey and meet you shortly." He turned to go, then suddenly returned to place a hard kiss upon his wife's mouth.

Richard went upstairs and Beatrice went into the kitchen. She spotted a fresh meat pie cooling on the window sill and instructed the servants to roast some venison on the spit. "Your master is hungry. Bring out the good wine and sweetmeats, too."

"Yes, my lady," said the cook.

Next, she went up to her bedchamber and, feeling utterly traitorous, scribbled a quick note to Edward. Beatrice then summoned Gretta and instructed her maid to have the letter delivered with haste.

The servants managed to produce a small feast of delicacies for their lord and lady, but every morsel Beatrice swallowed tasted bitter. While Richard ate heartily, her betrayal pricked her conscience like the sharp thorns of a wild rose bush.

***

"Damn him! Damn him to hell!" Richard shouted as he paced the floor of the main hall like a vicious animal.

Beatrice, who had been outside in the herb garden, came rushing in. "What is it, my lord?"

She noticed a richly attired messenger standing a few feet away. Richard turned on his heel and ripped the vellum sheet out of the messenger's hand. "*This!* This is what is wrong," he snarled, thrusting it into her hands.

She scanned its contents. "Oh…"

"Can you believe it? The Earl of Sussex finally agrees to my price and now, all of a sudden, I get this message stating that he wishes to break our deal."

Beatrice's stomach sank. "Has he given reason for his sudden change of heart?"

Richard pointed to the messenger. "Tell her."

The messenger, obviously uncomfortable, cleared his throat. "My lord has been 'informed' of the land's poor drainage, which he believes would render the soil infertile, my lady."

"Bullocks!" Richard shouted.

Beatrice knew the broken deal was Edward's doing. She felt extremely guilty for her part in this devious sabotage, but it was the price she was forced to pay to have Nick in her life.

As if reading her mind, Richard said, "I wouldn't be surprised if Edward is behind this!"

Beatrice's heart raced. "He's far away in Rochester."

Richard took a step forward and eyed her suspiciously. "You defend him?"

"No, my lord!" She paused. "I'm sorry things didn't work out with the earl."

Richard remained silent, but his eyes narrowed slightly as if trying to solve a puzzle. She quickly left the room before he sensed her guilt.

In the privacy of her bedchamber, Beatrice confessed to Gretta, "God is going to punish me for betraying my husband."

Gretta gave her mistress's hand a comforting squeeze. "You did it for the sake of your son, my lady. God will forgive you."

"My son grows quickly and I have yet to see him."

"It's for the boy's safety."

"I want to go to the monastery with Martin."

"You'd be taking an enormous risk."

"I only want to see him from afar. I'll summon Martin as soon as the opportunity arises."

"It will only cause you more grief."

Beatrice lowered her head in defeat. "Perhaps you're right. It would pain me greatly to see the boy and not be able to hold him in my arms."

"May I ask a question?" Gretta asked, changing the subject. "Why would the Bishop of Rochester not want the land in Westfordshire sold?"

"They're the most profitable plots of land we own, and they once generated much income for Edward—until my husband confiscated them."

Chapter 7

In the years that followed, Edward continued to scheme against his brother, but none of his devious plans came to fruition. The bishop's only victory was the Westfordshire sabotage. Sometimes Beatrice wondered if Edward had placed a curse on the land because there were no more potential buyers after the Earl of Sussex had changed his mind.

The relative peacefulness came to an end in the year 1135 when Henry I died. The king had not been well for quite some time, and he eventually developed a fever that killed him on the first day of December.

There was great turmoil in England following his death. Princess Matilda, the rightful heir, attempted to lay claim to the throne. Despite having sworn fealty, many nobles betrayed her by supporting Stephen, the king's nephew. The nobles with opposing views fought against one another. Matilda's supporters were soon outnumbered and Stephen, amidst all the confusion and fighting, usurped the throne.

Richard and Beatrice planned on attending the coronation of the new king. Several other members of the nobility would follow suit, having realized that it was far wiser to show support for Stephen than to fight or be executed for treason. Also, it was widely believed that Matilda would never succeed in attaining the throne.

Robert would finally accompany his parents to court for the first time. To celebrate the occasion, Richard surprised his eleven-year-old son with a new tunic of dyed red leather and a new sword.

Robert's eyes lit up as he accepted the finely crafted steel weapon from his father's hands. "It's best sword I've ever seen, Father, thank you!"

"If you're old enough to be officially presented at court, you're old enough to have your own sword."

"May I bring it with me?"

"Perhaps it would be best to wait until your next visit."

Robert looked at his father with disappointment.

Beatrice, who stood beside Richard, said, "Wouldn't you prefer to learn how to wield it properly before flaunting it in public?"

"I know how to use a sword," Robert retorted coolly.

"Of course, you do," she amended. "But—"

Richard held up his hand to silence his wife, then said to his son, "When we return from London you'll be given formal instruction along with my men. There is still much you have to learn."

"Aren't you forgetting something?" Beatrice whispered in her husband's ear.

"Oh, right," said Richard, handing Robert a leather sheath.

Robert fastened the sheath around his waist and slid the sword into it. Unprepared for its weight, the boy's legs buckled slightly and he was forced to regain his balance. Richard and Beatrice did their best to keep a straight face.

Robert's chest puffed out a little bit as he strutted around with his new sword. "Thank you for this splendid gift," he said to his parents. "I'll cherish it always."

***

Agnes added onions to a large cauldron of nettle soup, then cocked her head at the sound of an approaching horse. Peeking through the narrow slit in the window shutters, she said, "Martin is here."

Simon clenched his teeth in irritation as she smoothed her skirt and removed her apron.

Patting her unruly curls into place, she said, "You'd best notify the prior."

Muttering under this breath, Simon darted outside to fetch Bartholomew.

At the sight of the corpulent prior, Martin dismounted and walked toward him. "Greetings, Prior Bartholomew. I come bearing news from London."

Bartholomew nodded. "We have a new king."

"Crowned last month on the twenty-second day."

Bartholomew sighed. "I only hope that King Stephen can resolve at least some of the disputes that pit our barons against one another."

"We all wish for that in these dark times."

"If Prince William hadn't died—or if he had brothers—the situation wouldn't be so precarious."

"Henry left us with two choices: Matilda, a woman married to foreigner, and his weak nephew, Stephen."

Bartholomew lowered his voice and confessed, "Neither one is fit to rule, in my humble opinion."

"I agree with you, but what can we do except wait and hope for the best?"

The prior shrugged and invited Martin to his cell for refreshment and conversation. The visit was similar to the others, and another bag of gold was gifted to the prior with the admonition to spare nothing for the boy.

"Where is Nick?" Martin asked at length.

"He's with Jeremy. I'll fetch him."

Martin had met Jeremy the previous year, along with his mother, Sarah. Because the boys were as close as brothers, Jeremy had taken to spending weeks at a time at the monastery. Sarah was content to send her son to St. John's whenever he wished it.

Nick and Jeremy walked into the room with smiles on their faces—a visit from Martin was always a good thing.

"I have a gift for each of you," Martin said as he reached into a large leather satchel. He pulled out two wooden swords and handed one to each of the boys. "I'll teach you a few maneuvers now and, when you're old enough, I'll teach you to wield a real sword."

The boys thanked Martin for the gift and followed him outside. Using his own sword, Martin demonstrated correct posture, and how to properly parry and lunge. The boys mimicked the moves, using their wooden swords. Martin eventually left them to their practice and rejoined the prior. As usual, he was invited to dine with them and accepted the invitation.

During supper that evening, Martin vividly described Stephen's coronation celebration in London, which was celebrated with considerable pomp.

Gwen, twelve years old and quite the young lady, turned to Martin and requested, "Would you please bring me a pretty gown on your next visit? Like the ones the ladies wear in London?"

"Gweneth McFay," Agnes scolded.

"It's my fault," Martin interjected. "I fill her head with so many stories each time I come here."

"Please?" Gwen pressed, ignoring her mother's warning look. "I wish I could be a London lady!"

"Maybe someday you'll get your wish, Gwen," Martin said indulgently, then stood. "Alas, I must now take my leave. Thank you all for such a good meal."

"I'll accompany you to your horse," Agnes offered, wrapping a wool shawl around her shoulders.

Martin smiled. "There's really no need. It's cold out."

Agnes returned the smile. "I like the cold."

The moment they left the kitchen, peered through the crack between the shutters. The full moon cast its silvery light on Agnes's curly locks as she took Martin's arm. He overheard their laughter with a sinking heart.

***

Nick lunged with considerable speed at his opponent. "Take that! And that!"

"Arrrrgggghhhh! I've been stabbed!"

Jeremy staggered, then fell to the ground in a melodramatic theatrical display of death. Nick spun the wooden sword with ease before sliding it back in its makeshift sheath.

Jeremy leaned on his elbow and peered up at his friend. "I wish I was as quick as you, Nick."

"Practice, my friend."

"It was only last week that we received these swords and Martin taught us these moves," Jeremy protested.

Nick shrugged nonchalantly. "I must be a natural knight—

no, a *warrior*."

Jeremy had difficulty keeping up with Nick when it came to speed and agility. This was no doubt attributed to his inclination toward heaviness, which he had inherited from his mother.

Sarah, who was visiting Agnes for a few days, left the kitchen and went outside to check on the boys. Storm clouds quickly gathered in the late afternoon sky, and the cold wind made her shiver. She spotted her son and Nick across the vegetable garden by the dairy.

Cupping her mouth with her hands, she called out, "Jeremy, Nick, come inside!"

Hearing Sarah's call, Nick turned to Jeremy and said, "I'll race you."

Jeremy ran as fast as he could, but Nick won.

Gwen, who was coaxing the embers in the hearth with a poker, looked at them in irritation as they burst into the kitchen. "Close the door—you're letting in all the cold."

Agnes poured stew into wooden bowls. "You two must be hungry."

Nick and Jeremy nodded as they took their seats. They waited impatiently for the meal to be served and for everyone to sit around the table. The moment Simon had finished uttering a prayer of thanks, they picked up their wooden spoons and attacked the stew.

Gwen sat opposite them and stared in disgust. "You two eat like animals."

Nick sat up straight and ate with care. Jeremy, refusing to be bested by his friend, followed suit.

Simon laughed. "From little beasts to little lords. Ah, the power of beauty."

Jeremy's solemn brown eyes studied Gwen intently. "Will you marry me when I grow up?"

Nick elbowed him in the ribs and laughed. "No, silly goose. She's going to marry me!"

Jeremy frowned. "But I love her."

"That may be true," Nick conceded between mouthfuls of stew. "But it is *I* who will win her heart in the end," he stated confidently before winking at Gwen.

Gwen tossed her long black hair over her shoulders and fixed them with an azure stare. "I'm not going to marry either of you."

Stricken, Jeremy demanded, "Who will you marry?"

Gwen's eyes turned dreamy. "Martin, of course."

The boys scrunched up their faces and repeated in unison, *"Martin?"*

The adults ate and listened, trying hard not to laugh.

Gwen frowned in annoyance. "Yes, Martin. He's always kind toward me, and he told me that I was pretty. Obviously, he's in love with me."

Agnes covered her mouth with her hand to keep from snickering whereas Jeremy was at a loss for words.

Nick, who was very bright and possessed a quick tongue, retorted, "Martin is far too old for you. Besides, I think he fancies your mother."

Agnes dropped her spoon in surprise and Sarah let out a giggle. The boy was far too clever for his own good sometimes! Even Simon looked at Nick incredulously.

Gwen's face turned crimson. "Nicodemus St. John, you don't know what you're talking about!"

"Oh no? So, you believe that Martin will marry you?"

"When I'm old enough, *yes*."

"I see," Nick said, rubbing his chin. "Of course, Martin will be old and gray by then."

Gwen crossed her arms. "He will not!"

Nick paced around like a bent old man with his hand on his lower back, and Jeremy burst into laughter.

Gwen's eyes narrowed. "Stop that, Nick!"

"Do you plan to have many children with him?" Nick pressed. "If so, you'll need take his age into account."

"Martin is young and strong," Gwen retorted. "What do you know about such matters? You're a stupid boy."

"Gwen!" Agnes scolded.

The game had gone too far.

"I'm a clever boy," Nick corrected. "A *very* clever boy."

"Mother!" Gwen cried.

Agnes couldn't help smiling as she admonished, "Nick, please stop. Be good and finish your stew."

Nick obediently sat beside his friend and, between giggles, the boys finished their stew beneath Gwen's disapproving glare.

After dinner, Sarah, Simon, and Agnes remained at the table talking and sipping ale. It was Sunday, after all—their day to relax a bit. The children sat by the hearth, facing the fire. The freezing rain pounded against the shutters, but the golden glow and warmth within the kitchen was cozy. They had each been given a ceramic cup of hot mulled wine, watered down and heavily laden with honey. Every so often the adults would burst into laughter.

"I wonder what they're talking about and why we can't sit with them," Gwen muttered, eyeing the adults with curiosity.

"They want privacy to discuss *adult* matters," Nick said, waggling his eyebrows.

Jeremy shuffled his stool closer to Gwen. "I think of you as an adult, Gwen."

Nick narrowed his eyes at Jeremy and did the same thing. Before long, Gwen was tightly wedged between the two boys as they fought for her attention.

Gwen sighed. "I wish Martin was here."

"He's not going to marry you," Nick said. "So stop dreaming about it."

Jeremy peeked over his shoulder to make sure his mother wasn't looking before furtively kissing Gwen on the cheek.

She gasped in surprise. "What was that for?"

Jeremy shrugged. "If Martin won't marry you, I will."

Gwen gazed at the flames and Jeremy was crushed by her cold silence.

Nick frowned at his friend. "I've already told you, Jeremy. I'm marrying Gwen."

"Enough!" Gwen snapped. "Are you both daft? I'm not marrying either of you, so stop this nonsense right now."

Silence followed.

A moment later, Nick said, "Can I kiss you, too?"

Gwen rolled her eyes. "No."

"But you let Jeremy kiss you."

She sighed in irritation. "Very well. Hurry up."

Gwen tilted her cheek toward him. To her surprise, Nick gently kissed her lips. Placing her fingertips to her mouth, she stared at Nick askance. "Where did you learn to kiss like that?"

Nick smiled smugly and said nothing.

Jeremy glared at his overly confident friend, then turned to Gwen and demanded, "Aren't you disgusted?"

Gwen shook her head while staring at Nick.

In an uncontrollable surge of jealousy, Jeremy took hold of her chin and leaned forward. "Let me kiss you like that."

She slapped his hand away. "No!"

Jeremy frowned in the face of her rejection, and his mouth contorted into a sneer. Suddenly, he stormed out of the kitchen, slamming the door behind him.

The adults stopped talking.

Simon stood. "What happened?"

"It's my fault," Nick replied. "I was only teasing him. Forgive me."

Sarah said, "Jeremy is too sensitive, and he's inherited his father's bad temperament."

"I'll go talk to him," Simon offered.

Sarah stood. "No, let me."

She went outside into the storm, leaving Agnes and Simon staring after her and speaking in hushed tones.

Gwen looked to Nick and whispered, "Where did you learn to kiss like that?"

"I saw it in a little red book that's full of incredible pictures—but you can't tell anyone I've told you this."

"What little red book?"

"I found it hidden away in the library."

"Where is it now?"

"I don't know. Someone moved it."

Nick was an excellent reader and Bartholomew had recently given him free access to the monastery's library. It was obvious the prior adored the boy to allow such a thing, especially since books were so rare and expensive.

One day while perusing several volumes, Nick noticed a tiny book bound in red leather crammed behind the shelf. He struggled to free it from its hiding place and, when he opened it, he was shocked. The book was filled with detailed drawings of naked men and women in strange positions. He remembered one picture of a man with his mouth against a woman's mouth. Beneath the illustration was a single word: *kiss*. Nick put the book back where he found it and fled the library before anyone discovered his secret. When he next visited the library, the book was gone.

"I would like to see this book," Gwen said, taking hold of the poker to push a log further into the flames.

Sarah and Jeremy entered the kitchen soaking wet. By the look on Jeremy's face, he had been reprimanded severely by his mother.

Later, Jeremy told his mother that Nick had kissed Gwen on the mouth. Sarah immediately conveyed this information to Agnes, who then told Simon, who finally informed the prior. Upon hearing the news, Bartholomew became distressed and took action.

The time had come for Nick to move out of the living space that Agnes and Gwen shared. The children were getting older and, for the sake of propriety, Nick was given his own cell inside the monastery. None of the brethren objected since he was only a boy, but rules had to be followed. Nick adjusted to the changes in his life without preamble. Soon afterward, he began studying formally with the monks.

***

England continued to suffer greatly under King Stephen's rule, creating huge rifts between the opposing factions of the nobility. The political instability caused the crime rate to rise steadily, and anxiety reigned supreme within the kingdom. Bartholomew diligently sought news in order to keep his monks informed of what went on in the outside world. Fortunately, St. John's was so far removed from everything that it was practically unaffected by the turmoil.

CHAPTER 8
POITIERS, FRANCE
1139

The full moon peeked through the misty night sky while the crickets and frogs performed a symphony. As Edward crossed the moat, he took in the imposing fortress before leading his horse through the gate. It was his first time in Poitiers, and the weather was slightly milder than in England. Robert Fitzroy, Earl of Gloucester, rode beside him with a sheen of perspiration visible on his brow. They enjoyed a somewhat smooth journey across the English Channel, and were on their way to a secret rendezvous with the earl's half-sister, the Empress Matilda.

When Robert of Gloucester first approached the bishop to join their cause, Edward pondered on the matter for several days. The promise of power and a noble title in exchange for funds seemed like a fair trade. Edward realized that he could be tried and executed for treason against the monarchy, but the risk was worth the reward. Many English barons were already fighting against Stephen, anyway. The Welsh and Scottish leaders were also in constant rebellion. Given the strife and instability within the kingdom, Matilda was sure to seize the throne sooner or later.

French-speaking grooms and servants greeted the two Englishmen and ushered them inside. A huge log burned in the fire of the main hall, blue and gold tapestries adorned the walls, and there were fine pieces of carved furniture in the spacious interior. Matilda and her husband, Geoffrey of Anjou, stood in the center of the room.

Matilda looked like a queen in a lustrous samite gown of tawny gold with a black perse surcoat. Gold chains adorned her slender throat, and upon her finger was an emerald as green as her eyes. She held her head high and boldly eyed the men in a way that Edward found rather disconcerting.

In contrast, young Geoffrey looked boyish and awkward despite his expensive brocade surcoat and jeweled collar. He sported a beard in an attempt to look mature, but it only made him appear absurd.

Edward had been careful in his choice of dress. His scarlet cloak had a thick trim of vair along the bottom edge, and a bejeweled crucifix dangled from a thick chain around his neck. When he held out his hand, the large ruby ring on his finger flashed in the candlelight.

Matilda dutifully kissed the bishop's ring. "Welcome to my home, Your Excellency."

Edward inclined his head. "It's an honor to be here, Your Highness."

She smiled, but her eyes remained cold. "I'm pleased by your decision to join our cause."

Geoffrey interjected, "We must overthrow the usurper before London burns to the ground!"

Robert glanced at Geoffrey and Matilda raised her hand to silence her husband. She continued, "I have managed to round up a sizable army, but it's not enough. With your aid, we can give my cousin a good fight."

"I have sufficient men, Matilda," Robert assured. "But with the help of your uncle we will lead a successful military campaign against Stephen."

"God is on your side," Edward added piously.

"The sycophants supporting Stephen are the same men who swore fealty to you," Robert pointed out. "The usurper must face justice."

The servants brought a variety of fruit and tarts along with sweet wine.

Matilda offered Edward a goblet from a tray. "Wine, my lord?"

"Thank you," Edward said as he carefully accepted the expensive glass vessel.

She handed another goblet to her half-brother.

Edward discreetly observed the manner in which Matilda

and Robert treated one another. Did the latter feel resentment for being Henry's illegitimate son and therefore forced to support a woman's pursuit of the throne? If so, Robert did an excellent job of hiding his feelings.

"I believe we'll be ready to cross the channel in another fortnight or so," Matilda said after taking a delicate sip from her own goblet. "I'll send a messenger prior to our arrival. You'll have plenty of time to prepare your army."

"We'll be ready," Robert assured with conviction.

"You'll be greatly rewarded if we win," she reminded him. "Will you remain in Poitiers for a few days?"

"I can't stay long," Robert said. "I have urgent matters to tend to in England."

Matilda looked at him as slyly as a cat, and a slow smile spread across her face.

"You'll at least rest here for the night before you depart for England," she urged. "Surely, the bishop won't object to that."

Robert and Edward nodded and thanked their hosts.

"My uncle has discussed a few strategies…" Matilda trailed off, her eyes sliding toward Edward. "The bishop appears tired."

Taking the hint, Edward nodded. "I am, my lady."

Matilda rose from her chair and Geoffrey did the same. She turned to the pages that stood in attendance and told them to show Edward to his room.

"Goodnight," Edward said.

"We shall depart early," Robert reminded him.

Edward nodded and followed the handsome boy, leaving Robert with Matilda in the main hall. The last words he heard were Matilda's: *'I wish to hear the full details of your strategy, Robert.*

"Goodnight, my lord," the page said as he held the door open for Edward.

The boy couldn't have been older than fourteen, but he was quite tall and slender, with blonde curly hair and vivid hazel eyes. Edward, who enjoyed a pretty boy on occasion, managed to convince the boy to share his bed in exchange for a few coins.

***

Edward returned to London as stealthily as he had departed. Two months later, following a major rebellion in the southwest of England, Matilda invaded and led an attack against Stephen. Unfortunately, getting the usurper off the throne was not as easy a task as she, Robert, or her uncle, King David of Scotland, had anticipated. People soon began referring to the ongoing struggle between the two fighting cousins as the *Anarchy*.

It was not until 1141 that Matilda's forces captured Stephen at the Battle of Lincoln, but her attempt to be crowned at Westminster was met with bitter opposition and outright hostility from the people of London. She was forced to make a hasty retreat from the city for the sake of her own safety. Without a stable authoritative figure ruling England, more fighting ensued in the face of this military disaster. To make matters worse, Robert was captured in Winchester and Matilda was forced to free Stephen in exchange for her half-brother's freedom.

In 1142 Matilda was caught in a castle siege in Oxford. Had she not escaped across the Thames, she would have been captured by Stephen. Frustrated—and no doubt exhausted from years of fighting—Matilda returned to Normandy, which had been secured by her husband while she was fighting in England. Before long, she was fully absorbed in ruling Normandy and raising her son, and never made another attempt to claim the English throne.

***

Edward stared blindly at the sheet of rain outside the window. The shutters were open wide enough to allow the cold damp to permeate the room. Despite the fine mist on the bishop's fur collar and the wetness of his tunic, he didn't feel compelled to move. He'd been sitting in the same spot for so long that his serving woman had already come out twice to check on him. Now, she hovered by the hearth glancing at the supper dish on the table. The boiled cabbage was limp and cold, and the fat on the bacon slab had congealed.

Wringing her hands nervously, she inquired in a tentative

tone, "Your Excellency, your supper is cold. Shall I reheat it?" Edward failed to reply, so she pressed, "You've been sitting in front of the window for over an hour, my lord. Please come warm yourself by the fire lest you catch your death of cold."

Edward glanced down at the crumpled message in his hand and remained silent.

The woman didn't like the hardness of her master's mouth or the vacant look in his eyes. The bishop had seemed fine until the messenger arrived with news from Normandy.

"My lord?"

The woman waited for a reply and finally gave up.

Edward's eyes narrowed into two slits as he balled his hands into tight fists. After spending a fortune on Matilda's military ventures, he was left with nothing but empty coffers and empty promises. To add insult to injury, the bitch had no plans of returning to England anytime soon because there was 'too much work to do' in Normandy.'

It would take years to replenish his funds. Had Matilda succeeded in reclaiming the throne, he would have become as wealthy and powerful as Richard—an equal to his brother. Instead, he had nothing to show for the time wasted and the money spent. There were no spoils of war, no power, no title.

Oh, how he hated women!

Well...*not all women*. There was only one female on Earth worthy of his love, but she was so far removed from his grasp that she may as well not exist. He often fantasized about owning a great castle and having the word 'Duke' or 'Earl' or 'Count' in front of his name. In those dreamlike scenarios Beatrice would always run into his open arms and confess her love for him. Without lands or titles, his dream of winning Beatrice's love would never come to pass. Heaving a great sigh, he vowed never to be fooled by scheming women again.

Damn Matilda to Hell.

CHAPTER 9

The years passed quietly and quickly. Nick concentrated on his education, excelling in geometry, math, and science. He also enjoyed French and Latin, and seemed to possess a natural linguistic ability. Bartholomew was extremely proud of him, and whenever Martin paid a visit to St. John's, he would return to Beatrice with glowing reports of Nick's progress.

Jeremy eventually told his mother that he wanted to live at St. John's with Nick, embrace monastic life, and fight for God. Jeremy had used the term 'Warrior of God,' which Sarah found troubling. The thought of her son going off to fight in a holy war scared her, but knighthood seemed to be the dream of every young man these days.

The friendship between Nick and her son had not only endured, but also deepened throughout the years. Jeremy also took well to his studies and excelled academically. One morning while Jeremy and Nick were finishing their lessons, Bartholomew appeared in the doorway and led the two youths into an antechamber.

Looking at each one in turn, he said, "You're both at an age when you need to make a decision. We've instructed you in the ways of the Lord, hoping that someday you'll take the monastic vows, but only if you're inclined to do so. God has a plan for everyone, but He gives us the freedom to choose how we serve Him."

"We want to be knights," Nick assured.

"And monks," Jeremy added.

"I know, but there's more to being a knight or a monk than fighting and memorizing passages of the Bible."

Jeremy frowned, confused. "What else is there?"

"Well, there's the vow of poverty since the pursuit of material wealth can harm us spiritually. There's also the vow of obedience, where we obey God's laws and the Bible's teachings. There's the Cluniac vow of learning, which means we must spend much of our time reading and meditating on our studies." Bartholomew hesitated. "Finally, there's the vow of chastity, which means we must abstain from carnal knowledge."

Being young and inexperienced, neither boy knew exactly what carnal knowledge was, but they were certain it was sinful.

Nick scrunched up his face. "Will I be guilty of carnal knowledge if I get married?"

Bartholomew nodded.

"So, if I'm a monk I cannot marry?"

"Marriage is forbidden to monks."

Nick thought of Gwen. "What if I kiss a woman?"

Jeremy's eyes slid toward Nick as the prior replied, "That is also forbidden."

"Are women evil?" Nick asked.

"Of course they are," Jeremy interjected.

Bartholomew raised his finger. "No, Jeremy."

"Eve is evil," Jeremy stubbornly countered. "She led Adam into sin. She's the reason humankind suffers."

Bartholomew chose his words with care. "Eve was indeed sinful, but women aren't evil because they were created by God." Noticing Jeremy's puzzled expression, he added, "There are two kinds of women in this world—godly women, like your mother and Agnes, and wicked women, like Queen Jezebel. The latter can easily cause men to sin."

"How?"

"Leading them into temptation," Bartholomew replied, wishing the boy would stop asking so many questions.

"With carnal pleasures?" Jeremy asked.

The prior nodded. "That, too."

"What exactly are carnal pleasures?"

Bartholomew knew that he could not prolong the explanation of human sexuality any longer. With the patience and love of a paternal father, the prior proceeded to explain what happens to men and women as they age, how their bodies change, and how babies are created.

Nick and Jeremy listened in wide-eyed silence. It all made perfect sense now. The boys had been experiencing odd feelings of excitement in their male organs and having strange dreams. They would wake up bewildered, breathless, and wet. Neither one had said anything to the other for fear they had somehow sinned against God. It was a great relief to know that what they were experiencing was normal.

"Did Gwen go through this when she was fourteen?" Nick inquired.

Jeremy's eyes turned cold at the mention of her name.

The prior's face burned. "No."

"But her body changed," Nick pointed out.

It was true. Gwen had developed breasts and hips, and now looked like a woman instead of a girl. Bartholomew placed his face in his hands to gather his thoughts. "Women go through changes, too, but what they go through is…*different* than what we go through as men."

"How?"

"It doesn't matter," the prior snapped. "Forgive me, but Gwen isn't the issue here, you are," he said, pointing at each boy. "Now that you know all there is to know about manhood, you'll need to make some decisions soon. I suggest you take the next few weeks to pray and ponder on what we've discussed today."

Nick and Jeremy walked out of the monastery in quiet contemplation. Jeremy was the first to speak.

"What do you want to do?"

"I want to be a knight," Nick replied.

"Me too, but don't you want to be a monk as well?"

Nick thought for a moment. "Sometimes I do, but sometimes I want to see the world and what it holds for me. I've spent my entire life at St. John's. I love Prior Bartholomew and I love God, but I'm also curious."

"Well, I want to be a monk," Jeremy stated with unwavering conviction.

Ever since Jeremy had moved into St. John's, his demeanor had changed. He was serious and zealous. It was obvious to many of the brethren that he was well-suited for monastic life.

"Do you agree with what Prior Bartholomew said about women?" Nick inquired.

"What about them?"

"That they tempt men into committing sin."

"Yes."

"Aren't you curious about carnal knowledge?"

"The prior's explanation of copulation sounded very strange and unappealing—I won't risk losing my immortal soul for the sake of any woman." Jeremy made a face and added, "As far as I'm concerned, I think most women are evil—except for our mothers and my grandmother."

"What about other old women? Or very young girls, like infants or small children?" Nick asked, curious of where his friend stood on these matters.

Jeremy rubbed his chin. "I suppose they're safe."

"What about our Gwen?"

Jeremy pictured the raven-haired beauty with the brilliant blue eyes; the girl he had known since infancy. The girl who had slapped his hand away and cruelly spurned him. In his opinion, Gwen was the most dangerous woman of all. "I think it would be wise if we both avoided her." Nick was shocked to hear this, but said nothing. Jeremy continued, "There's something I should tell you, but I'm not sure how you'll react."

"You can tell me anything."

"I only have your best interest at heart."

"Now you're scaring me," Nick teased. "For God's sake, we're brothers—just tell me!"

"It's obvious that God has blessed you with the good looks He meant for me," Jeremy said in an attempt at humor. "I fear for you, my friend. I believe you're cursed."

"What are you talking about?"

"Your good looks are a burden, and I fear that you'll be tempted into sin."

"What nonsense!" Nick bellowed, slapping his friend on the back playfully.

Jeremy didn't laugh, however. "I'm serious. I see how the

women stare at you whenever we go to the village. Their hungry eyes follow you."

"You exaggerate. I've noticed no such thing."

"Gwen looks at you in the same manner." Nick was completely caught off guard by this statement, and his face flushed with pleasure. Seeing this, Jeremy accused, "You're pleased by this."

"What? No! She's practically my sister," Nick retorted, averting his gaze. "Your imagination is playing tricks on you, Jeremy."

"I can assure you it's not my imagination."

"If it makes you feel better, I'm not the least bit interested in Gwen or any other woman."

Jeremy regarded him dubiously. "I only felt it my duty to warn you, brother."

"I appreciate that. Shall we practice now?"

The boys walked to the cell they shared in order to fetch their wooden swords.

Unlike Jeremy, Nick didn't think what happened between a man and a woman was strange. In fact, he found it intriguing—something he would relish doing, especially if the woman involved was Gwen. The sudden thought made him pause in reflection.

"Let's make a pact," Jeremy suggested, cutting into Nick's thoughts. "Let's be brothers forever. If one takes the vows, the other must follow." When Nick hesitated, he frowned. "Do you want to serve God and go to Heaven or not?"

"I want to serve God."

Satisfied, Jeremy removed a small knife from his belt and cut his hand. He handed the knife to Nick, who did the same. The boys shook hands, their blood mingling within the firm grip.

"Brother," Jeremy said.

"Brother," Nick repeated.

The next day, Jeremy handed Nick a book. "I found this in the library."

Nick leafed through several pages. "This is about the

Knights Templar."

"I think we should join the Order."

After reading about the Templars, the warrior monks who protected Christian pilgrims in the Holy Land, Nick and Jeremy approached the prior and declared their mutual desire to someday join the Order of the Knights Templar. Bartholomew was a bit disappointed that they had not chosen the Cluniac Order, but was pleased nonetheless that they had chosen God.

As time passed, Nick and Jeremy associated less with Agnes, Simon, and Gwen, and more with the monks. As monastic novices who intended to take vows someday, they had daily responsibilities to fulfill. Their lives revolved round intense study, attending vigils and masses, and fighting practice. Free time was scarce.

Chapter 10

"I hope it's perfect," Beatrice said to Martin and Gretta as they walked through the crowded London streets.

"How can it not be, my lady?" Gretta countered. "You hired the finest blacksmith in London."

They made their way gingerly over garbage, human waste, and horse manure until finally arriving at the smithy. The pungent odors of burning wood, smoke, and steel hung heavily in the air.

A burly man wearing a leather apron and sporting a shaggy beard walked outside. "Your presence honors my establishment, my lady."

Beatrice smiled and inquired, "Is it finished?"

The blacksmith returned the gesture, revealing a missing tooth. "Aye, my lady."

He motioned for one of his apprentices to come outside. Like his master, the young man's face was covered with soot. In his hands was a shiny sword with a blade that measured about three feet in length. The apprentice handed the sword to his master, who held it out to Beatrice for inspection.

Beatrice did not attempt to lift the heavy sword, but took a step forward to examine it closely. The polished steel gleamed in the autumn sunshine, and the exquisitely carved hilt cradled a large onyx stone, which Beatrice had personally selected. The perfect birthday gift for a sixteen year old young man.

"Beautiful," Beatrice whispered. Turning to Martin, she asked, "What say you?"

A seasoned knight, Martin took the sword and handled it with expertise, tossing it effortlessly from one hand to the other. Then, taking a few paces away from the women, he began to lunge forward and practice other fighting maneuvers to test the sword's balance and craftsmanship. The women watched in awe.

When he was done, Martin handed the sword back to the blacksmith. "It's perfect, my lady."

The blacksmith beamed with pride.

"Good work," Beatrice said. "What of the other sword?"

The blacksmith had his apprentice fetch another sword. It was also well made and of good quality, but lacked the artistic finery of the first. Since Nick would need a fighting partner, Beatrice had provided a sword for Jeremy. She paid the blacksmith extra money for his fine work, and more importantly, his silence.

Beatrice walked a few steps away from the smithy, then extracted a letter from her sleeve and handed it to Martin. "This letter is for the prior."

Martin's brow creased in confusion. "It bears the Fitzwilliam seal, my lady."

"It's time he learned the truth about Nick."

"Are you sure you want to reveal your identity?"

"I am. I've given this much thought. I also want you to stay in Lewes for at least a month."

"An entire month? How will I explain my absence to Lord Richard?"

"Send word that a relative has summoned you from his deathbed. Richard will understand."

"As you wish, my lady."

"My son needs to learn how to properly wield a sword. You can show him the basics and he can practice between visits." Placing a hand on his arm, Beatrice added, "Godspeed, Martin."

***

When Martin presented the swords to Nick and Jeremy, the boys displayed joy and gratitude.

"No more wooden swords!" Jeremy exclaimed.

Nick aimed his sword at an imaginary opponent. "We're true warriors now."

"I'm glad you're pleased with your gifts," Martin said.

Nick asked, "Will you show us some new defensive moves before you go?"

"I plan on showing you many. I was told to remain here for

a month in order to train you." The boys looked at each other, amazed. "Now, if you'll both excuse me, I need to speak with the prior."

Once inside the prior's cell, Martin removed the letter from his satchel. "My master has instructed me to give you this. It will answer many questions."

Bartholomew said nothing as he stared at the official seal. After a moment he broke the wax and read the letter. He looked at Martin, perplexed. "Is this true?"

"I'm the loyal servant of Lord Richard Fitzwilliam of Kent and his wife, the Lady Beatrice," Martin replied. "My mistress believed it was time for you to learn the truth."

The prior had heard stories of Lord Richard's hot temper and jealous tirades against the chaste and comely Lady Beatrice. The troubadours even sang about it. As for the Bishop of Rochester, several rumors circulated about him—the majority involving whores.

"I know of the bishop's treachery, and the sibling rivalry between the two brothers." When Martin expressed surprise, Bartholomew added, "Just because I choose to live in a quiet monastery doesn't mean I'm ignorant. I keep abreast of politics and gossip almost as much as a royal courtier."

Martin chuckled. "I find that hard to believe."

Bartholomew raised a brow. "Do you? The monks here correspond with monks in monasteries all over England. There's a large number of our Cluniac brethren residing outside London. Oftentimes, local gossip slips in between the lines of encouragement and prayer."

"I see."

"Nick has asked questions in the past."

"What have you told him?"

"Exactly what you've instructed." Bartholomew held up the letter. "If Nick is truly the legitimate son of Richard Fitzwilliam, he should be among nobles of his rank—not here. He needs to know the truth. It's his birthright."

"That day will come, but not now. He's too young and it's still unsafe."

"The boys want to be knights—did you know that?"

"Yes."

"They dream of becoming Templars. I don't have the heart to tell them that the Order selects its members from the nobility."

"Then they shall *both* have the proper papers and titles if and when the time comes," Martin assured, confident that his mistress would provide whatever her son needed. "Until then, I beg you not to say anything."

Bartholomew was relieved at finally knowing the truth, but felt burdened because he was unable to share it with Nick. "Very well."

For an entire month, Nick and Jeremy spent the better part of each day learning how to fight with their swords. Both boys were swift, skilled, and strong. Their young, lean bodies were changing as they developed muscular arms, wide backs, and hard chests.

Agnes saw little of Martin during his visit. She looked forward to their conversations, but he was too engrossed with the boys. On the night before his departure, Martin suggested they take a walk after supper. She agreed, and they slipped out beneath the light of a crescent moon.

Martin said, "The boys kept me well occupied these last few weeks. My master will be glad to hear how much Nick has grown. He tells me that he and Jeremy are going to be knights someday."

"Aye, they talk of little else," Agnes confirmed. "Prior Bartholomew has been like a patient father, teaching them many things."

"Indeed he has." He paused. "Agnes, may I ask you a personal question?"

Her stomach clenched. "Certainly."

"Can you read?"

"A bit. My father was a clever man. Writing is a different story," she admitted with a self-deprecating chuckle. "I've little use for either of those skills since my life here revolves around domestic chores."

"The monastery is remote—far from the village and any gaiety life has to offer."

She shrugged. "I have a roof over my head and food on my table. I'm of good health and have a wonderful daughter...What more can a woman ask for?"

"Yes, but are you *happy*?"

Surprised by the intimacy of the question, she merely looked at him askance.

"Forgive me," he offered.

"There's no need for you to apologize, Martin."

"You're an attractive woman and..." he trailed off.

"Yes?"

He cleared his throat. "It seems like a waste that you're in the middle of nowhere cooking for monks."

"These monks have devoted their entire lives to God. It's an honor to serve them." *Was that bitterness she heard in her own voice?*

"Of course. I didn't mean for that to sound the way it did," he corrected. "What I meant was that you're *alone*. Why not find a man in the village to marry?"

Martin's suggestion felt like a blow. After all these years, she had always thought that someday he would...

Agnes caught herself. That he would what? *Propose marriage?* She almost laughed aloud at her own naiveté. Martin lived in a castle surrounded by noble courtiers. He was well-versed in courtly manners, and most likely treated every woman with the same level of courtesy.

"I'm far from alone," she responded coolly.

They returned to the kitchen in companionable silence, and Agnes never again entertained another foolish thought about Martin.

Nick and Jeremy bade Martin farewell the following morning. The boys promised to practice every day and to treat their weapons with respect.

Shortly after Martin's departure, Simon began paying special attention to Agnes. He would often return from the village with a pretty ribbon or a sweet tart, and on several occasions she caught him openly staring at her while she worked.

One morning, while Agnes and Gwen were in the dairy churning butter, Simon entered with a wrapped parcel. "Agnes, I've brought you something from the village. I hope you like it."

Agnes blushed and wiped her hands on her apron before accepting the gift. "You shouldn't trouble yourself on my account."

Gwen gasped in delight as Agnes held up a fine piece of wool dyed the color of mulberries.

Simon fidgeted. "Do you like it?"

"Very much," Agnes said. "Thank you."

"I thought the color would go nicely with your hair," he said. "And it will keep you warm in winter."

Agnes was touched. The fabric was of good quality and must have cost quite a bit. There was enough to make a frock for herself and perhaps one for Gwen. She glanced at her daughter, who was eyeing her with a grin.

"Well, I'd better get to work," Simon said, then left.

"He's been behaving so strangely lately," Gwen commented slyly. "I think he fancies you. Tell me, Mother, would you ever…?"

"Ever what?"

"Marry him?"

Agnes pondered her daughter's valid question. *Would she?* Simon was a good man—honest and kind. He wasn't unpleasant to look at, either. "I don't know."

"It would be nice to see you happily married. You've been a widow for far too long."

"What I desire most is to see *you* happily married. As for me, I was already blessed with a good husband once in my life."

"You can enjoy that blessing again with someone else," Gwen pointed out gently.

"True, but Simon has never spoken of marriage or even confessed love. It's nonsense to talk about it."

Gwen raised an eyebrow. "The only reason he hasn't

approached you is because of his intense shyness. Otherwise, he would have married you by now."

Agnes stood, flustered. "I should start dinner."

"I'll help you."

"No, stay and finish," Agnes instructed before slipping out the door.

Gwen remained in the dairy, smiling as she churned the butter. It would be a good thing if Simon and her mother got married. She hated the thought of her mother growing old without a companion.

"Gwen!" cried Nick as he ran into the dairy.

"Where's your shadow?" Gwen inquired coolly.

"Jeremy is praying." In his hand was a little red book. "Come away from the churn and see what I've found."

"What's in your hand?"

"Remember the red book I told you about years ago? The one I asked you to keep secret after I kissed you?"

The memory of Nick pressing his lips against her own made her blush. "Yes, but you said it was gone."

"Well, I just found it in the barn by the goat pen."

Gwen frowned, puzzled. "Do you think it belongs to Giles, the monk who tends the goats?"

"Impossible. He's too old and practically blind. There's no way he could even see these tiny drawings."

"Then who?"

"Definitely someone with keen eye sight."

"Hmm…"

"Well, go on and look at it," he urged.

Gwen opened the book with baited breath. She was shocked to see several sexual positions vividly displayed on page after page. What was a book of this profane nature doing in a monastery? As she studied the pictures, her face grew hot and her heart thumped fiercely. She would be in serious trouble if anyone caught her right now.

"Don't you find the pictures funny?" Nick inquired, his eyes doubtful.

Gwen studied one naked couple after another and soon felt

a stirring deep within her—a longing that ached to be filled. Her eyes slid discreetly toward Nick, and she was suddenly aware of his height and the breadth of his shoulders. Dropping her gaze to his wrists, she noticed the elegant bones that protruded slightly above his strong, beautiful hands. She imagined what those hands would feel like upon her bare skin...

Closing the book abruptly, she cleared her throat. "If I were you, I'd put this book back exactly where I found it and never tell anyone about it."

Nick frowned as he accepted the book from her hand. "What's wrong?"

Averting her gaze, she replied crisply, "Nothing."

"You're obviously upset about something."

"What do you care?" she snapped, overcome with an inexplicable emotion.

He appeared stricken. "Gwen?"

She wanted to throw her arms around him and speak sweet words Instead, she resumed her task and said, "You should run along now and find your shadow. He wouldn't approve of you talking to me."

Dejected, Nick hung his head and took his leave.

Gwen ran to the window and watched the sunlight play across his golden hair. She couldn't get the images from the book out of her head—she even pictured doing some of those acts with Nick. Her conscience felt guilty after such an unclean thought, and she sat down at the butter churn quietly reciting her prayers.

***

In the year 1145, Martin visited the monastery only once because Richard was forced to remain close to home in order to deal with squabbling nobles. Edessa, the oldest crusader territory of the Holy Land, had been captured the previous year by Zengi of Mosul, and news of this defeat finally trickled into Rome by summer. The loss of Edessa was felt in Christendom, and rumors of a possible crusade began to circulate throughout Europe.

In December 1145, Pope Eugenius III issued a papal bull

proclaiming a second crusade. When news of the pope's decree reached St. John's, Bartholomew immediately informed the monks. Nick and Jeremy were very excited at the prospect of fighting in a real holy war.

The tension hung as heavy as lead in the cold winter air as everyone waited for more news. December was so bitterly cold that the monks remained mostly indoors, leaving their cells only to eat and care for the animals in the barn.

One icy morning, Simon decided to confess his feelings for Agnes. He had been slowly courting her for years, but his intense shyness prevented him from asking for her hand in marriage.

Agnes sat at the table chopping kale for the evening's soup when he entered the kitchen with a pile of wood. After setting it down, he sat on a stool and watched her nimble hands. Although roughened from work, they were still graceful and sensuous. A few curled wisps of auburn hair escaped from her cap and he stared at the soft nape of her neck with longing.

"Agnes," he said.

She looked up from her task to meet his eyes. "Yes?"

"I've been wanting to tell you something for a very long time, but I don't know how."

A very long time, indeed, she thought as she noticed just how blue his eyes were. "Tell me."

"Agnes, I think…Well, I think that…"

She wasn't going to wait for his proposal any longer. Cupping his face in her hands, she kissed his cheek tenderly. "You're dear to me, Simon."

Taking her gesture as an invitation, Simon placed his hands over hers, and boldly leaned forward to cover her mouth with his own.

Melting into the kiss, she relished the touch of a man. She'd remained faithful to Tom's memory all these years, and as celibate as one of the monks she served on a daily basis.

Simon pulled away, and for the first time Agnes saw him as a *man*. She noticed the strength of his hands, the breadth of his shoulders, and the lines of his pleasant face. She liked how his eyes crinkled at the corners when he smiled. She leaned her head forward to welcome another of his kisses.

"God, I've dreamt of this day over and over. I never believed it would come true," he said against her mouth as his hands roamed throughout her supple body.

"We can't," she whispered. "We shouldn't…"

He kissed her neck. "We *can* and we *should*."

"Simon, we're in a monastery," she said breathlessly as his hands cupped her breasts.

"No, we're in a kitchen *near* a monastery," he corrected her between kisses.

He took her nipple into his mouth and she gasped aloud.

Agnes could scarcely breathe. "Simon…"

Simon didn't respond, but continued to suck on one nipple while his fingers teased the other. Agnes never suspected he was capable of such passion and she never imagined she could respond to him in such a manner.

He urged her to sit on the kitchen table and positioned himself between her thighs. She looked at him knowingly as his hand slipped beneath her skirt.

"Marry me, Agnes."

"Yes, Simon, but we must stop—"

He placed a finger over her lips. "Let me have you."

Agnes nodded and they made love with such intensity that it left them breathless afterward.

Chapter 11

Agnes and Simon were married in the spring of 1146. Bartholomew was sad to lose such an industrious pair of workers, but piled many blessings upon them. As a wedding gift, the prior provided them with a pair of chickens and a goat. Simon eventually secured work for both of them at a local inn at the village.

Gwen remained at the monastery as a kitchen maid. With Simon and her mother gone, she felt completely and utterly alone.

***

Bernard of Clairvaux, the Cistercian preacher whose rigid ideals were becoming increasingly popular with zealots, began a preaching tour in order to rally support for the Second Crusade. Bartholomew, who openly dismissed many of Clairvaux's teachings as fanatical, supported his campaign nonetheless, and encouraged the monks to pray for the souls of the crusaders. Nick and Jeremy were in a perpetual state of excitement and spoke of little else except the recapture of Christian territories, and defeating the Infidel.

All this talk made Gwen very nervous—not because she didn't believe in the motive behind the crusade, but because it meant that Nick would leave Lewes. She prayed fervently for God to miraculously kill the Infidel Himself to prevent Nick from fighting. Her greatest fear was that he would die in battle and never return.

Summer came quickly that year, bringing with it heat and longer days. Gwen missed her mother tremendously. Virgil, the new kitchen knave who replaced Simon, wasn't nearly as efficient as his predecessor. Perhaps it was because he was old, fat, and lacked the energy. Regardless of the reasons, Gwen was forced to work harder to make up for the man's slack.

Nick and Jeremy practiced their sword fighting more than

ever before. Jeremy still kept a strict schedule of Bible reading and theological studies, but Nick would oftentimes sacrifice those lessons to practice his sword fighting alone. On those occasions, he preferred the privacy of the courtyard by the kitchen, and Gwen would watch him from the window as she prepared the meals. Sometimes, while she was outside tending the garden or in the dairy, Gwen had caught him staring at her with great intensity. Whenever she met his eyes, he would quickly avert his gaze and continue to practice in silence.

Gwen churned butter in the coolness of the dairy one hot morning when she heard the familiar hissing sound of metal cutting through air. She stopped her task, wiped the moisture from her brow, and stretched her back. From the tiny window she spied Nick attacking an imaginary opponent with strong jabs. The heat had caused him to shed his tunic, and his strong chest glistened with perspiration. Flashes of light bounced and gleamed off the polished blade of his mighty weapon.

Nick possessed an animal grace that she found both impressive and intimidating. His shoulder length hair was the color of pale honey, which gleamed like spun gold in the bright sunlight. He kept it tied back neatly with a strip of leather. The expression of concentration on his face was so fierce that it made him appear much older than his nineteen years.

While Gwen watched from the dairy, the images of the forbidden red leather book came to mind. As if sensing her wicked thoughts, Nick stopped his imaginary attack and turned around to capture her gaze. They stared at one another for several seconds before Gwen quickly retreated from the window with a racing heart. Her hands trembled as she resumed churning the butter.

Nick appeared in the doorway a moment later. "Why are you spying on me?"

Gwen kept churning, her eyes downcast. "There's water in the cup if you need a drink."

Nick picked up the earthenware cup and drank thirstily. "Thank you." She nodded without looking at him. "You shouldn't spy on others."

"I wasn't spying, I was watching you."

"Why were you watching me?"

Flustered, she said, "You look foolish."

"Foolish? How?"

"You're fighting with air."

"I'm *practicing*, not fighting."

She carefully kept her eyes averted and remained silent. To meet his gaze would be to confess what was in her heart, and she couldn't expose such vulnerability to anyone.

Frustrated, he left the room.

Gwen stopped churning the moment he departed and edged close to the window. Her eyes followed the line of Nick's shoulders and lingered at the muscular cords of his neck. He was getting stronger by the day, and with that physical strength came a drastic change in his personality. He was serious now, almost to the point of brooding. Thanks to Jeremy, he talked incessantly of war and the glory of God.

Where was the sharp-witted boy she once knew? The one who kissed her and begged her to marry him?

She returned to the churn with blurred vision, and focused her attention on the task at hand. She usually thought of Nick when she was alone in her bed at night. That way, no one would see her tears.

Later that day, Bartholomew sent Nick and Jeremy into town to purchase some supplies.

While they hitched a mule to the cart, Gwen exited the kitchen with an empty basket. "Would you mind getting some things for me?"

To her surprise, Nick suggested, "Why not come with us? You're better than we are at selecting foodstuffs."

Jeremy frowned. "I'd rather Virgil accompany us."

"Virgil is sick," Gwen explained.

"Can't he go tomorrow?"

"Jeremy, that's enough," Nick said. "Get into the cart, Gwen. I'll notify the prior that you're coming with us."

Jeremy didn't offer his hand or even cast a glance in her direction as she scrambled into the cart. Miffed by his lack of courtesy, she glared at him. Jeremy moved over on the wooden plank that served as a seat, deliberately allowing a wide space between them.

Offended, she said, "I don't have the plague."

Jeremy ignored her comment.

"Tell me what I did to offend you," she pressed. "You've been treating me like a stranger for a long time."

Jeremy snorted and turned his face away. Exasperated, she simply gave up. They sat in total silence until Nick returned.

The journey was short and uncomfortably silent. When they arrived in the village, Jeremy jumped down from the cart and began walking away.

"Where are you going?" Nicked demanded.

Jeremy glanced at Gwen before replying, "I'll get the supplies. You can stay with her and shop for food."

"Come along, Gwen," Nick said.

To her delight, they gravitated closer to one another as they walked past various stalls filled with merchandise. Nick patiently stood by her side as she paused to examine pots and wooden spoons, and aided her in selecting dried and fresh bunches of herbs, fruits, vegetables, sausages, and breads.

"Thank you for inviting me," Gwen said.

"You deserve a respite. I know Virgil doesn't pull his weight in the kitchen."

"How do you know?"

Nick shrugged. "Well, the other monks have made comments, but I've noticed that you often appear tired."

She chuckled wryly. "Working in the kitchen has destroyed my beauty."

"Far from it," he countered, then blushed.

Gwen gently brushed her forefinger against the back of his hand. "I'm glad that you don't loathe me."

A shiver of pleasure ran up his arm as he met her eyes. "Why would I?"

"Jeremy can't stomach the sight of me."

"Jeremy embraces some extreme views, one of them being an aversion toward women."

"Let me guess—we're evil temptresses."

"I'm afraid so."

She frowned. "Does that include his own mother?"

"No, but…" At the sight of Gwen's expression he hastily added, "I don't agree with his views."

"Thank God for that."

"Are you hungry?" he asked. When she nodded he said, "Let's buy some chewets for the ride home."

"I'm fond of them," she admitted, her stomach growling at the thought of the fried meat pies.

"Me too."

"I know. In fact, I know all of your favorite foods."

There was so much he wanted to say. "Gwen…"

Hopeful anticipation lit up her eyes. "Yes?"

"Nick!"

It was Jeremy. Gwen cursed under her breath.

"I need your opinion on something," he said as he glared at Gwen.

Nick said to Gwen, "We'll meet at the cart. Make haste."

She watched him walk away with Jeremy, who gave her a withering look. She tried not to feel resentment toward her childhood friend, but Jeremy had changed in the last few years.

She wandered through the market alone, stopping only to buy the things she needed for the kitchen. Two men playing an organistrum shoved past her, almost causing her to fall over. Several children ran after the men, dancing and giggling to the cheerful music. She shook her head and laughed softly.

"Good day, fair lady," said a deep voice.

Gwen turned around and spotted a ruggedly attractive man behind one of the stalls. Dressed in a fine linen tunic the color of midnight, his brown wavy hair fell to his shoulders and he possessed a pair of eyes the color of charcoal. Several bolts of good fabric were displayed before him. Gwen didn't remember seeing his stall the last time she had been in the village.

She took a step closer. "Are you new here?"

The man took in her cerulean eyes, ebony hair, and trim waist. "I've been here for almost two months. Haven't you noticed my stall? Everyone else has."

"I don't live in the village."

"Where do you live?"

"I work at St. John's."

"An enchanting lass like you so far from the gaiety of town is surely a sin." Gwen blushed and smiled. Encouraged by this, he asked, "What's your name?"

"Gweneth."

"*Gweneth* is a nice name," he said, walking around to the front of the stall.

"Thank you, sir."

"Ranulf St. George, wool merchant. At your service." He then snatched Gwen's hand, kissed it, and made a sweeping gesture with his arm as he bowed low.

Unaccustomed to male attention, Gwen was both flattered and surprised by the gallant display. "St. George, like the dragon slayer?"

His eyes twinkled. "Aye."

"It's a fine name."

"Not as fine as you are, my sweet girl."

Nick approached the stall in time to see the wool merchant kiss Gwen's hand.

"Here, this is for you," Ranulf said as he handed Gwen a pair of blue silk ribbons. "You can tie up that pretty hair of yours and stay cool in this heat."

She shook her head. "Oh, I couldn't possibly—"

"Please, they're only ribbons. A mere token."

"You are most kind."

Ranulf winked. "The color matches your eyes."

Nick's first instinct was to hit the man, but he prudently decided to place a protective arm around Gwen's shoulders. "Come away, Gwen, we must get going." When they were out of Ranulf's earshot, he added, "You shouldn't talk to strangers."

"He's a wool merchant and his name is Ranulf St. George."

"Prior Bartholomew has warned you never to talk to strange men when you go into the village."

Ignoring his chastisement, she played with her new ribbons. "He was quite handsome, don't you think so?"

His eyes narrowed. "I would not know."

"Kissing my hand like that—such chivalry."

He scowled. "That's enough."

Satisfied by his jealousy, she decided not to provoke him further.

Jeremy was already in the cart waiting for them. "She should be stoned," he said, staring in their direction.

At first Gwen thought he was referring to her, but then she realized he was talking about an old woman standing a few feet away. Despite the heat, the old crone wore a black cloak and her scraggly gray hair fell in tangles past her shoulders.

Jeremy continued, "Everyone knows she's a witch."

Sensing that she was being watched, the old woman turned her head and glared at Jeremy, Nick, and Gwen.

"No one has ever said a word against her," Nick pointed out as he helped Gwen into the cart.

"That's because everyone is afraid of her," Jeremy retorted. "Mad Margaret should be driven out of this village."

"*That* is Mad Margaret?" Gwen inquired, surprised. She had heard Prior Bartholomew speak of the woman once or twice, and always with the warning to steer clear of her at all costs.

Jeremy barely looked at Gwen as he nodded in response to her question.

"Jeremy, the old crone is only mad—loss of wits doesn't make a person a witch," Nick said in Mad Margaret's defense. "Simon told me so."

"Regardless of what Simon said, she's a witch."

Nick, who was busily doling out the chewets he had purchased from the baker, replied with a mere shrug. He was hungry and didn't want to discuss the matter further. Gwen bit into her chewet as her eyes scanned the crowded market in search of Mad Margaret. As if by magic, the old crone had disappeared without a trace.

***

Beatrice and Gretta sat in the cool shade of an elm tree in the castle's large courtyard. Twenty feet away, undeterred by the summer heat, Robert practiced his sword fighting with one of Richard's knights. At age twenty-one, he was handsome, strong, and the sole heir of his father's fortune. There were several nobles of high station seeking marriage alliances through Robert, but Richard was still holding out for the best offer.

Richard stepped out into the courtyard to speak with his son and Beatrice gazed in wonder at how two men could look so much alike despite being twenty years apart in age. Robert put down his sword and approached the elm tree once his father had gone back inside. He took a seat on the grass beside his mother.

Beatrice placed her hand on her son's shoulder. "You seem anxious. What troubles you, my son?"

"The king wants his nobles to support the crusade, and Father intends to go."

"I know."

"Father wants me to go with him."

Beatrice nodded, fighting back tears. She had argued with Richard that morning. She didn't want her son to go to war. Richard pointed out that Robert was no longer a boy, but a man with responsibilities and obligations to fulfill. She conceded, for she knew her husband was right. Robert would be taking Richard's place in the near future, and he had to set the example for all the men who served in their army.

"I'm *apprehensive*," he confessed. "I'm ashamed to even tell you such a thing. Don't think me a coward."

She met her son's eyes with empathy and love. "There's no shame in feeling fear, Robert. I'm sure the king himself is anxious at the thought of entering that strange land and fighting those barbarians. Fear doesn't make anyone a coward; if anything, it makes you wise. It's our duty as Christians to fight the Infidel with every ounce of strength in our being."

"I want to fight."

"You will, you'll be victorious, and you'll return to England as a hero," she assured him.

A servant approached them and handed Robert a chalice of

watered wine. He drank thirstily, then kissed his mother's cheek before returning to practice.

Gretta quietly reached for her mistress's hand and gave it a squeeze. "He'll be fine, my lady."

"Dear God, I hope so. I've already lost one son; I can't bear to lose the other."

***

The summer days passed, each one warmer than the next. Nick began avoiding Gwen after their outing to the village, and she was convinced that Jeremy had something to do with it. At first she was deeply hurt, but the seed of resentment festered in her heart, and the pain turned to anger.

Gwen and Virgil traveled to the village for supplies every once in a while, and she would make it a point to visit Ranulf at the market. The merchant took a liking to the girl, and rode to St. John's whenever he had the opportunity to do so. Ranulf eventually introduced himself to the prior, and respectfully asked permission to court Gwen. Bartholomew granted it, for he had always known the day would come when Gwen would marry and have a life of her own. Soon, he would have to find someone to take her place in the kitchen.

Ranulf's visits not only broke the monotony of Gwen's lonely life, it gave her the opportunity to spite Nick.

On a breezy afternoon in early September, Agnes paid her daughter a surprise visit at St. John's.

"You look well, Gwen," said Agnes after they had shared a warm embrace.

"As do you, Mother. Where is Simon?"

"There's so much work for us to do at the inn, but being an indulgent husband, he allowed me to come see you today."

"Come, sit. I was preparing something to drink."

Agnes entered the room and sat down at the familiar table. The smell of chamomile, mint, and lavender filled the air. For years she had brewed the same drink for her daughter, now she watched as Gwen poured the steaming liquid into two ceramic cups.

"How are Nick and Jeremy?" Agnes inquired before taking

a careful sip. "How is Prior Bartholomew?"

"Prior Bartholomew is as strong as an ox." Gwen paused, her expression odd. "As for Nick and Jeremy, I believe they're faring well. They practice their sword fighting daily in preparation for the crusade, and when they're not out clashing swords, they're praying."

Agnes frowned slightly. "Sarah said Jeremy intends to take the vows."

Gwen rolled her eyes. "Jeremy is more zealous than all of St. John's monks combined."

"I see," Agnes said, peering closely at Gwen.

"He's developed an aversion to women. To him, we're all evil temptresses."

"Surely, Nick doesn't treat you in such a manner."

"We don't speak to each other the way we used to when you and Simon were here," she admitted, her eyes sad. "Jeremy pressures him to stay clear of me."

"Would you be happier in the village? Now that Simon and I have secured a bigger home, you can live with us."

The last thing Gwen wanted was to invade her mother's privacy. Agnes deserved to be happy with Simon, not fret over her grown daughter.

Gwen smiled at her mother. "Thank you for the offer, but I'm fine here."

"What of Ranulf?"

"He comes to see me whenever he can."

"Has he spoken of marriage yet?"

"He's implied it once or twice."

"Do you fancy him?"

Gwen shrugged. "He's a good man, I suppose."

"He's older and has a thriving business. You wouldn't have to work as hard as you do now. You could possibly afford a servant if you married him."

But he isn't Nick, Gwen thought.

"You're twenty-two and still unmarried," Agnes pointed out. "It's my fault for keeping you here in this isolated place."

"You remained unmarried for several years."

"I was a widow—there's a difference. Is Ranulf courteous and kind toward you?"

"He treats me well enough."

"I see no reason why you shouldn't at least consider marriage. You don't want to live at the monastery for the rest of your life, do you?" Gwen said nothing and Agnes reached for her hand. "I want to see you content and cared for. You could do a lot worse than Ranulf."

Gwen fought to keep the tears at bay and smiled. "I'll give it serious thought, Mother."

Agnes left her daughter with much to think about.

The following day brought rain, but that didn't deter Nick and Jeremy from their daily practice. They were sparring outside the dairy and Jeremy suddenly slipped on the wet grass. He thrust his sword forward with more force than intended, and the blade cut the top of Nick's shoulder. Blood oozed from the wound as Nick grunted in pain and fell to his knees.

Jeremy's panicked cry prompted Gwen to look out the window. Dropping the bunch of parsley in her hands, she ran out into the rain and knelt beside Nick.

Jeremy stood, white-faced and trembling beneath a canopy of rain.

Gwen said, "We need to get him inside."

They helped Nick to stand, then brought him into the kitchen.

Gwen fished for a clean cloth, then pointed to a wooden stool by the fire. "Remove his tunic."

Jeremy helped Nick to sit, then looked at the blood-soaked fabric and retched. "I can't."

Glaring at him, she pushed him out of the way and peeled the wet fabric off of Nick's torso.

Seeing the torn flesh, Jeremy paled. "Dear God."

Gwen examined the wound and determined that it was deep. Taking the cloth, she applied pressure to the cut. "Now's not the time to be squeamish. There's hot water in the kettle. Pour some into a bowl."

Jeremy did as he was told and placed the bowl on the table.

"I need some air…"

"Stay," Gwen snapped as she dipped the cloth in hot water before cleaning the wound. Nick winced in pain and she put her lips to his ear. "It's deep and it will need to be dressed."

"Only a scratch," Nick countered through stiff lips.

Turning to Jeremy Gwen said, "Here, hold this and apply pressure to staunch the bleeding." She took Jeremy's hand and placed it over the cloth on Nick's wound. He visibly flinched at her touch and she rolled her eyes. She noticed that he turned his face away in order not to look at the blood.

Gwen grabbed the stone mortar and pestle from the shelf and placed them on the table. She began to pick the leaves off of various dried herbs that hung in neatly tied bunches from the low rafters. Agnes taught her daughter the art of preserving and using various roots and leaves, just as her ancestors had in Ireland.

Nick watched in amazement how quickly and gracefully Gwen moved throughout the kitchen. When she approached him with the odd-smelling concoction, he smiled slightly.

"You should consider alchemy," Nick teased.

Sitting naked from the waist up, she couldn't help but notice his fine physique. Nick caught her gaze and she blushed. "Remove the cloth, Jeremy."

"I'm going to be ill," Jeremy said, his face green.

"Not here," she snapped.

"Go wait by the door, brother," Nick suggested.

Jeremy lingered by the doorway while Gwen gently smeared the herbal remedy into the cut and patted it down. Despite the pain of his wound, Nick enjoyed the feel of her smooth hands upon his bare skin.

"All done?" he asked.

"Not yet," she replied as she tore off a strip from a cloth of clean linen. "I need to dress the wound."

Nick admired the way her fingers moved so deftly. "If not an alchemist, then a physician."

"It takes a sword wound to revive your sense of humor, I see," she commented, ripping off another strip.

"I didn't realize it was dead."

Ignoring his comment, she warned, "You'll surely catch your death of cold if you keep practicing in the rain—that is, of course, if Jeremy doesn't kill you first."

"How can one catch cold in early September?" Nick countered. "I must practice even more now that Prior Bartholomew has given me his blessing to fight when the time comes."

"And when will that be?" she inquired, barely able to disguise her fear.

"Soon."

"You're definitely going?"

"Of course he is," Jeremy replied on Nick's behalf.

Nick looked to Jeremy, then Gwen. "It's my duty as a knight and as a Christian."

"We want to be Templars," Jeremy announced.

Gwen met Jeremy's gaze. "You had better get over your squeamishness of blood because you'll be seeing plenty of it in battle." Turning her attention back to Nick, she whispered, "When will you be back?"

Nick shrugged and winced at the pain in his shoulder. "It could be months—even years. I don't know."

"Most likely years," Jeremy interjected from across the room. "And I'm *not* squeamish."

Gwen fought the urge to slap Jeremy across the face.

"Do you have something hot to drink?" Nick asked, changing the subject.

Gwen ladled some broth from a small cauldron into a wooden bowl. "Here."

"Thank you."

Nick allowed the flames in the hearth to warm him as he sipped the broth. Gwen's eyes discreetly traced the muscles of his chest and shoulders.

"The rain is letting up. I should fetch the swords lest they rust," Jeremy said before running outside.

Gwen took advantage of the little time they had alone. "Nick, do you really want to become a monk?"

He regarded her for a moment. He knew that Prior Bartholomew recently granted the village wool merchant permission to court Gwen. Obviously, she was keen on the idea. What would it matter if he left for the holy war?

Gwen didn't care for him—she never did.

"Well?" she prompted.

"I do," he affirmed, his face like stone.

Jeremy returned with the wet swords and set about drying the steel with a cloth to prevent rust.

Although terribly disappointed by his response, Gwen did her best to hide it. "Let me sprinkle some of this into the broth," she said, kneeling before Nick. "It will help ease the pain."

Nick watched as her long delicate fingers crumbled dried herbs. He breathed in the comforting steam before placing the bowl to his mouth. Gwen caught herself admiring his lips. Oblivious of Jeremy, they stared at one another in utter silence.

"*Gweneth*."

She stood and turned toward the door. "Ranulf, what are you doing here?"

Ranulf, who was almost ten years Nick's senior, regarded the younger man with a flicker of rivalry before his face softened into a smile for Gwen. "I have business in Brighton and St. John's is on the way."

"How thoughtful," she said flatly.

Nick stood, staggering slightly. "I'll be going now."

Gwen placed a hand on his arm. "Sit, Nick, you need to rest for a moment. You've lost quite a bit of blood."

Nick shook his head. "Jeremy, help me to my cell."

Gwen and Ranulf watched as Jeremy and Nick slowly made their way to the door.

Nick looked back over his shoulder and met Gwen's eyes. "Thank you."

Ranulf placed the parcel on the table, walked to the hearth, and put his hands out toward the flames. "I've brought you a fine cut of cloth, my dear."

"Thank you," she said distractedly.

She went to the window and watched Nick, which annoyed

Ranulf. He placed both hands on her shoulders and spun her around to face him. The wretched kitchen knave could enter at any moment, and he wanted to steal a kiss.

"I missed you," he confessed before leaning down to claim her lips.

Gwen closed her eyes and pretended it was Nick.

***

Christmas was quiet that year. Virgil, who had no family, was kind enough to pull a monk from the ranks to help him in the kitchen, thus allowing Gwen to spend Christmas with Agnes and Simon. It was good to be around the glow of their mutual happiness. She returned to St. John's shortly after the New Year. Had Nick noticed her absence? Gwen waited for him to come visit her in the kitchen, but he never did. In fact, the only time she ever saw Nick was from a distance, and he was usually accompanied by his fleshly shadow, Jeremy.

In the early spring, Virgil suggested that they go into the village to procure food for the annual Easter feast. Bartholomew insisted on it being abundant after the weeks of self-denial due to Lent.

Virgil took his basket and wasted no time in visiting the food stalls in the market. Gwen remained close, offering her opinion on various items. She noted Ranulf's absence that day. This wasn't unusual since the nature of his trade required frequent travel.

"What do you think of these? We could bake them into the tarts," Virgil said, pointing to a basket of dried apples. "Fresh would be better…"

She didn't reply because her attention was on the old woman staring at her and whispering from across the narrow lane. It was Mad Margaret.

"Or we could use dried berries," Virgil said.

An icy shiver crept up Gwen's spine and she felt the hairs on the back of her neck stand on end. Mad Margaret's eyes were locked on hers and the old hag began to whisper.

"Gwen?" Virgil snapped.

Gwen swung her head to face him. "What?"

He sighed in irritation. "Apples or berries?"

"Prior Bartholomew is fond of apples. We could make apple cakes. The monks would love it."

Virgil turned around to negotiate price with the vendor at the stall. Gwen gasped in unexpected surprise when she turned and found Mad Margaret's face only inches from her own!

The old woman's hand came down in a vice-like grip on Gwen's wrist. "Don't worry, child. He'll return to you."

"Who? Ranulf?"

The old crone shook her head. "Not the wool merchant, the other man—the one you *truly* love."

Gwen's eyes widened in shock. "How do you...?"

"*Gwen!*"

Mad Margaret released Gwen's wrist.

"What are you doing speaking with that witch?" Virgil demanded.

"I wasn't speaking…I mean, I turned around and she was right here!"

To Gwen's surprise, Mad Margaret was nowhere to be found. It's as if she disappeared!

"Never mind. Here," he said, placing a burlap bag of dried apples in her arms. "Is that too heavy for you to carry?"

Gwen shook her head and followed Virgil to the next stall. Her mind raced as she thought of Mad Margaret's words. The old woman had lost her wits.

Gwen and Virgil prepared a fine Easter meal for the monks. Like Bartholomew, Virgil believed that after the denial of Lent, they deserved to gorge themselves on good food. Knowing the departure for the crusade was imminent, it would possibly be the last banquet for Nick. For this reason, Gwen went out of her way to prepare each dish with care and much love.

The apple cakes were baked to perfection, along with savory meat pies. Gwen even made little decorations on them with the leftover dough; flowers and animal shapes, even a few initials. The monks would be delighted by this extra-added touch. The prior had purchased two lambs with the money Martin provided, and Virgil roasted the tender meat with fresh herbs.

They baked bread and churned butter laced with honey—a special treat. The prior allowed the monks to drink wine freely, too.

Later, they set about cleaning up the kitchen. After a while of scrubbing plates, Virgil rubbed at his hands.

Gwen knew he suffered from arthritic pain. "You've done enough today, Virgil. I can finish the rest."

"Are you certain?"

"I am. Goodnight Virgil."

The knave departed and she was soon lost in her thoughts, humming quietly to herself as she washed the remainder of the ceramic cups and wooden spoons.

"May I come in?"

To her surprise, it was Nick. "Are you sure Jeremy would approve?" Regretting her rudeness, she amended, "Forgive me. Of course, you can come in."

He walked into the room. "That was quite a feast that you and Virgil prepared for us today. I wanted to thank you. I especially liked my meat pie with the letter 'N.'"

Gwen smiled as she wiped her hands dry. "I thought since you'll be departing soon…" She couldn't bring herself to finish the sentence.

"I know you're upset about us leaving."

"It's more than that, Nick."

"Jeremy is zealous, but he cares for you, Gwen. You're like a sister to him."

"I could care less what Jeremy thinks or feels about me." She paused to let her words sink in. "I only care about what *you* think and feel about me."

"I care greatly for you. After all, you were the one who found me in that wretched basket."

"Is that what I am to you, then? A sister?"

He noticed her hands. They were red from kitchen work but still elegant, like her mother's. "What am I to say, Gwen? What can I say?"

She gave him a tight little smile. Every inch of her body craved to be close to his, yet she turned her back on him and resumed her task. "You've already said quite enough," she said quietly.

"Gwen—"

"You're welcome, Nick. It was a pleasure preparing a feast in honor of our Lord."

And with those words, she dismissed him. Nick wanted to say more, but refrained. He watched her for a moment, but she continued to ignore him. Dejected, he left the doorway and walked toward his cell. When he was gone, she hung her head and wept.

***

By the spring of 1147 it was evident that English troops would be helping the French king, Louis VII and the German emperor, Conrad III in their fight to recapture the Holy Land. A group of Anglo-Norman and Flemish sailors prepared to depart in May from Dartmouth and Richard Fitzwilliam would be among them.

Beatrice oversaw the preparations for the journey. Food, supplies, clothing, weapons, and a variety of other items were carefully divided into rations and packed for the large number of men who would be accompanying Richard and Robert.

A week before their departure, Richard found Beatrice in the castle's chapel. She was on her knees, praying for God to watch over her husband and son during their upcoming journey.

"Beatrice," Richard said softly.

She mumbled a few more words and crossed herself before standing up to face her husband.

"The Earl of Sussex and Lord Dunn think it wise for us to travel to Dartmouth together. I agree with them," he informed her.

"So, you are leaving early?"

"I leave on the morrow to meet with them before heading to Dartmouth. Is everything ready?"

"All is packed and ready, my lord."

There was a moment of silence before Beatrice burst into tears. Richard pulled her into his arms.

"Richard," she said, her voice trembling with anxiety. "I

want you to know that I've never been unfaithful to you." He knew exactly what she was referring to, but remained silent. "I love you and I've longed for the day when you would tell me that you're finally ready to accept your son."

"Beatrice—"

"Please, Richard, let me say what I have to say. I want my son. For twenty years I've lived without knowing who he is, and—"

"Beatrice—"

She cut him off again. "I want that to change."

His wife's boldness surprised him. "We'll talk of this at a later date, I promise."

Encouraged by his words, she said no more. Arm in arm, they left the chapel and made their way out to the main hall where there was a flurry of activity as the men prepared for their departure.

Later that night, as Richard lay in bed with his wife, he told her that he loved her. His desire for her was heightened by the fact that he was going away. He didn't know when—or if—he would see her again, and made love to her with urgent passion. They lay in a silent embrace for a long time before falling asleep.

The cruel dawn was upon them too quickly and Beatrice tried to be strong and composed for the sake of her men. Richard dressed with the help of his valet, while another servant polished his sword one final time before handing it to his master.

"I must go," he said at length.

"I need to see Robert," Beatrice said.

"Make haste, woman. My men and horses are awaiting me downstairs."

She slipped into a velvet surcoat and followed her husband out into the courtyard. Her son was about to mount his steed when she ran to him. "Godspeed, Robert," she said as she embraced him.

Robert returned his mother's embrace and kissed her cheek tenderly. "I'll see you soon, my lady."

Richard gave her one last hard kiss on the mouth before mounting his own horse and leading the large group of nobles and knights out of the castle's courtyard. Beatrice watched the men until they were out of sight before slowly making her way back into the castle.

Suddenly, a thought struck her. Richard's meeting with the other nobles allowed her some time to travel to St. John's to see her son. According to Martin, Nick and Jeremy were also departing from Dartmouth with the troops. She would ride to the monastery at once.

***

The evening before Nick's departure to Dartmouth, Gwen went to his cell. She had never before done anything so bold, but she couldn't bear for him to leave without saying goodbye. With nervous trepidation, she knocked on the door.

"Gwen," Nick said in surprise.

"Are you alone?" she inquired, her eyes scanning the small space.

"Jeremy is in the church, praying."

There was an awkward silence. Nick noticed that her eyes were red and swollen from crying.

"I wanted to say farewell," she explained. "Do you really want to be a monk for the rest of your life?"

Nick's first instinct was to hold her close and not let go, but that would go against everything he'd been taught. "You've asked me this before."

"Do you?" she prompted, placing a hand on his arm.

Nick remained perfectly motionless, his heart beating out of control. Gwen came closer still and he felt the warmth of her body as he met her eyes. Her supple lips were inviting, and he instinctively placed a hand on her waist. Before they realized it, their lips pressed together in a kiss. A wild hunger took hold of him and he wanted nothing more than to pull her inside the room and lock the door.

They jumped apart the moment they heard footsteps. It was Jeremy, and he stopped short when he turned the corner. Nick and Gwen stood staring at him with guilty expressions on their faces.

"Gwen came by to say farewell," Nick explained.

Jeremy gave her a brisk nod, mumbled a thank you, and went into the cell. Nick, who was still stunned from the kiss, said nothing more. She stared at him with pleading eyes before lowering her head. Hot tears streamed down her cheeks and she wiped them away with the back of her hand.

"Forgive me," she said before walking away.

"Gwen, wait."

Gwen ran outside and continued to run toward the well. The evening was warm and the rumble of thunder in the distance threatened rain. There, in the quiet solitude by the ancient well, she gave in to her grief.

Nick stretched out on his cot and stared at the ceiling after Jeremy blew out the candle. Would he ever see Gwen again? Was he making a mistake? It was too late for such questions. There was no turning back now.

The next morning, Bartholomew fought back tears as he helped Nick and Jeremy prepare for the long journey ahead. Martin had provided two fine steeds along with clothing, supplies, and food. With their swords at their sides and their purses full, the two young men said farewell to the kind prior.

Gwen entered the courtyard carrying a large bundle wrapped in cloth. "I baked fresh bread. There's some hard cheese and sausage, too."

Jeremy accepted the bundle with a grateful nod. There was an awkward moment as she waited for them to say something. Bartholomew, sensing the uneasiness between the three of them, suggested that they pray. After the prayer, Gwen looked up at Nick and caught his eye. No words were spoken, but she could sense that he wanted to say something.

Bartholomew held out two scrolls, each emblazoned with an official royal seal of the Holy Church. The young men stared at the formal documents with puzzled expressions. "Martin instructed that I give you these. They're official proclamations of your noble birth."

"Noble birth?" Nick repeated, stunned.

"These are forgeries?" Jeremy demanded.

"I didn't have the heart to tell you sooner, but the Templars fill their ranks with members of the nobility. Both of you may now join the Order, if you desire. Simply hand those over to the Grandmaster."

Jeremy crossed himself. "Praise be to God. Tell Martin thank you." Then, turning to Nick, he said, "Do you see? This is the will of God. It's our destiny."

"It's a forgery," Nick pointed out.

Jeremy shrugged. "Yes, but for the good of God."

"Be careful not to not break the seals of those letters," Bartholomew said. "Farewell, my sons, and Godspeed."

"Farewell," they replied in unison.

Nick turned to hold Gwen's gaze for a moment. Then, both men turned their horses around and headed for the main road.

Beatrice had just reached the crest of the hill that lay behind the monastery when Nick and Jeremy crossed the courtyard. Shading her eyes against the blinding rays, her heart jumped in her chest when she saw Nick for the first time. There was no mistaking his proud, noble bearing and golden hair.

She kicked her horse and made him advance down the hill at great speed. They had to pass through the village in order to reach the road leading to Dartmouth, and she wanted to get a better look at Nick. She dismounted near a well on the main road and waited.

Before long, she saw their horses in the distance and pretended to draw water from the well. When the two men were abreast with the well, she looked up and gazed into her son's eyes for the first time.

Nick commanded his horse to halt and dismounted. "Here, let me help you."

He studied the attractive older woman discreetly as he pulled up the bucket with ease. Beneath her dark cloak she wore a sumptuous gown of velvet patterned with gold. What was a noblewoman doing at a well in the middle of nowhere?

Beatrice stepped aside, her eyes never leaving his handsome face. "Thank you."

He handed her the bucket. "May I ask what brings you to these remote parts?"

Jeremy sighed loudly in irritation. "We should get going, Nick."

Beatrice shot the impertinent young man a look before replying, "I'm visiting my family in Lewes."

"It's a fine village. I bid you good day, my lady," Nick offered before mounting his horse.

She squinted up at him. "You're both knights?"

"Aye."

Noticing the horse's bulging saddle bags, she added, "Your heavy provisions suggest a long journey."

Jeremy interjected, "We're on our way to Dartmouth and set sail tomorrow, so we really must be off."

Undeterred by Jeremy's rudeness, she asked of Nick, "To fight in the crusade?"

"Aye, my lady," Nick replied. A strange, inexplicable feeling of warmth came over him as he looked into the mysterious woman's clear, blue eyes.

"Godspeed to you both," she said. "May the Lord bless and watch over you."

The young men thanked her and urged their horses forward.

Beatrice stood frozen in the middle of the road and watched until her son became a speck on the horizon. She then fell to her knees and offered up a prayer to God, asking that He protect her husband and her sons.

CHAPTER 12

One hundred and sixty-four ships filled with English, Flemish, French, and German crusaders sailed from Dartmouth on the nineteenth day of May in the year 1147. Fate, however, had other plans for the devout Christian warriors. Five days after their departure a vicious storm forced the ship onto the coast of Portugal, and they ended up in the city of Oporto.

Afonso Henriques, son of Henry of Burgundy, was the self-proclaimed king of Portugal. Power-hungry and ambitious, he was determined to seize Lisbon, which was currently being held under siege by the Moors. Afonso's goal was to bring the city under Christian control. Unfortunately, he had only about fifteen thousand lances and shields with which to arm its men. Desperate, Afonso and his soldiers were forced to come out in shifts and exchange weapons with one another.

The king attempted to persuade the crusaders to help him with his military endeavor. In return for their assistance, the crusaders would receive remission of their sins since the pope had decreed that aiding Portugal was as good as fighting in the Holy Land. The material rewards from the plundering also served as a temptation to many of the noblemen. The leaders of the Christian troops negotiated with the king and finally agreed to help, but it was not until the end of June that they actually journeyed to Lisbon.

Nick and Jeremy stood on the prow and gazed at the beautiful city as their ship approached the harbor. Atop a great hill stood a fortified citadel within sturdy *cerca Moura*—Moorish walls—and to the left and right, the impressive city descended to the banks of the Tagus River. Nick pulled the fresh, salty air into his lungs and squinted from the sunshine that reflected off the water like polished silver coins.

Lisbon was wondrous and strange with a multicultural mix of inhabitants due to the lack of a stabilized religious rule. The buildings were jammed so closely together that it was virtually impossible to find a street more than eight feet wide. The Moors built their houses and markets in well-defined spaces, adorning their homes with vibrantly colored tiles.

As they followed the other crusaders through the streets, Nick and Jeremy took in the sights, sounds, and smells of the advanced city. Most of Lisbon's inhabitants were good looking. One sultry girl tossed Nick a smoldering glance and he shyly returned the smile only to catch Jeremy's disapproving glare.

The crusaders eventually set up camp outside the city gates, and the noble leaders congregated to discuss their plan of attack. Among these men were the bishops of Portugal, the Earl of Sussex, Afonso Henriques, Gilbert of Hastings, and the Earl of Kent.

The Knights Templar had helped Afonso recapture the nearby city of Santarem a few months ago, and were now preparing to help in the recapture of Lisbon. Jeremy, upon hearing this news, grew very excited and looked forward to meeting the famous warrior monks. He continually praised God for guiding them toward their destiny, and offered many prayers of gratitude.

As thrilling as their adventure was turning out to be, Nick couldn't stop thinking about Gwen. He was well aware that he had hurt her by deliberately avoiding her company, but he did so to avoid Jeremy's tiresome sermons against the female sex. He had always assumed that Gwen knew how much he cared for her, but now he was no longer certain.

***

Gwen sat listlessly in the garden tossing stale breadcrumbs to the birds. Several weeks had passed since Nick's departure and she missed him terribly. She had grown accustomed to hearing the clash of swords every day and seeing him from afar. Now, there was only silence.

"*Gweneth!*"

She turned her head at the sound of Ranulf's voice. "I'm in the garden."

He greeted her with a kiss, then said, "I've come to ask you something."

Gwen braced herself.

"I've come to ask for your hand in marriage. I spoke to your mother yesterday, and she and Simon both approve. The prior has offered us his blessing, too."

Gwen was fond of Ranulf, but she didn't love him. Only one man occupied that space in her heart, and for all she knew he would never return to Lewes.

Ranulf took her hand. "I can provide you with a house and fine clothing—even a servant to help you."

"You're too kind."

"I don't want you to think of me as merely kind. I want you to think of me as a husband. Say yes, Gweneth."

She looked into his dark eyes, searching for something that wasn't there. He leaned forward and kissed her, but all she could see was Nick's face. She had made a fool of herself by crying in his cell, and he had offended her the following morning by not bidding her goodbye.

The thought of having her own home, pretty clothes to wear, and even a servant to command was tempting. Ranulf was offering her a better life than the one she had now. What did she possibly have to lose?

"I'll marry you, Ranulf."

"We'll marry at once."

"No," she countered a bit too hastily. Seeing Ranulf's puzzled expression, she said, "I can't abandon my post—it may take a while to find a replacement for me."

"I'm willing to wait." His face lit up and he gathered her into his arms. "I'll be the best husband. You won't be sorry."

***

Lisbon continued under siege throughout July, August, and September. Other troops had arrived to help, and the crusaders grew hopeful.

On the first day of October, while the men of the camp were eating their supper, Jeremy suddenly grabbed Nick's shoulder. "Look!"

Nick spied a large army of crusaders on horseback sporting

white linen tunics over thigh-length hauberks. Emblazoned in red on the front of each tunic was the Cross of the Order of Christ; the symbol of the Knights Templar. Several of the knights at the frontline carried long flags with three pointed tails bearing the Order's red cross.

The crowds parted to allow the army through, and they went straight toward the nobles. Jeremy watched the warriors ride past with an expression akin to awe, while Nick studied their hardened stares, battle scars, and lined faces. The Templars were known for being the fiercest fighters—usually the first into battle and the last to leave. It was rumored that they fought with a zeal so profound it could only come from God.

"I can hardly wait to join the Order," Jeremy admitted.

One of the Templars glanced at Nick as he passed. The knight's vacant eyes held the coldness that comes from shedding the blood of men.

Temperatures dropped as night fell, and fires flared around the camp. Nick reclined on the soft grass. Wrapping his wool cloak around him, he gazed up at the starlit sky. As usual, images of Gwen crept into his mind. Her silky hair, azure eyes, and radiant smile caused physical pain in his heart. In Lewes, he had taken for granted that she was always nearby and he found comfort in her daily presence. For the first time in his life, Gwen was no longer orbiting around him, and the coldness of her absence was difficult to bear.

Nick heaved a troubled sigh. If he joined the Order of the Knights Templar, he would no longer be able to speak with Gwen. The rigid rules the warrior monks embraced regarding women prompted many of them to forsake their own mothers. Nick had always believed that he was destined to become a warrior of God, but his destiny came with a high price.

Near the end of October the noble leaders decided to take Lisbon by force from the Moors. Nick, who by this time was well known throughout the camp as a skillful fighter, had been biding his time by teaching other men how to properly wield their weapons. In addition to swords, many of the crusaders were armed with maces, maritels, and axes.

On the eve before the attack, while Nick was demonstrating defense techniques to a group of onlookers, the Earl of Kent approached him. Nick had seen the gray-eyed man consorting with Afonso and Gilbert on many occasions.

Richard watched Nick for a long time before pulling him aside. "You're a skillful fighter and so is your companion," he said, motioning toward Jeremy. "What's your name?"

"Nicodemus St. John, but I go by the name of Nick."

"Well, Nick, I'm Richard Fitzwilliam and I want you and your companion to fight alongside my knights when we attack early tomorrow morning."

Jeremy became excited when Nick informed him of their assignment. After supper, they led their horses to the far side of the camp where the nobles slept. They were welcomed by Richard, who immediately rounded up his men to discuss attack strategies.

Later that night, while Jeremy slept, Nick remained awake for a long time. There was something strange in the air. The full moon cast a luminous glow upon the camp, and an inexplicable tranquility fell over him. In that moment, he was sure something great would happen tomorrow. Shivering with emotion, he offered a heartfelt prayer to God—the first since his arrival.

The next day dawned chilly with a dense fog rising from the Tagus. The troops were ready and anxious. The bishops offered prayers to God on behalf of the Christian fighters. Horses stomped and grunted; men spat and wielded their weapons at imaginary opponents, practicing for the real fight that was soon to come. An intense, vibrating energy encircled the camp as they prepared to attack the city gates.

Afonso and Gilbert rode ahead of the crusaders. Nick and Jeremy were in the front lines, riding alongside the highborn men. They stopped several yards from the gates, constantly scanning for enemy soldiers along the city walls. They had to be cautious since the Moors were experts in the art of archery—seldom did an arrow miss its target.

"There, Father!" Robert cried, pointing at the western ramparts.

Richard motioned to Nick, who followed his gaze. An archer stood on the parapet, aiming his arrow at the crusaders below. There was no time to spare—the Moors would sound out the alarm at any minute. Afonso urged his army forward and they charged for the gates.

One of Afonso's soldiers had scaled the wall in the middle of the night and now held the doors open for the Christian army to enter. The noble gesture cost the man his life, but his sacrifice allowed the crusaders to infiltrate the city. Once inside, the Moors defended their territory while calling out to Allah for strength and perseverance. A few of the Moorish archers pulled back their bowstrings and let the arrows fly, but there were too many Templars climbing the walls. The arrows took out only a small number of crusaders.

A blood-curdling scream caused Nick to spin around. One of the Moors on horseback was riding toward him with raised saber, ready to strike. The man's black eyes were wild as his mouth opened in a battle cry. Nick instinctively swung his sword. In all the years of training, his sword had only made contact with the steel of another sword, or a wooden post, or a burlap figure filled with straw. Now, for the first time, it made contact with human flesh. The English steel blade sliced through the studded leather breastplate of the Moor's armor, past the padded tunic underneath, and finally into the man's chest. Bleeding profusely from the huge gash, the Moor came at Nick again with fanatical persistence. This time Nick slanted his sword and aimed at the man's neck. Blood flew from the wound in a wide arc before the Moor fell off his horse and was trampled in the melee.

Nick couldn't tear his gaze away from the dead Moor. He had never before killed a man and his entire body shook violently from the shock of it. A piercing scream yanked him back to the present, and he caught sight of a Moor riding directly toward Lord Richard. The nobleman had his back turned, however. Nick urged his horse forward and intervened with a quick, hard jab to the man's belly. It was a fatal blow; *his second kill*. The Moor collapsed upon his horse's neck as the animal galloped away. Richard caught Nick's eye for an instant to express gratitude before continuing to fight.

The bloody battle raged on and, for a while, the Christians thought they had been defeated until a swarm of Templars penetrated their midst. The warrior monks fought as viciously as lions, slaying several Moors in a short time. Nick and Jeremy directed their horses toward the Templars and bravely fought alongside them. The fighting eventually ceased when the remainder of the Moors retreated and the troops headed eastward.

Exhausted and bloodied, the Christians appeared dazed as they scanned the area to survey the damage. Lisbon was littered with the bodies of the dead and injured, and the ground had become a gritty mixture of soil and blood. The color red was everywhere: on the walls, on the streets, and on the men. Nick spotted Jeremy several feet away, his face as white as snow. The carnage was gruesome—torn throats, ripped bellies with steaming intestines exposed, decapitations, amputations…

Many soldiers dropped to their knees and bent their heads in prayer. Jeremy took a step and staggered before bending at the waist and vomiting several times. The contents of his friend's stomach hit the ground with a splash, emitting a sickly steam in the cold air. Nick swallowed his own bile and squeezed his eyes shut just as a cheer of victory rang out among the crusaders.

God had won.

In the following days there was much celebration and prayers of thanksgiving being offered to God. The stalwart soldier who had sacrificed his life to open the doors of the gate was named Martim Moniz. Afonso Henriques officially declared him a hero, and masses were sung in his honor.

The initial shock and horror Nick and Jeremy had experienced immediately after battle was soon forgotten as they joined in the celebrations. Like women who forget the pain of childbirth the moment they hold their babies, the two young men forgot the carnage and were filled with elation from their holy victory. The fact that God was being given all the credit for Lisbon's recapture further ignited their Christian zeal.

In a surge of emotional determination, Nick and Jeremy joined the Knights Templar. The Order's Grandmaster accepted their official papers without the slightest hesitation, and the young men solemnly took the vows of celibacy and obedience. As an outward sign of their godly devotion, they cut their hair. The tonsure was the common style adopted by the warrior monks, and Nick winced slightly as he watched his golden locks fall to the ground.

"Don't you feel different?" Jeremy asked the next morning.

"Aye, cooler," Nick replied, running his hands through his shorn hair.

"That's not what I meant."

Nick grinned. "I know what you meant."

"Do you know how much our lives are going to change? We'll send word to Prior Bartholomew at once."

Nick nodded but his mind was elsewhere. No matter how hard he tried to force Gwen out of his head, she haunted his thoughts daily. He sometimes envied his friend. At least Jeremy knew who he was and what he wanted out of life. Nick, on the other hand, wanted to serve God, but secretly fostered forbidden desires for a woman.

Emperor Conrad III and King Louis VII of France were in the Holy Land fighting the Turks. The troops in Lisbon received word that the German and French troops had suffered terrible losses. Since the Templars were in a position to send several hundred knights to their aid, they would depart for the Holy Land immediately. The vast majority of crusaders, feeling they had already contributed to the cause by fighting in Portugal, made other plans. Few would accompany the Templars.

On the eve before their departure Richard said to Nick, "You're a fine swordsman and a true warrior. I'll pray for God to watch over you and your friend, Jeremy." Then, putting his hand on Nick's shoulder he added, "I also want to thank you for coming to my aid in battle. You saved my life."

"It was God who saved you, my lord," Nick said. "I was only His instrument."

Richard patted Nick's back in a gesture of camaraderie.

"You're a good man, my friend. I won't forget you. Godspeed."

As Nick watched Richard walk away, he couldn't shake the feeling that there was something familiar about him. As if reading Nick's thoughts, Richard looked over his shoulder and met the young man's gaze.

***

After several months of waiting to hear news from Nick, Gwen finally gave up hope and married Ranulf in December of 1147. It was a small ceremony performed by Prior Bartholomew and attended by some of Ranulf's relatives. Gwen looked lovely in a cream colored frock with a pale blue surcoat. Her long hair was braided into two long plaits and tied with the two blue ribbons Ranulf had given her on the day they had first met.

The wedding celebration took place in Ranulf's cottage since the ground was already covered with snow. Agnes and the other women had spent the previous day preparing for the small feast. Roasted chickens, stewed rabbits, fresh bread, various tarts, dried fruit, and wine graced the long wooden table that dominated the big kitchen.

Gwen sat beside her new husband at the table, her spirits high from the wine and merrymaking. Ranulf smiled at his young, beautiful bride and placed his hand upon her thigh under the table. She returned the gesture somewhat nervously. She knew the rudimentary facts about copulation but, being a virgin, she was anxious. According to Ranulf, who liked to boast, he was quite experienced with women. Oddly, knowing this tawdry fact about her new husband didn't stir any jealousy within her.

Agnes approached her daughter at one point during the celebration. "Simon and I are so happy for you."

Gwen caught Simon's eye across the room and he raised his cup to her. "I'm happy, too, mother. Ranulf is a good man, just as you said."

Later, after the guests bade the couple goodnight and bestowed blessings upon them, Gwen took a good look around the cottage. It definitely needed a woman's touch, but it was far better than her accommodation at the monastery. Ranulf bolted the door and turned to his bride. They were now completely alone for the first time. Without a word, he gripped her shoulders and kissed her hard.

"Stop, Ranulf," she said playfully against his lips. "You're hurting me."

Ranulf pulled away, his face stern. "You're my wife, do you understand? I have the right to kiss you."

Ranulf leaned in for another rough kiss and Gwen struggled to free herself from his embrace. He gave her a quick slap across the face.

Gwen reeled back, her hand rising to touch her burning cheek. "What was that for?" she demanded, truly frightened. He had never displayed any violence or unsavory traits during their courtship.

"That was for your behavior earlier." When she looked at him askance, he continued, "I saw how you stared at my cousin, Lars—dancing with him and carrying on. That kind of loose behavior ends today."

"He asked me to dance. I could hardly refuse."

"Next time, make up an excuse not to."

She doubted the opportunity to dance with the pleasant young man would ever arise again. "As you wish, Ranulf."

"I want to lay down the rules tonight. You're no longer under the prior's care. You're my woman now."

Gwen's eyes filled with unshed tears.

Realizing that perhaps he had been too harsh, Ranulf embraced his young bride. "Gweneth, you're so lovely. I fear you'll be tempted by someone younger or more handsome than me," he confessed, his voice nearing tenderness.

"I've sworn my loyalty to you on this day before God. Please don't fear such treachery from me."

Ranulf picked her up effortlessly and took her into the bedroom. After placing her on the wide truckle bed, he began to remove her clothes. He then removed his own clothes and she was in awe at seeing a naked man for the first time. His member was erect and engorged and she stared at it fearfully.

Following her gaze, he frowned. "What? Is it not to your liking?"

"No!" When he scowled, she hastily amended, "I mean…I've never seen one before. Will it fit?"

Ranulf laughed and kissed her again, only this time he was gentle. As Gwen kissed him back, his hand slipped between her thighs. He broke from the kiss to spit in his hand and smear the liquid on her womanhood. Suddenly, he forced his member inside of her and she cried out. He continued to move within her, each thrust harder than the last. She gritted her teeth against the pain and was relieved when he finally stopped and collapsed on top of her.

"Why are you crying?" he demanded as he looked down at her face.

"You hurt me."

"It hurts the first time, but then it gets better."

Ranulf kissed her forehead, then rolled off of her and fell asleep with his hand on her breast. Turning her face to the side, Gwen wept silently as she reached down between her legs. There was pain and blood, too. This was not at all what she had expected; not at all the loving union her mother had described.

My God, what have I done?

Gwen curled up into a fetal position and fell asleep. She dreamed of Nick and his golden hair gleaming in the sunshine.

CHAPTER 13

Beatrice had received only two messages from Richard since his departure. The first letter was dated August 1147 and stated that their ship had gone astray in Oporto. According to Richard, the nobles were negotiating terms to aid in the recapture of Lisbon from the Moors, and they were slated to depart in the near future. Not knowing how long Richard would remain in Oporto, Beatrice refrained from sending a reply. The second letter, which didn't arrive until almost a year later in July 1148, described in detail the military victory in Lisbon. The letter went on to state that Richard and Robert, like many other nobles, would remain in Portugal for several months in order to partake of the spoils of war. Beatrice replied immediately stating that all was well in Kent Castle, and closed the letter with affectionate words to her husband and son.

Several months later on a cold November morning in 1148, Gretta burst into her mistress's bedchamber in a state of sheer panic.

Beatrice, who had been sleeping soundly, was startled awake. "What's the meaning of this?"

"My lady, look out the window!"

Beatrice scrambled out of bed and threw open the wooden shutters. An icy wind rushed into the room as she leaned forward on the sill. The castle was completely surrounded by an army! In the courtyard below, Richard's knights—the few who had remained to watch over the castle and womenfolk—had been rounded up and were being held captive.

"Oh God!" Beatrice cried.

Taking deep breaths, she forced herself to calm down. Within a few moments, the women heard the sound of footsteps in the hallway. Gretta ran to the door and threw the bolt, locking them safely within the bedchamber. Loud banging filled the silence as several men attempted to break through the heavy oak door. Still in her linen night shift, Beatrice quickly donned a fur-lined surcoat. Gretta began to cry.

Beatrice gripped her shoulders. "Calm yourself."

Her maid had every reason to cry, however. An invasion usually meant rape or death to the castle's womenfolk. Beatrice fetched the sharp dagger she kept hidden beneath her mattress. One of the door's hinges was already destroyed—only a few more hard thrusts and the door would soon give way.

"Oh, my lady, I'm so frightened," Gretta whimpered.

"Courage," Beatrice said firmly, handing her maid an iron poker from the hearth. "Go stand in the corner, try to stay out of sight."

The door flew open with a loud bang as the hinges fell to the floor. Several dirty, armed men invaded the room. Beatrice inched closer to the opposite wall, wielding the dagger.

"*Do not touch them!*"

The command came from the hallway. Beatrice kept her head high as she stared defiantly at the soldiers. They were of the worse kind, too—*mercenaries*—landless fighters up for hire, their lord being any man who paid them in coin. The men moved aside to let their employer through.

Noticing the dagger, he said, "Drop it, Beatrice."

Shocked, Beatrice dropped the dagger. "How could you do this? Richard is away fighting in the name of God and you invade his castle? You of all people!"

Edward sniffed. "Your husband is a traitor."

"Liar!" she spat, lurching forward with balled fists.

Beatrice was about to strike when one of the men quickly intervened by placing the tip of his sword at the base of her throat. Gretta screamed.

"I wouldn't do that if I were you," Edward warned. "As lady of the house you should show your guests some hospitality."

"How dare you," Beatrice sneered.

"Careful, my dear. As the wife of a traitor you should consider yourself fortunate that my men haven't killed you. Alert your household and have them prepare a meal for my soldiers. These men are tired and hungry."

"I will do no such thing!"

Edward eyed Beatrice for a moment before taking a few steps forward and placing his lips to her ear. "Here's a little piece of advice for you: *do as you are told*. These soldiers haven't seen a woman in a *very* long time. You and your little maid are quite lovely. Since they're being well paid to obey *my* orders, it would be wise for you to remain on my good side."

Beatrice's anger turned into real fear as she looked at the men. Each man stared back at her with lust in his eyes.

"I'm the only one who can protect you," Edward added before retreating.

"Come, Gretta, let's awaken the household," Beatrice said before pulling the collar of her surcoat tightly to ensure modesty.

Edward had stooped lower than she could ever have imagined! To lay siege upon a nobleman's household while he was away on a holy crusade was dishonorable. When that household belonged to your brother, it was unforgivable.

Later that day, after the army had dined on the castle's food and ale, Beatrice and Gretta took refuge inside the solarium. There were mercenaries throughout the entire castle. Beatrice's bedchamber afforded no safety or privacy now that the door had been knocked off its hinges. Gretta bolted the door of the solarium as her mistress nervously paced the floor.

"What am I going to do?" Beatrice asked desperately. Fearing that Edward's men were eavesdropping outside the door, she lowered her voice. "They didn't kill all of our knights, did they?"

"Only a few. Lord Richard's men are under watchful eye," Gretta replied.

"Are you sure of this?"

"I'm repeating what one of the pages told me."

"What of Martin?"

"I don't know, my lady."

"Our only hope is to send word to the king and to Richard." She bit her lip thoughtfully. "But *how*?"

"I'll attempt to sneak out in the middle of the night," Gretta suggested.

"No. Edward's men will hunt you down and God only knows how the bishop would punish us afterward."

"You can say that I fled from fear, that I deserted you." Beatrice shook her head but Gretta persisted. "My lady, it's our only hope."

"It's too dangerous."

"Perhaps we can send one of the men."

"If Martin is alive, he could do it. He's accustomed to sneaking off undetected."

The women crept into Beatrice's bedchamber where ink and vellum were readily available on her writing desk. Gretta stood watch inside the doorway as her mistress scribbled a letter to the king describing their plight. Beatrice folded the letter into a tiny square and tucked it between her breasts.

"Gretta, fetch a basket and fill it with all the salves and ointments you can muster," Beatrice instructed. "Be sure to include clean linen strips."

Gretta scurried to fulfill the task, then accompanied her mistress downstairs. Beatrice found Edward seated at the head of the great dining table where Richard normally sat.

Edward looked up, pleasantly surprised. "Beatrice."

In her most respectful tone she asked, "May I please see my men?" Indicating the basket in Gretta's hands, she added, "My maid and I would tend to their wounds, and offer them some bread and wine. You've kept them in the stables without warmth or food—they must be cold and hungry."

"Very well. Beware, Beatrice, you'll be accompanied and watched like a hawk," he warned as he motioned for the guards to escort the women to the stables. "Bring the men into the kitchen."

"Yes, my lord," said one of the men.

Beatrice hesitated. "Will you allow them to sleep indoors at night? Please, Edward, they're good men."

"I'll do it for you."

"Thank you."

As Edward's men escorted Richard's knights into the

kitchen, Beatrice quickly counted how many were left and concluded that five had been slaughtered that morning. To her relief, Martin was among the survivors. The men gathered around the warmth of the kitchen's large hearth and gratefully accepted the loaves of bread and flasks of wine doled out to them. Beatrice and Gretta tended to the men's wounds under the watchful eyes of Edward's soldiers.

"Thank God you're alive," Beatrice whispered to Martin as she cleaned the cut in his arm.

"We were outnumbered and caught completely by surprise, my lady," Martin whispered.

Beatrice's back was turned to the mercenaries as she pretended to examine Martin's wound. "I need you to take a message to the king," she whispered. "It's tucked between my breasts. Go on, take it."

She leaned over to apply a linen strip to the cut and he saw the folded note in the shadowy cleft between her breasts.

"Forgive me, my lady," Martin whispered as he grabbed the corner of the note and pulled it out.

Beatrice straightened and went over to the next man who needed his wounds cleaned. Out of the corner of her eye she noticed Martin tucking the note up his sleeve. All she could do now was pray.

Edward barged into Beatrice's room the following morning. "Where did you send him?"

Beatrice sat up in bed and pulled the coverlet up to her chin. "Edward, what are you doing here? The sun hasn't yet risen and already you make demands on me."

"The man who crept past my guards—where did you send him?"

"I have no idea what you're talking about."

"One of your men escaped from the kitchen. Are you suggesting that you know nothing about this?"

Feigning surprise, she replied, "Nothing, my lord."

Edward left the room in a huff. Gretta emerged from the antechamber, frightened.

"Gather whatever needs mending and our sewing supplies,

we can take advantage of the light in the solarium."

The women readied themselves in silence and proceeded to the solarium an hour later.

"Martin should make it to London by nightfall," Beatrice said. "God willing, the king will send help in the next day or so. We must stay clear of Edward and his men in the meantime."

They occupied their time with sewing while praying silently, and only stopped to partake of the midday meal. The women spent the day in a state of nervous agitation mingled with hope. When the sun began its descent, one of the mercenaries rudely strode into the solarium without knocking on the door.

"The bishop expects you to join him for dinner and demands that you don your finery," the big oaf muttered directly to Beatrice.

Appalled by the man's lack of manners, Beatrice could only nod in response.

Gretta eyed the man with disgust as he left the room. "Don your finery?" she repeated, shocked.

"God help me," Beatrice murmured.

"What are you going to do, my lady?"

"I don't wish to anger Edward in any way, so I have no choice but to get dressed and join the bishop for supper. Come Gretta, perhaps I can charm him into thinking he's made a grave mistake."

Gretta helped her mistress bathe and change into a formal brocade gown of tawny gold trimmed with vair. Beatrice selected a gold necklace with a large sapphire pendant that hovered in the hollow of her throat, deepening the blue of her eyes.

"Be careful," Gretta said before Beatrice left the room.

Edward sat at the head of the table dressed in one of Richard's fine leather tunics. It had been a long time since Beatrice had seen her brother-in-law dressed in something other than clerical robes. As she approached the table, she noticed it was laden with dried fruits, nuts, cheeses, breads, and roasted meats. She also glimpsed the fine wine, which was reserved for special occasions. Edward had raided Kent Castle's stores.

"Ah, Beatrice. You are the definition of beauty," Edward said, standing up to take her hand.

They stood facing one another and she couldn't help comparing him to Richard. It was uncanny how alike they were in stature and features. One of the castle's pages came forward to pull out her chair and she met the young man's eyes.

Noticing the exchange, Edward said, "I'm not the monster you think I am."

Beatrice would have preferred to sit at the opposite end of the table, but Edward insisted she sit at his right hand; a place reserved for wives and honored guests. "Perhaps you should tell that to the families of the five men you killed yesterday morning."

Edward sighed in irritation as he took his seat. "I invited you to dine with me with the hope that we could speak like two civilized individuals."

This conversation required wine so she motioned for the page to fill her goblet. It felt strange to sit at Edward's right hand instead of Richard's. "What do you wish to speak with me about?"

Edward drank deeply of his own wine before replying, "It's not my desire to harm you or your household."

"Then why are you here?"

"I want my share of land and a title."

Beatrice stared at him, astonished. "You have no legal right to demand such a thing, Edward. The laws of primogeniture—"

"The laws be damned!"

After several seconds, she said softly, "You're the Bishop of Rochester. Isn't that good enough for you?"

He pounded his fist against the table. "No!" When she averted her face, he amended, "Forgive me, Beatrice, but it's not enough. Richard has been given everything from the moment he was born, and it's not fair."

She met his gaze evenly. "So this is your game?"

His eyes were pure steel. "I play no games."

"What do you call this?" she challenged. "Are you not

playing the role of lord and master by seizing Richard's castle, wearing his clothing, and dining with his wife?"

Edward's face turned red. "It should have been me," he cried passionately. "I should have been firstborn. *This* is my rightful place—not the Church."

"This is Richard's rightful place. Not yours."

"Leave us," he said to the page and to his men.

She tried to think of ways to reason with her brother-in-law. Then, a thought struck her. *Had he finally slipped into the realm of madness?* "It's not too late to correct this mistake," she said gently.

"What mistake?"

"Taking over my household. You can still withdraw your men and depart in the morning. God will forgive you, and I won't say anything to Richard."

"What about the knights and the servants? Do you think they'll describe this as a friendly visit?"

"I'll convince him of your remorse and your wise decision to retreat. Please, Edward." She reached to touch his hand but refrained. Her fingertips rested on the tabletop and Edward stared at them. "There's a chance for you to redeem yourself."

He raised his eyebrow. "Do you honestly think Richard would believe that I was remorseful?"

Rather than reply, Beatrice drank deeply. She wanted to feel completely numb and blot out the nightmare. She was dealing with a madman.

Edward continued, "There's no turning back for me."

Emboldened by the wine, she said, "You'll burn in Hell for this, you know."

"Dearest, I plan to burn in Hell for many reasons." He paused. "Shall we eat?"

They ate in silence for several minutes. Beatrice could manage to swallow very little under Edward's heavy gaze. Relief swept over her when one of the mercenaries ran into the room.

"Your Excellency, two riders have been spotted in the distance," the man announced.

Edward frowned. "Do they carry flags or banners? Can you identify them?"

The man scrunched up his face. "They're too far away and it's hard to see in the moonlight, my lord."

Edward stood and so did Beatrice.

"May I go to my room?" she asked.

He nodded before following the man upstairs to the battlements.

"Two messengers are approaching the castle as we speak," Beatrice said to Gretta once she was inside the safety of her bedchamber. "I think the king may have sent them."

Gretta crossed herself. "Thank God."

Beatrice massaged her temples. "My head is heavy from the wine. I need to sit down."

Gretta picked up an ivory comb, then quietly unraveled Beatrice's long, thick plaits with deft fingers. She was about to comb her mistress's hair when the door flew open. Edward barged into the room accompanied by two of his men.

"Leave us," he said to Gretta.

The maid waited for her mistress to nod before obeying the bishop.

Edward turned his attention to Beatrice. "Are you still going to deny knowledge of your man's escape?"

Beatrice said nothing and, to her horror, he held up the letter she had written to the king.

Holding it out for her inspection, he continued, "Martin was chased down and apprehended by one of my men. He had this with him, and it's written in your hand. You were a fool to take such a risk."

"Edward, please—"

"Now, your man will pay for your folly." Turning to his men, he said, "Kill him and lock the knights in the dungeon."

"No!" Beatrice cried. "This is my fault. Martin was only obeying my direct command, and my knights have done nothing to deserve such wicked punishment."

Edward studied her beneath hooded lids. Beatrice's flaxen hair was loose and wavy from the braids she had worn earlier, and her face was flushed with worry. She had never looked so delectable.

"Please, Edward," Beatrice said softly.

The men were about to carry out their orders when Edward said, "Wait. Flog the offender and teach him a lesson. His life has been spared thanks to his mistress's generosity."

The bigger of the two mercenaries asked, "What of the knights, my lord?"

"Let them be for now."

The guards departed and Beatrice sighed with relief. "Thank you."

"Send your maid to tend to your man's wounds," Edward advised. "He'll need it."

Beatrice hastily summoned Gretta and sent her downstairs with a basket of salves to care for Martin. The thought of him being flogged made her sick to her stomach, but at least she'd managed to spare his life.

Edward shut the door after Gretta left the room, then turned to Beatrice and said, "Take off your clothes."

Shocked, she cried, "No!"

"I swear to God, Beatrice, if you don't do as I say, I'll have every knight and servant killed tonight—including that milk-faced ninny of a maid."

With trembling fingers, Beatrice removed everything except her flimsy linen shift, which failed to hide the contours of her breasts or the shadowy patch between her legs.

Edward's eyes dilated. "You're so beautiful," he whispered. His hand reached out to touch her cheek and she pulled back. He attempted to touch her once more and she avoided him yet again. Angered, he took hold of her shoulders. "You were always too good for me."

Beatrice tried to struggle free as he leaned forward and planted a hard kiss upon her unyielding mouth. She bit his lip hard.

"You little bitch."

Edward gave Beatrice a look she'd never seen before and, for the first time in her life, she was truly afraid of him. He pushed her onto the bed and when she tried to scramble away, he slammed her back down on the mattress. She struggled wildly as he sat astride her, pinning her arms over her head with one hand, while the other went beneath the linen shift.

"Edward, I beg you!"

"Submit quietly, and your man will receive a moderate flogging. Resist and scream, and it will end badly for him."

Beatrice whimpered in response to the vile threat. Despite Edward's schemes against Richard, he had never been vicious or violent toward her. They had always maintained a certain level of respect with one another. As she stared into his piercing gray eyes she saw something that chilled her blood.

Gazing down at her body, he said almost reverently, "I've dreamed of this moment so many times…"

"Don't do this," she whispered.

He tore open the top of her shift to reveal her breasts. Sighing contentedly, he cupped and kneaded them, placing his mouth greedily on each nipple and sucking hard.

"Stop, Edward!"

Edward's breathing grew shallow as he hardened, his member throbbing with the pain of anticipation as he freed it from beneath the tunic.

He had waited so long…

Pulling the shift up to her waist, he smothered his sister-in-law's body with his own and entered her roughly. Beatrice turned her face into the cushion in order not to scream. With each violent thrust he thought of Richard and how good it felt to take his brother's wife.

"Oh, God, Beatrice…oh, God!' he cried. His eyes closed in ecstasy at finally having her, and it was with the greatest sense of satisfaction that he emptied his seed into her body.

Afterward, Edward glanced down at Beatrice with a victorious expression on his face. He dressed quietly and left the room. Beatrice reached down between her legs and grimaced at the sight of semen on her fingertips. She wanted desperately to rid herself of his filth, but she couldn't bring herself to bathe. Instead, she lay motionless on the bed, crying silently.

Gretta came into her mistress's bedchamber much later and found Beatrice staring blindly at the ceiling. It was obvious she had been ravished. "My lady!" she cried, covering Beatrice's body with the coverlet.

Martin received a moderate flogging in exchange for Beatrice's sexual submission. Unfortunately, one of the deep welts in his back got infected, and he developed a severe fever. He died two weeks later, and Beatrice deeply grieved the loss.

***

Edward had planned on returning to Rochester for Christmas in order to meet with a cardinal visiting from Rome, but he was unable to travel due to inclement weather. Beatrice cursed the snow every time she passed her window.

The bishop had forced himself on her several times, and she submitted to the abuse for the sake and safety of her knights and servants.

There was still no news of Richard or Robert.

Sometimes, snippets of gossip trickled in from foreign vendors who came into contact with castle servants. Most of the news was banal—trivial matters such as scandals, divorces, and executions. Beatrice discovered that the king, in celebration of the victorious conquest in Portugal, planned on spending Christmas in London at the Tower. The massive fortress had been built by Duke William of Normandy almost a century earlier as a result of the Norman Conquest.

On the first day of March in the year 1149, Beatrice knew she was pregnant. For two decades her womb had remained fruitless. Now, shockingly, under such dire circumstances, it nurtured life. She remembered the day long ago when she had asked Edward to help find her son. After offering a detailed description of the baby, Edward's eyes had gone soft and she recalled his words: '*It could have been our child, Beatrice.*'

Edward could never know. *Never*.

She informed Gretta of her predicament. "I can't bring this child into the world. You must help me."

Gretta told the bishop that Beatrice was sick, and convinced him to let her buy medicine in the nearby village. He agreed, but only if she went accompanied by two of his men.

Gretta walked ahead of the men, mindfully keeping a good distance between them. She stopped before the home of an old healer known for her skill. The front door was wide open and the aroma of various herbs and roots wafted from within the shadowy interior.

The men wandered across the street to chat with a pair of scantily dressed village women. Gretta suspected they were whores.

One of the men eyed Gretta and said, "What are you gawking at, girl? Hurry up and tend to your business."

An old woman with white hair motioned for Gretta to come inside as she placed an armful of foul smelling leaves in a wooden bowl.

"They smell terrible but they're quite potent," she commented as Gretta wrinkled her nose. "Here for a remedy, girl?"

Gretta cast a nervous glance over her shoulder at the men across the street. "My mistress wishes to end a pregnancy."

The old woman's eyes went to the fat leather pouch at Gretta's waist before snipping leaves and roots from the various bunches that hung literally everywhere. Next, she slowly ground the herbs together with a mortar and pestle, adding drops of oil every so often.

The process took so long that one of the men came to the door and demanded, "What's going on in here?"

The healer poured the herbs into a pouch and handed it to Gretta. "That should help lessen the pain when the blood flow gets too heavy," she said loudly. Eyeing the man, she added, "Oh, hello. Does your wife suffer from menstrual cramps, too?"

He blushed and frowned. "I'll be waiting outside."

"Thank you," Gretta whispered gratefully.

The woman procured a vial containing black liquid. "Tell your mistress to drink all of this at once. I warn you, it's terribly bitter. She'll become violently ill, but she won't die. The poison—"

"Poison?" Gretta interjected. "Why not whip up a potent emmenagogue?"

"They don't always work." Lowering her voice, the healer added, "Everyone in the village knows what's going on inside that castle. This poison will force the bishop's spawn from her ladyship's womb. *Guaranteed.* Your mistress is to take *that* once the baby is out," she added, pointing to the pouch of herbs in Gretta's hand.

"What if she's too sick?"

"Those leaves are the antidote to the poison. They *must* be consumed. Crush them into wine or whatever you can get her to keep down."

Gretta nodded, handed the woman several coins, and left the cottage. The men took hold of the maid's arm and escorted her back to the castle.

Later that afternoon Beatrice drank the potion. She had never tried to rid herself of a babe before, and she was frightened of what was about to happen. It wasn't long before she felt ill. Her nausea grew greater with each passing minute until the vomiting began in earnest. Gretta fretted about, trying to do everything possible to make her mistress more comfortable, but nothing seemed to help. Thankfully, the bishop stayed clear of Beatrice's room.

"Dear God, Gretta! The old crone means to kill me," Beatrice gasped as she wiped her mouth with a linen cloth. Never before had she felt such pain in her belly. She vomited again, but only bile came out.

"She said you would be ill, and assured me that you wouldn't die, my lady," Gretta soothed. "The baby will be forced out eventually."

"Oh, Lord, let it be soon!"

A moment later Beatrice suddenly doubled over as a sharp spasm overtook her body. The miscarriage was messy and painful. Gretta immediately cleaned up the tiny fetus and the blood. She removed Beatrice's soiled shift, cleaned her body, and helped her mistress into a dark blue surcoat that would conceal bloodstains.

"Burn everything," Beatrice said thickly as she got into bed. "There must be no evidence of the horror that has transpired here."

Gretta hurled the bloodied shift and the fetus into the greedy flames of the hearth. Next, she crushed the antidotal leaves into a large drinking vessel and added some water, a dollop of honey, and a splash of sweet wine. "Here, my lady," she coaxed, placing the vessel to Beatrice's lips. "The old woman said you must drink all of this after your body rids itself of the babe."

Beatrice turned her head away. "I can't…"

At Gretta's insistence, Beatrice gradually consumed the contents inside the chalice. Within a few moments, her body felt numb and the pain subsided. The potion had a soporific effect, too, quickly inducing sleep.

Gretta remained at her mistress's side throughout the night. Beatrice's head felt heavy and her mouth was as dry as sawdust when she woke up the next morning.

"My lady," Gretta said with a look of relief.

Beatrice was surprised as she moved to sit up in bed. Not only was her pain virtually gone, but she was famished. She drank some watered wine, and later ate small chunks of bread sopped in beef broth.

Edward appeared in the doorway. "Yesterday, your maid told me that you were ill. I'm relieved to see that you're doing better today. There's color in your cheeks."

Hearing his voice, she lifted her chin and met his gaze. The dark blue of her garment deepened the blue of her eyes, making them mysterious. The hatred Edward saw reflected in them caused his heart to tighten in his chest. He had loved her the best way he could, all the while hoping that she'd eventually love him back.

He continued, "I was worried about you."

"Thank you for your concern."

"I never want to see you in pain, Beatrice."

She laughed without humor, and it was a bitter sound. "Edward, you have caused me more pain than I could ever have imagined."

He visibly flinched at the offense. "I only wanted what Richard had…I'm sorry."

Her eyes studied him from beneath her lashes. Did she hear a hint of regret in his voice?

A letter from Richard finally arrived two days later. Luckily, the messenger was intercepted by one of the castle's servants outside the gates. The young man had the presence of mind to hide the correspondence and send the messenger on his way. Later, he managed to smuggle the letter to the kitchen knave, who handed it to one of the scullery maids, who gave it to Gretta, who finally placed it in Beatrice's eager hands.

According to Richard's letter, he and Robert were still in Lisbon at the request of King Afonso, aiding the monarch in establishing the new Christian kingdom. Beatrice frowned when she read her husband's next words: *'Why haven't you replied to my letters?'* Edward had no doubt intercepted and destroyed Richard's letters without mentioning a word. Beatrice's cheeks flushed with fury at her brother-in-law's arrogance. How dare he keep such precious news from her! Richard ended the letter with the words, 'God is with us,' which made Beatrice grimace since she felt abandoned by Him. God had done nothing to protect her form Edward.

Beatrice reread the letter before hiding it, and felt hope for the first time in months. Later, when the midday sun spread its warmth and melted most of the snow, she took it as a good omen. By sunset there were great golden puddles in the vast courtyard.

Edward announced his imminent departure to Rochester, and Beatrice offered a silent prayer of thanks to God—the first in many weeks, in fact. He appeared in her bedchamber the night before his departure, and she cursed God for forsaking her yet again. He took his pleasure as she lay motionless, fervently hoping against pregnancy. She couldn't endure taking another batch of that wretched poison. When he finally collapsed on top of her, he pressed his lips to her temple.

"Hold me Beatrice…*just once*," he whispered.

When she failed to comply, he wept.

Beatrice was shocked by this display of…? She couldn't even guess what transpired within Edward's warped and troubled mind. Eager to be rid of him, she forced her arms to move.

When her hand tapped his side, he squeezed her and cried harder. "Don't hate me," he pleaded. "Please…"

Cringing from the wetness of his tears against her neck, she managed to whisper, "Don't cry, Edward."

Taking her words as an attempt at tenderness, he kissed her mouth. "I love you…God, how I love you."

Beatrice lay frozen as his body, wracked with sobs, convulsed against her own. His shrunken member was cold and flaccid against her thigh and she fought the urge to push him off. After a few minutes he composed himself and began to dress.

"I wish I didn't have to go, but there are urgent matters that need my attention. I'll return within a fortnight." He paused, hoping for some comment or reaction on her part. "Some part of you must love me, Beatrice."

"Is that what you're waiting for?" she snapped. "For me to love you? *You*?"

The last word was spoken with derision and it cut Edward to the bone. "Am I not good enough? Smart enough? Handsome enough?" When she remained silent, he persisted, "Is it because I'm not as wealthy as Richard? Because I have no land to call my own?"

Beatrice averted her face and ignored him.

Defeated, he whispered, "Farewell, Beatrice."

She watched him go without a word. When Gretta emerged from the shadows a second later, she said, "Richard is still in Lisbon. I must send word to him."

Gretta, who had waited patiently in the anteroom for the bishop to conclude his business, glanced over her shoulder furtively. "We must be careful. Remember what happened to Martin."

Beatrice winced at the harsh reminder as she made her way to the desk. Her hands shook uncontrollably as she procured a piece of parchment. "I'll be more careful this time."

"My lady, you are not well."

"I won't be well until my husband returns."

Edward selected four men to accompany him on his journey, admonishing the remainder of the mercenaries to keep a close eye on Beatrice and her household. He also warned his sister-in-law not to attempt anything that would lead to 'dire consequences.'

Predictably, Edward's men became lax the moment he was gone. Without supervision, they were free to eat, drink, and divert themselves without restraint. Unable to leave the castle unmanned and, knowing they would be severely punished for laying a hand on Beatrice, the men satisfied their lust by summoning the village whores to Kent Castle.

Long after the soldiers had enjoyed their fill of wine and women, Beatrice quietly crept down to the main hall. Several men were already snoring, while others could be heard laughing outside with their paid female companions. She clung to the shadows as she made her way to the stables where Richard's knights were imprisoned. Predictably, there were no guards posted there.

She pulled out a spare key from within her sleeve and stuck it in the big iron lock. Quietly, she slipped into the large wooden structure, causing a few horses to stir. The knights were gathered together on the hay, most of them asleep. The few who were awake rose to their feet and bowed to their mistress.

Beatrice handed one of them the folded message. "Your lord should still be in Lisbon with the Portuguese king. Take this letter and see that it gets to him. The bishop's men are in the main hall as we speak. Most of them are drunk…we won't have another chance like this one." She shook the shoulder of the nearest sleeping knight. "You must not dally, go now!"

One knight appeared concerned. "Wait!" he said to the others. "My lady, what will happen to you when the bishop returns and finds us gone?"

"Edward will blame this folly on his men. I'll be sure to mention their negligence. Now, go!"

"Why not come with us?"

"I can't abandon my household or my servants," she explained. "I must remain here for the sake of their safety. Otherwise, Edward's men would wreak havoc."

"You're a good and brave lady," he said.

The men filed out of the stables as quickly and silently as possible. Beatrice left the stables as stealthily as she had entered them, and within minutes she was back in the safety of her bedchamber.

"Thank God," whispered Gretta, crossing herself.

Beatrice was out of breath and shaking from head to toe. "Thank Him, indeed."

Chapter 14

Gwen grew accustomed to marriage and the duties of being a wife, but she was far from happy. The first year with Ranulf was particularly difficult. He worked hard and traveled often, but she was never permitted to accompany him. She quickly learned that her husband had a roving eye and a love of drink—a combination that led him to be unfaithful in his marital vows.

Nevertheless, she tried hard to make their marriage work. Despite the slaps and shoves he imposed on her whenever he was drunk or jealous, which was often, she maintained a cheerful disposition. To ease his wife's loneliness during his frequent absences, Ranulf came home early one evening and gave Gwen a golden-eyed kitten. She was delighted, especially since it was the nicest thing her husband had done for her since their wedding day. The creature was so tiny it looked like a small pile of gray fur in the palm of her hand.

"Do you like it?" he asked.

"Very much. Thank you, Ranulf."

"I've already named him, too. Methuselah."

"An odd name for a cat."

"Well, I hope it lives a long time," Ranulf said before sitting down to eat his supper. "Did you bake bread? You know how I hate stale bread."

Gwen placed the tiny kitten in a basket before fetching a warm loaf from the hearth and placing it on the table. She stroked Methuselah's soft fur as she watched Ranulf eat in silence. Afterward, he dragged her off to bed, took his pleasure, and went to sleep.

Life continued in this uneventful routine until one morning in the spring of 1149. While Gwen was planting seeds in the garden, she became dizzy and fainted. After regaining consciousness, she slowly got up and went back inside the cottage. The following day she was overcome with nausea and became ill every morning afterward. When her mother came to visit, Gwen confessed her symptoms.

"How long since your last monthly?" Agnes inquired.

"Almost two months. Do you think I'm with child?"

"I do."

Gwen suddenly appeared anxious. "I hope Ranulf will be happy with this news."

"He'll be overjoyed." Agnes reached for Gwen's hand. "You and Ranulf will be good parents."

Gwen hesitated. "Ranulf is a fine provider…"

She couldn't tell her mother that Ranulf spent many nights in taverns with other women, or that his lovemaking was rough, or that he sometimes hit her.

"I saw Prior Bartholomew at the market two days ago," Agnes said, changing the subject. "He recently received news from Nick and Jeremy."

Gwen's heart skipped a beat. "What news?"

She listened intently as her mother relayed how Nick and Jeremy had fought bravely in Portugal before joining the Order of the Knights Templar.

"They are helping the French and German crusaders fight the Turks," Agnes concluded.

"When will he—*they*—be coming home?"

Agnes noticed Gwen's odd slip of the tongue. "No one knows. It could be months or years."

Or never, thought Gwen. She said nothing but her expression spoke volumes.

Agnes realized her daughter's sudden sadness with concern. "Is anything wrong?"

"It's nothing."

Agnes knew she was lying. "Tell me, please."

"Ranulf no longer speaks sweetly to me, nor is he gentle. I feel that I displease him most of the time."

Agnes embraced her daughter. "Do your best to appease him, and he'll eventually soften. Men are different than us. Women possess bigger hearts and have greater capacity for compassion. Men, on the other hand, were made to fight wars."

Gwen nodded, forcing herself to smile. "You're right. Perhaps I'm being too sensitive."

"Things will change now that you're with child."

Not wanting to discuss the matter further, Gwen suggested that they start preparing the evening meal. Agnes chatted about what to expect during pregnancy as she helped her daughter with the cooking, and stayed until the shadows grew long.

Later that evening as Gwen served Ranulf his supper, she said, "I have to tell you something."

"What is it?" he asked between spoonfuls of stew.

"I'm with child."

Ranulf stopped eating and put down his spoon. His expression was one of shock, then gradually his mouth spread into a wide grin. He picked up his wife and spun her round and round. "Well done, Gweneth!" he cried gleefully. "Well done!"

"Be careful, Ranulf!" she warned as she laughed.

Her husband set her down and kissed her heartily on the mouth. "This pleases me greatly, it truly does!"

Gwen smiled as he nuzzled her neck. Hopefully, their marriage would improve.

CHAPTER 15

The full moon cast its silvery glow throughout the forest as a white swirling mist arose from the river. Nick heard a woman weeping, but as he walked toward the sound his feet became heavy as lead. The sobs grew louder and he forced himself to move with great effort. Sitting on the grassy riverbank, the familiar figure was barely discernable in the milky haze.

He stepped onto the moist grass. "Gwen!"

She met his gaze, her eyes glistening in the pale moonlight. He knelt and took her face into his hands. Tenderly, he kissed each eyelid, the tip of her nose, and, finally, her lips. The salt of her tears remained on his tongue as he inhaled the scent of her hair.

"Nick," she whispered as she slowly leaned back toward the earth. She was pulling him down with her...

"Nick...Nick!"

At the sound of Jeremy's voice Nick sat up in his cot. Drenched in cold sweat, his heart pounded out of control. His member was painfully hard.

"Wake up! You're dreaming," Jeremy said. "You've been tossing restlessly for quite some time."

"Forgive me if I disturbed you," Nick murmured.

"What were you dreaming about?"

Nick stared blankly at his friend. "Fighting the Turks."

Before walking out the door, Jeremy said, "The bells will toll soon."

"I'll be ready shortly."

The ancient abandoned mosque where Nick and Jeremy now resided had been converted into a monastery by the Templars. Nick sighed as he rose from the narrow cot, which afforded little comfort. Rubbing his aching back, he glanced out the window and took in the summer sky. The orange glow of the coming dawn was smeared across the smoky horizon. He could see the distant lights of the great city beyond the wide plain. There was already activity stirring as merchants prepared for the open markets. If he closed his eyes, he could almost smell the saffron, cinnamon, and cumin. The mosque lay on the outskirts of the city center and took almost half hour to reach by foot.

Splashing cold water on his face from a large clay basin, Nick attempted to erase the memory of his sensual dream. It wasn't the first time Gwen had crept into his peaceful slumber, and he was sure it wouldn't be the last.

The bells for Nocturn rang as he dressed hurriedly. Sometimes the rigid schedule of the Templars tired him; Nocturn at three in the morning with chanting and meditation, Lauds at seven, followed by Holy Mass, Nones at midday, Vespers in the late afternoon before supper, and finally Compline at half past nine in the evening. It was enough to tax the body and mind of anyone, let alone a warrior who was already pushed to the limit from so much fighting.

The schedule didn't seem to bother Jeremy. His friend relished every opportunity to worship God. Back at St. John's, the monks were more lax and Nocturn was practiced after dawn rather than before, allowing the brethren a few more precious moments in bed.

Nick rushed out of his cell and into the chapel where the monks were already chanting. Several of them turned around to give him a reprimanding look—Jeremy included. He took his place and tried to concentrate, but his mind kept drifting back to England…and to Gwen.

After leaving Portugal, Nick had marveled at the many sights their journey afforded them. While passing through Spain, the mosque in Cordoba with its countless pillars had left him awestruck, but nothing could have prepared him for the wonders of Constantinople. From atop the distant hills, the great city glistened in the sun like a shimmering jewel. When they finally arrived in Anatolia, they were forced to stop their march at the order of Emperor Comnenus, ruler of Byzantium. Their goal was to continue on toward Jerusalem, where they were supposed to meet up with the other Templars who were aiding the crusaders. Louis VII, who had suffered tremendous losses and had already left in January, entrusted the responsibility of the campaign to the Templars and Conrad III.

The following days were relatively peaceful and the Templars spent their time in prayer and preparation for the next attack. The last battle they fought had proved less than successful, and once more a cry went out to the lords of Europe for help.

Unfortunately, the Infidel was a cunning enemy, and wouldn't wait for the reinforcements to arrive before attacking the Christians again. Everyone was tense with anticipation and, although many refused to admit it, overcome with fear. The eerie stillness of the days could only mean an onslaught of battles to come, and the masses offered were more like rallies to lift everyone's spirits.

Some of the more zealous monks gave short sermons on God's infinite power and described in detail how the Infidel would perish. A strong camaraderie permeated the brethren unlike anything felt by the monks in the past. Jeremy, swept up in the religious fervor, claimed that he was filled with Holy Spirit and therefore one of God's earthly instruments. He, too, offered fiery sermons and uttered proclamations with authoritative conviction.

One night while the two of them were washing up before bed, Jeremy announced, "Nick, I feel that God is directing my steps and shaping my destiny. Each day I grow stronger! I can't even describe the joy in my heart."

Nick, who was accustomed to hearing outbursts like these throughout the day, said nothing. Jeremy's constant preaching had grown wearisome. It was as if his friend lived in a constant state of blissful rapture.

"Don't you feel the same way?" Jeremy pressed.

Jeremy's tone and the manner in which he had asked the question made Nick frown. "I suppose so."

"Well, it certainly doesn't seem like it."

Nick was taken aback momentarily. "I can appreciate your zeal but, unlike you, I hate these wars." To lighten the mood he added with a grin, "And the cots we're forced to sleep on are surely the most uncomfortable beds in Christendom. I'm doing penance every night."

Jeremy failed to see the humor in the last statement and stared at Nick in amazement. "How dare you say such a thing?"

Nick shrugged, nonplussed. "I'm only being honest."

"Perhaps you would prefer to fight on the side of the Infidel. I hear Saladin is fond of earthly luxuries, and that his soldiers sleep on satin pillows inside their tents."

In truth, Saladin was a wise and educated ruler, and if his soldiers really did sleep on satin pillows Nick believed it must be for a good reason. During their travels he had quickly ascertained that Islamic cities were far more advanced than Christian cities. The Moors excelled in astronomy and mathematics, and employed superior habits of hygiene. Moorish architecture was not only intricately and beautifully constructed for pleasure, but also ingeniously designed to remain cool indoors while desert sandstorms raged and temperatures soared outside. In short, each Islamic city they passed left him with a sense of awe. If the Moors were truly evil—the Infidels—why had they been blessed with so much knowledge and talent? Nick once posed this question to Jeremy, who immediately retorted that Satan often disguises himself as an angel of light.

Nick smiled to break the tension. "I would relish the feel of a satin pillow right about now." When Jeremy's face remained as hard as stone, he became exasperated. "Oh, come now! What happened to your sense of humor? Did you lose it on the battle field? God isn't an unreasonable tyrant, you know."

Jeremy appraised Nick coolly. "I'm familiar with God's ways, and it is my duty to make them known to others." He shook his head sadly. "I worry about you, Nick."

"Well, there's no need for you to worry."

Jeremy chose his words carefully. "Your heart isn't in this, and it hasn't been for a long time."

"Who has made you my judge?"

"God has," Jeremy replied evenly.

Nick's eyes grew steely as his temper reached its limit. "Well, since you and God are on such intimate terms perhaps you may let Him know that I'm tired. I've fought hard for His cause this past year, and I find it tragic that blood must be spilled in such copious amounts to satisfy Him."

Jeremy flinched. "I'll pray for your soul, brother."

"Unlike those noblemen in Portugal who spilled blood for the sake of titles, land, and spoils, I did it for God," Nick pointed out. "You have no right to judge my heart."

Jeremy went to bed in silence, leaving Nick by the window. He blew out the single candle and gazed up at the night sky, resting his elbows on the sill. The stars were particularly bright due to the waning moon. After two months in Damascus, no real progress had been made. The Christian forces enjoyed some small victories, but the city still lay in the power of the Turks. Nick caught sight of a falling star. *Was he truly meant for this way of life? Had he made a grave mistake?* He had been asking himself these questions since his departure from Lisbon, and he felt guilty for doubting his decision.

Nick slept fitfully that night and woke up at dawn to the sound of battle horns. An army of Turks had been spotted on the plain. Accustomed to fighting at a moment's notice, the warriors were ready. The Grandmaster busily assembled everyone in the courtyard and spoke words of encouragement. Horses grunted as their hooves stomped impatiently on the sandy ground, sending clouds of dust into the air. Nick and Jeremy mounted their steeds and rode out with the others in uniform precision.

Nick stole a sidelong glance at Jeremy. He remembered the first time they had seen the Templars in Lisbon. How impressive the warrior monks had seemed atop their horses with their silver hauberks gleaming in the sun beneath pristine white tunics emblazoned with red crosses. He and Jeremy were now part of that powerful army.

How long ago it seemed.

The Turkish army had formed an intimidating line on a high plain to the east. Arrows were already piercing the morning sky, obliterating the light of the sun. Nick watched as dozens of his brethren fell from their horses, arrows protruding from every imaginable part of their bodies. A piercing battle cry went out and the monks charged at the enemy with ferocity, slaying any Turk within reach.

"May you burn in Hell!" Jeremy cried to the man whom he had just ruthlessly slain with his sword.

The Turk dropped off his horse like a sack of wheat before his corpse was brutally trampled by the animal's hooves. Jeremy's initial squeamishness had long since vanished, and he now fought with a zeal that Nick found both impressive and terrifying. Nick, on the other hand, didn't share his friend's bloodlust. In fact, it was becoming increasingly difficult to fight these squabbles.

"Allah hu akbar!"

The cry came from Nick's immediate left. He swiveled in his saddle in time to see a Turk charging at him with his saber held high in the air. Nick's horse reared as he dodged the blade and plunged the English steel of his sword into the man's rib cage. The Turk dropped to the ground.

A pair of terrified black orbs stared at Nick as the man's mouth yawned open in a soundless cry; he was still alive. Nick could not tear his gaze from the Turk's face as he silently fought for his life; his expression filled with pain and sorrow. For a moment everything grew silent and still all around them. Nick saw no hatred in those exotic dark eyes. It was only a man—*a human soul*. The spell was broken when the hooves of a Templar's horse cracked the Turk's skull in two. The man's brain splattered onto the scalding, arid sand.

Nick squeezed his eyes shut against the gory scene as he fought a wave of dizziness. The screams of the dying filled his ears, causing his head to throb viciously. It sickened him to kill, and he wondered if God really approved of such an atrocity. Was He not a God of *Love*? Another Turk screamed in anguish as a Templar cut off his hand. Disgusted, Nick urged his horse to the edge of the battle field and fought defensively.

It became painfully clear that the Infidels were winning, so the Christians retreated. The Turks cried out victoriously in their strange language as they watched the Templars ride off in defeat. As he fled the scene, Nick searched for Jeremy among the slain and wounded on the sandy ground. He breathed a sigh of relief when he caught sight of his friend slumped in the saddle.

Nick noticed that Jeremy was clutching his side. "How badly are you hurt?"

Jeremy's head turned and Nick glimpsed the whites of his eyes before he fell forward onto the horse's neck. Nick grabbed the reins from Jeremy's hand and led both horses toward a low plain. By now the Turks had already taken over the mosque, leaving the Templars homeless. They couldn't turn back.

Nick dismounted and tended to his friend. "Jeremy, can you hear me?"

Jeremy groaned. "I'm wounded…"

"You're going to be fine," Nick assured. He helped Jeremy dismount and eased him onto his back beneath a dying juniper tree offering little shade. The blistering sun was merciless.

"I'm cold…"

Nick lifted the hem of Jeremy's hauberk to examine the wound beneath. What he saw made him tremble with grief, and he bit his fist to prevent himself from committing the sin of blasphemy—he wanted nothing more than to curse God and his bloody wars. The deep puncture in Jeremy's belly bled profusely. Nick lifted his head and saw that Jeremy's saddle, as well as the horse's flank, was drenched in blood.

Jeremy shivered despite the intense heat. "Nick," he whispered. "I can't see."

Nick's own vision was blurred by tears. "God's teeth, Jeremy. You can't leave me here alone."

"Don't weep for me. I go to God now…Heaven." Nick shook his head and Jeremy smiled. "I'm so happy…I fought for Him."

Nick felt guilty about their quarrel. "Forgive me, Jeremy. Forgive my lack of faith…my lack of friendship. I've always loved you like my own brother."

Jeremy convulsed in pain and his eyes took on a vague expression. His last words were a sigh. *"I know."*

Nick bent his head and wept. He reached over Jeremy's body to remove his friend's sword and noticed the red corner of a small book peeking out from beneath the hauberk. He pulled it out and froze. After a moment, he leafed through the pages and saw the familiar erotic scenes.

"Jesus Christ," Nick said aloud.

How long had the book had been in Jeremy's possession? Nick had no idea, but he now understood his friend's aversion toward women. Seeing the sexual images no doubt ignited Jeremy's passion, thus making it difficult for him to remain chaste in mind and body. No wonder he had contemptuously referred to them as 'evil temptresses.'

As Nick closed the book, his eye caught sight of something on the inside cover. He reopened the book to see a rough sketch of a girl's face, and immediately recognized Gwen's sharp features, pretty mouth, and almond-shaped eyes. He stared at the image, stunned at having discovered his friend's secret. Jeremy's contempt toward Gwen became crystal clear in that moment: unrequited love.

"I'm so sorry, my friend," Nick whispered.

Later, he and his brethren buried Jeremy, along with the other faithful monks who had died for God. The relentless sun slowly sapped their strength as they dug a mass grave. The Grandmaster uttered a quick prayer on behalf of their souls, and decided to travel west to the closest Christian camp. The last thing the exhausted men wanted to do was ride in the heat of the day after fighting and burying the dead, but they had no choice. Without food or water, they would soon perish.

Nick rode silently for hours, grieving the loss of his friend. His throat burned with thirst and his mouth felt gritty. He grew dizzy from the intense sun and vomited twice. In his mind's eye, he saw Jeremy's pale face and the Turk he had slain in battle.

S*o much blood...so much death*.

Nick's eyes slid toward his companions. Did they harbor the same regrets as he did? He should have departed for England after their military victory in Portugal, but he had chosen to follow Jeremy. Now, his friend was dead and he was stuck fighting a war he no longer believed in. Gazing up at the cloudless expanse of sky, he wondered how God would feel if he abandoned the army. Without an official discharge, he would be considered a deserter and killed on the spot when caught. Unless, of course, he had a head start. He fixed his gaze on the knights riding in front of him. Some were slumped over with exhaustion, while others hung their heads in defeat. They were weak, hungry, thirsty, and demoralized—would the Grandmaster expend their precious energy to search for one deserter who would most likely die alone in the desert?

The giant orange sun bore down upon the horizon by the time the Templars arrived at their destination. They were greeted with indifference by the Christian troops who were just as severely weakened and discouraged. As rations were doled out, discussions for another attack were already underway. Nick silently consumed the small portion of unpalatable food and stale water allotted to him, then went to sleep.

Each day brought more war strategies and grandiose plans. The Grandmaster and his officials preached emphatically in an attempt to rekindle the troop's zeal. The knights were quiet, solemn, and there was something in their eyes: *doubt*.

On the third day, Nick was assigned the first shift of the night's watch. He and another monk were responsible for keeping an eye on the northwestern border of the camp, and another pair of men were assigned the southeastern border.

"I'll sleep now while you watch, then we'll switch," the monk said. He was young, possibly younger than Nick.

Nick nodded in agreement and pretended to scan the horizon for intruders while the young man spread his cloak over the sand and knelt on it. After uttering a quick prayer and crossing himself, he settled down to sleep. The moment Nick heard his companion snoring, he untethered his horse, stuffed rations into the saddle bag, and slithered away from the camp with the stealth of a seasoned warrior.

God could fight His own Holy Wars from now on.

Chapter 16
Lewes, England
June 1149

Gwen opened one eye slowly and saw a gray paw directly in her line of vision. As consciousness gradually crept back, she could feel the cat's sandy tongue rubbing against her cheek.

"Methuselah," she groaned.

The cat mewed loudly at the sound of his mistress's voice and gently tapped his paw against her face. Gwen tried to open the other eye, but it was swollen shut. Her body fared no better as she attempted to move. Peering up at the window, which was at an odd angle from her vantage point on the floor, she realized by the bright sunshine that it was morning.

The door opened and the new servant, Leah, stood frozen in the doorway with a basket in her hands. Ranulf had recently hired the girl under the pretense of helping Gwen during the pregnancy.

"Mistress Gweneth!" Leah cried, leeks and carrots spilling onto the floor as she dropped the basket.

Gwen gradually became aware of a cold stickiness between her legs. She tried to speak, but her lips were cracked and swollen.

"Holy Virgin, help us!" Leah cried out in horror when she saw the front of her mistress's frock.

Gwen already knew.

Leah gently helped her mistress to bathe and change before fetching the midwife.

The middle-aged woman arrived shortly afterward. She examined Gwen's bruised face before carefully prodding her midsection and nether region with expert hands. "You're lucky he didn't kill you this time. I'm sorry for your loss, Gweneth."

The midwife advised Leah to administer a healing salve and

a calming draught before taking her leave.

Gwen stared up at the ceiling as Leah went to work in the kitchen. The tears refused to come, but she knew that when they did, she would be unable to stop them.

During the first few months of her pregnancy, the friction in their marriage had increased rather than decreased. Gwen felt ill often, and was rarely in the mood to perform her wifely duties in bed. Ranulf flirted with Leah in the hope that the girl would satisfy his lust. When Leah firmly rejected his advances, Ranulf began drinking heavily and visiting whorehouses. Since his needs weren't being met at home, he felt justified in his deplorable behavior.

Last night, Ranulf had come home drunker than usual. Gwen rejected his lewd advances and he yelled at her, claiming that she was a 'useless wench.' Angry and humiliated, Gwen confessed her regret at having married such a drunken lout, and threatened to leave if he didn't change his ways.

Unaccustomed at being told what to do—especially by a woman—Ranulf responded to her ultimatum with several punches to her face and stomach. When she fell to the floor, he mercilessly kicked her in the belly. The last thing Gwen remembered was his foot coming toward her head.

Agnes and Simon rushed to Gwen's side the moment Leah sent word. Agnes's eyes filled with tears at the sight of her battered daughter.

Simon's face paled. "What has he done to you?"

Gwen reached out for Agnes's hand. "I lost the child."

"No...oh, no," Agnes cried.

Simon frowned. "Where is he?"

"I don't know. He beat me and left me for dead."

"That good for nothing—"

Agnes placed a hand on Simon's arm and shook her head, giving him an imploring look. "Not now."

Simon's mouth tightened. "I'll wait outside. Let me know if you need anything."

"This is my fault," Agnes confessed to Gwen. "I encouraged you to marry Ranulf."

"How could you possibly have known he would turn out to be an abusive drunkard?"

"I still beseech your forgiveness."

"There is nothing to forgive."

Several days passed with no sign of Ranulf. When Gwen finally received news that he had taken up with another woman, she was glad. At least for the time being, she was safe.

Four weeks after her beating, Gwen felt almost normal again. She still had some ugly bruises, but she could walk with considerable ease and work in the garden. Agnes visited her daughter daily.

"Move in with us," Agnes urged. "There's no need for you to stay here with this beast."

"Ranulf has been gone for a month."

"He'll be back eventually."

"I don't want to cause any trouble for you and Simon."

"We love you and want you to be safe."

"I'm sure Ranulf will be very remorseful when he returns…he usually is whenever he mistreats me."

"Mistreats you?" Agnes repeated incredulously. "Beating your wife to the point of killing your unborn child is more than merely *mistreating* you. He could have killed you!"

Gwen lowered her gaze. "I know, mother."

"Leave him and come live with us."

Gwen shook her head. "Ranulf will come looking for me. As my legal husband, he has the right to demand my return."

Agnes's eyes filled with frustrated tears. Her daughter was right. Any escape from Ranulf would only be temporary. Besides, his large family was well-connected in Lewes and could make life difficult for them.

Later, when she was alone, Gwen sat by the hearth and Mad Margaret eventually crept into her thoughts. Leah had once commented on the witch's knowledge of flower lore and her gift of foresight, which, according to many, came from the Devil. That didn't deter young girls from purchasing love potions, or married women from seeking cures for infertility.

Do I dare? No one would know.

Mad Margaret's cottage was located on the outskirts of the village; a pleasant enough walk by day, but not by night. Gwen waited until the sun was low on the horizon before setting out in Ranulf's cart. The mule he owned was getting fat and could use a bit of exercise.

The evening was unseasonably chilly, and she pulled her wool cloak tightly around her shoulders. Like many other garments she possessed, the fine cloak had been a gift from Ranulf. Gwen shuddered at the thought of her husband. Not a day passed that she didn't rue her decision to marry him. Oh, how she longed for her former life at St. John's! Better to be lonely than in bad company.

"Why did you leave me, Nick?" she whispered.

The reply came in the form of a hooting owl. The moon rose slowly above the cultivated fields flanking each side of the narrow road. There were no dwellings this far out and every noise made her jump. She almost screamed when a shadowy figure crossed the road ahead, then she realized it was only a wild hare.

A flicker of light in the distance captured her attention. Since Gwen had never been so far out of the village, she assumed the light came from Mad Margaret's cottage and veered the cart in that direction. The full moon created eerie shadows on the trees, making the leaves shimmer like silverfish.

Before long, Gwen came upon a small wooden cottage. She got down from the cart and made her way through the overgrown grass to the front door. She stepped onto the stone slab and hesitated before knocking on the withered door.

To her surprise, the door swung open immediately to reveal Mad Margaret's toothless grin. Her straggly gray hair hung loosely down her back and, to Gwen's horror, she wore a necklace of human teeth.

"Come in, child," she said, yanking Gwen inside with surprising strength.

The interior of the cottage was dim despite several lit candles, and their tiny flames created flickering shadows that danced on the walls. Gwen paused mid-step as she noticed some of the shadows gyrating in a manner inconsistent with the rest, giving off the impression they had lives of their own. Something moved in the corner and she whipped her head around. It was a cat, and its yellow eyes glowed like two luminescent orbs in the dark. A low fire burned in the hearth and a thick gruel bubbled in a small iron cauldron. Gwen inhaled and did her best not to make a face. The sticky sweet scent in the air carried an underlying stench of rot—like overripe apples sprinkled with mold.

"Come along," the witch said, breaking into Gwen's thoughts. "I'm surprised it took you this long."

The walls of the cottage were darkened by smoke, making them appear almost black. One wall flaunted a collection of skulls from several animals. Gwen was considerably taller than her strange host, which forced her to duck her head in order to avoid hitting the countless bunches of herbs and roots hanging from the low rafters. Gwen recognized some of the plant species, but the majority seemed exotic, not native to England. She wondered if the old woman grew these herself.

"Aye," Mad Margaret said as if in reply to Gwen's thoughts. "I have a fine garden around the back."

Gwen's eyes widened in surprise—and fear. The witch circled her uninvited guest slowly, her eyes taking in every inch of the blue eyed, raven-haired beauty. Her gaze finally came to rest upon Gwen's coin purse.

"I hope I haven't disturbed you, Mad—" Gwen stopped, mortified. "*Mistress* Margaret."

The witch's eyes twinkled mischievously and a smile played upon her lips. "I know the villagers call me Mad Margaret. To be honest, I rather fancy the name. I knew someone would come tonight; in my mind's eye I saw a young girl wanting a love potion, not you." She pointed to a crooked stool beside a round table. "Sit."

Gwen cleared her throat nervously as she took a seat. "I came here because—"

"I know why you're here, Mistress Gweneth."

The old crone went about the cottage gathering various

items. She returned to the table with a small copper bowl, a silver plate, and a handful of dried leaves. She placed the leaves in the bowl and procured a small glass vial from her pocket containing a murky liquid. As she poured a few drops over the leaves, Gwen saw the color was brownish red. *Old blood.* Mad Margaret reached her hand into a large ceramic bowl on the mantel and extracted several small bones. Gwen studied the delicate bones and tried to discern whether they came from birds or rabbits.

"Neither. They're the bones of a human infant," the old witch muttered, never looking up as she dropped the bones onto the leaves. "Don't worry, I didn't kill the little mite—his mother did after drinking the emmenagogue she purchased from me."

Gwen shivered in fear as Mad Margaret took hold of her hands and stared at the palms for a long time.

"What do you see?" Gwen asked in a shaky voice.

The witch's brow creased in confusion. She looked up at Gwen, but said nothing. She picked up the copper bowl and shook it so the leaves, blood, and bones mixed together, making a sickening sound. Mad Margaret's eyes rolled into the back of her head as she chanted something in a strange tongue. Then, as if some invisible force had taken hold of the bowl, it dipped forward out of her hands, and the contents landed neatly— unnaturally—on the silver plate.

Gwen's hand flew to her mouth to stifle a cry. She was about to flee the room, but Mad Margaret's hand shot out like a viper and clamped down upon her wrist. "Be still, child, and take courage. The answers you seek are coming."

Gwen trembled as she fought down panic.

The witch leaned over the table to read the leaves, bones, and blood, then sat back with a surprised expression. "I must see the soles of your feet."

"Why?"

"They'll show me where you've been and where you're headed. If they reveal the same message as the bones, I'll inform you of your destiny."

Gwen obediently removed her leather slippers and exposed

the soles of her feet to the witch.

Mad Margaret muttered to herself, oblivious of Gwen's worried expression. "The soles tell me the same thing as the bones," she stated with a sigh as she got up and began cleaning everything off the silver plate.

Gwen put on her shoes and wondered how long she would have to wait before the old woman revealed the information she so desperately desired.

Mad Margaret regarded the young woman out of the corner of her eye and smiled smugly. She would be important someday—best not to tease her too much. "You are destined to become the wife of a powerful nobleman. Even though you are of low birth, you will be a lady with a great title and riches beyond your imagination." She paused and her expression grew serious. "Love will find you, but with it will come death."

Upon hearing this, Gwen recoiled. "*Death?* Whose death?"

"Neither I nor the bones can tell you who will die." The old crone took a step forward and touched Gwen's cheek, making her wince involuntarily. "It will be someone very dear, and your wealth won't console you."

Gwen's shoulders sagged in defeat. The reading had been grossly inaccurate. She was already married, possessed no title, and was far from wealthy. Believing she had wasted her time, she decided to give the witch one more chance. "What about children?"

Mad Margaret grinned but the gesture lacked mirth. "Your *current* husband's violence almost damaged your womb, but the young heal quickly. Worry not, for you'll conceive again."

Icy fingers raced up Gwen's spine. Eager to leave, she flung the coin purse at Mad Margaret before racing to the door and throwing it open. A young girl stood on the stone slab, causing her to stagger back in surprise.

The girl peeked into the cottage and inquired, "Is Mad Margaret in? I wish to purchase a love potion."

Gwen glanced over her shoulder and Mad Margaret winked at her. Terrified, she fled.

Chapter 17

After the Christian victory in Lisbon, the shrewdest of the noblemen wisely remained in Portugal long after the departure of the crusaders. Included among those ambitious men were Richard and Robert Fitzwilliam, who aided Afonso in maintaining order within the land while the king established new laws.

As reward for his help and loyalty, Gilbert of Hastings was appointed Archbishop of Lisbon by King Afonso. A friendly liaison was firmly established between the English and the Portuguese. The Second Crusade had ended with a humiliating defeat in the Holy Land, and by 1149 it was clear that the only shining victory to come out of the entire effort was the establishment of Christian rule in Portugal.

Worrying Rumors of King Stephen's inability to control the squabbling English nobles reached Richard's ears. Matilda had long desisted from obtaining the English throne, yet the civil war raged on. Rebels used the war as an opportunity to increase personal wealth and power, and rumors of clergymen siding with these treasonous men circulated throughout the kingdom.

Richard had written to Beatrice several times, but received no word in return. One night, he dreamt of Edward seated at the head of his table. Beatrice stood beside him with her hand on his shoulder, and a smug smile played upon his brother's lips. So vivid was the dream that Richard woke up searching for his sword. He wasn't superstitious, but the dream frequently haunted his thoughts.

On a brisk October morning in 1149, while Richard and Robert were out hunting with Afonso, a messenger approached. "I have a letter for the Earl of Kent."

Richard held out his hand and took the folded vellum with much excitement, but the joy left his face as soon as he read the letter's contents.

Noticing Richard's expression, the king inquired, "Is there something wrong, Lord Richard?"

Robert echoed the king's concern. "Father?"

Richard crumbled the letter angrily, instantly regretting his decision to remain in Portugal. "My brother has betrayed me yet again." Meeting his son's gaze, he added, "He's overtaken Kent Castle."

Robert's face paled as he thought of his mother. "We must leave at once."

A hawk alighted on Afonso's gloved wrist and he placed a tiny leather hood over the predator's head. The hawk's razor sharp talons were bloodied from the rabbit it had captured. "A nobleman laying claim on a household while its lord is away on a holy crusade is despicable." He met Richard's eyes. "You must return to England and reclaim your castle, yet you've lost several men. I'll help restore your army. It's the least I can do to repay you for your loyalty and service."

The next few days were spent in preparation for Richard and Robert's journey to England. True to his word, Afonso gave Richard enough money to replenish his army with mercenaries before sailing off to Kent. If Edward was still in Kent Castle, he was no doubt intercepting Beatrice's letters. For this reason, Richard didn't risk informing his wife of his imminent return. He dispatched messengers to his English allies, requesting their aid to reclaim his home.

Richard and Robert suffered a treacherous journey across the English Channel. The ship pitched and rolled upon the angry waves, making many of the mercenaries seasick. The storm lasted well into the morning and the men fell to their knees in a prayer of thanksgiving when it finally ended with no casualties on board.

Upon reaching England, Richard was both pleased and relieved to discover that his allies were ready to fight for his cause. Their cooperation couldn't be attributed completely to Fitzwilliam loyalty, however. The majority of them despised the Bishop of Rochester, and wanted to see him brought down. When Richard learned that Edward wasn't in residence at

Rochester, one of his allies sent a spy to Kent. The spy returned confirming Richard's worst fear, and his first impulse was to strike at once.

Robert, who had inherited Beatrice's infinite patience, said. "Father, wouldn't it be wiser to attack in the middle of the night when my uncle least expects it?"

Richard nodded. "You're right, my son."

The army set out at dawn the following morning. Richard's hatred for Edward made his heart feel like a lump of ice within his chest. They stopped at a river to allow the men and horses a brief respite. There was a sizable forest to cross before reaching Kent.

Richard addressed the men as they drank water and stretched out on the grass. "We'll reach the castle before nightfall. I'll lead a few men inside while the rest of you remain hidden in the woods. Edward's men will be on the battlements. We'll overtake them and sound the alarm. When you hear the signal, attack."

One man asked, "How will you enter undetected?"

"There's a secret passage," Richard replied. "The narrow tunnel leads from the dungeon to a small clearing in the forest. It served as a means of escape during an attack or a siege."

Robert's brow creased in confusion. "Why didn't you ever tell me about this? Does mother know?"

"I planned on telling you when the time was right. No, your mother doesn't know."

"What about my uncle?"

"The passageway is revealed only to firstborn sons when they inherit."

The men eventually mounted their horses and continued on their journey. The afternoon slipped into twilight, and the half-moon provided enough light to see clearly, but not enough to reveal their hiding places among the dense wall of shrubs and trees.

The castle was nearly three hundred yards away. Fires burned at intervals along the ramparts, crisply outlining Edward's sentries. Richard chose thirty men and quietly proceeded to the small clearing in the forest. Robert was among them.

The men stood aside as Richard swept his right foot across the grass in search of something. When the side of his boot hit a hard object, he bent toward the ground and took hold of a steel ring. He pulled hard on the ring, which was attached to a square metal door. When the door flipped open, it revealed a hole in the earth barely big enough to let a man through. The men climbed down to the bottom and Richard lit a small torch. Its fiery glow revealed a section of the underground corridor. Richard proceeded to lead the way, and eventually stopped before an ancient wooden door. With a quick shove, he opened the door and came face to face with a stone wall.

"Where are we?" Robert whispered.

"On the other side of the dungeon wall," Richard replied as he felt around the center of the wall for a metal lever. "Ah, there it is."

To everyone's amazement, the wall creaked and shifted just enough to allow a man to slip through. Richard was on the other side a second later, standing in the middle of the dungeon's corridor. After checking to make sure no one was around, he motioned to the men. One by one they slipped through the crack.

The moment the dank, moldy smell permeated Robert's nostrils, he cringed in disgust. He had always thought of the dungeon as the castle's bowels, avoiding it at all costs. The torch in his hand revealed a film of greenish slime on the stones.

Moving silently, they reached the stairs leading up into the castle. Richard removed his sword and held it aloft. The men followed suit; they were tense, ready to fight. Richard met their gazes and gave them a curt nod before snuffing out the torch. They moved together with the effortless synchronicity of seasoned soldiers. When the men reached the top of the stairs, they turned down a wide hallway. Richard stopped when he heard voices coming from the doorway beyond, and everyone behind him froze.

Two of Edward's mercenaries stood inside the doorway

leading into the main hall. Richard motioned to one of his men, who nodded in understanding. Together, they pounced on Edward's men like giant cats, instantly slitting their throats. The slain guards fell to the floor without a sound.

Richard stepped over the corpses before crossing the room. The men waited until he reached the far wall and gave the signal before following his lead. Richard put his finger to his lips then pointed to an alcove. Four of Edward's men were stationed past the great hall by the castle's main entrance. Richard and his men slit their throats, too.

"Six of you will come upstairs with Robert and me," Richard instructed. "The rest of you will go to the battlements where Edward's men are stationed. You have the advantage of surprise. Signal the others the moment you can."

He pointed to the narrow stairwell, which spiraled upward to the battlements, before leading his own small group in the opposite direction. Richard crept upstairs toward the castle's sleeping quarters. The corridors were lit at intervals, creating ominous shadows on the hanging tapestries.

Someone shouted and the thunder of approaching hooves impregnated the night's silence. Did Edward's sentries spot Richard's men before they had the chance to launch a sneak attack?

"Damn," Richard cursed under his breath. "Stay close to the walls and shadows," he whispered to the others as he snuffed out a nearby torch.

It was only a matter of time before they were discovered. Hopefully, his allies would arrive quickly.

***

"Wake up, Your Excellency! We're under attack," the burly mercenary cried out from the doorway.

Edward's eyes flew open and he ran to the window. An army had infiltrated the courtyard below, and the sound of steel swords clashing above meant the ramparts had been breached.

"This is my brother's work," he sneered. "Bring Beatrice here *now*."

When the big man entered Beatrice's bedchamber, he found

both women at the window. Their jubilant expressions vanished at the sight of him. Without a word, he grabbed hold of each woman's arm and forced them out of the room. Beatrice glanced over her shoulder and, to her immense surprise and relief, she caught sight of Richard and Robert peeking around the wall of the opposite hallway. Her face lit up with joy, but Richard put his finger to his lips. *Silence.*

Edward paced frantically as the women entered the bedchamber. Beatrice smiled smugly, which only irritated him further.

"I warned you of this day," she said.

"Silence, woman!"

Beatrice chuckled at his fury. Her impudence earned her a sharp slap across the face from the bishop's bejeweled hand. Edward's demeanor toward her had changed drastically after his return to Kent. He no longer sought her bed and she often caught him staring at her with contempt. Finally, their feelings for each other were mutual.

Knowing her husband and son were alive gave Beatrice the strength to endure whatever Edward had in store for her, even if it meant death. "Does hitting me make you feel like more of a man, Edward?"

Edward composed himself and regarded her coldly. "Guard!" When the man appeared in the doorway, he said, "Lock them in the dungeon."

"No!" Beatrice protested.

"Oh, yes," Edward countered coldly. "This is Richard's doing, I know it. When he searches the castle for you, he'll assume you've been abducted. You can scream all you like down there—*no one can hear you.* I know this because your cruel husband locked me in one of the cells as a prank when we were children. It took hours for my father's men to find me."

His eyes took on a distant look as he spoke of his childhood. Beatrice saw hatred and pain, but that didn't deter her from saying, "Perhaps they should have left you there to rot."

Edward looked at her sharply, and gradually, his scowl turned into a demented smile. "Perhaps I should leave *you* there to rot." The surprised look on her face satisfied him. He had poured out his love for her on many occasions and the cruel vixen had only spurned him. The bishop waved his hand. "Take them away."

Gretta cried hysterically. She feared the dungeon and believed it to be haunted by ghosts. Beatrice, on the other hand, remained calm and held her head high as she was led away.

It was dank and eerily silent as they entered the crude stone hallway that led to the place where prisoners were once kept and tortured. Gretta stood very close to Beatrice, and when the mercenary opened an iron gate, she whimpered.

"Get in," he said.

Beatrice peered inside the cell before stepping over the threshold. She heard the squeak of mice and wondered if the fat kitchen cats were getting lazy. The silliness of such a thought at a time like this made her almost laugh aloud. Gretta refused to enter the cell, and after being unceremoniously shoved, she landed in a heap at Beatrice's feet.

"Stupid brute," Beatrice mumbled as she helped her maid to stand.

The man slammed the gate shut and locked the women inside. It was dark in the small cell, and the idea of being left for dead in the airless space was enough to drive anyone mad.

"What are we to do, my lady?" Gretta asked in a shaky voice.

"We'll wait," Beatrice answered with a calmness she didn't feel.

"What if no one comes?"

Placing her lips to Gretta's ear, Beatrice whispered, "Do not fear. Richard and Robert are here. I saw them when that oaf fetched us from my room."

"What if Lord Richard didn't see us being led down to the dungeon? What if the bishop escapes and your husband believes we're with him?"

Those thoughts hadn't occurred to Beatrice, and she soon felt the first wave of panic. If Edward succeeded in escaping, surely her husband would do a thorough search of the entire premises before chasing after his brother... *wouldn't he*?

"I'm *sure* Richard will find us here." Gretta began to sob quietly and she added, "Pray to God, Gretta, it will occupy your thoughts."

The maid obediently clasped her hands together and began to pray. Beatrice strained her ears to hear what was going on upstairs, but the stones were so thick they obliterated any sound. There was a battle going on and she had no idea which side was winning.

***

Richard watched as his wife and her maid were led to the dungeon. They would be safe in a cell for the time being. Motioning for Robert and the other men to follow, he crept down the hall to his bedchamber. He found Edward at the window with his back turned.

"Did you really think you would get away with this, *brother*?" Richard demanded.

Edward whipped around with a start and stared at his older brother with unmasked hatred. "Richard!"

"You wear my clothing, you set yourself up in my chamber—you're lower than a serpent." Richard unsheathed his sword and his men did the same. He raised his hand to still them. "This is my battle."

Edward unsheathed his sword. The two brothers circled each other like territorial animals. Edward was the first to strike with a forward lunge. Richard sidestepped and turned with an uppercut, nicking the bishop's chin with his sword tip.

"You bastard," Edward cried, wiping the blood off his chin with his hand.

"I was always a better fighter than you. Surrender now and all you'll face is the king's judgment and prison."

"I have no fear of you!" Edward spat as he lunged at Richard again, this time with both hands gripping the sword hilt.

Richard deflected the blow with a powerful strike of his own. The two men continued to fight, steel blades clashing. Robert watched in awe as his father fought against his uncle with precision and grace. There were footsteps heading toward the bedchamber, and Richard's allies steeled themselves for a fight. A handful of Edward's mercenaries flooded the room, only to be pierced through with ready swords. They fell down dead, causing the other mercenaries to step over them as they entered.

Richard's men fought fiercely. Meanwhile, Edward was beginning to tire. Richard took the opportunity to cut into Edward's right shoulder, thus weakening his fighting arm. It wouldn't be long before Richard disarmed his opponent. He took a quick glance to assess the fighting at the other end of the large room.

Edward, wounded and in pain, dropped his sword and fell to his knees. Richard kept the tip of his sword at his brother's chest. "You'll be stripped of everything," Richard seethed. "You'll live like the most common peasant in prison."

"I would rather you kill me now," Edward retorted.

Richard was tempted. "I don't want your blood on my hands, even if you are a liar and lack honor. Death is too good compared to what I have in store for you."

Edward, unwilling to accept defeat, decided to play his last card. A slow smile crept to his lips. "Such a pity that my time in Kent has to end so soon. Your wife has been enjoying my company immensely." Richard clenched his jaw and he continued, "She has the most adorable little mole on the inside of her left thigh…"

Richard raised his sword and was about to strike when he heard Robert cry out.

"*Father!*"

Richard turned and spotted Robert on his knees, the hilt of a sword sticking out of his chest. The blade had gone clean through. Richard's legs went weak and his sword fell to the ground. He ran to Robert's side, cradling his son in his arms. Edward took advantage of the dire situation and fled the room.

Edward's men lay dead, along with two of Richard's men. The allies were downstairs; they had overtaken the castle.

"Oh God! Oh God!" Richard repeated over and over as he held his son's head against his chest.

"We won, Father," Robert whispered.

"Aye, son," Richard agreed, tears blurring his vision.

Robert looked down at the hilt and paled. "Funny, I can't feel anything…"

"Robert—"

"I wish I could see Mother before I die."

One of the knights had already left to fetch Beatrice.

***

"Lady Beatrice, you must come with me now! Lord Richard has sent me to fetch you."

Freed from their cell, Beatrice and Gretta fled upstairs to Richard's bedchamber where her husband was cradling Robert in his arms.

Beatrice sank to her knees. "Oh, Robert…"

"Don't cry, Mother, I'm in no pain," Robert assured in a weak voice. "I fought bravely."

Beatrice kissed his face, the salt of her tears mingling with the taste of his young skin. "I love you Robert, oh God. Two sons lost…two sons lost, please don't die!"

"I had a brother?" asked Robert on the verge of unconsciousness.

Beatrice nodded and continued to hold his hand. Robert closed his eyes and said nothing more. Richard turned to Beatrice and held her tightly in his arms as she wailed with pain. There was cheering outside and downstairs.

Richard had won.

Edward managed to escape to the stables during the melee. The pain in his shoulder was excruciating. He cursed his brother and urged the horse forward, galloping toward the dark forest.

CHAPTER 18

By the time Nick arrived in England in the autumn of 1149, the entire crusade seemed like a distant dream. Only the loss of Jeremy and his occasional nightmares made it a painful reality. Riding his powerful war horse through the familiar villages of his homeland, he saw everything through different eyes. Even the village of Lewes seemed strange upon his arrival.

War changes a man forever.

Nick contemplated life while urging his horse through the narrow streets. The villagers gazed up at him not as a mere man, but as a warrior, a knight, a *hero*. If only they knew he was a deserter; a man who would have been killed like a disgraceful dog if caught by his Grandmaster.

Several young boys ran up to him inquiring if he was in need of a squire. He had been one of those boys, once. It seemed so long ago. Nick patted them on the head and sent them on their way. He also noticed many girls admiring him as he passed.

The first person he sought was Sarah. He rode out to her cottage and knocked on her door.

Sarah almost didn't recognize the powerfully built man who stood before her. "Oh, Nick," she cried, embracing him. "You've come home! Where is Jeremy?"

He hesitated. "I've returned to England alone."

Alarmed, she demanded, "Why did he stay behind?" Seeing the look on his face, she cried, "Oh, no...*no*."

Nick embraced her. "I'm sorry, Sarah."

Sarah wiped her eyes and pulled away. "Thank God Jeremy had you as his friend and brother."

"He fought bravely for God. You should be proud."

Sarah nodded, the tears streaming down her cheeks. Jeremy's sword was wrapped in burlap and tied to his saddle.

Nick retrieved the weapon and gave it to her. "This is your son's sword. It helped to recapture Lisbon from the Moors and to fight against the Turks in the Holy Land."

Sarah slowly picked up the heavy metal sword and gazed upon it with reverence. Nick had cleaned any traces of blood from the steel and polished it until it shone, but the scars of battle showed themselves in the many nicks and dents.

"Thank you," she said softly.

Nick politely took his leave, promising to return soon. He mounted his horse and rode to the inn to see Agnes and Simon. They greeted him warmly, and were distressed to hear the tragic news of Jeremy's death.

"Poor Sarah!" Agnes lamented.

Nick nodded sadly. "I gave her Jeremy's sword."

"I'm sure she's grateful for that."

At length, Agnes said, "Here, come and sit by the fire while I get you something to eat." She scurried about, first filling a ceramic cup with ale then setting a plate of steaming stew before him. "Careful, the stew is hot."

Nick inhaled the savory steam. "You two look well. Marriage suits you both."

"Aye," Simon agreed with a smile. "The inn keeps us busy. We own it now."

Agnes added, "The innkeeper fell ill a few months ago, and since he had no children or relatives, he willed it to us. We couldn't believe our good fortune."

Nick was happy for them. It was good to see the people he cared about doing well in life.

Simon said, "Gwen will be so happy to see you."

Nick felt the color rise in his cheeks. "How is she?"

Agnes turned her face away. "She's better now."

Nick frowned. "Was she ill?"

A strange look crept into her eyes as she reached for his hand. "Go see her."

Nick looked askance at Simon, who motioned for him to step outside. "Let me show you the garden out back while your stew cools."

Agnes was on the verge of tears and busied herself by patting down the dough on the table. The two men walked outside toward the back where a large plot of earth boasted vegetables and herbs. Along the edge of the garden were some apple trees, the branches bare from the recent harvest.

"You should see Gwen as soon as you can," Simon said, his face serious.

"Has something happened to her?"

"She lost her child."

"Her *child?*" Nick repeated, barely able to disguise the pain in his voice.

"You didn't know that Gwen got married?"

Nick shook his head. "How did she lose the child?"

"Gwen married the wool merchant—"

"Ranulf St. George."

"He's quite a bit older than she is and very jealous. When she came to be with child this past spring, we were hopeful…" Simon hesitated. "Ranulf usually goes away for days on end, but when he's home, he spends most of his time in taverns with women. One night, he came home drunk and he beat her."

Nick staggered slightly. "While she was pregnant?"

"Aye. He beat her so badly it almost killed her. Agnes is sick with worry daily and so am I."

Nick's fists were balled, his jaw set in a tight clench. "Where does she live?"

"Nick—"

"Where does she live?"

For the first time Simon saw Nick not as a young boy, but as a seasoned warrior, a man to be reckoned with…a dangerous man.

Gwen's cottage wasn't far from the inn. It was larger than most of the homes in the village and very well kept. There was a small herb garden in the front of the yard and a big vegetable garden in the back. A girl stood in the center of the latter feeding a cluster of cackling hens. She froze at the sight of Nick.

"Is this the home of Mistress Gweneth?"

"It is, sir," Leah replied.

"Tell her Nick St. John is here to see her."

Leah went inside the house. A few moments later she came

out again. "My mistress bids you to enter."

Nick smiled inwardly at the thought of Gwen having a servant as he was led inside the nicely furnished cottage. The girl offered Nick a seat by the fire and a pewter mug filled with ale. She also placed a small dish of aged cheese on the table beside him before going back out into the garden and closing the door. Nick was so busy looking around that he didn't notice Gwen standing within the shadowy interior of her bedroom.

He stood up immediately. "Gwen!"

She didn't move, keeping her face in profile. "It's a pleasure to see you again, Nick," she said quietly. "What an unexpected surprise."

There was something strange about Gwen. She was different—certainly not the feisty girl once knew. "I've thought of you often." He felt awkward when she said nothing. "I wish you could have seen the things that I've seen. You would have loved Portugal."

"I'm sure I would have." She paused before confessing, "I was so worried. I was afraid you'd never come home. I prayed for you every day."

"Well, God must have heard your prayers because He spared my life."

"But not Jeremy's."

"How do you know?"

"I sent Leah to Sarah's house with some tarts. My maid returned and told me the news shortly before you arrived. Sarah must be inconsolable."

"Jeremy died a warrior, fighting bravely for his God."

"*His* God…not yours?"

Nick ignored her question. "Why do you remain in the shadows instead of coming out here and greeting me properly?"

Gwen chuckled mirthlessly. "*Properly*? You're not supposed to talk to me, remember? According to Prior Bartholomew, you're a Templar Knight."

"My beliefs where women are concerned are the same as they've always been. I'll never stop talking to you, or Agnes, or Sarah—or any other woman."

"You're a rebel."

Nick's face grew serious. "Come here, Gwen. Let me look at how married life has been treating you."

"You've already spoken with my mother and Simon." There was a long pause before she said in a strained voice, "You should go now, Nick. Thank you so much for stopping by."

"Please don't shut me out."

"You shouldn't have come. Not today…*not now.*"

"I know about your husband. I know about the child you lost. Please…"

Gwen sobbed softly as he approached. "NO!" she shouted, backing into the shadows further. "Go, now!"

Nick hesitated. She had never spoken to him in such a manner and it hurt him. He turned to go, but something stopped him. "I care about—I've cared about you all of my life. I won't leave you now in your time of need."

"You left me long ago!"

Nick strode into the bedchamber and gently cupped her shoulders. Gazing down remorsefully at the top of her bent head, he whispered, "I did, and I'm so sorry."

"I don't want your pity."

"Let me look at you." He took hold of her chin and lifted her face toward him. "My God," he whispered.

Gwen averted her gaze as he silently took in her swollen eye, bruised cheek, and the cut on her forehead.

After Ranulf had tired of his whore and returned home, he had apologized profusely to Gwen for having beaten her so viciously. He mourned the loss of their unborn child, and had vowed never to raise his hand to his wife again. Even though Ranulf still frequented the taverns and whorehouses, their marriage had improved somewhat. Until last night.

"Why do you stay?" Nick demanded.

"I'm legally bound to him."

"You can go live at the inn."

"And bring my troubles to my mother's doorstep?" Gwen shook her head. "Ranulf would never allow it, anyway. He'd drag me back here by my hair, if need be."

The fury building within Nick's chest was making it hard for him to breathe. Staring at her bruised eye, he inquired, "When did *this* happen?"

"Last night."

Gwen explained how Ranulf had come home drunk and when she accidentally dropped his supper dish, he became irate. Hungry and irritated by her clumsiness, he had struck her hard in the face, bruising her eye and cheek in the process. She fell to the floor where a shard of the broken plate cut her forehead.

"Where is he?" Nick asked through clenched teeth.

"Please, you don't understand."

"Oh, I understand perfectly," he countered icily. "Ranulf is an angry drunk who beats you, and his fists killed your unborn child. Perhaps the next beating will cost you your life."

"He's not always like that!"

"How can you defend him?"

"He takes care of me. Where else am I to go?"

"I see. You put up with him because he provides you with a pretty cottage, a servant, and fine clothing." Nick regretted his words instantly, but it was too late.

Gwen's mouth tightened into a thin line. "I want you to leave."

"I did not mean to—"

"Please, just go," she said, turning her face away.

Nick left the cottage feeling frustrated and angry.

***

"There's nothing I can do, Nick," Bartholomew said apologetically.

The two men sat facing each other in the refectory while eating supper. The monks had already eaten, thus allowing them a measure of privacy to speak freely. Nick's return was a joyous event, but the prior felt the sting of Jeremy's loss. Nick described the battle that led to his friend's death, but omitted the fact that he had deserted his brethren.

Nick put his head in his hands. "For God's sake, Ranulf committed murder!"

"Some would see it that way. Others may think the Lord

took the babe because it wasn't meant for this world."

"That's absurd."

"I agree, but that's the truth. If I could annul the marriage, I would."

Bartholomew broke off a chunk of bread and placed it in his mouth as Nick inquired, "Could you write a letter to the archbishop? Or to the Pope?"

The prior shook his head. "It would do no good. Gwen isn't a member of the nobility; she has no power, no importance. As much as I hate to say it, her case would most likely be ignored."

Nick violently pierced a chunk of boiled carrot with the tip of his knife and placed it in his mouth. "Where is Ranulf now?" he asked between chews.

"Off in search of fine silks and other fabrics to sell, I suppose. According to Gwen, he travels often and he's a shrewd merchant."

"But a shamefully abusive and violent husband."

"It's not our place to judge others, Nick."

"Prior Bartholomew, how can you sit there and defend Ranulf after what he's done to our Gwen?"

The prior sighed tiredly. "I'm not defending him."

"She defended him, too."

"Ranulf is a lost soul. His love of drink interferes with his better judgment."

Nick shook his head and pushed his plate aside. "I have lost my appetite."

"You can't carry on like this, my son. I know how much you care for Gwen. You're upset about what happened, and so am I, but there's nothing we can do. She is legally married to him and therefore his property." The prior paused. "It's getting late and you should get some rest."

"It will be strange sleeping in my cell tonight without Jeremy," Nick admitted.

Bartholomew crossed himself. "May his soul rest in peace. God never forgets those who sacrifice their lives for Him. You can rest assured, Nick. Jeremy has been given a place of honor in Heaven and is smiling down upon us as we speak.

Goodnight."

Nick bade the prior goodnight and returned to his old cell feeling guilty for not being honest with him. Jeremy's cot was still there, as were his books and a few of his belongings. Stretching out on his cot, he stared up at the ceiling. The moonlight cast an eerie glow over the sparsely furnished room. He couldn't stop picturing Gwen's beautiful face, battered and bruised by Ranulf's fists. He eventually fell into a fitful sleep, and the sound of her crying haunted his dreams.

For the next few days Nick enjoyed the peacefulness of the monastery. He devoted much of his time to study and meditation. Gwen's dire situation occupied his thoughts and he needed to see her again. The sun had begun its descent one afternoon when Nick decided to ride into the village.

Crickets chirped in the autumnal twilight as Nick approached Gwen's cottage. He was about to knock on the front door when he heard singing. Following Gwen's voice to the rear of the dwelling, he stopped outside the window and peeked through the narrow slit of the partially closed wooden shutters. She stood in the center of a large wooden tub filled with water, washing herself with a cloth. Her slick, wet body glistened in the golden glow of candlelight. Her legs were lean and long, her waist trim, and her breasts firm. She was singing an old Irish tune softly to herself, completely oblivious of being watched. Careful not to make a sound, Nick silently admired her beauty. When he felt himself hardening with lust, he cursed under his breath while offering a quick prayer to God. Such despicable behavior was improper for a monk, and his highly trained conscience prickled with guilt.

A door creaked open not far from where he stood, followed by the sound of footsteps. Nick held his breath in anticipation of seeing Ranulf. After a moment, the footsteps quickly ran back inside and closed the door with a loud bang. Through the window slit Nick saw the serving girl he had seen the other day.

"I let the cat out, Mistress Gweneth," the girl said.

Gwen nodded. "Will you fetch the lavender oil?" The girl went to a cupboard, took out a small vial, and added a few precious drops to the water. "Thank you Leah, that will be all for today. Goodnight."

She rubbed the scented water into her skin and sniffed her arm in satisfaction. The piercing floral scent permeated the air. Slowly, Gwen leaned back in the tub and relaxed. A smile of pleasure spread across her face as she inhaled the sweet steam. Nick's chest tightened; he longed to smell every inch of her skin...

"God forgive me", he whispered to himself.

As he took a step away from the window he accidentally stepped on a cat's tail. The animal let out a loud hiss, causing Gwen to leave the tub and come to the window.

She peered out the slit, whispering, "Ranulf? Is that you?" She paused. "Methuselah?" When there was no response she returned to her bath. "Methuselah, you mischievous cat."

Nick let out a slow sigh of relief. He shouldn't be lurking outside a married woman's window, even if that woman was Gwen. As he turned to go, he heard heavy shuffling footsteps coming down the dirt road. Quickly, he hid behind the nearest tree and waited. It was Ranulf.

Staggering in his drunkenness, he let himself into the house and Nick heard the sound of a large splash. Creeping back to the window, he saw that Gwen had gotten out of the tub and bolted the door from the inside. Her wet, naked body was a lovely sight to behold. He watched in awe as she tiptoed back to the tub and quietly slipped back into the water.

Within seconds, Ranulf pounded on the door. "Open the door, woman," he demanded, slurring his words.

"I don't feel well." She proceeded to feign a cough in the hope that her husband would go away.

The banging on the door became more insistent. "Open the damn door!"

Nick could see Gwen's knuckles turning white as she gripped the sides of the tub. He unwittingly placed his hand on the hilt of his sword.

"I swear to God if you don't open this door I'll knock it down!" Ranulf bellowed.

Gwen sat frozen in the tub, her muscles tense. "Please, Ranulf, I'm sick with my monthly pains. Go to bed and I'll join you in a bit," she replied sweetly.

This seemed to appease the beast and he mumbled something sexually obscene before shuffling away from the door. Gwen eased back against the tub and closed her eyes in obvious relief. "You probably reek of ale and whores you filthy pig," she whispered audibly at the door. She would never dare say these words to Ranulf's face, however. Then, covering her face with her hands, she cried silently.

Nick wanted so badly to comfort her, to take her away from this place, but the laws of man and God forbade it.

How could I have left you alone, Gwen? How could I have allowed you to fall into this mess?

He retreated from the window and found his way back to the main road where his horse was tethered. The ride back to the monastery was difficult as his mind raced with thoughts. Nick fell onto his cot without removing his clothing, and remained awake for hours.

After performing the morning mass, Bartholomew approached Nick as he was exiting the church. "A letter arrived yesterday from our brothers in London."

"What news?"

"After overtaking his brother's castle, the Bishop of Rochester has fled Kent." *Your good for nothing uncle, may he rot in Hell*, the prior wanted to shout.

"Who's the bishop's brother?"

Your father. "Richard Fitzwilliam, Earl of Kent."

"I met the man in Lisbon along with his son, Robert."

The prior arched a brow in surprise. "Oh?"

"Good men," Nick stated. "Where is the bishop now?"

"No one knows."

"What happened?"

"Lord Richard retaliated against his brother with an army and recaptured his castle. Unfortunately, his son died in the fight."

"Poor Robert," Nick said. "He was a fine young man."

"The funeral mass will be held at Canterbury Cathedral tomorrow." The prior paused. "Perhaps you should attend."

"I shall indeed pay my respects to Lord Richard."

"You haven't been yourself lately, my son," Bartholomew said. "You seem withdrawn and sad. I know you're still grieving over Jeremy, but I believe there's more to it than that."

Nick stared at the man whom he loved as his own father. How could he tell the prior that he had fled the Templars due to an extreme lack of faith? And then there was Gwen. How could he confess carnal desire for a woman whom he should love as a sister? Or that he wished Ranulf dead? Such sinful, forbidden thoughts shouldn't exist in his mind let alone be uttered aloud.

Bartholomew peered deeply into Nick's eyes and saw conflict and pain; a tortured soul. "When you're ready to speak, I'll be here waiting with an open heart to help you however I can. You can trust me, Nick."

"I know," Nick said gratefully, as he placed his hands on the prior's shoulders.

Bartholomew nodded, satisfied. Nick turned and made his way down the stone stairs. The pale morning sunlight fought through several dark clouds in the pewter colored sky. He shivered and suddenly longed for the comforting heat of the bright Mediterranean sun.

CHAPTER 19

Richard approached Beatrice's bedchamber and paused in the doorway. She had taken ill since the death of their son. Gretta hovered around her mistress constantly in an effort to persuade her into taking some nourishment. The maid curtsied to Richard as he entered and moved away from the bed.

He knelt down and took his wife's hand in his own; it was frail and icy cold. "Today is Sunday," he said gently. Beatrice, pale-faced and red-eyed from countless tears, stared blankly at the ceiling. "Robert's funeral...He would hate to see you like this. He loved you so much and spoke of you often while we were away."

She nodded, knowing he spoke the truth, and struggled to sit up. Gretta came forward to assist her mistress.

"You must eat first," Richard said, nodding to Gretta.

Gretta left the room to fetch some bread and broth.

As soon as they were alone, Beatrice gripped Richard's arm and pulled him close. He was surprised at her strength.

"I want my son."

"Dearest, he's dead," Richard said gently.

"*I want my son.*"

This time, Richard understood exactly what she meant. Beatrice wanted to replace Robert with the baby boy she lost so long ago. He didn't know what to say. Edward's reference to markings on intimate parts of her body still rattled through his grief-stricken mind. The thought of it made the bile rise in his throat. She had been through so much and he wanted to avoid this conversation—*for now*.

Taking her husband's silence as reluctance to grant her wish, she became agitated. "I want my son," she persisted. "He's *your* son and deserves to be restored to his rightful place, which is here with us."

Richard sighed deeply, running a hand through his hair. He

didn't want to discuss this topic on the day of Robert's funeral. "Let's not speak of this now, my love."

Beatrice rose on her knees and suddenly gripped his shoulders. Using all her strength, she forced him to face her squarely on the bed. Richard was completely taken by surprise, temporarily lost his balance, and almost fell over. *Had she lost her wits?*

"It's Edward, isn't it?" she demanded angrily. "Your brother has been trying to destroy you for years. He hates you—even though he wants to be you—and will do anything to bring you down! How much more proof do you need? For God's sake, Richard, open your eyes!"

He looked at her for a long, hard moment. "Answer this question for me, wife: how is it that Edward knows about the mole on the inside of your thigh?"

Beatrice's face turned red and her teeth came together in an angry snarl. "Your brother *raped* me. He threatened to harm me and our household if I didn't submit to his lust, so I did."

Gretta arrived with the tray of food as Beatrice was in the middle of making her confession. Seeing the stunned expression on her master's face, she hovered warily in the doorway.

Beatrice continued, "You're silent, husband. Do you doubt me? Ask my maid if you don't believe me."

Richard looked to Gretta. "Speak."

"The bishop hurt the Lady Beatrice. I cared for her wounds after he—after he…" Gretta trailed off, crying.

"Enough!" he cried, tears welling up in his eyes.

Richard had never expressed his emotions so openly before, so Beatrice didn't know how to react.

"I'm sorry I wasn't here to protect you," he whispered.

Beatrice embraced her husband while giving Gretta a meaningful look. They would keep the aborted child a secret—there was no need to hurt Richard further. Gretta nodded, then discreetly vacated the room.

Richard pulled away. "I never meant to hurt you by taking the boy away. My brother led me to believe the child was his."

Since they were finally airing their differences, she asked, "What would ever possess you to think that I would commit adultery with your brother?"

"Weeks before you gave birth, Edward implied that the child you were carrying wasn't mine. He was so sure of it, so smugly confident—if we weren't at court I would have struck him. This incident, on the tail of your midnight rendezvous with Edward, only added to my suspicion. What's a husband to think?"

"*My* husband should have known better. Edward has been plotting against you for years!"

"You're right."

"You played into his hands, Richard."

"Forgive me."

Beatrice could only glare at him in hurtful silence. "Give me my son. Have him come home, recognize him as your flesh and blood, then I'll forgive you."

"I entrusted the babe to one of my most loyal men. When he returned assuring me that the boy would be well taken care of, I never asked any questions. I don't know where our son is."

"*I do.*"

His face registered surprise. "That's a story you can tell me after the funeral. We must see to Robert now."

A while later, Beatrice stood by Richard's side, their backs to the high altar. No money was spared for Robert's funeral; it was a grand affair. The archbishop himself conducted mass while several members of the nobility stood in attendance. The great cathedral was filled with kinfolk and allies who had come to pay their last respects. Robert's body was covered in sheer linen, his arms were folded upon his chest, and his hands were curled around the hilt of his polished sword.

Beatrice did her best to stay calm as she accepted words of kindness and comfort. One man in particular suddenly caught her attention. Standing with his back to her, his honey colored hair and broad shoulders seemed familiar. She held her breath as the young man turned and walked toward Richard.

"Lord Richard, I was most distressed when I heard about your son. He was a fine young man," Nick said as Richard gripped the young man's hand firmly.

Beatrice remained in shocked silence when Richard turned to her and said, "This is Nicodemus St. John. He fought alongside us in Lisbon."

Nick regarded the fair-haired woman with a flicker of recognition. "My lady, I'll pray for your son's soul."

Nick inclined his Beatrice stared at her son's retreating back in stunned silence.

Richard said, "Nick and I met in Portugal. He's a fine young man and a skillful warrior."

"*He's much more than that, Richard.*"

***

"Prior Bartholomew, I need to speak with you," Nick said after Vespers. "It's a serious matter."

"Do you need to confess something?" When Nick nodded, Bartholomew led him into his private chamber and bolted the door. "Speak, my son."

Nick confessed, "I left the Order without the Grandmaster's permission."

"You deserted them?"

Nick dropped his eyes in shame. "In the middle of the night, like a common thief. The knights were too tired, too beaten down to give chase." He paused. "We had just suffered a terrible defeat."

"Why would you do such a thing?"

"I lost Jeremy and I couldn't…" he trailed off, shaking his head. "I've seen things that no man should see."

"War is brutal, but keep in mind that you fought for God." Nick met Bartholomew's gaze and the prior shuddered as he peered into the warrior's eyes.

"Did I?" Nick rubbed his temples, troubled. "I have so much blood on my hands…I've killed many men."

"You killed Infidels. You killed evildoers."

Nick recalled the dying Turk's desperation; the man's eyes haunted his dreams.

The silence stretched until Bartholomew finally said, "In God's name I absolve you of your sins."

As Bartholomew made the sign of the cross, Nick was uncertain whether he wanted absolution and the thought shocked him. "What about the crime I've committed?"

"Desertion is serious, but I doubt the Grandmaster will trace you here. After all, the documents you handed him stating your noble birth were produced in London, not Lewes. I'll also write a letter sanctioning your decision to leave the Order on the grounds of conduct not befitting a monk."

"But I haven't done anything to—"

The prior raised his hand to silence Nick. "I know, but better to be seen as an immoral sinner released from his monastic vows than to be tried as a deserter."

"You're releasing me from my vows?"

Bartholomew nodded and was sad to notice the relief on Nick's face. "It's the safest thing to do under the circumstances. I doubt the Templars will come looking for you here, but if they do, I'll be ready."

A monk approached them. "Prior Bartholomew, a messenger is here for Nick."

They went outside where a man on horseback held out a scroll with an official seal. "Nicodemus St. John?"

Nick took the letter and read it, then looked at the messenger in surprise. "Is this some kind of joke?"

"The Earl of Kent never jokes," the messenger replied before riding off.

Nick turned to Bartholomew and said, "The letter states that *my parents*—Richard Fitzwilliam and his wife, Lady Beatrice—wish to see me."

Bartholomew sighed tiredly. "Finally."

Nick frowned. "What?"

"Your parents have finally called you home."

Stunned, Nick demanded, "Wait—you knew I was their son and never told me?"

"Come to my cell, I want to show you something."

Nick followed the prior to his chamber.

Bartholomew unlocked a drawer and retrieved the gold and ruby crucifix. "This was wrapped in your swaddling clothes the day we found you. At first, I didn't know what to make of it, then Martin told me the truth when you were older. I wanted to tell you, but he swore me to secrecy. He said it was for your safety."

"My safety? I saw Lord Richard and his wife at the funeral. They said nothing about this to me."

"They must have their reasons."

Nick examined the stunning crucifix. "I met Lord Richard in Lisbon—nothing was said then, either."

"Your questions will be answered soon."

"Robert was my brother," Nick said with sudden realization as he fastened the exquisite crucifix around his neck. "I must go to Kent Castle at once."

First, he would visit Gwen. He wanted to apologize for their last encounter, and share the news about being reunited with his parents. He'd spend the night at the inn and depart for Kent in the morning. He rode to the village in the late afternoon.

"Nick," Gwen said, surprised to see him at her door.

"I promise not to upset you this time," he said, his gray eyes twinkling in the mellow golden light.

"I was harsh with you and I'm sorry."

"I'm here to seek *your* forgiveness. Seeing you hurt like that made me lose my wits."

Gwen's eyes slid toward the neighboring cottage down the road then back to him. Her expression was apprehensive. "I would invite you inside, but Ranulf is away on business and my serving girl, Leah, has left for the night. I'm alone."

"I see," he said, following her gaze.

If Nick went inside while Ranulf was not home, a nosy neighbor could easily get the wrong idea.

"I should have come earlier in the day. I wasn't thinking. Perhaps I should go…"

"Wait," she said, placing a hand on his arm. "I'm going to sup with Simon and my mother tonight. Join me."

"Nothing would please me more."

She gasped when she noticed the crucifix around his neck. "Where in the world did you get that?"

"I'll tell you during dinner," he teased. "Come."

"You would keep me in suspense?"

"I would."

They walked to the inn and he followed Gwen into the large, cozy kitchen. A rustic wooden table was set with earthenware jugs filled with wine, fresh loaves of bread, nettle soup, hard cheese, and crispy sausage.

"What a pleasant surprise!" Agnes said as she embraced him. She noticed the crucifix immediately. "Where did you get that?"

"I asked the same thing, but Nick wishes to keep us in suspense," Gwen said.

Nick cleared his throat. "I have a surprise for all of you. Let's first enjoy our meal, shall we?"

Before long, they were eating, laughing, and talking. The food was good, the wine was strong, and the company was pleasant. Gwen sat back for a moment with a wistful expression. Agnes caught her daughter's eye. The simple food, the friendly banter, the intimacy of the evening; Gwen was reliving her childhood in that moment.

"What's your surprise, Nick?" Agnes demanded, "You're cruel to keep us in such as state of curiosity."

"The crucifix you see around my neck was wrapped in my swaddling clothes the day I was found, and it belonged to my family." Three sets of eyes stared at him in surprise. "Today, I discovered that I'm the son of Lord Richard Fitzwilliam and his wife, the Lady Beatrice."

A collective gasp of shock went around the table before Simon said, "The Earl of Kent is one of the most powerful men in England."

"This is astounding news!" Agnes exclaimed. "When are you going to see them?"

"Tomorrow," Nick replied.

"You'll stay here and rest before your journey."

"That was my intention. I mean to pay, of course."

"Nonsense," Simon said.

Throughout Nick's incredible revelation, Gwen sat back in

frozen silence. She had heard of the powerful nobleman, and was completely stupefied to discover that Nick was his son. She recalled her visit to Mad Margaret's cottage…

Noticing Gwen's silence, Nick said, "I thought you would be happy for me."

Gwen took a long sip of wine before feigning a smile. "I am. This is wonderful news."

Nick thanked Agnes for the meal before following Simon outside for a breath of fresh air.

As soon as the men left, Agnes asked, "What's wrong, Gwen? You looked as pale as death a moment ago." When Gwen heaved a sigh and stared down at her lap, Agnes said quietly, "You love Nick."

Gwen tilted her head upward and what Agnes saw in her daughter's eyes confirmed her suspicion. With a jealous husband like Ranulf, this situation could lead to tragedy. "Your husband must never know the truth, do you understand?"

"I hate him, Mother."

"I know…but I shudder to think of the consequences if Ranulf suspected your feelings for Nick."

"Do you think Nick loves me?"

Agnes sighed sadly. "I believe he does."

Both women gazed out into the night where they could see the outline of the men in the pale moonlight.

Nick insisted on accompanying Gwen back to her cottage after supper. At that late hour, the tavern's patrons would be roaming about in search of trouble. A comely woman like Gwen was a prime target for any ruffian. They set out from the inn in silence and walked uphill to the main road. It was a cold autumn night with a crisp, clear sky. One of Gwen's hands clutched her cloak tightly around her throat, and the other was tucked into the crook of Nick's arm.

"The stars are so bright tonight," she said.

Nick followed her gaze. "They are, indeed. Tell me, are you truly happy for me?"

"I am. Your real family has finally made themselves known to you. I can only imagine your excitement."

"You, Prior Bartholomew, Simon, Agnes, and Sarah will be my family forever," he said. "Nothing will change."

"You're the son of high-born nobles. They may frown upon your association with people of lower rank," she pointed out gently.

"No one can control what I feel or what I do. As overjoyed as I am, I've lived my entire life without my parents. I don't *need* them," he declared passionately.

Gwen slid her hand down his arm and took hold of his hand, squeezing it affectionately. She was truly touched by his words.

"What a fine lass you have there."

Two men reeking of ale appeared before them. Nick stepped in front of Gwen. It was an instinctive gesture.

"Step aside, *friend*. Let us see the pretty girl behind you," the man sneered.

The other added, "We never see such women where we come from."

Nick drew himself up to his full height. "Go find your beds and sleep away the effects of your drink."

"Youth makes fools brave."

Nick retorted, "And ale makes men daft."

"Perhaps my friend and I will show you just how daft we really are."

The man removed a dagger from his belt and unexpectedly took a jab at Nick's arm. The gesture was more to frighten than to cause any real injury. With lightning speed, Nick unsheathed the sword from the scabbard hidden within the folds of his cloak. The pale moonlight glinted off of the wicked steel blade. The two men took a step back, shock registering on their faces despite their drunkenness.

"This sword has killed many men in Lisbon and in the Holy Land. It can handle two more," Nick warned.

The men bowed their heads and stepped back from the warrior, muttering their apologies.

Gwen breathed a sigh of relief as Nick sheathed his sword. It was the first time he had ever revealed such ferocity in her presence, and it sent a strange thrill through her.

"I'm sorry you had to witness that," Nick said.

"You're bleeding!"

"That worthless drunk stabbed me."

"Come," she said, leading toward her cottage.

Gwen opened the door, lit a candle, and led Nick to a small stool before the hearth. She coaxed the embers into flames, then mixed herbs in a bowl.

"This is a familiar scene," Nick commented.

She smiled. "Aye, the day Jeremy injured you with his sword. You were both soaking wet." On a more serious note, she added, "You must miss him terribly."

Nick nodded, his eyes distant. "I do."

Gwen stood before him with the bowl in hand. "I need you to roll up your sleeve." She examined the cut and declared, "It's not as serious as the last wound I tended, but it should be cleaned and dressed."

Taking a piece of linen dampened with wine, she proceeded to clean the blood on his arm. Gwen marveled at the hardness of his muscles, which were much more defined than she remembered. There were scars on his skin, too. *Battle scars.* She stole a sidelong glance at him and noticed that his eyes were closed. She took the opportunity to examine his sensuous mouth, strong jaw, and thick neck. At that moment, his eyes opened.

She averted her gaze. "Almost done."

Nick caught her hand. "Look at me."

"Let me finish so you can be on your way and rest up for your journey tomorrow."

"Stop addressing me as if I'm still a boy at the monastery. Whatever shred of boyhood I possessed when I left St. John's was lost on the battlefields." He placed both hands on her waist and spun her around to face him. "I want you to *look* at me."

Slowly, she met his gaze. The confession of love was apparent; there was no need for words. A slow tear crept down her cheek. "Oh, Nick…"

"I know," he whispered.

Gwen lowered her head. He cursed himself for having

ignored his true instincts. Growing up in a monastery and becoming a monk had seemed like the natural thing for him and Jeremy to do. Had he taken heed of his doubts and followed his heart, Gwen would not be married to Ranulf…she would be his.

"I should never have married him," she admitted. "I should have waited for you."

"There was no guarantee that I would come back. I could have died, like Jeremy did."

"I would have been better off alone in that monastery hoping for your return, than trapped in this loveless marriage with a violent man."

"If Ranulf ever hurts you again…" Nick placed his hand upon the hilt of his sword. "I swear, he'll meet a cold, steel reckoning,"

"Don't talk like that."

Gwen tried to pull away, but Nick refused to release her. He stood up, his hands tightening around her waist as he drew her close. It was the first time he had ever held a woman in such a manner. He reached out to touch her hair before gently tracing his fingertips along the contours of her face.

Gwen stared at him breathlessly, not daring to speak or move lest she break the wondrous spell. Slowly, he bent forward and buried his face in the softness of her neck. The sweet crispness of lavender mingled tantalizingly with the warm scent of her skin. Nick found the combination intoxicating and instinctively began to kiss her smooth throat.

Gwen shivered, melting against him. Nick's mouth moved to claim her lips and she opened them. The kiss gradually progressed from tender to passionate, his mouth exploring hers hungrily as his hands ran up and down the length of her back. When her hands gripped his shoulders and pulled him closer, he hardened against her thigh.

Pulling away reluctantly, he whispered, "I must go."

Gathering every fiber of self-control he possessed, he left the cottage.

Nick awoke at dawn feeling both exhilarated and uneasy. Gwen was a married woman. He couldn't leave for Kent without at least speaking with her, so he set out for her cottage after sunrise. When he arrived, he was met with sounds of hysterical weeping and Gwen's serving girl calling out for help. Nick ran to the door and pushed it open.

"Help me, sir, please," Leah pleaded as she struggled to help her mistress up from the floor.

Nick was sickened by the sight of Gwen's bruised cheek and bloodied lips. He stooped down and picked her up effortlessly in his arms. She winced in pain as he carried her and placed her gently upon the bed.

"Nick," Gwen whispered hoarsely.

"I'm here."

"I hate for you see me like this."

He fought to keep control over his rage. "Why did he do this to you?" She said nothing. *"Why?"* She shook her head, refusing to answer. "I'll seek him out this instant and run him through with my sword if you don't tell me."

"He came in this morning in a rage," she explained.

Leah ran into the room. "Mistress Gweneth! Your husband returns!"

Nick pushed past the girl and unsheathed his sword.

"No, Nick!" Gwen cried, trying to sit up on the bed. "He's drunk and violent—you'll get hurt!"

He shot her a look that immediately made her regret her words. "Never underestimate me again, Gwen."

Gwen wasn't accustomed to seeing this side of Nick and prudently kept quiet. She was overcome by respect as she watched him leave the room.

Ranulf staggered into the cottage reeking of ale. "Where are you hiding, you worthless bag of bones? I'll thrash the life out of you!"

"You'll not lay a hand on her ever again," Nick said.

Ranulf was caught off guard and spun around. "Ah! So you're the so-called *hero*, the monk my wife is so fond of—the scoundrel who was in my house last night while I was away," he sneered. "Tell me, monk, did Holy Mother Church teach you to commit fornication with the wives of hardworking men?"

"I have never dishonored you or your wife."

"Never dishonored me, eh? People talk in this village. They saw you come in here after dark."

"Then those people should have also seen me leaving a moment later. Your wife merely dressed a wound that I incurred while protecting her from two rogues in the street. Perhaps she would have told you the whole story if you had given her the chance instead of pummeling her with your fists."

Ranulf frowned in outrage. "A man has the right to treat his woman as he wishes."

"Any man who raises his hand toward a woman is a coward," Nick retorted, his grip tightening on the hilt of the sword.

"How dare you insult me under my own roof?" Ranulf spat, unsheathing his own sword.

"How dare you beat your wife and kill your unborn child," Nick seethed, his anger finally taking over. "You're nothing but a violent whoremonger."

Ranulf lunged forward with lethal intention, and Nick sidestepped the lunge effortlessly. With the tip of his sword, he managed to slice off the lower tip of Ranulf's ear.

"Bloody bastard!" Ranulf spat as he placed his hand over the stinging remainder of his earlobe.

"I suggest you sheath your sword," Nick warned.

"And I suggest you sheath your tongue, monk!"

Ranulf lunged forward again, this time grabbing a lit candle and tossing the hot wax in Nick's direction. It landed on the side of his neck and burned the skin, but it wasn't enough to distract the seasoned warrior. Nick lifted his sword and pierced Ranulf's right shoulder.

Ranulf cursed. Gripping his sword with both hands, he slashed at Nick's chest. Nick jumped back as the tip of the tip of Ranulf's sword scratched his collarbone. Nick wondered where the wool merchant had learned to fight. No doubt the alcohol gave him far more bravado than wisdom.

"Sheath your sword now and I'll spare your life, you drunken fool," Nick said. "Continue to lunge at me and I'll defend myself the only way I know how."

"Damn you!" Ranulf shouted, trying again to run the monk through with a fierce lunge. "I'm going to disembowel you!"

Nick defended the blow with a steely clash of his own sword. With feline grace, he stepped forward and slashed Ranulf's throat. Leah screamed as Ranulf's blood oozed from the lethal wound.

"I tried to warn you," Nick said flatly to the dying man.

Ranulf dropped his sword and stood motionless for a moment, attempting to speak. Only gurgling sounds escaped his lips before he collapsed onto the floor. Gwen, who had managed to crawl out of bed, clung to the doorway. She had watched the entire scene in silence and her face was white with fear.

Nick placed his sword on the table and stood beside Gwen. She was watching the pool of rich, red blood expand beneath Ranulf's head with a look of shock. "Come away, Gwen," he said, placing an arm around her shoulders and leading her outside to get some fresh air.

Leah went out to fetch Agnes and Simon. When they arrived at the cottage, Gwen could muster no emotion other than relief. Agnes embraced her daughter as she eyed the corpse on the floor. The nightmare was over.

"I should summon the magistrate," Simon said. "He should know our side of the story as soon as possible."

The magistrate came in the company of another man. Nick explained what had occurred and Leah confirmed his story. Gwen was also questioned as a witness. Agnes gave her a calming draught after the ordeal and she fell asleep. The men took the body to the chapel where Ranulf's family would make final preparations.

While Gwen slept, Agnes and Leah scrubbed the kitchen floor. The blood turned the soapy water pink.

Simon took Nick aside and said quietly, "Ranulf's family will be very angry."

"*We're* angry," Nick retorted.

"That we are. He killed our grandchild and could have easily killed Gwen, too, but his family doesn't seem to take that into consideration." Simon looked around. "Ranulf's uncle will surely lay claim to this cottage."

"His uncle? What of his parents?"

"Both dead."

"What of Gwen?"

"She'll come to live with us." Simon paused. "I fear for you and Gwen. Who knows what Ranulf's family is capable of?"

"There's nothing to fear," Nick assured. "Ranulf was the first to draw his sword. I tried to dissuade him from fighting, but he stubbornly persisted. I had no choice but to defend myself. Leah and Gwen have already given their testimony." He paused. "I'll deal with Ranulf's family if and when the time comes."

Nick remained in Lewes for a few days in order to keep an eye on Gwen. Shortly after his departure for Kent, Ranulf's uncle sent a message to Gwen. He wanted her out of the cottage by the end of the month. She could have challenged him in court, but decided against it. At this point, she wanted nothing more than to walk away from her old life and be left in peace.

CHAPTER 20

Nick emerged from the forest and gasped when he saw Kent Castle. An impenetrable wall encircled the imposing Norman fortress, and he spied the guards on the parapets. Richard's knights gathered together as Nick urged his horse forward, and they watched from above as he crossed over the drawbridge.

A groom appeared in the courtyard to take his horse, as a page exited the castle. "Good day to you, my lord. You must be thirsty," he said, holding out a silver chalice.

Nick accepted the watered wine with gratitude and drank it thirstily. No one had ever called him 'lord' before and it felt strange. He followed the page through the castle's impressive entrance and into the vast main hall.

"Please, sit," the page said before taking his leave.

Narrow windows lined one wall of the enormous room, while the opposite wall boasted a series of tapestries. Nick studied the colorful embroidered figures, and quickly discerned that each panel told part of a story. He walked toward the giant works of art to have a closer look. In the first tapestry, five richly dressed men hunted in a forest. In the second scene, a man pointed to a beautiful white unicorn drinking from a stream. The third scene depicted the unicorn fleeing while the men tried in vain to capture it. In the last tapestry, a fair maiden sat feeding the unicorn from her hand while the men looked on in awe. An inscription in Latin was neatly embroidered beneath her feet: '*Castitas. Obstinata Pudicitia. Decus Muliebris.*' Nick translated the words in his head: 'Chastity. Resolute Purity. Womanly Honor.'

"It is said that only a chaste virgin with a pure heart can coax a unicorn to eat from her hand," came a deep voice from behind him.

Nick tore his eyes from the tapestry and turned around to face Lord Richard. His beautiful wife stood at his side, staring at the crucifix around Nick's neck.

Richard continued, "Thank you for coming, Nick. I imagine our message came as a shock to you."

Nick took in the man's height and build, the gray eyes, the facial features…how had he not noticed their mutual resemblance before now? He replied, "It did."

"I can only hope that you understand the reasons for our actions."

Beatrice took a step toward him. "Don't you recognize me, my son? The day you and your friend departed for the crusade, I was the woman at the well."

"I remember," Nick said.

"I thank God daily for your safe deliverance," she admitted, her voice trembling slightly with emotion.

Two servants entered holding trays laden with fine wine and silver bowls filled with dried figs, nuts, and sweetmeats. A tray of freshly baked tarts and pastries emitted such a mouth-watering scent that Nick's stomach growled involuntarily. The servants set out the food, poured wine into the three goblets, and left.

"Please, eat," Beatrice said as she pushed a bowl of dried figs toward Nick. "These are my favorite."

Nick tried one and smiled at her as the sweet fruit delighted his palate.

"There's much we have to discuss," Richard stated.

"Let him eat first, Richard," Beatrice interjected. "Our son has journeyed long and must be hungry."

"Forgive me," Richard said as his wife held out the tray of baked goods.

Nick assuaged his hunger while Richard updated him on the current state of affairs in Portugal.

At length, Nick asked, "Why was I abandoned at the monastery?"

The bluntness of the question erased the smile from Beatrice's face. She poured out more wine and settled in her seat as Richard recounted the events that led to their son's abandonment in Lewes.

Nick remained silent as his father spoke. He ran his hands through his hair and took a deep breath when Richard had concluded. At length, he pointed to the crucifix around his neck. "And this?"

"I placed it in your basket before you were taken away," Beatrice explained. "It's a priceless heirloom in my family and I wanted you to have it."

"I'll wear it every day, my lady," Nick promised.

"I want to ask your forgiveness," Richard said. "I was a fool for allowing my conniving brother to create a wedge between me and my wife."

Nick met Richard's gaze. "I forgive you."

Beatrice cried out in relief at Nick's words. "Oh, thank God." She crossed herself and added, "Your uncle is an evil man. He's been the cause of so much grief in our lives." She fought back tears at the memory of Robert.

"Your rightful place is here in Kent," Richard added with a sweep of his arm. "Everything I own will one day be yours."

Beatrice couldn't contain herself any longer. "May I embrace you, Nick?"

Before Nick could answer, she wrapped her arms around him and held him close. He was stunned at first, then kindly returned the embrace. As Richard watched the exchange between mother and son, he couldn't help noticing how much Nick's gray eyes resembled his own.

Nick was shown to an airy bedchamber that afforded him a view of the forest. The room was grand and luxuriously appointed with finely carved wooden furniture and vibrant tapestries. The comfortable bed was canopied in sumptuous red velvet. As Nick touched the soft feather mattress he thought of his narrow, stiff cot at the monastery.

"I hope everything is to your liking," Beatrice said from the doorway.

"Very much, Lady Beatrice. Thank you."

"You may call me mother, if you wish. You're a grown man now, and perhaps it doesn't feel right to call a total stranger that…" she trailed off, her face crimson.

In an attempt to put her at ease, Nick replied, "I appreciate that honor, my lady. It's indeed difficult to call a stranger 'mother,' especially a beautiful woman who appears much younger than her years."

Beatrice beamed with joy at his compliment. "You have no idea how long I've waited for this day. As soon as I discovered your whereabouts I had my most trusted manservant, Martin Sinclair, visit you as often as possible."

"How is Martin?"

"He's dead, thanks to the Bishop of Rochester."

Nick was deeply saddened by this news. They talked of Martin and life at the monastery. He told Beatrice about Gwen, Agnes, Simon, Bartholomew, Jeremy, and Sarah.

"Martin mentioned them so often that I feel like I already know them," Beatrice admitted. "I would like to meet all of them in person."

"Jeremy was killed in battle this past summer," Nick said quietly.

Beatrice's face fell. "I'm very sorry."

"I'm sure everyone would be honored to meet you and Lord Richard."

"Your father and I plan to hold a banquet in your honor. Every serf and ally for miles will come and swear fealty to you, just as they have sworn fealty to your father. I want you to invite your friends. We'll send a carriage to fetch them." Nick looked uncomfortable, so she inquired, "Is there something amiss?"

Nick hesitated, searching for the right words. "My friends and I are *simple*. We don't know about proper courtly behavior, nor do we own any fine clothing that would befit such a grand occasion."

"Don't worry, my son. Leave everything to me."

"Thank you...*Mother*."

Later that night, Richard, Beatrice, and Nick dined, drank, laughed, and cried until the late hours of the night. Nick was physically and emotionally exhausted by the time he fell onto the feather bed. He was soon fast asleep with a smile on his face.

Gwen, Agnes, Simon, and Bartholomew were welcomed like royalty at Kent Castle. Sarah, who was still mourning the loss of her son, insisted on remaining in Lewes. Nick was distressed to hear that she had become reclusive despite Agnes's attempts to include her in their lives.

The small party arrived the day before the banquet, and Richard and Beatrice went out of their way to make their guests feel comfortable.

During supper, Nick leaned toward Gwen and whispered, "Well? What do you think?"

Gwen's eyes lingered on the fine silver bowls and chalices, the decadent food set before her, and the costly jewels on Beatrice's fingers. "I can't even imagine what this must be like for you."

"They're good people," Nick pointed out.

"I don't doubt it."

Nick licked his lips nervously. "Lord Richard—my father—said that my rightful place is here now."

Gwen pretended to pick at a bit of lint on her skirt in order to avert her gaze. "Lord Richard is right. You're next in line as Earl of Kent."

A bout of laughter interrupted their quiet conversation. Gwen and Nick glanced up to see Bartholomew recounting a funny story. While the prior appeared to be at ease, Simon and Agnes seemed uncomfortable and out of place in their surroundings.

On the morning of the banquet, Beatrice found Nick pacing the floor of his bedchamber with a slight furrow in his brow. He stopped and looked at her in surprise. "Oh, good morning."

"Good morning, Nick. You seem agitated."

Nick shook his head. "It's nothing."

"I came to tell you that your father and I enjoyed entertaining your friends at supper last night. What a charming bunch—and the prior has quite a sense of humor…" she trailed off. "Nick, what ails you?"

"What if father's allies reject me?"

"Reject you…how?"

"What I mean to say is: what if they don't accept me? I haven't had a privileged upbringing, and I fear that many may not view me as…"

"A noble?" she asked, finishing his sentence.

"Aye."

"Ah." Beatrice rubbed her chin thoughtfully. "The good prior was provided with plenty of coin so that my wishes where your upbringing was concerned were carried out to the letter. I wanted you to learn how to read, write, and speak proper English, but also French and Latin. I made sure that you learned arithmetic, history, geography, and the sciences. Martin reported to me regularly on your progress. When you were older, you were trained in the skills of combat by one of your father's best knights. I procured the finest blacksmith in London to create your sword." Her eyes wandered to the magnificent weapon laid across the desk within its scabbard. "It's true that you may have lacked certain luxuries, but you always ate the best food that money could buy, and were afforded a better education than many of the noble sons I personally know. And from what your father told me of your fighting skills in Lisbon, you received excellent training in that department, as well."

Nick walked up to his mother and took her hands in his. "Please don't be offended by my words. I'm very grateful for all that you've done for me, and I'll never forget it. I'm nervous."

"Trust me, you have no reason to fear the English nobility. God knows how I wish you could have grown up here. It pains me that you and Robert never had the chance to enjoy each other's company as brothers."

"I don't want to see you upset. You've given me so much, but there's still one thing I lack—and I don't wish to shame you or father."

"What do you lack?"

"I'm ignorant in the ways of courtly manners and don't know how to dance. I don't want to come across as boorish or coarse at the banquet."

Beatrice's face brightened. "Well, it's early enough in the

day for you to learn a few things before the evening's festivities. Come, let's go downstairs." When he hesitated, she raised an eyebrow. "What is it?"

"My friends…they may also wish to prevent looking like fools."

She laughed lightly. "I'll have the servants summon them to the main hall. Meet me there in a few moments."

Nick, Gwen, Agnes, and Simon stood together in the main hall a half hour later. Bartholomew was in the castle's chapel praying, and would spend the remainder of the morning in study. Beatrice stood in the center of the room. With a graceful, sweeping gesture, she invited them to sit at the head table, which had already been set by the servants.

The group walked toward the table and Beatrice put up her hand. "Never enter a room unceremoniously. Gentlemen, hold your heads high and keep your shoulders straight. Ladies, you must *glide* into the room, chin parallel to the floor."

The little party looked quite impressive as they made their way to the table. The men knew enough to help the women take their seats before taking their own.

Once everyone was seated, Beatrice took a seat opposite so she could be easily observed. "Hands must be washed before the feasting begins."

A page came forward with a copper bowl filled with rosewater and a clean linen cloth. She gracefully washed her hands, dried them on the cloth, and waved the page away with a 'thank you.'

"Please note that I'm eating alone," she pointed out. "When my husband is seated beside me, it's considered gallant of him to feed me choice bits from his trencher in order to avoid me having to soil my hands."

There were quite a number of table rules to follow, such as not dipping meat into the salt dish, never scratching oneself, or placing elbows on the table. Etiquette also demanded that diners not pick at any vermin— such as lice or fleas—not spit, and not clean their noses while seated at the table.

Next, Beatrice called out to one of Richard's knights to

demonstrate some basic dance steps. The man, who was on guard duty, entered the room awkwardly and laid down his weapon in order to accommodate his mistress's wishes. Surprisingly, he was a decent dancer.

Richard strode into the main hall a while later and the knight paled at the sight of his jealous master.

Richard stopped. "What's the meaning of all this?"

Beatrice motioned her head toward the others. "A few dance lessons before the banquet."

Richard stifled his laughter as Simon stepped on Agnes's foot. Beatrice gave him a warning look, which made him want to laugh even harder. "Carry on, man," he said to the knight before taking his leave.

Gwen and Agnes later enjoyed the luxury of being pampered by servants. Beauty concoctions made up of dried flowers, herbs, and milk were applied to hair and faces. After bathing, a servant combed Gwen's long, black tresses. The hair was then woven with ribbons into two long plaits that hung to her waist. Agnes's hair was coiled and tucked into simple copper templers.

While the women underwent beauty ablutions, two gowns had been laid out for them. Upon seeing their expressions of surprise, one of the servants explained, "They are gifts from the Lady Beatrice."

Gwen's crimson silk gown was trimmed with costly vair along the sleeves and hem. Agnes's brocade gown was the color of amethyst with tiny seed pearls sewn across the neckline. Neither woman had ever worn anything so fine.

The men, looking regal in their attire, admired the ladies as they entered the main hall. Gwen's gaze was fixed on Nick, who wore a black leather tunic under a sable velvet robe lined with ermine. A gold and emerald ring glittered on his right hand. His father, resplendent in dark green velvet, stood by his side.

Earlier that day, dozens of serfs acknowledged the new heir and swore fealty to him. Now Nick would repeat the process with Richard's allies. Jewels glittered in the candlelight as splendidly clad lords and ladies awaited their hosts. Richard,

Nick, and Beatrice, appearing elegant in their finery, made a grand entrance. They took their seats in the center of the room, and the ceremony of swearing fealty began. The noblemen formed a line and swore their allegiance to Nick, promising loyalty and aid in battle when called upon. When the ceremony was over it was time for merrymaking.

Nick took his seat at the high table by Richard's right hand, while Beatrice took the seat to her husband's left. Gwen sat beside Nick, then Agnes, Simon, and finally, Bartholomew.

Gwen's eyes swept across the entire room. Recalling Martin's stories of fine lords and ladies, parties, and dancing, never once did it occur to her that she would be a character in those fairy tales. She sat back in her chair and sighed contentedly. Stealing a sidelong glance at Nick, she noticed his grim expression.

"What ails you?" she inquired softly.

Nick shook his head and forced a smile. "Nothing."

"Stop worrying. They approve of you."

Nick reached under the table and took hold of her hand. Their eyes met for a brief moment before Richard tugged on his son's sleeve to get his attention. "Do you see that man there?" he asked, discreetly motioning toward a white-bearded nobleman in gold brocade. Nick placed a chalice to his lips and nodded. Richard drank from his own cup before continuing, "That's the Earl of Derbyshire. He's wise, and one of my most precious allies, providing me with useful information when needed. It's all a game, my son—keeping them on your side. Always remember that one favor repays another."

Nick greedily soaked up everything his father taught him. "And who is the young lady seated beside the earl? His granddaughter?"

Richard smirked. "Ah, no."

When the old man's crooked finger ran over the curve of the young woman's breast, Richard looked pointedly at his son and offered a wry smile.

Throughout the evening, Richard offered pertinent information regarding the important noblemen present.

Occasionally, Nick managed to slip a few harmless snippets of gossip to Gwen for her amusement. At one point during the meal he speared a juicy piece of roasted venison with the tip of his knife and offered it to her. Gwen took the morsel into her mouth slowly, without taking her eyes off of him.

Knowing the gesture aroused him, she smiled wickedly. "Thank you, *my lord*."

Nick shook his head in mock disapproval. "Two days in a castle and you've already become a courtly vixen."

Ignoring his comment, she said, "*My lord*…it has such a powerful ring to it, don't you agree?"

"It does, but I'm unaccustomed to such a title."

Richard stood up to make an announcement and the room fell silent. "As you already know, I have recently lost one son only to rediscover another. Most of you are aware of my brother's wickedness, and how the Bishop of Rochester has wreaked havoc within my household. I was wrong to have sent my own flesh and blood away." Richard paused for a moment, and gazing down at Beatrice, he continued, "And I was wrong for doubting my faithful wife, who has graciously forgiven me."

Beatrice was both touched and surprised by this public declaration. Richard placed his hand on Nick's shoulder. "Tonight's feast is to honor my son, Nicodemus. I propose a toast to his health."

The crowd responded with a cheer and held up their cups. The minstrels began to play and soon everyone danced merrily.

One of the noblemen engaged Nick and Richard in conversation. Within a few minutes, Nick noticed Gwen being led across the hall by a handsome man. She even laughed when he whispered in her ear.

"What do you think should be done with the land in Devonshire?" the nobleman asked of Nick.

Richard noticed his son's eyes following the pretty girl. Had he inherited his father's jealous nature?

Distracted, Nick had missed part of the conversation. He tried to look thoughtful and replied, "I believe I should consult with my father before offering you any reply."

The man nodded in approval as he winked at Richard. "Already you show wisdom, young man."

"You must forgive my ignorance in these matters, my lord," Nick offered humbly.

"Listen well to your father because he's shrewd."

Nick agreed, thanked the man for his kind words, and excused himself before walking toward Gwen.

The handsome man caught Nick's eye and smiled as he approached. "Ah, our guest of honor."

Nick inclined his head politely and tried to recall the man's name. As if reading Nick's mind, Gwen said, "This is George Burlington, Count of South Bedford."

"Welcome to Kent," George said amicably. "I owe a lot to your father."

"How so?" Nick inquired.

"When my father died, Lord Richard helped me retain my estate after my uncle had attempted to lay claim upon it. The matter grew so heated that it was brought before the king. Because of Lord Richard's alliance and his intervention, I won the case. My uncle hates me to this day." George paused. "You're also the victim of a meddling, unscrupulous uncle."

Nick nodded. "I've never met the bishop, however."

"Perhaps that's a good thing." George's arm made a sweeping gesture toward the other guests. "Everyone here is an enemy of the Bishop of Rochester."

"May I ask why?"

"He has wronged each of us in one way or another. In my family's case, the bishop tried to confiscate my mother's lands in Burgundy, claiming that women were not allowed to own land according to canon law. This desperate and ridiculous outburst came shortly after his own lands were confiscated by your father. Since my mother's family is French, and the land given to her was a gift from her father, the bishop's allegations were seen as an insult and an outrage."

Gwen made a face at Nick. "Your uncle seems to make trouble wherever he goes."

"The few nobles who support the bishop do so out of

convenience," George explained. "The greedy, rebellious barons in the north, for example."

Gwen was completely absorbed in the conversation and enjoyed at being drawn into such a web of intrigue. She and her mother led such uneventful lives in comparison.

"Lord Burlington," said a page after begging their pardon for the interruption. "Your lady mother bade me tell you that she's retiring for the evening."

"I'll be along shortly," George said to the page. To Nick and Gwen he added, "My mother relies on me heavily since my father passed on. My lady," he said, taking Gwen's hand and pressing his lips to her knuckles. "It was a pleasure to have made your acquaintance. I hope our paths cross again soon. Good evening to you both."

"What a charming man," Gwen commented as she watched him walk away.

"It seems as if he took a liking to you." Nick said, unable to mask the jealousy in his tone. "I'm sure many gentlemen gathered here tonight feel the same way."

"Oh? I didn't notice."

Nick held out his hand. "Shall we dance, my lady?"

As they moved in tune to the music, Nick and Gwen were completely oblivious to the liveried servant who had been watching them throughout the entire evening, and who stealthily crept out of the castle, unobserved.

CHAPTER 21

Edward placed a coin in the outstretched palm of the whore who had just serviced him. The buxom woman smiled while tucking the money into the top of her gown, the ample cleavage of her breasts swallowing it.

"Thank you, my lord," she purred.

The bishop's hand found its way to her backside and he gave her bottom a squeeze before watching her depart with a satisfied grin. Stretching lazily on the large bed, he conjured memories of the couplings he and Beatrice had shared. No woman could ever compare. There was a knock at the door.

"Enter," said the bishop, annoyed.

A servant appeared. "Your Excellency, Will is here to see you."

"Send him in." A moment later, a young man entered the room and inclined his head. Edward poured some wine from the pitcher on the bedside table. "Any news?"

"The nobles swore fealty to him without question. In fact, everyone present readily accepted the young man with great enthusiasm, especially after the speech your brother gave on his behalf. There's a woman who is close to Nicodemus; her name is Gweneth McFay."

"What do you know of her?"

"I know she was raised alongside your nephew. They seem very fond of one another." As an afterthought, he added, "Her husband was slain recently."

Edward's eyes narrowed. "Slain?"

"Aye, my lord, by your nephew's own hand."

Edward drank the contents of his chalice and said, "Tell me more."

Will saw the excitement in the bishop's eyes. Being one of Edward's best spies, he relished moments such as these. "Gweneth's late husband, Ranulf St. George, was a known drunkard and brute. Nicodemus tried to defend the girl, and Ranulf drew his sword against him."

Edward's mind turned somersaults as he threw back the covers and got out of bed. This information was precious, indeed. "Nicodemus killed this man?"

"In self-defense."

The bishop waved his hand dismissively. "What exactly is the relationship between this Gweneth woman and my nephew?

"Judging by the way they looked at one another at the banquet, I would venture to say that they're in love."

The bishop refilled his chalice, then filled another one and handed it to Will.

"Thank you, my lord," Will said, surprised at the gesture.

"St. George…why does that name sound familiar to me?" Edward mused. "I want you to find out who Ranulf's family is and track them down."

"Yes, my lord," Will replied before taking a sip. The wine was superb.

Edward removed a leather coin purse from his belt and tossed it at Will. "Bribery money—you know what to do with it. Now, go!"

Edward's mind brimmed with the possibilities of this new information. If Gweneth and Nicodemus were lovers, then Ranulf's death could be ruled a murder resulting from adultery.

Robert's unexpected death had automatically moved Edward to the head of the line in terms of legal inheritance, but the reinstatement of Nicodemus Fitzwilliam made his nephew the next contender for the Earldom of Kent. If he could get Nicodemus out of the way, however…

***

"Where are you?" Nick called out.

Everyone at Kent Castle was groggy from the previous evening's festivities. After the midday meal Gwen had insisted they go outside for some crisp, autumn air.

Nick continued to look around. "I'm not enjoying this game…you were always better at hide and seek."

Silence.

"Gwen!" He paused, shivering from the cold. "Very well. I'm going inside where it's warm."

Nick walked a short distance and darted into a large bush. He had used this trick many times during his childhood. As expected, Gwen crept out from her hiding place to see if he had truly gone inside.

He jumped out and blocked her path. "Aha!"

Gwen gasped in surprise. Her cheeks and nose were red from the cold. "Cheater!"

"How dare you call me a cheater," he retorted, feigning offense. "We Fitzwilliams are noble and good."

She gave him an exaggerated curtsy. "Oh, a thousand pardons, *Lord Nicodemus*."

"That will be enough out of you!" he cried, tickling her.

"Stop tickling me, you rogue!"

"*Rogue?*" he repeated and tickled her even more.

"Stop! Stop!" she giggled.

Nick stopped abruptly and kissed her. He hadn't kissed Gwen since the night when she dressed his wound in her cottage. She opened her mouth to allow his tongue to explore the sweet cavity, and he went mad with desire, gripping a handful of her hair in the process.

Nick pulled away. "I need to ask you something."

A hundred butterflies fluttered in her stomach as she gazed at him in anticipation.

He continued, "You know I'm fond of you—no, fond isn't the right word. The truth is that I love you. I have always loved you, Gwen. I want us to marry." Gwen's face broke into a grin then she quickly sobered. Puzzled by the two extreme reactions, he inquired, "What is it? Have I offended you with my proposal?"

"No, but…"

After a silent pause, he prompted, "But?"

"I'm not of noble blood. I'm only Gwen—a simple girl with no title or dowry. Your parents would prefer a more suitable match for you. After all, you're the son of the Earl of Kent. That's no small thing, Nick."

"I won't wed some milk-faced lady simply because it's expected of me. You're *my* Gwen. No newly acquired title or fortune will ever change how I feel about you."

"What about your monastic vows?"

He lowered his head. "Prior Bartholomew has already released me from my vows." Gwen stared at him askance and he added, "I have too much blood on my hands, and my conscience weighs heavy."

Gwen sometimes caught the haunted look in Nick's eyes and wondered what horrors he had witnessed abroad. Was he plagued by demons?

"Say you'll be my wife," he said, lifting his head to meet her gaze.

"It's all I've ever wanted."

He picked her up and spun her around until she squealed for him to stop. Then, he kissed her again and again. The future seemed bright and, for the first time since his return, he was genuinely happy.

The betrothal was kept private and the wedding would be very small due to the fact that Gwen was a recent widow.

Agnes, Simon, and Bartholomew departed the following day but Gwen remained in Kent. For the first time in her life she had her very own room. How drastically her life had changed in a matter of months!

Beatrice gave her future daughter-in-law a gift in the form of a lady's maid. The girl's name was Eunice, and to Gwen's delight, she was amicable and clever.

***

News of Ranulf's death at the hands of a warrior monk spread throughout Lewes and its neighboring villages. The wool merchant's drunkenness and violent tendency were widely known. Stories of him beating his pregnant wife—and killing their unborn child—had already been circulating for months. Nicodemus St. John was known for his heroic deeds abroad, and the monastery readily vouched for him and his exemplary conduct. No one believed that the death was anything other than an act of self-defense on the part of the peaceful young man. Yet, despite this, Ranulf's family demanded justice.

A royal messenger arrived at Kent Castle while Richard sat with his son in the main hall going through the chamberlain's accounting books.

The messenger handed Nick a sealed letter and said, "I was instructed to bring you to London, my lord."

Nick broke the seal and read the letter, then passed it to his father.

"This is preposterous," Richard said. "Is my son being charged with murder?"

The messenger shook his head. "He's only being summoned for questioning."

Beatrice and Gwen entered the room and were apprised of the situation.

Richard turned to his son. "I'll accompany you."

"As will I," added Beatrice.

"And I," said Gwen.

"No," Nick said. "I wish to go alone."

"Let me go with you," Gwen insisted. "I'm a witness, and the king may wish to question me."

The messenger said, "She's right, my lord."

"Gather your things quickly," Nick consented.

The stable groom was already waiting outside when they entered the courtyard. The golden palfrey she mounted had been a betrothal gift from Nick.

"Are you ready?" Nick asked from atop his horse.

Gwen looked over her shoulder to see Richard and Beatrice waving to them with grim expressions on their faces. An icy wind stirred and she nuzzled her chin into the warm fur of her heavy cloak. She urged her horse to keep up with Nick and the royal entourage. The riding lessons she began several days ago would be put to the test now.

Nick stole a sidelong glance at Gwen. "Everything will be fine," he said quietly.

Chapter 22

Gwen took in the crowded buildings and dilapidated houses as the king's messenger led them through the overpopulated streets of London. Dark smoke wafted upward from various dwellings and melted into the amber sky. It had taken the better part of an entire day to reach London, and her body was sore. The dusting of frost on the ground was mixed with mud, horse manure, and every kind of filth imaginable. She imagined London as a vibrant city—not a dingy landscape. Even the people appeared colorless and unhappy as they tended to their daily business.

Seeing the look of disgust and surprise on Gwen's face, Nick said, "Not what you expected?"

She urged her horse closer to his. "No."

"This is not half the city that Lisbon is," he commented. "Or Constantinople for that matter."

Two beggars reached up to touch Gwen's leg as she rode past. "Spare a coin, milady?"

Filthy and dressed in rags, their toothless grins resembled sneers. She reached into her purse and tossed a few coins at them. The beggars blessed and thanked her as they scrambled for the money.

They rode on until they came to a large wall with an impenetrable iron gate. The gate creaked open slowly to allow them passage, then closed with a heavy thud. Royal guards peered down from the parapets.

Once inside the courtyard, the castle's servants came out to greet them. As the son of an influential nobleman, Nick was afforded the courtesy and respect of an invited guest as he was led to a lavishly decorated room where the king sat in attendance with his men. The courtiers watched the young couple with interest as they approached Stephen. They bowed low before the king and only rose with his permission. Gwen was surprised to see Ranulf's aunt standing beside a man in bishop's robes. Suddenly, she experienced a terrible sinking feeling in the pit of her stomach.

"Welcome, Lord Nicodemus Fitzwilliam," Stephen said. Looking at Gwen, he added, "I expected you to come alone. Who is this?"

"May I present Gweneth McFay, Your Majesty," Nick replied. "She is Ranulf's widow."

Stephen frowned. "You're accused of slaying her husband, yet she accompanied you. How interesting."

"It was in self-defense," Gwen blurted out.

"Insolent girl!" Ranulf's aunt muttered.

Stephen raised his hand to silence both women. "How dare you speak out of turn in my presence? You will speak when spoken to."

Both women bowed their heads in remorse.

"I killed Ranulf only after he attacked me," Nick stated. "I was raised as a monk and I've fought for God as a Templar, killing the Infidel in His name, but I'm not a murderer."

"You're a trained fighter and Ranulf was a merchant. He was at a severe disadvantage."

"With all due respect, Your Highness, Gweneth was also at a disadvantage when Ranulf beat her so viciously that he killed their unborn child. Should this woman not be defended in the same manner?" Nick challenged.

Stephen quietly pondered Nick's words.

Edward interjected, "She's not only a helpless woman to you, is she, *nephew*?"

The bishop's last word was uttered with such disdain that Nick flinched. He had not expected to meet Edward under such circumstances.

"Did you know that Ranulf was a distant relative of mine?" Stephen asked.

Both Nick and Gwen shook their heads in absolute shock. The bishop's face, however, was oddly smug.

Turning toward Gwen, Stephen added, "Your late husband's father was my mother's half-brother. Ranulf was a bastard—as was his father—but his royal connection, although thin, is why I feel compelled to give consideration to this case."

Ranulf had never mentioned his distant kinship to the king, and Gwen wondered if he even knew of its existence.

"What is this woman to you?" Stephen demanded of Nick.

"When I was abandoned on the steps of St. John's Monastery, it was Gwen who found me. She's the daughter of Agnes McFay, the woman who raised me. We grew up together."

"You love her," the king said, making it sound more like an accusation.

"I do."

"See, Your Highness? He admits it. He killed Ranulf in order to have this woman for himself," Ranulf's aunt said angrily.

"That's not true and you know it," Gwen retorted.

The king raised his hand again. "Mistress Gweneth, were you a good and faithful wife?"

Gwen's eyes shone with indignation. "Yes, sire."

"If that's true, why did your husband beat you?"

"My husband was a very jealous man who drank heavily. He also spent much of his time with other women. I have no idea why he liked hurting me, sire. Neither does my serving girl, Leah, who witnessed many beatings."

"I'm told that young Lord Nicodemus was seen going into your cottage at night," Edward pointed out.

Gwen met the bishop's cold gaze. "We had dined with my mother and my stepfather earlier that evening and Nick accompanied me to my door. Two drunken rogues attacked us with knives. Nick warded them off, but got cut in the process. I only dressed his wound, nothing more. He left my home immediately afterward."

The king smiled wryly. "It seems to me that you're frequently in need of rescuing." The king paused and a few courtiers within earshot chuckled. "Perhaps you should employ an armed guard."

"Forgive me if that's how it sounds, Your Majesty, but I can assure you that isn't the case."

Stephen stared at her for a moment. "You *are* quite pretty, Mistress Gweneth. I can see how you would attract unwanted attention from strangers. It's no surprise that your late husband was a jealous man. I would be, too."

Gwen felt her face grow hot and lowered her head.

Edward didn't like the turn the situation was taking. "Your Majesty, I think it's worthy to note that Nick and Gweneth are to be married soon."

"Is this true?" Stephen asked, surprised.

The bishop had finally played his ace card and Nick noticed the gleam in his cold, gray eyes. The king studied the couple while absentmindedly stroking his chin. His bejeweled fingers flashed in the candlelight.

"It's true," Nick replied honestly. "But it has nothing to do with me killing Ranulf in self-defense."

"Are you certain of that? After all, she's a lovely prize to be had," Stephen pointed out.

"I swear to you, sire, Ranulf would be alive today had he not drawn his sword and lunged at me."

"Why hasn't your father apprised me of your betrothal? As king, my approval should've been sought."

"I only spoke to my father about the matter recently. I'm sure my father has every intention of giving you proper notification and requesting your formal permission and blessing."

Edward stepped forward. "Your Majesty, may I—"

The king held up his hand. "You may not." The bishop glared at the young couple as Stephen continued, "Mistress Gweneth, do you swear upon your life that your husband's death was an act of self-defense?"

"Yes."

The king turned his gaze on Nick. "And you tried to reason with the man before running him through?"

"Several times, sire, but Ranulf was filled with rage and drink."

"I believe you both," Stephen declared.

"Majesty," Edward interjected. "You cannot—"

"You dare tell your king what he can or cannot do?" Stephen snapped. He swept a hand toward Gwen and added, "This woman is simple. She doesn't strike me as a conniving adulteress who schemed to have her husband murdered. I would expect *that* sort of deviant crime from a sophisticated courtier—or my cousin, Matilda—not an honest country girl from a monastery. As for Lord Nicodemus, *your nephew*, I have heard nothing but good things of this man."

Gwen and Nick stole a look at Edward, who was seething with rage.

"What of my nephew?" Ranulf's aunt asked.

Stephen raised an eyebrow. "Is it true that Ranulf beat his pregnant wife to the point of killing his own unborn child?"

"Aye," she admitted reluctantly. "But he was drunk, sire, and didn't do it out of wickedness."

Stephen folded his hands in a gesture of finality. "Ranulf's death was not an act of wickedness, either. It was self-defense. An eye for an eye."

Edward was outraged. "Should he not stand trial?"

Stephen frowned. "The enmity between you and your brother, Richard, is well known to me. I suggest you stop channeling your hatred toward your nephew and set your mind on godly matters." Turning his attention back to Nick and Gwen, he said, "I'm satisfied with what I've heard here today. You're both welcome to stay for supper and spend the night. Lord Nicodemus, please extend my regards to your father and mother when you return to Kent in the morning."

Having been dismissed by Stephen, they bowed gratefully before backing away from the king's presence. Nick shot a menacing look at his uncle before leading Gwen to a quiet corner.

"I told you all would be well," he said. "Stephen has a slew of squabbling nobles and rebellious barons to worry about. The death of a mere merchant is trivial in comparison."

"Ranulf never informed me of his relation to the king."

"Perhaps he never knew. After all, it's an illegitimate

kinship." Nick paused. "How did Edward know about Ranulf's familial ties to the monarchy—and our betrothal for that matter? Unless…there's a spy in our midst."

"At your father's castle?"

"Where else? No one knows about our betrothal except our parents and Prior Bartholomew. It must be one of the castle's servants."

"There are so many of them."

"Don't worry, we'll sniff out the traitor eventually."

"I find it hard to believe that your uncle—*a bishop*—attempted to use Ranulf's kinship to the king as a valid reason to have you punished for murder."

"He's done worse things than this, I'm afraid. Let's not talk of him. We're innocent in the eyes of the king, and he's invited us to stay the night. We may as well enjoy the food and whatever entertainment has been devised for the evening. In the morning we'll return to Kent."

"I never imagined I'd be within these royal walls, let alone addressed by the king himself."

Nick smiled. "Well, my love, consider yourself a courtier now. The king publicly stated that you're a prize, which will gain you popularity within the court."

She batted her eyelashes playfully. "He did say that and, I must admit, I'm flattered."

He tossed her a mock frown. "Should I be jealous?"

She giggled and slipped her arm into the crook of his elbow as they followed the other courtiers to supper.

Chapter 23
Kent, England
December 24, 1149

"Look at how pretty you are," Simon said.

Agnes, who stood beside her husband, moved forward to place a crown of holy sprigs and evergreen on Gwen's head. "Perfect," she whispered, eyes misting.

Gwen stood in the center of the room in a gown of buttery velvet trimmed with mink.

It was close to midday when she made her way to the castle's chapel. Her recent state of widowhood prompted the couple to have a small ceremony with a select group of nobles. Nick stood by the altar in a dark blue tunic with the Fitzwilliam crest embroidered on the front. When he caught sight of Gwen, his face broke into a smile and he held her gaze steadily as she made her way toward him.

The couple clasped hands and the priest began the wedding ceremony. Nick drowned happily in the blue depths of Gwen's eyes, relishing every minute of the magic spell she was unwittingly casting over him.

After the ceremony the guests descended the stairs into the main hall, which was decorated for Christmas. Boughs of holly and spruce adorned the great hearth where a roaring fire offered welcomed warmth. Richard provided the finest food and entertainment to delight the guests. There were musicians and troubadours performing for everyone's pleasure.

At one point, a troubadour recited praises in honor of the bride's beauty and virtue. Gwen offered the handsome man her hand, and he kissed it gallantly before taking his leave and bestowing his attention on another lady. She sat back for a moment enjoying the realization that now she would be addressed as *Lady* Gweneth. The thought inspired her to reach for Nick's leg under the table and place her hand upon his thigh.

The gesture caught Nick totally off guard and he practically choked on the wine he was drinking. Coughing slightly, he looked at her with an expression of surprise and pleasure at her boldness.

The wine flowed freely, and the intoxicated guests enjoyed themselves. The feasting and dancing continued after the sun had set. Nick, who was dancing with Gwen, suddenly caught her in his arms and spun her around. When he stopped, he planted a hearty kiss upon her mouth. Laughing against his lips, she put her arms around his neck.

When she pushed back from the kiss, her eyes were drawn toward the back of the room. The servants had lit the torches and she saw something moving amid the shadows of the opposite wall. It was Mad Margaret. The old witch's black eyes glittered as she stared at Gwen knowingly, and a wicked smile touched her lips.

Gwen gasped aloud, blinked, and the vision was gone, disappearing as quickly as it had appeared.

"What did you see?" Nick asked, following her gaze.

She shook her head and tried to smile. "The wine…I'm tired, that's all."

It was a half-truth, and she felt guilty about already having to keep something from her new husband. Nick decided to let the matter drop.

Gwen's eyes searched the shadows again. Had the old crone really been there or was it simply a figment of her imagination?

In honor of the holy day, songs were sung in honor of Christ and the traditional yule log was paraded before the guests, then thrown into the fire. Everyone would attend Christmas Mass in the morning before feasting again at midday. It was almost midnight when the couple excused themselves and made their way to the nuptial chamber. As Nick and Gwen left the main hall, the guests cheered and wished many blessings upon them.

Gwen could feel Nick's uneasiness as they entered the large bedchamber, which Beatrice had prepared especially for them. They were pleased to see gorgeous tapestries and a big canopied bed with burgundy velvet trappings. A pitcher of evergreens stood atop the bedside table emitting a fresh scent, along with a plate of dried figs, two goblets, and sweet wine. Candles burned everywhere.

"Your mother is very thoughtful," Gwen said.

She stared at Nick until he met her eyes. His discomfort was obvious, and she knew it was due to his virginity. Gwen took his hand and pressed his palm against her face, nuzzling her cheek against it as she closed her eyes. She heard his sharp intake of breath.

"Gwen, I…"

Without a word, she slowly traced the features of his handsome face with her fingertips. He was a strong, imposing warrior, yet her touch made him as weak as a child. The woman had a power over him that both frightened and enchanted him.

Gwen moved closer and stood on the tips of her toes in order to kiss his face sweetly until he sought her mouth, then she responded to *his* passion. Nick, who had never been intimate with a woman, appreciated the fact that Gwen was tactfully allowing him to be the aggressor, while cunningly taking the lead in lovemaking. It was an irresistible combination and before long, they were on the bed.

Their lovemaking was tender and passionate. The closeness was beyond anything either of them had ever experienced before. Nick emptied his seed into her and the pleasure was exquisite. Gwen, too, cried out in ecstasy, having never experienced such sweet release. When it was over, Nick gathered her into his arms and closed his eyes. They lay still for quite some time, both satiated and content.

"I had no idea that it could be like this," Gwen whispered.

Nick, who was almost asleep, opened his eyes and saw her watching him. There were tears in her eyes. He wanted badly to please Gwen, especially since she had known the lovemaking of another man.

"This was so beautiful…so perfect," she continued. For the first time in her life, she had *made love*. It was a far cry from the rough, unpleasant tumblings she had endured with Ranulf.

Nick understood. In a way she, too, had been a virgin. "Sleep, my love," he said softly.

Gwen curled up beside him and was soon asleep. She dreamed of summer fields and flowers, but the distant sky was ominous. A storm was coming...

***

The New Year was celebrated quietly at Kent Castle, and the family welcomed 1150 with hopefulness and gratitude. Nick and Gwen spent the remainder of that winter, and all of spring and summer in a state of perpetual bliss.

When the stifling heat of summer became too much to bear in London, King Stephen departed for the cool breezes of his country residence. Hunting parties and summer fetes were organized to delight and refresh the king and his courtiers. Richard and Beatrice were summoned to court, but Nick and Gwen were not. Although they found it odd, Richard said nothing on the matter. Besides, the newlyweds were so enraptured with one another, they didn't seem to care.

With the end of summer came the harvest. Nick and Richard were constantly busy overseeing the work of their serfs, while Gwen and Beatrice oversaw the storage of grain and the salting of meats. Winter would be upon them soon, and the Fitzwilliam larder had to be filled in order to sustain their household. Beatrice was both pleased and impressed with Gwen's domestic skills.

During the first week of October, Gwen approached Beatrice in the solarium. "May I have a word, my lady?"

Beatrice put down her sewing and glanced at Gretta. "In private?"

Gwen caught Gretta's eyes and smiled. "No, I have good news to share." She paused. "I'm with child."

Beatrice embraced her daughter-in-law and cried tears of joy. "This is the most felicitous news, my dear." Turning to her maid, she asked, "Isn't it, Gretta?"

"Indeed," Gretta beamed happily. "God be praised."

Beatrice wiped her eyes. "Does my son know?"

Gwen shook her head. "Not yet. I wanted you to be the first

to know."

Beatrice's eyes watered upon hearing this. "Thank you, Gwen."

After the midday meal, Gwen and Nick walked hand in hand in the garden. It was a chilly afternoon, and the sun shone in a clouded sky. The trees surrounding the castle were ablaze with color. Red, orange, and yellow leaves floated down from the high branches. Gwen pulled the fur-lined cloak tightly around herself as they walked, and Nick placed his arm around her for added warmth.

She looked up at him and smiled. "Nick?"

He kissed the tip of her nose. "Yes?"

"I have something to tell you."

His brow creased in worry. "What is it?"

Surprised at his expression, she asked, "Why do you look so serious?"

"Sometimes I worry that you're not happy here."

"Why would you think such a thing?"

"I know that you're fond of my parents, but surely you miss your mother and Simon."

"I do—very much."

"If you want to leave here—"

"I love your parents and I love it here." His gray eyes reflected the color of the sky. The powerful arm around her shoulders made her feel safe. Pulling him toward a stone bench, she sat down. "Sit, my love."

"What do you want to tell me?"

"I'm with child."

For a moment, he seemed stunned. Then, suddenly, his face broke into a joyful grin and he pulled Gwen onto his lap. "You've just made me the happiest man in England. I love you."

"I'll give you a fine son, my love. I know I will."

"Son or daughter—it matters not, as long as the babe is healthy."

Gwen loved him more than ever in that moment.

That evening, while they supped, Nick turned to his father

and said, "I have joyous news, Father."

Richard wiped his fingers on the bread trencher and glanced at Beatrice, who was smiling from ear to ear. "It seems as if you already know about this news, wife."

"I do," she confessed.

"Gwen is with child," Nick said.

Richard appeared shocked, then patted his son's shoulder before rising from his seat to kiss Gwen's cheek. "This is good news, indeed."

Gwen blushed and Nick squeezed her hand. Richard took his seat and drank a toast to his son and daughter-in-law. Setting down the chalice, he added, "I expect you'll want a home of your own now."

"We're happy here," Nick replied.

Richard put up his hand. "You and your wife shall have your own home. Now we must decide which one of the family properties would be the most suitable."

Beatrice asked, "What about Cabot House?"

"In London? Hmm…" Richard mused, scratching his head. "I was thinking of Pembroke Place."

"But it's so far away," Beatrice protested. "I wish to be close to my grandchild."

"Aye, that's true," Richard agreed.

Beatrice pondered the matter. "Penway Manor!"

Richard nodded. "It's big enough and near Kent."

"And closer to Lewes so that Gwen can visit her mother more often," Beatrice added.

Gwen lit up at the last statement.

"Penway Manor it is, then," Richard said decisively. Then, turning to Nick he added, "We should ride out there soon."

Nick and Gwen thanked Richard profusely for his generosity. Later that night, while they were in bed, Gwen cried silent tears of joy. Not only was she married to a man she adored, but she was also carrying his child. In addition, she was rich beyond imagination, and had just acquired a grand home from a set of loving in-laws. She couldn't think of any woman in England more fortunate than she, and her heart overflowed with gratitude. Looking to her sleeping husband, she gently kissed his brow. It wasn't long before she was dreaming of an infant boy with gray eyes.

Lord Dunn arrived at Kent Castle three days later. Richard, who had been expecting his old friend, led the burly man to a private chamber. Lord Dunn took a seat by the warm fire as a servant came in with a tray of refreshments.

"Ah, mulled wine—my favorite," he said, accepting the hot ceramic cup from a tray.

The buxom girl smiled at the old nobleman, and he playfully tweaked one of her nipples. She almost dropped the tray, but regained her composure at the sound of Richard's throat clearing in disapproval. Looking at her master, she blushed deeply, offered him the other cup and scurried out of the room.

"Such a fair, young thing. My wife seems to find the ugliest girls to staff our household," the old man lamented comically.

Richard chuckled. "She knows what a scoundrel you are with the ladies."

Lord Dunn took the jest in stride. "No more of a scoundrel than you once were."

Richard patted his old friend on the back amicably. "That was a *long* time ago."

Lord Dunn took a hearty swallow of the hot wine, allowing the spices to play upon his palate. Some of the murky red fluid found its way to his white beard. "Have you heard anything regarding the bishop?"

"Edward has been in hiding since my return. After fleeing Kent, he reappeared in London to accuse my son of murder then vanished immediately afterward. My spies are out searching for him, but so far, nothing."

"The Devil take his soul."

"My brother will pay for what he's done. If not in this life, then the next."

"I heard a rumor that he gave the king a handsome contribution."

Richard smiled wryly. "Edward is always scheming."

"Stephen is a weak king, Richard." Lowering his voice, the

old man added, "I often wonder if Matilda wouldn't have been a better choice."

"She is Henry's daughter, after all."

Lord Dunn toyed with his beard. "Aye."

Richard drank the remainder of his wine quietly before announcing, "I do have some good news."

Lord Dunn seemed as eager as Richard to change the subject. The Bishop of Rochester caused the bile to rise in his throat. "What news?"

"I'm going to be a grandfather."

Lord Dunn raised his cup. "That's good news, indeed. Gweneth seems like a fine girl despite—" he trailed off.

Richard finished the sentence in his head: *...despite the fact that she isn't of noble birth.*

Lord Dunn set down the cup. "Forgive me, Richard. I didn't mean…"

Richard shook his head. "I know people are talking, but I don't care. As long as my son is happy. I feel I owe him at least that much for what he's suffered—and Beatrice as well."

"I would have done the same thing, my friend."

"Thank you for that."

"Gweneth is a clever girl, and I'm sure the king will feel the same way when you officially present her at court. Have you received an invitation for Christmas?"

"Not yet, but when it arrives I'm sure Lady Gweneth will be accompanying us," Richard replied, deliberately using his daughter-in-law's proper title.

"The Earl of Sussex will be there, as will the Duke of Wallingford and the other barons," Lord Dunn paused before inquiring, "Do you think Edward will be there?"

"I've been wondering that myself."

"Are you prepared for that possibility?"

Richard blew out a breath. "Stephen is aware of Edward's treachery toward me, yet he does nothing."

"The Bishop of Rochester has strong allies and deep pockets. Perhaps the king's failure to execute judgement on your behalf has more to do with self-interest than lack of regard for your case."

"There are rumors that Gilbert of Hastings—"

Richard was already shaking his head. "When I left Portugal there was still too much work to be done. I doubt we'll see Gilbert's face any time soon." He paused thoughtfully. "How was your harvest this year?"

The men went on to discuss the profits of the recent harvest, compare crop yields, and criticize politics.

***

By the end of the third week of Advent, an official summons arrived for the *entire* Fitzwilliam family to attend the royal Christmas celebration. Nick and Gwen would be present, which finally relieved Richard of the growing resentment he'd been nurturing toward the king for his snobbery. Beatrice began to plan for her family's journey to London, and Gwen was called upon to help with decisions on clothing, jewelry, and gifts.

"This is so foreign to me, Lady Beatrice," Gwen confessed. "At the monastery, things were so simple…"

Gwen's apprehension was almost palpable and Beatrice did her best to appease the girl's fears. "As you know, there are three Christmas masses and each will be celebrated at Westminster Abbey with the king."

"Every noble family will be there?"

"Only those invited by the king. You should be honored, my dear." Beatrice could sense that Gwen was nervous about the prospect. "You'll need a different gown for each mass, and of course for the twelve nights following Christmas Day."

"I don't think I have enough clothing."

"That's why my seamstresses will work around the clock, if needed. Besides, I'm sure that you can fit into some of my garments."

Gwen's tall, slender frame was similar to that of Beatrice's, and her pregnancy was still in its early stage. At three months, the slight bulge in her stomach was barely perceptible.

"Thank you," Gwen said gratefully.

"Come, let's see what we can find," Beatrice said as she took Gwen's hand and led her into a large chamber.

Gretta, who was never far from her mistress's side, followed. As she removed several articles of clothing from Beatrice's trunks, Gwen marveled at the wealth Nick's parents possessed. There were various fur lined mantles and capes in sumptuous shades: blue perse lined with ermine, scarlet buckram trimmed with vair, and gold brocade edged with miniver. Bliauts of mottled silk, cauls, and veils as sheer as gossamer.

After Beatrice had selected her own wardrobe for the trip, she turned her attention to Gwen. "Now for you, my dear," she said as she led her daughter-in-law to a highly polished looking glass.

With two servants carrying the valuable garments to and fro, Gwen felt like a queen as she stared at her reflection. Very few garments would have to be made for the occasion—a new caul, a few veils, and an overtunic in green silk.

"Now for the jewelry," Beatrice said, smiling.

Gwen gazed at the gilded chest Gretta held in her arms, which appeared heavy. The maid set it down with a slight grunt and Beatrice opened the lid to reveal an array of rings, brooches, necklaces, bracelets, and earrings made of silver and gold. Some of the pieces encased various precious stones, such as topaz, onyx, ruby, emerald and sapphire. Gwen's head spun from the sheer luxury of it all! Appropriate pieces were selected and the chest was taken back to its secure location.

Beatrice placed her arm around Gwen and said, "When you're being officially presented to the king, you must look, walk, talk, and act as a noble lady."

"But I've already met the king," Gwen pointed out.

"Not as a *Fitzwilliam*." Beatrice led her daughter-in-law to the window so the other servants wouldn't overhear her next words. "I cannot stress enough the importance of making a good impression at court. It's for Nick's sake that I'm telling you this, my dear."

"I'll do my best."

Beatrice smiled. "I know you will."

Chapter 24
London, England
December 1150

The Fitzwilliam entourage arrived in London two days before Christmas. Fortunately, the only snowfall in December had been mild, making the journey fairly easy. Beatrice and Gwen, along with their maids, had traveled in an enclosed wooden carriage lined with fur skins for warmth. Nick rode on horseback alongside his father and the other men. A dozen of Richard's finest soldiers and three of his best archers had been chosen to accompany them on the journey for protection. The women, their precious jewels, and their costly clothing were a temptation for bandits.

Grooms, squires, and pages scrambled over the icy cobbles to receive the large party. Gwen was glad when Nick finally came to the carriage in order to offer his hand for her descent.

She took his hand, stepped down from the coach, and allowed herself to be led inside. Following Richard and Beatrice, they twisted through cold stone passages and up several stairs. The servants apprised them of their expected presence at dinner the following day, promised to have food and drink sent to their respective guest chambers, and took their leave with polite curtsies. Richard and Beatrice bade Nick and Gwen goodnight before retiring to their chamber.

Gwen was relieved to be alone with Nick and in front of a warm fire. It wasn't long before a page entered with bread, meat, and wine. They ate hungrily. Tired from the journey, they sought the warmth and comfort of their bed and soon fell asleep.

The sound of the rain pounding against the shutters disturbed Gwen's slumber. Nick was still sleeping soundly. Quietly, she went to the window and peeked outside. The rain fell hard, and she was grateful they had arrived last night before it started. Shivering, she crawled under the warm covers.

It was nearly midday when Beatrice knocked on their door. She had come to check on Gwen's appearance before accompanying her daughter-in-law to the main hall where the courtiers were gathered. Richard had risen early, and was already meeting with various noblemen.

Beatrice walked in as Eunice held a polished looking glass before her mistress. Gwen looked regal in a midnight blue perse trimmed in white ermine. Her hair had been braided, and the sheer veil over her head was held in place by a silver and gold circlet. A single pearl rested in the center of her forehead.

Nick also looked like the perfect gentleman in a brocade tunic and mantle lavishly lined and trimmed with vair. Expensive jewels glistened on the hands of the young couple, as well as around their necks.

Nick spread out his hands. "Good morning, Mother. How do we look?"

Beatrice smiled in satisfaction. "Perfect."

The Fitzwilliams were expected to present themselves to the king before partaking of the dinner feast. Two well-dressed pages accompanied them to where Stephen was seated upon a raised dais. Beatrice and Gwen stood slightly to the side as Richard and Nick stepped forward and knelt. The women followed suit and waited until the king told them to rise. The men noticed how the king's eyes lingered on their wives.

"Lord Richard," Stephen said. "It pleases me to see you here with your family."

"Thank you, sire."

"Lady Beatrice, you are a vision. Welcome," Stephen said courteously.

"Thank you, sire," Beatrice replied, keeping her eyes downcast in modesty.

Stephen's gaze went to Nick. "We meet again, and you've brought your lovely wife."

All eyes turned to Gwen. Several of the lords and ladies moved closer to shamelessly eavesdrop.

"Come forward," Stephen said.

Gwen struck an elegant figure as she bowed low before the king.

"Your Majesty, may I present my wife, Lady Gweneth," Nick said proudly.

Gwen stood quite still as the king studied her for a moment, his eyes taking in her lovely face, rich clothing, and expensive jewels. She was as regal as any highborn lady, and Stephen wondered if this girl was truly of low birth. Perhaps she, too, was left on some remote doorstep as an infant. He knew that was not the case, however, but it would make it easier for her to infiltrate the royal court and avoid the inevitable gossip.

"Welcome," Stephen said simply.

The women were dismissed, but Richard and Nick remained in order to discuss affairs of state. Beatrice led her daughter-in-law into the throng of guests. Several ladies approached in order to greet them, and find out more about Gwen. Many of them knew about Nick and the trouble Edward had caused, but Gwen was still somewhat of a mystery.

To Gwen's immense relief, Beatrice did most of the talking. She informed the ladies that her daughter-in-law was from a vague, ancient family in Ireland, and that the newlywed couple would be moving into their new home after Epiphany. It was the only information Beatrice divulged, and it seemed to satisfy the courtiers' insatiable curiosity for the time being.

The women complimented Gwen on her fair skin, and before long, they were discussing beauty concoctions. Since Gwen had a vast knowledge of herbs and roots, she had much to contribute to the conversation.

As the temperature plummeted outside, the rain turned to snow, and by Christmas morning a white blanket covered the ground.

The Bishop of Rochester didn't show his face in court. Richard was relieved, yet at the same time vexed by his brother's mysterious absence. Edward was a schemer, and was no doubt plotting something somewhere.

The sumptuous Christmas Day banquet was served in high style. In addition to the main hall being decorated with greenery, crisp white linen tablecloths were spread over the trestle tables. The golden glow of candles made the vast main hall appear cozy. At the high table, pewter trenchers were accompanied by matching spoons and silver goblets with copper stems. The lower tables were set with wooden trenchers and ceramic drinking vessels. In the center of every table was a display of greenery and red holly berries.

Roasted venison piled high on platters, along with pigeon pies, braided breads, and a variety of fish were served to the guests. There was even a splendid peacock, which had its feathers painstakingly replaced after being roasted. When the traditional Yule boar was carried out by four large servants, everyone applauded the roasted beast with an apple in its mouth.

Gwen thought she would burst from consuming so much food, and was relieved when the last course finally arrived at the table. It consisted of fruit, nuts, puddings, and small cakes. The servants also served wine sweetened with honey and spices. Glancing at Nick, she noticed that his face was unusually serious, his eyes fixed. Following the direction of his gaze, she saw a young man seated at one of the lower tables.

"What's wrong?" she asked.

"That man over there looks so familiar."

"He should—he's a servant at Kent Castle."

Nick's head whipped toward her. "Are you sure?"

"Quite sure."

"I don't recall seeing him in our entourage."

"He didn't come with us."

Nick leaned over to whisper in his father's ear. Richard followed Nick's gaze, and frowned. Gwen saw that father and son were watching the man like two hawks stalking their prey.

The man happened to look up and caught Nick and Richard staring at him. After saying a few words to his dining companions, he stood and casually walked away from the table.

Nick and Richard also stood and followed the man.

Beatrice turned to Gwen. "Where are they going?"

"I think they wish to speak with one of your servants," Gwen replied, puzzled.

Beatrice shrugged. "Have you tasted this pudding?"

***

"Do you think he's a spy?" Nick asked as they strode over the flagstones.

"Yes. Most likely one of Edward's," Richard replied.

The man ducked into the kitchen and they ran after him. There were tables laden with bowls, animal carcasses, vegetables, and cauldrons of various shapes and sizes. Red-faced servants scurried about carrying trays of food and pitchers of wine. The man ducked under a nearby table, scurried to the other side, and went out through a doorway like a frightened rabbit.

Nick pointed. "There he goes!"

"Get that man!" Richard shouted to the servants.

Nick ran after the man, leaving his father in his wake. The frigid air stung his cheeks as his powerful legs carried him through the snow with ease. He spotted some of the king's guards several yards ahead and called out to them. The guards unsheathed their swords and moved to block the fleeing man.

Nick unsheathed his sword and placed its tip at the man's throat. "Who are you?"

The man remained silent and one of the guards struck him in the face. "Answer!"

Richard arrived and stood beside Nick with his sword unsheathed. He motioned for the guards to step back and allow them privacy. The king's men walked away, but remained wary.

"I've seen you in my home, yet you didn't ride here with my men," Richard said. "Who are you?"

Silence.

Richard lowered Nick's sword and replaced it with his own, pushing the blade through the man's skin. The spy cried out as beads of blood escaped the small wound. "It would be a shame to soil this pure white snow with your blood. Tell me who sent you here."

"No one sent me, my lord," he lied.

Richard lowered his sword and let a drop of red blood fall from its tip onto the pristine snow. "Ah, such a shame...like a stain on a fine tablecloth." He put the sword to the spy's throat again. "The next puncture will redden the snow even more. I ask you again, who sent you here?"

The man panicked. "The Bishop of Rochester."

Richard lowered his sword. "Where is he hiding?"

"I don't know."

Richard took a step forward and was about to raise his sword when the man hastily added, "I swear, my lord, I don't know. Your brother sends me to various locations to report what I see."

"Does he summon you to Rochester?"

"Not anymore—he abandoned his home well over a year ago."

Richard's eyes narrowed. This was not good. "Where do you meet?"

"Various locations. A messenger usually arrives with instructions stating where and when to meet. After I've met with the bishop, he departs immediately afterward. I have no idea where he resides—no one does."

"I think he speaks the truth, father," Nick said.

"What's your name?" Richard demanded.

"My name is Will."

Richard studied the man. "I could kill you right now for your treachery."

Will shivered from cold, but mostly from fear. "Please spare me, my lord," he begged. "I do this work to feed my family...my mother, she is sick—"

"Cease!" Richard snapped. "Since it's Christmas, and I'm in a merry Christian mood, I'll spare your life—"

"Thank you!" Will interjected.

"*If* you work for me, instead," Richard said, finishing his sentence.

Will's face lit up with surprise. "My lord?"

"I, too, am willing to pay handsomely for your services. If you refuse, I'll kill you. Choose your fate now." Will nodded eagerly. Richard gave him a tight smile. "I take it you agree to my terms?"

"If you spare me, I'll tell you everything."

"I also want to know what you've told Edward so far."

Will didn't relish the thought of betraying the powerful bishop, but he had no choice under the circumstances.

Richard motioned for one of the guards to come forward and tossed the man a coin. "Keep him under lock and key until I come for him," he instructed. "I don't wish to trouble the king with this trivial matter."

"Aye, my lord," replied the guard while holding Will's arm in a firm grip. "He won't be going anywhere. Our dungeons—"

Richard cut him off. "There's no need to take him to the dungeons *yet*."

Will's relief was palpable as he inclined his head at Richard in gratitude. "Thank you, my lord."

"I'll lock him in one of the tower rooms and place a man by the door," the guard said.

Richard and Nick watched the guards take Will away before heading back to the main hall. Once they were inside, each man took his seat and joined the celebration as though nothing had taken place.

Later that evening after most of the guests had retired, Richard made his way up the spiral staircase of the tower with Nick in tow. He could see the flickering orange light of a torch as he reached the top of the stairs. A guard stood before a massive wooden door and a set of keys jangled from his leather belt. The guard unlocked the door and allowed the two noblemen entrance. The tiny, dimly lit room contained a table and a chair. Will looked up when the noblemen walked into the room.

"Tell us what you've told my brother thus far," Richard demanded as soon as the door was shut behind him.

Will licked his dry lips nervously and disclosed everything. Richard paced the room while Nick stood quietly by the door. When the spy finished speaking, he lowered his head in shame.

Richard was exasperated, yet impressed with Will's ability

to spy so effectively. "Listen carefully. You'll meet Edward and tell him there was nothing to report except that I was here with my family and we had an enjoyable Christmas. Do you understand?"

"Yes, my lord."

"I want you to find out where the bishop goes and what he does. I need to know where he's hiding. Once you have acquired this information, you will ride to Kent and be richly rewarded."

"What if I can't get the information you need?"

"I'll kill you the next time I see you." Richard knocked on the door, and when the guard opened it, he said, "This man is free to go."

The guard glanced over Richard's shoulder and cocked his head toward the staircase. Will got up from his chair and bowed low to the noblemen before hastily taking his leave.

"Oh, and Will," Richard called out after him.

Will stopped and spun around. "My lord?"

"Happy Christmas."

***

As was customary, the Fitzwilliams presented the king with a New Year's gift. Beatrice had purchased a costly set of Venetian glass goblets with gilded stems and Stephen seemed very pleased with them. They departed for Kent the day after Epiphany.

Nick and Gwen planned their move to Penway Manor shortly afterward. Beatrice kindly arranged for a number of servants to accompany the couple to their new home. Trunks were packed and heaped onto covered carts, and two dozen soldiers would serve as armed escorts.

Beatrice held her son tightly as she bade him goodbye on the morning of their departure. It was a cold, clear morning in early February. Richard also gave Nick a hearty embrace and patted his back. Gwen, her small belly protruding despite the looseness of her gown, stood quietly to the side until her in-laws approached to bid her farewell.

"I'll visit you shortly," Beatrice promised.

"Hopefully you'll be there for the birth," Gwen said.

Beatrice nodded and embraced her, then stood aside so that Richard could kiss her cheek and say goodbye. Nick helped Gwen onto the front of the cart, which had been covered with oilcloth and lined with fur skins for warmth. Two cushions had been placed upon the wooden seat for comfort, and Gwen settled in quite nicely in her cozy enclosure. She wrapped a fur lined wool cloak tightly around herself and waved goodbye. Nick mounted his horse and led the party toward Penway Manor, which was located near the border that separated Surrey and West Sussex.

Eunice, who sat beside her mistress, tried hard to stay awake in order to entertain and distract Gwen from the monotony of the journey. The slow rocking eventually won over and she fell asleep, much to Gwen's amusement. They traveled the remainder of that day, stopping to rest in a village before nightfall. It would be another half day before they reached their destination. Gwen's back ached from a combination of the pregnancy and the ride.

The weather remained clear and cold throughout their journey, and when Nick finally caught sight of the manor in the distance, he breathed a sigh of relief.

Four round towers stood majestically at each corner of the rectangular stone structure. From the top of each tower flew a black banner with the gold Fitzwilliam lion in the center.

They reached the manor and Gwen was glad to stand and stretch. The few servants who lived at Penway and maintained the property had been notified of their arrival. The bedchambers were recently aired, the fires lit, and fresh rushes were scattered on the floor. The servants who had traveled with them wasted no time in joining the others in the kitchen to prepare a hot meal for their new lord and lady.

Nick and Gwen were served bread, butter, and wine to tide them over until supper. After the small meal, they set about exploring their new home. It wasn't nearly as large as Kent Castle, but still bigger than what was needed to live comfortably. The main hall was roomy enough to hold an impressive banquet, and the solarium was located between the two most spacious bedchambers. Nestled between the main hall and the kitchen was the chapel, and the servants' quarters were located on the lower levels. Gwen, who couldn't tolerate foul smells during her pregnancy, was relieved that the latrines, stables, dairy, and hen houses were kept in the back, far from the main building.

"Well, do you like it?" Nick inquired.

Gwen smiled. "I love it…and I love you."

He bent his head and kissed her softly. "I think we're going to be happy here."

"I *know* we'll be happy here.'

Nick kissed his wife again, this time with far more passion. Despite being tired from the journey, Nick carried his wife to the bedchamber where they made love slowly and tenderly, relishing the feel of the velvet coverlet beneath their bare bodies.

Afterward, as they lay in each other's arms, Nick said, "Invite your mother and Simon as soon as you wish."

She smiled. "I'll send word tomorrow."

CHAPTER 25

The last week of February brought a tempestuous snowstorm. Despite the harsh traveling conditions, Richard was summoned by the king. There was a serious matter of state that had to be addressed as soon as possible. Beatrice didn't want her husband to go, but knew she had no choice in the matter.

Two days after Richard's departure, Gretta came into her mistress's bedchamber to announce a male visitor.

Beatrice frowned. "Did the man give a name?"

"No, my lady. He insists on speaking with Lord Richard, and refuses to reveal his identity. There's something familiar about him, however."

"Have him wait in the main hall. I'll be down shortly." Then, as an afterthought, she added, "Have two of Richard's men stand close by."

Beatrice donned a red brocade surcoat before going downstairs. As she had requested, two armed knights waited outside the door. A wiry man wearing a wool cloak of good quality and two gold rings upon his right hand warmed himself by the hearth. The hilt of a sword was visible at his side. Judging by his appearance, the stranger was neither noble nor a peasant.

Upon seeing Beatrice in the doorway, the man bowed low. "My lady, I'm here to speak with your husband regarding an urgent matter."

"My maid told me that you refused to give your name," Beatrice pointed out.

"I have valid reasons for my refusal."

"You must be Will, the spy my husband apprehended in London."

Surprised, Will said, "My lady?"

"Don't deny it. My husband told me everything. Your reason for coming here must be important for you to travel in such unfavorable weather conditions."

"It is," he assured.

"Richard was summoned to court."

Will rubbed his chin anxiously, unsure of what to do. "This is most distressing news."

"You can spend the night here and ride to London tomorrow morning."

"I can't risk going there, nor can I send a messenger."

"I see." She paused. "You can tell *me*."

Will regarded her for a long moment, debating whether or not to follow her suggestion. He finally concluded that if Richard trusted his wife, so would he. "What I have to tell you must be revealed in private."

Beatrice nodded. "Come."

She led the spy through a side door, up a flight of stairs, and down a long hallway. "In here," she said, ushering him into the castle's quiet chapel.

Will crossed himself as he entered the sacred space, and quickly knelt before the statue of the Virgin Mary. Beatrice did the same before sitting on the wooden bench against the wall and inviting him to do the same.

"I saw the bishop two weeks ago," Will said.

"You actually spoke to Edward?"

"Aye. I told him that I had seen your family during Christmas, but had nothing out of the ordinary to report—as your husband had instructed. The bishop then sent me here to spy on you."

"This is why you're here now?"

"That's part of the reason, yes, but there's more. I have just come across some information that will be of great interest to Lord Richard—the Bishop of Rochester plotted against the king."

"What do you mean?"

"He sided with Matilda and Robert of Gloucester, and aided them financially when they led their initial attack against King Stephen."

Beatrice narrowed her eyes. "That was several years ago. Robert of Gloucester is dead, and Matilda is preoccupied with

Normandy."

"Yet the strife within our kingdom continues. Madam, we are still in a civil war."

Will was right. "Do you have solid proof of Edward's treason?"

"I have a network of informants who can be easily bribed to obtain it," he replied confidently.

Beatrice stood and paced the stone floor of the chapel. "Richard must be informed of this news at once."

"No, my lady! What if the message is intercepted?"

"You have a valid point. I'll summon my husband on the pretense of illness. He knows that I would never call him home unless it was important." Will nodded in agreement and she regarded him with a raised brow. "As for you…where did you stay the last time you *infiltrated* my home?"

Will blushed guiltily. "The servant's quarters."

"I have every servant accounted for, how did you slip in unnoticed?"

Will squirmed uncomfortably. "Well, one of the kitchen maids—"

Beatrice put up her hand. *"Enough!"* She wasn't surprised that the clever spy had charmed one of the young kitchen girls and shared her bed. She sighed in disapproval and continued. "You have permission to carry on as you've done in the past, but if you impregnate the girl, you'll be forced to marry her. I keep a respectable Christian household."

"Yes, my lady."

"You had best earn your keep, spy, lest you evoke my husband's anger," Beatrice warned as he headed for the door.

***

Richard circled the chair in which Will sat. He had departed for Kent the moment he read Beatrice's letter. "Where is Edward now?" Richard demanded after the spy had repeated what he had told Beatrice.

"My guess would be the Kingdom of East Anglia."

"Where the northern barons are still fighting," Richard mused aloud.

The rift between Stephen and Matilda gave the rebels a perfect excuse to wreak havoc across the English countryside. With neither side winning at the war's onset, the barons turned to fighting for their own gain. Even though Matilda had already given up and fled the country, the rebels continued to fight for power in the northern territories—and were successfully gaining ground.

Richard leaned against the window sill and gazed across the bleak winter landscape as unanswered questions flitted through his mind. Was Edward trying to persuade the barons to revolt against the king? If so, could it be at Matilda's request with the promise of a reward? It seemed unlikely that she would be involved, given that she was busy ruling Normandy with her husband. Besides, her last attempt at claiming the English throne nearly cost Matilda her life. No, this was most likely Edward's own doing. Richard knew full well that his brother would stop at nothing to get his hands on lands and titles.

"Have you told me everything?"

"Aye, my lord."

"You'll be rewarded, Will, but not yet. I want you to stay here in Kent until Edward summons you."

Richard sent one of his most trusted soldiers to deliver a message to the king warning him of the Bishop of Rochester's rebellious plot. He hoped the message reached Stephen before Edward summoned Will.

***

Gwen sat sewing in the solarium with Eunice when Nick entered the room. The solemn look on his face made her frown. "What ails you, my love?"

Nick lowered his head and offered her the piece of parchment he held in his hands. "This arrived for you," he said softly. "It's from Simon. Your mother is ill."

"What? Oh, no!" Gwen's eyes watered. "I knew it would happen sooner or later…*she* said so."

"What are you talking about?" Nick asked, confused.

"*Love will find you, but with it will come death.*"

"I don't understand."

Gwen's tears streamed down her cheeks. "Everything has been so wonderful—I knew it wouldn't last. Now, I must pay the price for my happiness."

Nick feared Gwen would harm herself and their unborn child in a fit of hysteria. "Eunice, would you please prepare a draught to calm my wife?"

Eunice set down her sewing. "At once, my lord."

Nick placed both of his hands firmly on Gwen's shoulders and forced her to look at him. "Calm yourself, my love, and tell me what you're crying about."

Gwen shook her head and wiped the tears from her eyes. "You'll never look at me the same way again."

"Please, Gwen, I want us to have no secrets." He kissed his wife's forehead. "I'll love you no matter what you tell me."

Encouraged by his words, Gwen led him to the window seat. "When you were away fighting the Turks, I went to see Mad Margaret. I was brokenhearted by your departure and Ranulf treated me so badly…I was desperate. Please don't think too badly of me, Nick."

He pulled her close and whispered, "I don't think badly of you. Tell me what Mad Margaret told you."

"She predicted that I would marry a nobleman and be a great lady—rich beyond my imagination."

He shrugged, nonplussed. "The old crone was right."

"I know, and that's why I fear her last prediction: '*love will find you, but with it will come death.*'"

Nick sensed that his wife was truly afraid. "Gwen…"

"Don't you see?" she demanded desperately. "I have found love—so much of it, in fact, that now I must pay for it by losing someone dear to me. My poor mother."

"Don't fret. Mad Margaret's ramblings could be wrong. Your mother is as strong as an ox."

"I shall go to her at once."

Nick looked down at his wife's pregnant belly. "In your condition? In this cold weather?"

"Oh, Nick…*what are we going to do?*"

"I'll fetch her myself," Nick assured. "Summon the

physician now—I plan to take him with me, along with two servants."

Gwen squeezed his hand in gratitude. "I'll have the servants prepare a bedchamber."

"All will be well, my love," Nick promised. "Your mother will be here soon enough, and she'll recover."

Agnes arrived in a covered cart wrapped in warm furs with Simon by her side. Nick, who had barely slept in his effort to get his mother-in-law to Surrey as quickly as possible, was exhausted. As soon as she was settled comfortably in her chamber, he sought out his own bed and slept heavily.

"All this fuss," Agnes whispered through cracked lips.

Simon's brow creased as he gazed down at his wife's pale face. "You've been weak and feverish for days."

Gwen held a cool cloth to her mother's forehead while the physician prepared a lungwort and lemon balm to aid in sweating out the fever. "Simon, why didn't you notify me sooner?"

"I thought she would get better," he admitted sadly. "Had I known it was this serious…"

His eyes became shiny with tears and Gwen reached out to clasp his hand. "We'll do all we can for her."

An hour later Gwen was on her knees in the private chapel, fervently praying for her mother's recovery.

By midday the sun shone brightly, thus melting much of the snow. Nick, Gwen, and Simon were about to partake of the midday meal when one of the guards on the battlements cried out. Richard's army approached, causing quite a stir within the household since his visit was unexpected. Nick ran out to greet him and Gwen followed suit, proudly holding out the welcome cup for her father-in-law. She noticed that the horse's legs and hooves were caked with mud.

Richard took the cup, drank the wine, and dismounted. He and his men were clad in hauberks with swords at their sides; an army ready for battle. "I'm here to collect my soldiers," he said.

"What happened?" Nick inquired.

"Edward is consorting with the northern barons—he's inciting a rebellion."

"You got this information from Will?"

"Aye. The king has been apprised of Edward's treachery and has declared the Bishop of Rochester a traitor; an enemy of England. My brother is one of the most wanted men in the kingdom. The king is meeting me tomorrow in East Anglia, so I must leave now."

Nick hated to leave his pregnant wife and sick mother-in-law, but duty compelled him to join his father. "Gwen, I must go with him."

"Oh, no," she whispered.

Nick put his lips to her ear. "How can I refuse to help my father after all he has done for us?"

"But, my mother," Gwen blurted out.

Richard looked at her askance and Nick explained, "Agnes and Simon are here. Agnes is sick."

"Your mother is a strong woman." Richard said consolingly. "She will recover."

Gwen met his gaze. "I hope you're right, my lord."

Richard offered her a tight smile. "My prayers will be with her."

Nick motioned to his squire and the young man ran out to saddle his master's horse. "I'll don my hauberk and fetch my sword."

Richard noticed that Gwen looked tired and said kindly, "You should rest, Gweneth, for your sake and that of your unborn child. Beatrice is already making preparations to be here for the birth."

"I'm grateful for that."

There was an awkward silence and Gwen suggested that he come inside to partake of some refreshment. Richard declined, stating that they had more than enough provisions. He could see that Gwen was distraught and was holding back tears.

"Gweneth…"

"My lord?"

"Everything will be fine," Richard assured.

Nick returned in his war gear and Gwen gasped involuntarily; he looked so menacing. The hauberk was stretched across his muscular shoulders, and in his right hand he carried the mighty sword Beatrice had given him years ago.

Richard felt proud in that moment. "I'll wait outside the gates," he said in order to allow the young couple a bit of privacy.

"Godspeed, my lord," Gwen said to her father-in-law.

Richard inclined his head, mounted his horse, and rode away. Nick and Gwen stared at each other before he bent his head and kissed her lips. The kiss was passionate and tender at the same time.

Gwen suddenly flung her arms around his neck. "Please don't go. Don't leave me."

"These men swore fealty to me, Gwen. I am duty and honor bound to fight alongside them. I'll return to you soon," he promised softly in her ear.

"I love you," she said, squeezing him tightly.

"And I love you."

She kissed the gold and ruby crucifix around his neck, then tucked it beneath the leather tunic he wore over his hauberk. "Now it's closer to your heart," she said, holding back tears. "Be careful, my love."

Nick smiled down at her before heading toward the courtyard. Gwen watched him walk away, admiring his powerful, feline grace. He mounted his horse in one smooth motion, turned to look at her once more, then mouthed the words: *I love you*.

An inexplicable fear took possession of Gwen and she began to tremble. She couldn't control the hot tears that streamed down her face as she watched her husband and father-in-law lead the army north. She stood in the doorway until she could no longer see them in the distant fields.

"Godspeed, my love," she said aloud, then turned to go upstairs in order to tend to her sick mother.

***

Richard gazed across the moonlit terrain and saw nothing.

Stephen's army should have been at the meeting point by now. According to his spies, Edward had taken residence in a nearby fortress and his mercenaries were camped out by the shore.

The sound of a twig snapping underfoot made Nick unsheathe his sword. "Father," he whispered.

Richard's hand was on the hilt of his sword. "Wait." He breathed a sigh of relief as the figure of a wiry man emerged from the darkness.

"My lord, the bishop is supping with one of the clergymen in town," Will said.

"When did Edward arrive?"

"We arrived this morning."

"How many men are with you?" Nick asked.

"Two hundred, my lord," Will replied.

"Father, we're severely outnumbered."

"Aye, but Stephen and his men should be here soon, and he'll have more than both of our armies put together."

Nick glanced around. "So, do we wait to attack?"

"Yes. There's no need to shed blood until the king arrives." Richard said. "If Edward has any scruples, he'll surrender."

Nick knew his father's reason for not smiting the traitors immediately was due to practicality and not cowardice. Wars were expensive, and noblemen sought to preserve their armies and resources for as long as they possibly could.

"We'll remain here and wait," Richard instructed. "Go now, Will, before someone discovers your absence."

Will bowed and obediently disappeared through the trees. He had not walked fifty paces into the forest before someone pounced on him, and put a knife to his throat. "The bishop was right about you, Will," said the man who held him captive.

Will tried to remain calm, but the cold steel against his skin was making it difficult to do so. The man's breath was a putrid combination of rotting teeth and stale ale. A figure materialized from behind one of the trees. To Will's horror, it was the bishop himself.

"Thank you, Will, you have served me well. Such a shame it has to be the last time," Edward said coolly, then flicked his wrist.

The man slit Will's throat then cleaned the knife on the front of his greasy leather tunic. Will opened his mouth to protest, but only faint gurgling noises came out. He fell face first into the dirt.

"Well done," Edward said to the man. "Now, get the rest of the men."

The last time Edward met with Will, the spy claimed that he had 'nothing to report,' which was highly unusual. Will *always* had some tidbit of information to impart. Suspicious, Edward sent someone to spy on Will.

Richard and Nick were quietly pondering their current situation when they heard a battle cry.

Richard began shouting commands and his soldiers wasted no time obeying them. Within minutes, the men were ready with swords and shields in hand. The thunderous sound of hooves pounding the earth simultaneously filled the night. The soldiers looked to their lord for instruction.

"Hold," Richard shouted.

The rumble got closer.

Richard raised his arm. "Archers, ready!"

The best archers were already lined up in position with arrows pointed toward the trees. Behind them were rows of soldiers on horseback.

"Hold," Richard shouted again.

The horses whinnied and stomped, the anxiousness of the soldiers palpable in the tension-filled air. Even Nick, a seasoned fighter, was fidgeting in the saddle.

At the sight of Edward's mercenaries emerging from the trees, Richard lowered his arm. *"Now!"*

The arrows made a whirring noise as they cut through the air and hit their targets. Several of Edward's men were immediately killed and others fell, wounded.

"Again!" Richard commanded.

The archers quickly reloaded their bows and fired again, causing more of Edward's men to fall.

It was normally Richard's strategy to utilize the archers as much as he could before sending in the riders and foot soldiers. This was practical in terms of expenditure and deterred the enemy's army, making them weaker.

He had the archers reload two more times before ordering forth his mounted horsemen. Since many of Edward's men were injured or killed, the odds had evened out between the two forces.

English sword clashed against English sword. Nick had never fought with his fellow countrymen, and it seemed morally wrong to do so. He tried to maintain his position close to his father, but it was difficult. The fighting went on for a long time before Stephen's army arrived on the scene.

Edward's army was soon surrounded and forced to surrender. Edward, who fought defensively on the outskirts of battle, attempted to flee. Nick chased after him, with Richard following close behind.

Nick urged his horse into a hard gallop, then reached out for the reins of his uncle's steed, gripping them tightly in his right hand. Yanking with all his might, he forced the beast to slow its pace. The leather cut into the flesh of Nick's hand, but he was determined not to let the bishop escape.

Once the horse came to a complete halt, Edward sat still and silent in the saddle with his head lowered. Richard and two of his knights came up beside them. One of the men disarmed the bishop by taking his sword.

Richard sneered at his brother. "It is over, Edward. The king will hang you for treason." When Edward said nothing, he lowered his voice and added, "I'll make sure the last thing you see before you die is my face."

Nick glanced at his uncle in confusion. Why wasn't the bishop responding?

Richard continued, "Did you really think you could hide forever, you coward."

Many of the soldiers urged their horses closer in order to witness the bitter exchange between the two brothers. The powerful Bishop of Rochester was being humiliated and brought low before everyone.

Richard spat at his brother. "I hope you burn in Hell!"

Edward finally met Richard's gaze and smiled slyly. With lightning speed he removed the sharp knife hidden in his belt. Nick, who was still beside Edward holding his horse's reins, suddenly felt the wind being knocked out of him.

"No!" Richard cried, jumping down from the saddle and running to his son.

Nick looked down and saw the hilt of Edward's knife protruding from his chest. He glanced at the soldiers then at his father with a bewildered expression. Richard's men had Edward surrounded, each one holding a sword inches from the bishop's throat.

"My God!" Richard cried as he helped his son dismount and recline on the grass.

Nick felt an excruciating pain in his lungs and knew he was going to die. Both lungs would soon be filled with blood and cut off his air supply. He had witnessed many Infidels die in this manner.

Richard held his son in his arms. "I'm sorry for everything, my son. I shouldn't have gone to fetch you in Surrey. I should have let you stay with your wife…oh, God forgive me!"

"Take care of Gwen and the child," Nick whispered.

"Of course…they'll have the best of everything," Richard assured. *How was he going to break the news to Gweneth?*

"Give her this," Nick said as he struggled with the top of his tunic. Richard helped him remove the gold and ruby crucifix from around his neck. "Tell her I've never loved any woman but her…"

Richard nodded, the tears stinging his eyes.

Nick's face was white in the moonlight, his brow covered in a sheen of sweat. He swallowed hard. "Thank you—and mother—for everything…" The pain was unbearable, but he fought to maintain consciousness. "Tell Gwen…*I'll see her in Heaven.*" The last sentence had been uttered in an almost inaudible whisper as Nick took his last breath.

"God forgive me," Richard said before crossing himself and crying out in pain.

How could God be so unjust?

Edward looked down his nose at his brother and chuckled. "I've taken *two* sons from you, Richard."

Richard's soldiers lowered their swords at the bishop's callous comment. They knew better than to deprive their master of the pleasure of killing his enemy. Richard raised his sword with both hands and let out a mighty cry as he ran toward Edward, the blade swinging wildly. Edward's muscles tensed as he prepared to die. Much to everyone's surprise, however, Richard stopped short. Edward looked puzzled.

"Death is too good for you, Edward…too *easy*," Richard said menacingly.

Edward appeared utterly mortified by his brother's comment. It was now Richard's turn to laugh, and he did so—*maniacally*.

"Oh, no, no…death is *far* too good," Richard sneered.

Stephen, who had witnessed the entire scene, applauded in approval. Richard turned to face his king. "Well said, Lord Richard…a very wise choice. Death would be far too good, indeed. Since you've endured so much loss due to your brother, and since you're the one who alerted me to his traitorous plan, I'll allow you to decide what's to be done with him."

Richard thought for a moment. "I would have him stripped of everything he owns until he is as poor as a beggar. He should be publicly humiliated and sentenced to live in dire solitude within your royal dungeons until the day he dies." He paused, eyeing his brother with contempt. "I can't think of a worse punishment, sire."

"Neither can I," the king stated. "As for your son, he will be given an honorable burial for his bravery as a loyal knight. I'm sorry for your loss, my friend."

Edward appeared truly frightened as the king's men tied him up. The prospect of spending life in a dark, dank cell would terrify anyone, especially someone like Edward who lived for his material comforts. Death would have been preferable.

The two brothers locked eyes. Richard recalled their days as children, when Edward would follow his big brother around like a shadow. How had it come to this? As if reading Richard's mind, Edward's eyes watered. Was that regret Richard saw in them? If so, it was far too late for redemption. There was a gripping pain in his belly as he averted Edward's gaze. His heart sank to low depths as he turned his horse around and urged it southward.

***

The sun was rising over the distant hills as Gwen entered her bedchamber. She had sat by her mother's side throughout the entire night. The high fever had made her mother incoherent, but Richard was right; Agnes was strong. The fever broke before dawn, and Simon insisted that Gwen rest at least for a little bit. Reluctantly, she agreed.

Dropping to her knees, she thanked God for sparing her mother's life. She also prayed for Him to watch over her husband and father-in-law while they were away fighting for the king.

"Amen," she said aloud and crossed herself.

Rising to her feet, she rubbed her lower back and winced. It seemed that every muscle of her body ached and her eyes burned from exhaustion. The baby in her belly was kicking hard, no doubt feeling his mother's agitation. Eunice had already turned down the bed, and there was a ceramic mug filled with hot mulled wine. Gwen drank deeply, and without bothering to change her clothing, dropped onto the soft bed and fell asleep immediately. A few hours later, she awoke to the sound of Eunice's voice.

"*Lady Gweneth…*"

Gwen sat up groggily.

Eunice stood at the foot of the bed, anxious. "It's your mother, my lady, she's awake and asking for you."

Gwen found Simon wearing a huge grin and holding Agnes's hand. "It's a miracle," he said simply.

"How do you feel, Mother?"

"I'm famished," Agnes replied.

Gwen turned to one of the servants. "Fetch some bread and broth."

"And boiled eggs," Agnes added.

The fire in the hearth burned brightly and it was almost too warm. Simon opened the window shutters just a crack to allow fresh air into the room. Peering through the opening, he said, "Look, Gwen."

Gwen pushed open the shutter. In the distance, she saw the Fitzwilliam banner billowing in the breeze. It was Richard's army. "They're home!" she cried excitedly. "I'm going to the battlements to get a better view."

Simon watched the approaching army, his brow creasing deeply in concern. When he turned around, Gwen was gone.

Gwen was filled with joy that her mother had recuperated, and now her husband was home. After the stress of the last few days, she felt as if a heavy load had been lifted from her shoulders.

Gwen fetched a warm cloak from her chamber before entering the tower that led to the battlements. She looked forward to the spring when she could go up there and admire the green fields and trees of the encroaching forest. Her step was light and she hummed softly as she ascended the spiral stairs.

It had only been a few days, but she missed Nick—his kiss, his touch, his company. They would celebrate Agnes's recovery then they would make love, and she would have him remain in bed with her until late afternoon.

The door that led to the rooftop was thick and made of solid oak studded with iron. Gwen couldn't open the door, no matter how much she pushed and pounded. She saw Simon coming up the last curve of the stairwell toward her. His face was as white as a sheet. "What is it, Simon? You look as though you have seen a ghost."

Simon said nothing, but continued to stare at her with troubled eyes.

"I can't open this door," Gwen said. "Will you try?"

He hesitated. "Let's go downstairs."

"What's wrong with you? Please open the door."

Defeated, he averted his eyes. "As you wish."

It took three strong shoves to open the massive door. Gwen ran to the edge of the stone ramparts. She could see the army more clearly from this vantage point.

"Do you see Nick?" she demanded, her hand shading her eyes from the sun.

Gwen's eyes took in the mourning flag before turning to the familiar war horse trotting alongside her father-in-law. Nick wasn't in the saddle. She felt a sudden sinking feeling in her chest and she knew.

She knew.

Mad Margaret's prophecy…fulfilled. She had been given her mother in exchange for Nick. The world spun out of control and she felt the ground give way beneath her feet. Simon caught her before she fell.

Richard arrived at Penway Manor and went up to Gwen's chamber where she lay motionless on her bed.

"She knows, my lord," Simon informed Richard. "She saw you from the battlements."

Richard knelt by the bed and took Gwen's hand in his; it was cold and limp. "Forgive me."

Her eyes stared upward blankly and Richard knew she was still in shock.

He bent over her hand and gave in to bitter tears.

Simon had the courtesy to walk out of the chamber in order to give him some measure of privacy. After wiping his eyes roughly with the back of his hand, Richard reached into the pouch at his side and took out the crucifix. He placed it in Gwen's hand and closed her fingers around it before taking his leave.

Simon waited until almost evening in order to tell Agnes that Nick was dead; he wanted to make sure the fever did not return.

"My God," Agnes cried, her eyes filling with tears. "Our little Nick…"

Simon nodded sadly. "Richard has left for Kent. His wife will be devastated."

Agnes shook her head sadly at the thought of Beatrice. A mother's worse nightmare was to lose a child, and she had lost two sons. "I need to see Gwen."

"You're not yet fully recovered, Agnes."

"She shouldn't be alone," Agnes pointed out.

Simon gripped his wife's hand. "I'll check on her."

The thought of her daughter needing her gave Agnes renewed strength. She would mourn for Nick later, but now she had to be strong for Gwen.

Agnes made her way to her daughter's chamber and paused in the doorway. "I had to come to her, Simon."

He didn't argue with his stubborn wife, but instead helped her to settle in beside her daughter. Gwen embraced her mother and cried like a child. Agnes gave Simon a look and he left the room.

"Oh, Gwen…we all loved him, but no one as much as you," Agnes said softly. "But now you must be strong for the sake of your child. I know how you feel, my sweet girl. I went through the same thing."

"It hurts so much…"

"Nothing consoled me when Tom died—except *you*. Tom lived in you, just as Nick will live in your child."

Gwen wept uncontrollably. "Oh, Nick…"

Agnes stroked her daughter's cheek. "You and I have loved and have been loved in a way that many women only dream of. Like your father, Nick died young—in the prime of life, but he left behind so much. I'll never regret loving Tom and you should never regret loving Nick." Gwen met her mother's eyes. Agnes smiled slightly and wiped the tears from Gwen's cheek. "Be thankful to God for the time you two enjoyed together."

"I am grateful, Mother. I love him so much."

"And he will always love you, Gwen."

Gwen looked down at the gold and ruby crucifix in her hand, then placed it around her neck. Nick would live in her heart forever.

Chapter 26
Surrey, England
Spring 1150

"Push, my lady!"

Gwen gritted her teeth against the pain and pushed with all her might. Beatrice and Agnes were present for the birth, and both women sympathized with her pain.

The midwife shouted, "Add more feverfew to the fire!"

"No!" Gwen cried. "I detest that vile smell."

"I hate it, too," Beatrice admitted softly.

"Very well, my lady," the midwife conceded. "Push!"

Gwen had been in labor for hours, and was spent from exhaustion.

"You can do it, Gwen," Agnes urged.

Gwen took a deep breath, pushed hard, and felt the baby come out. Beatrice and Agnes craned their necks to catch a glimpse of the child, and both of them smiled.

"What is it?" Gwen asked wearily.

"A fine boy," the midwife announced triumphantly.

Gwen closed her eyes in relief. She would have loved either sex, but a son would have pleased Nick.

The midwife cleaned the baby, wrapped him in linen, and handed him to Gwen.

"Hello," she cooed sweetly.

Both grandmothers were around the child. The boy's eyes were as gray as his father's, and the downy hair on his head the color of honey.

"He looks exactly like Nick did when he was born," Beatrice commented tearfully.

"He's precious," Agnes said, smitten.

Richard, who had been waiting outside, approached the bed and regarded his grandson with pride. The future Earl of Kent and his mother would be provided with the very best for as long as they lived.

"What will you name him, my lady?" the midwife asked.

"I shall name him Richard Thomas Fitzwilliam," she said. "It would have pleased Nick."

Both Richard and Agnes were touched by her choice. Gwen held the child close and kissed the top of his soft head. The boy's eyes were wide open and he looked around at everyone with curiosity. He seemed full of life and wonder. Suddenly, his tiny hand shot out and took hold of the gold and ruby crucifix around Gwen's neck. She had never taken it off since the day Richard had given it to her, not even when she bathed.

"That belonged to Nick, your father," she said softly to her son. "Actually, his name was Nicodemus St. John and I was the one who bestowed that name upon him. It's quite a story, and I'll tell you about him someday when you're older."

Gwen held the baby close and kissed him tenderly. She knew in her heart that Nick was looking down on them and, for the first time since his death, she faced life with a renewed sense of hope and joy.

Did you enjoy this novel? The author would appreciate your review on Amazon. Thank you.

Turn the page for a sample of the intriguing bestseller, SABINA: A Novel Set in the Italian Renaissance.

SABINA

A Novel Set in the Italian Renaissance

C. DE MELO

Copyright 2009 C. De Melo
www.cdemelo.com
All rights reserved
ISBN-13: 978-0999787809 (C. De Melo)
ISBN-10: 0999787802

"Let all Italy know, and all Christendom too, of the power, the strength, and the glory that the Florentines have at present in Tuscany."

–Historian Benedetto Dei describing "Florentie bella" in the book: *La cronica dall'anno 1400 all'anno 1500.*

CHAPTER 1
LUCCA, TUSCANY
AUGUST 1, 1477

It was the first day of August and mercilessly hot. Not a single drop of rain had fallen for nearly a month, causing the crops, livestock, and Tuscans to suffer. Sabina Rossi sat on a stone bench outside her father's villa quietly reading a book, its pages well-worn from frequent use. It was a special book, and she took great pains to keep it hidden from her father's prying eyes.

Placing her fingertip on the page, she looked up at the cloudless sky. The endless expanse above her head was lapis lazuli, the noble blue favored by artists when painting the Madonna's cloak. She gazed into the distance, visually tracing the uneven line of Monte Pisano, the mountain separating Lucca from its rival city, Pisa. According to legend, God had deliberately placed it there to prevent the *Lucchese* from looking at the *Pisani*.

The distant bells of San Michele broke her reverie, and she recalled to mind its colonnaded façade. At the church's pinnacle, flanked by two angels, stood a large statue of St. Michael spearing the great dragon. Each metal feather of his sculpted wings quivered in the wind, making it seem as if the archangel could take flight at any given moment.

The crow at Sabina's feet hopped around to capture her attention. Throwing another crumb from the chunk of stale bread in her lap, she inquired sweetly, "Still hungry, Mendi?"

The savvy bird visited her about the same time every day in order to receive a free meal, so she eventually nicknamed it Mendi—a shortened version of *mendicante*, or beggar.

"Sono disgraziato!"

Startled by the sound of her father's voice, Sabina tossed the book into a nearby rosemary bush as Mendi flew away with an agitated cry.

Don Antonio strode into the courtyard. "Where are you?"

"Here, Papa," Sabina replied.

The old man stomped toward his daughter with a scowl on his face. "Why do you disgrace us? Have you no shame?"

"What's wrong?" she asked, her face as innocent as an angel's.

"You continue to swim naked after I strictly forbade you to do so! People will think you're a common slut!"

"No one was around, so I decided to take a quick swim."

"No one was around, eh? Donna Francesca saw you on her way home from the market. She was so shocked that she dropped her basket. What were you thinking?"

"It's so hot, Papa. Who wouldn't relish the feel of cool water on their skin on a day like this? I didn't mean to offend anyone."

"Sabina!" Cecilia exited the villa carrying a potted plant with her three year old son, Paolo, in tow. "Did you pluck the leaves from my basil plant?"

Sabina regarded her older sister with disdain. Since the death of her husband, Cecilia had ceased to care for her appearance and had gained weight. The twenty-three-year-old widow looked tired and matronly.

"Well? Did you?" Cecilia pressed, frowning at the bare stems.

Don Antonio peered at Sabina suspiciously. "You're not still concocting silly love potions for those stupid village girls, are you?"

Although she remained silent, he saw the familiar look of guilt on her face and proceeded to administer a sound beating. Sabina cringed from the assault as Cecilia attempted to placate their father.

The old man eventually regained his composure and balled his hands into fists. "What am I going to do with you, Sabina?"

Paolo spotted the book in the rosemary bush and picked it up.

Cecilia moved toward her son. "What do you have there?"

Sabina snatched the book from her nephew's hands and placed it behind her back. "It's only a silly book of poetry."

"Let me see it," Don Antonio demanded.

Sabina shook her head and his face darkened in anger. Knowing her father's temper, she relented.

He leafed through the pages. "A book of poetry, eh?"

"Papa—"

"Not only do you sit here reading books of witchcraft, but you lie to *me*—your own father!"

"It's not witchcraft, it's botany."

"Botany, my elbow! You should be reading the Bible or reciting prayers or anything that may save that soul of yours, which I'm certain is bound for Hell!" Turning to Cecilia, he added, "Why didn't you stop her from committing such mischief today?"

"I was gone for most of the afternoon," Cecilia explained. "Donna Filomena is sick, so I helped her look after the baby."

Don Antonio sighed tiredly, then narrowed his eyes at Sabina. "When you're not writing silly poems, you're reading silly books."

"You simply lack appreciation for literature, Papa."

"I *do* appreciate literature," the old man corrected. "What I don't appreciate is a rebellious daughter. Why can't you be like Cecilia? She goes to church willingly, while you have to be forced. She engages in Christian works, while you mix potions. Cecilia has never given me reason to worry, but you give me nothing but grief!" He paused, his face a mask of anger. "As God is my witness, I will see you married before the month's end. I've already begun discussing the arrangements."

"Arrangements?"

"I'm planning your future," he said, calmly adjusting his sleeve.

Sabina smiled, unfazed. "Very well."

"You're going to marry Signore Tommaso Caravelli."

The exceptionally wealthy widower lived in Florence. Twice married and still without an heir to inherit his sizeable fortune, he was one of the most sought-after men in Tuscany.

Sabina stood, the smile vanishing from her face. "That's quite funny, Papa…I almost believe you."

"You *should* believe me."

"I would rather you marry me off to a Pisano than to that old Florentine! He's almost old enough to be your father!"

"Bite your tongue, girl! Signore Tommaso is several years younger than I am, and strong enough to keep you in line."

Despite the harm done to her precious basil plant, Cecilia interceded on her sister's behalf. "Father, you cannot be serious. Signore Tommaso is in his fifties—he's far too old for Sabina."

"He's exactly forty-nine."

Cecilia winced. "That's a thirty-year age difference."

The old man snorted. "I'm getting too old for your sister's constant mischief. She needs a husband—not a foolish young man with his head in the clouds—but a strong man with worldly experience who won't tolerate her impudence." When Sabina shook her head defiantly, he added, "If you refuse to marry him, I will personally escort you to the convent of your choice."

"I'll be good, I promise," Sabina said. "I'll never swim naked or do anything that upsets you."

He crossed his arms. "You'll be obedient and do as I say."

Sabina crossed her arms, too. "I will not marry him."

"Do you realize how wealthy he is? Or the kind of life he can provide for you? There are countless women who would jump at the chance of marrying such a man."

"Then let him choose one of those women for his bride."

"You stupid, foolish girl! I should beat you until some good sense enters that hard head of yours."

Sabina's chin began to quiver. "Please, Papa…"

Don Antonio almost felt pity, then he remembered how she had recently cost him a considerable sum by letting out the neighbor's goat as a prank. The animal never returned, forcing him to offer monetary compensation. "You will either marry Tommaso or dedicate your life to God. The choice is yours to make."

"That's what I should have done at your age," Cecilia mused aloud.

Sabina frowned at her sister. "What?"

"I should have become a nun instead of getting married. They must enjoy a peaceful existence."

"Well, that kind of dull life may be appealing to you, but not to me."

"There's nothing wrong with dedicating your life to God," Don Antonio snapped. "It's a selfless and noble endeavor. Perhaps a convent would be a better choice for you, after all."

"Forgive me, Papa," Sabina said contritely. "I meant no disrespect."

His expression softened. "I can't continue to support you forever. Tommaso is willing to wed you without a dowry because he's desperate for an heir, and needs a strong young bride to provide him with one."

Sabina pursed her lips. "You expect me to be grateful?"

"You have no dowry."

"No, but I'm a Rossi. Does our noble name not account for anything? I'm sure our blood is purer than the common sludge coursing through Tommaso's veins."

"Our noble name is *all* we have now—a chance like this will not present itself again." Don Antonio was aware of his daughter's stunning beauty and how it drew the attention of the local men. Her chastity was in constant danger, so the sooner the girl was married, the better. "Tommaso is dining with us tomorrow evening."

"*Tomorrow*? When were you planning to tell me?"

The old man's patience was exceeding its limit. "I was on my way to tell you now, only Donna Francesca intercepted me at the gate. Tommaso wants to meet you before the official betrothal."

"Of course. All men wish to inspect a broodmare before making a purchase. I'm assuming it won't matter if I like him or not, will it?"

"*Sabina is going to marry Signore Tommaso! Sabina is going to marry Signore Tommaso!*"

Hearing her nephew's childish taunt, Sabina ran into the house and went straight to her small bedchamber, bolting the door. Going to the window, she gazed at the neat rows of olive trees growing beyond the stone walls of the courtyard. Her late grandfather, Bernardo, had planted those trees before her father was born. They were tall and thriving now, but barely producing enough crop to make a profit.

Sabina was in this miserable predicament because of her grandfather and his bad gambling habit. She couldn't be angry with him, however. In life, Bernardo had been a charming man whom she had loved dearly.

"Open up," Cecilia cried from the other side of the door.

Ignoring her sister, she looked past the olive trees to the distant hills of the sun-scorched landscape. The grass was the color of straw thanks to the unusually dry summer. Oh, how she desperately longed for rain.

The Republic of Venice was never scorched or dry. In fact, there was plenty of water in La Serenissima; the very streets there made of it! She could run away to Venice and...

And what, you silly girl?

Shortly after her mother's death, her father became ill. He eventually recovered, but his health was never the same. Money was tight and the lack of decent suitors put a strain on the Rossi finances. To make matters worse, Cecilia was forced to return home with an extra mouth to feed after her husband died. Her father was right; he could not support the four of them forever. She would have to marry Tommaso.

"Sabina, please open the door," Cecilia implored.

"Go away. Leave me alone."

"Papa is right. You won't get another opportunity like this one. Stop behaving like a spoiled brat and be grateful."

"If you feel so strongly about it, sister, then you should marry him!"

She expected an angry reply, but instead she heard Cecilia's frustrated sigh and retreating footsteps.

Chapter 2

Sabina's contrary mood the following day prompted Don Antonio to threaten his daughter once again with a cloistered life in a remote convent. She was ordered to bathe and prepare for the evening's festivities while Cecilia and two kindly neighbors cooked an elaborate meal to impress their guest of honor.

Sabina spent a considerable amount of time fuming and pacing the floor of her bedchamber. Rather than wear something pretty for the special occasion, she chose a somber black frock with high neckline and long sleeves. Unmarried girls usually wore their hair loose—and Sabina was no exception, often allowing her thick, dark locks to cascade down her back. Despite this, she fashioned her hair into a severe style by coiling her tresses into a knot at the nape of her neck. When she was done, she smiled smugly at her reflection in the looking glass.

Cecilia pounded on the bedchamber door. "Make haste, Sabina! Signore Tommaso will be here at any moment."

"I'm almost done," Sabina replied in a cheerful voice.

Don Antonio and Cecilia exchanged a look of hopeful surprise, but when Sabina finally emerged from the room, their faces fell.

"You look like Mother," Cecilia commented.

Don Antonio was about to tell his stubborn daughter to change into something more suitable when he heard a carriage outside the door. "Santo Cristo, he's here." He gave Sabina a stern look and warned, "Behave." She rolled her eyes and crossed her arms. *That wretched girl*, he thought while opening the door for his guest.

"Buona sera! Your presence honors my humble home, Signore Tommaso. Please, come in."

Tommaso mumbled a polite reply, practically pushing past

the old man in order to get a better view of Cecilia and Sabina. The young women gaped in admiration of the Florentine's clothing, correctly assuming that his lavish outfit was worth more than both of their entire wardrobes put together.

Tommaso cut a fine figure in his knee-length black velvet robe trimmed with fox fur. Beneath the robe he wore a tunic fashioned from green silk with silver embroidery around the collar. He offered the sisters a gallant bow while studying each of them in turn. One was plump and rather plain, but she wore a decent gown of good quality linen. The other, although dressed like an austere matron in black, had an exquisite face with eyes the color of emeralds.

Tommaso turned to Don Antonio. "Which one is to be my bride?"

Before her father had a chance to answer, Sabina replied, "I am."

Ah, the beauty is to be mine. Tommaso masked his relief with a grimace. "She doesn't look hearty enough to bear children."

Sabina was about to take a step forward and give a sassy retort, but her sister restrained her with a painful pinch to her upper arm.

"I assure you, she's as healthy as an ox, Signore," Don Antonio gently contradicted. "Sabina will bear you many sons."

Feigning interest in Cecilia, Tommaso asked, "What about her?"

"Oh, my daughter Cecilia is a widow and has a small son."

The Florentine waved his hand dismissively and heaved a theatrical sigh of resignation. "I suppose Sabina will have to do."

"How dare you come in here and—"

Cecilia's hand clamped down over Sabina's mouth.

Tommaso raised an eyebrow. "I see she possesses a fiery spirit, Don Antonio. No wonder you wish to be rid of her."

The old man's face resembled the color of ripe pomegranates as he glared at Sabina, who stared back at him with fearless defiance.

Tommaso continued to study the untamed beauty with amusement. "Please remove your hand from your sister's mouth," he said calmly to Cecilia. "I would hear what she has to say."

Cecilia looked to her father, who nodded with obvious reluctance. Her hand had been so tightly cupped around her sister's mouth that rosy imprints of fingers were splayed across Sabina's cheek.

"Well?" Tommaso prompted. "Go on and speak your mind."

"How dare you come in here and inspect us as though we were farm animals that you wish to breed. How dare you comment on my appearance when you're practically old enough to be my father and—" Sabina was about to make a rude comment about his lack of good looks, but it would be untrue. Tommaso's face was lined, yes, but also strong and distinguished—almost handsome.

Tommaso eyed her expectantly. "And?"

Don Antonio stood aside, silently wishing for the earth to swallow him whole while Cecilia nervously bit her lip.

"You should know that I'm not the type who merely sits at home praying over rosary beads and doing needlework," Sabina warned. "I don't plan on changing my ways, either."

"Sabina!" Don Antonio cried.

Tommaso never broke eye contact with Sabina as he placed a hand on the old man's shoulder to restrain him. "I'm devout but not overly zealous, so I don't expect you to pray any more than you already do. Also, I don't need any more tapestries on the walls of my palazzo."

Sabina crossed her arms. "I dislike being told what to do."

Mortified, Don Antonio covered his face with his hands.

"That makes two of us," Tommaso admitted quietly as he patted the old man's back in a gesture of comfort. "Anything else, Signorina?"

"That's all I have to say…*for now.*"

The relief in the air was almost palpable.

"It seems as though you and I have much in common, Sabina," Tommaso said. Turning to Don Antonio, he inquired cheerfully, "Well, when do we eat? I'm absolutely famished."

The three of them stared at him in surprise.

"What can we do about Sabina?" Tommaso asked in response to the curious stares. "Shall we thrash her within inches of her life? It won't change how she thinks or feels, will it? Besides, I like her spirit. I think she'll make a fine wife."

The old man's eyes widened in disbelief. "You still wish to marry my daughter?"

"Of course I do." Taking a step closer to Sabina, Tommaso whispered, "Hopefully, you'll grow to like me someday."

Don Antonio and Cecilia looked immensely relieved as they sat down at the table. Sabina was silent throughout the meal as Tommaso regaled them with tales of his travels. At one point he noticed a book on a stool, carefully bound in red velvet.

Reaching for it, he inquired, "What's this?"

Sabina stood. "Please, Signore, I insist that you give me the book."

Realization dawned on him when he noticed the pages were written by a neat, female hand. "This is your writing."

She was tempted to snatch the book out of his hands, but her father shot her a warning look. "Yes, it is."

"I would love to know what sort of things my future bride writes about." Sabina remained stoically silent. Not wanting to torment the girl further, he relinquished the book. "You have pretty penmanship."

"Thank you," she replied, clasping the book to her chest.

The evening soon came to an end and Don Antonio insisted that his guest spend the night. "After all," he reasoned, "you'll be my son-in-law soon, and I hope you will think of this as your home in Lucca."

"I appreciate the offer, Don Antonio, but I have urgent business early in the morning." Tommaso bent over Sabina's hand, and said in a low voice meant only for her ears, "*Goodnight, Tempesta.*"

Sabina received a thorough tongue-lashing from her father, then helped her sister clean up. Cecilia swept the floor while Sabina scrubbed the plates, lost in thought. She was relieved that Tommaso was not the ogre she had imagined—after all, she could do worse.

Three days later, a messenger from Florence arrived at the villa with a posy and a small wooden box.

Cecilia went to the kitchen door and called out to her younger sister who was picking rosemary in the garden. "Something has arrived for you! Come inside!"

Sabina took the box from her sister's hands once she entered the kitchen. "What's this?"

"Open it and find out."

Sabina opened the box and pulled out a string of pearls. Perfectly round orbs gleamed in the sunlight pouring in from the window.

"Oh, my!" Cecilia exclaimed. "There's a note and flowers, too." She shuffled inside and picked up a piece of vellum from the scarred wooden table. "Here, let me read it to you."

"I can read just fine," Sabina said, taking the note from her sister's hand.

" 'My dearest Sabina…Your beauty and spirit have enchanted me, and I look forward to our next encounter. Until then, enjoy the humble token I have sent you. Your servant, Tommaso.' "

"He's incredibly generous and kind," Cecilia pointed out. "You're a fortunate girl."

Sabina put the necklace on with her sister's help, then placed the flowers in a ceramic pitcher filled with water.

"Sabina? Are you home?"

Cecilia frowned as she peered out the window. "It's that good-for-nothing Marco! You should send him away. Signore Tommaso won't appreciate men visiting you now that you're officially betrothed."

Marco's tall, stocky frame filled the doorway. "I heard you're getting married to Tommaso Caravelli," he said sourly. "Is it true?"

Cecilia took it upon herself to reply. "Yes, it's true. My father has arranged for Sabina to marry—and about time, too!"

Sabina intercepted. "Come with me, Marco."

Cecilia moved to block her path. "Papa and Signore Tommaso wouldn't approve of you wandering off alone with Marco now that you're spoken for."

"I will handle things the way I see fit," Sabina retorted as she exited the house with Marco in tow. When they were out of earshot, she added, "My father is forcing me to marry him."

"What about us?" Marco asked, his brown eyes lacking their usual twinkle. "How will we continue to see each other if you're married and living in Florence?"

Sabina looked over her shoulder to make sure Cecilia was not following them. "Let's walk far from the house."

They followed the stream that snaked behind the olive grove and led into a wooded glen. Hidden beneath a thick canopy of trees, Marco gripped Sabina's shoulders and pulled her against him.

"You're hurting me, Marco."

Easing his grip, he noticed the expensive pearls around her neck for the first time. "Are those from him?"

"Yes."

"My God, what is your father thinking? He's too old for you."

She felt a strange urge to defend Tommaso, but refrained. "There's nothing I can do."

"Marry me, instead."

"What?"

"Marry me."

In all the time they had known each other, and throughout the many embraces they had shared, Marco had never mentioned the word 'marriage.'

When they were children, Marco ran with a pack of older boys who enjoyed making mischief and wreaking havoc on younger, weaker children. He was the imp, the bully who had teased her incessantly—sometimes even cruelly. The moment she blossomed into a young woman, his demeanor toward her changed from aggressive to possessive. At first, she resisted his amorous advances, but he was persistent. To make matters worse, her mother died unexpectedly. With her father overcome by illness and grief, and Cecilia caring for a husband and child, she had no one to turn to for comfort. Marco came to the rescue, filling the sudden, agonizing void in her life with his constant company and piquant humor. In exchange for this emotional salve, she had finally given in to his physical demands.

Although Marco was attractive, their relationship was far from the romantic ones described by troubadours.

"I can't marry you," Sabina stated firmly.

Taking hold of her chin, he bent his head and plundered her mouth. Unable to resist the familiar comfort of his body, she wound her arms around his neck and played with the dark curls at the nape.

"Are you ready to give this up," he asked against her lips, his big hands trailing down the length of her spine.

"I'll learn to live without it, and so shall you."

The house was far enough away to allow Marco to ease Sabina onto the soft grass and lift her skirts. His lovemaking was urgent, and he took his lustful pleasure as selfishly as a common stallion. She bore his considerable weight and hard thrusts placidly, knowing it was the last time they would ever be together in a carnal sense.

Satiated, Marco placed his head on her bosom afterward. Trailing a blade of grass along her collar bone, he said, "Don't marry him."

She stifled a yawn. "I can't disobey my father."

He raised himself on his elbow and stared at her in disbelief. "Since when are you the good, obedient daughter? The role of martyr doesn't suit you at all."

"Hush or I'll find a potion that will turn you into a toad."

"Be careful, Sabina," he warned, his face serious. "You'll end up burned at the stake someday if you continue to make such jests."

Despite Marco's blatant disregard for the divine admonition against the sin of fornication, he came from an extremely devout and superstitious family.

"Who said I was jesting?" she challenged with a twinkle in her eye.

Marco frowned at her in disapproval. He knew the love potions Sabina created for the village girls weren't real—or at least he hoped they weren't. "You try my patience at times."

"Then I've succeeded in my task."

To break the tension, he tickled her roughly. "Vixen!"

"Stop that, Marco Alfani!"

Lowering his head, he kissed her heartily on the mouth. "Marry me."

"I cannot," she replied, wriggling out of his grasp and smoothing the creases from her skirt.

"Let me speak to your father and ask for your hand in marriage."

"No!"

Marco's expression was one of puzzlement verging on anger. "Do you *want* to marry him?"

"Do you realize that you've never told me you loved me? What difference does it make if I marry you or Tommaso? Neither of you love me. I'm only a pawn to be used in a game played by men."

"Please, let me ask your father for your hand."

"Why? Is my marriage to another man an assault on your pride?"

Marco appeared wounded. "I do love you, Sabina."

***

Marco arrived at Don Antonio's villa later that day. Cecilia and Sabina were both in the kitchen preparing supper while Paolo played at their feet.

"Don Antonio, may I have a word with you, please?" he said from the doorway as he fidgeted nervously with his hands. Despite the August heat, he had worn his best wool tunic in an attempt to look presentable and there was a sheen of perspiration on his brow.

Don Antonio eyed the uninvited guest suspiciously. He never cared much for the young man who eyed his daughter like a stud seeking to rut, but said, "Come in, Marco. What can I do for you?"

Marco cleared his throat. "As you know, sir, I'm a simple

man but I come from a decent family."

"Yes, your father is a good man and I've known him for many years."

Encouraged by this, Marco continued, "I don't have much now because I'm still young, but I'm a hard worker. I would like to ask—"

"—for my daughter's hand in marriage."

"Yes, I want to marry Sabina."

"She is already spoken for."

"But, Don Antonio—"

"I'm sorry, Marco. The answer is no."

Although his pride was deeply wounded, Marco inclined his head respectfully and gave Sabina a wistful glance before taking his leave.

Don Antonio sat down at the table and allowed his daughters to set a plate of steaming stewed tripe before him. "Have you been allowing Marco to court you?" he asked, staring pointedly at Sabina.

Sabina poured wine into his cup and re-corked the bottle. "You know how Marco has always been fond of me."

"That's not what I asked you."

"We are not courting."

Cecilia snorted. Don Antonio glanced at his eldest daughter before fixing his gaze on Sabina. "Well, whatever is going on between you two must end. *Now.* You're going to be married soon, and I will not have you sullying yourself or our family name, do you understand?"

"Yes."

"I'm serious, Sabina."

Placing a loaf of bread on the table, she said, "I know, Papa."

"Don't worry, Father," Cecilia said. "Sabina is not so foolish as to throw away her entire future."

"I hope you're correct," he said. "I'm entrusting her into your care."

Cecilia's eyebrows shot upward. "Into my care?"

"Yes. From now until the wedding day, don't let your sister out of your sight."

Chapter 3
Florence, Tuscany
August 28, 1477

Was there ever a city more glorious than Florence? It was no wonder the royal courts of Europe recognized it as the epicenter of art, culture, and classical expression. Tommaso had sent a carriage to fetch his bride and her family a few days before the wedding. When the vehicle passed through the massive city gates, Don Antonio pointed out the Medici crest—a gold shield with several red balls. Since the Medici commissioned many public artworks and paid for structural repairs, the family's coat of arms was ostentatiously displayed throughout the city. This cunning strategy served as a visual testament to any foreigner entering Florence that Medici authority was both unchallenged and absolute.

The horses were forced to slow their pace within the crowded streets, thus allowing the occupants inside the carriage to marvel at the grand palazzos and public statues carved from dazzling white Carrara marble. The elegant piazzas teemed with Florentines, many flaunting expensive jewels and sumptuous clothing. The majority of people wore red, but not just any red; *Florentine Red* was currently the most fashionable color in Europe. Sabina mentally likened it to the color of blood—vibrant, yet deep, and extremely flattering to the complexion. Some wore Florentine Red in the form of plush velvet with a luxuriously thick pile while others sported brocade with decorative flowers and leaves fashioned from gold or silver thread.

"Red everywhere," Paolo chirped.

"What a clever boy you are," Cecilia cooed as she kissed the top of her son's head.

"Florence is overflowing with wealth and it shows," Don

Antonio mused aloud, his gaze fixed on a well-heeled pair of gentlemen.

The city consisted of successful bankers, artists, sculptors, wool and silk merchants, carpenters—too many talented people to mention. The staggering net worth of some bourgeoisie families rivaled that of royal princes.

The carriage turned down an impossibly narrow street and finally came to a stop in front of a long stone wall with an iron-studded wooden door at its center. Above the door was Tommaso's family crest, marking the residence as the Palazzo Caravelli. The carved stone shield portrayed a cylindrical tower with an eagle poised atop Guelph crenellations. Two servants appeared, helping them alight from the carriage. Sabina and her family followed them into a courtyard surrounded by low stone buildings and a tower that appeared to be at least five hundred years old. There was a cistern in the center of the courtyard and a bronze fountain fashioned like a mermaid.

"Welcome," Tommaso said as he emerged from within the shadowy interior of the tower.

Greetings were exchanged, then Sabina eyes were drawn to the ceramic bas-relief sculpture of the Madonna and Christ child adorning the wall behind his head. The exquisitely carved figures, along with the boughs of decorative leaves and fruits framing the charming scene, were painted in brilliant white, yellow ochre, and blue.

Following her gaze, Tommaso smiled. "Do you like it?"

"It's lovely."

"You have good taste. Luca della Robbia's work is in high demand." Taking her hands into his own, he said, "I trust that you'll find your chamber comfortable. If there's anything you or your family requires, please don't hesitate to ask the servants."

She was charmed by his courteous hospitality. "Thank you."

Motioning to the servants, he instructed, "See that our guests are given some refreshment and show the ladies to their bedchambers."

Turning to Don Antonio, he inquired, "Would you care to

take some wine with me under the shade of my fruit trees before going to your room, or would you prefer to rest first?"

"I would be delighted to have some wine with you."

"Very well," Tommaso said as he put his arm around the old man in a friendly gesture. "Ladies, we shall see you at supper."

The cool interior of the palazzo was a relief from the heat outside. Sabina, Cecilia, and Paolo ascended a long flight of stairs separating the servant's ground floor from the *piano nobile*. Sabina took in the attractive surroundings, liking her new home instantly. She smiled in delight when she entered her new private quarters, which were spacious and well-lit. The wide bed boasted a canopy fashioned from the softest yellow silk. The servants had carefully strewn lavender and tansy onto the comfortable straw and down-filled mattress in order to give the bed a pleasant scent while simultaneously repelling bedbugs. There was an antechamber for bathing and a sitting room with a small writing desk.

The Rossi family enjoyed the best of what Florence had to offer, including the hospitality of their gracious host. Sabina, who had always taken an interest in the arts, immediately noticed that the paintings and sculptures of Florence possessed a different style than those of Lucca. Many of the themes were the same—Annunciation of Christ, Madonna Enthroned or the martyrdom of various saints, but in Florence the figures seemed to be alive. The Virgin Mary was often depicted as a pretty young woman flaunting current fashion rather than a stiff matronly figure in traditional dark blue cloak. Instead of static religious effigies, Florentine sculptors adopted the style of ancient Greece and Rome to create idealized gods. One could easily imagine these impressive figures stepping down from their marble pedestals at any moment to walk among the people.

Interestingly, it was common for wealthy Florentine families to commission religious paintings for their private chapels with their own likenesses included in the holy scenes. Family members stood alongside Jesus or their patron saints dressed like royals and dripping in jewels. Sabina wondered if these people were trying to be seen as godly, or if they were attempting to drag God down to their level. Although unsure of the answer, she was certain that Florentine art was magnificent.

Artists, architects, sculptors, writers, philosophers, and musicians thrived under the patronage of guilds and generous commissions from wealthy families. Tommaso mentioned the names of the city's most prominent families and Sabina committed a few of them to memory: Strozzi, Pazzi, Rucellai, and Tornabuoni. Of these great families, none was more generous in their patronage than the powerful House of Medici.

The day before their wedding, Tommaso and Sabina attended Holy Mass in the church where they would be married.

"This is the Basilica of San Lorenzo, a revered church in the city," Tommaso stated proudly. "Brunelleschi, who is considered the most talented architect in the city, designed the basilica's interior."

"Did the Medici pay for this church?" she inquired, her eyes darting to the Medici coat of arms displayed throughout the church.

"Yes."

Sabina was again impressed by the wealth and power of Florence's leading family. "Will I have the honor of meeting them soon?"

"Most certainly."

After the service, Tommaso led Sabina to the front of the church. On the floor before the high altar was a big circle of porphyry, a rare and expensive Egyptian marble the color of mulberries—a stone normally reserved for emperors. "Lorenzo's grandfather, Cosimo, was buried beneath the circle upon which we are standing. So beloved is he by the Florentines that they've bestowed upon him the Latin title of *Pater Patriae*, or—"

"Father of the Fatherland," Sabina supplied.

"Correct," he beamed. "Cosimo adopted the turtle as his personal emblem during his lifetime, thus alluding to his infinite patience. He was a man who waited for the right moment to strike. The great grandfather of Lorenzo, Giovanni di Bicci, was buried in the sacristy beneath that communion table." Sabina followed his pointed finger. "His location is also marked by a circular slab of costly porphyry."

"What about that beautiful porphyry sarcophagus over there?" she asked, indicating the iron grate in the sacristy's wall.

"That's the final resting place of Lorenzo's father, Piero, commonly known as Piero il Gottoso. The Medici are plagued by gout, thus the nickname. Do you see how the sarcophagus rests on four turtles? It's an homage to Cosimo."

The precious materials and prestigious locations of the tombs hinted at the Medici family's enormous pride, but Sabina wisely refrained from voicing such an unkind speculation.

***

The last day of August dawned clear and predictably hot. Tuscany was still in the midst of a drought with no relief in sight. True to her father's words, Sabina would be married before the month was over. Tomorrow was the first of September and, by then, she would be the legal wife of Tommaso Caravelli. She was pleased that her future husband treated her and her family like royalty. She had even been allowed to bring Mendi, who was now calling out loudly from his wired brass cage near the windowsill. The bird took flight at whim throughout the day, yet always returned in the evening to roost.

Every fine lady in Florence possessed a talented lady's maid, so Tommaso had procured one for his bride as a wedding gift. A girl by the name of Teresa plaited Sabina's hair, expertly coiling the braids into two rolls at the top of each ear then tucking the rolls into templers adorned with pearls. She then pinned a length of silk as sheer as mist to the headdress, allowing a measure of the fabric to fall in front of her mistress's face.

Sabina admired her reflection in the highly polished looking glass. The long-sleeved gown she wore was cut from gold brocade with an intricate pearl design sewn into the front panel of a snug-fitting bodice.

A page eventually knocked on the door, signaling that it was time to go. Tommaso had arranged for a litter to carry his bride the short distance to the church.

Don Antonio began his familiar speech the moment he saw his daughter descend the stairs. "We have long since lost the family fortune—thanks to your grandfather's gambling—but our name is still one of great fame, going as far back as—"

"—the first fathers of Tuscany," Sabina interjected with a huff. "I know, Papa. The Rossi family were once the great Guelphs who possessed considerable wealth...*I know*...but we are not rich and we no longer hold any power, political or otherwise."

"Show some respect, Sabina," Cecilia snapped.

Sabina shot Cecilia a withering look before taking her father's hands into her own. "Don't worry, Papa. I won't disrespect our good family name," she assured in a gentler tone.

Hurt by Sabina's initial harshness, Don Antonio nodded sadly.

"Forgive me," Sabina offered before entering the litter.

Cecilia placed her arm around her father's slumped shoulders. "Come, our carriage awaits."

As a rule, Tommaso Caravelli avoided ostentatious behavior whenever possible. Unlike some noblemen who flaunted their wealth by strutting around like peacocks in the latest fashions, he preferred understated elegance. While he adhered to this personal code of conduct, he had no qualms bending the rules where Sabina was concerned. It was a popular custom in Florence for veiled brides to ride to the church on a white horse on their wedding day, but that was not good enough for Tommaso. He insisted that his future wife be transported to the basilica in a gilded litter with the Caravelli crest painted on the door.

Family, friends, and curious onlookers gathered to see Tommaso Caravelli get married—again. They stared at the golden litter as it was carried up the stairs of San Lorenzo by two liveried pages, then gaped as Sabina emerged from the velvet-lined interior with all the pomp of a queen arriving at her own coronation. She walked into the church, drawing the eyes of many lustful men and envious maidens. Tommaso stood by the altar looking handsome in a brocade tunic of deep amber, the golden beads sewn into the fabric gleaming in the candlelight.

The moment Sabina stood beside the groom, the priest began the long, monotonous marriage ceremony. Everyone appeared relieved when Tommaso lifted the sheer veil from the bride's face and kissed her cheek. Invited guests made their way to the Palazzo Caravelli in the blazing heat of the midday sun to partake of the marriage feast.

The lavish meal was served in the spacious main hall, which was airy and cool. The cooks prepared roasted fowl, stag, hare, and swan, each served with various sauces. Fresh breads, aged cheeses, and stewed vegetables accompanied the meats. Honeyed treats of every size and shape mixed with nuts, fruits, or rare spices were available in abundance for those with a sweet tooth. Acrobats and troubadours performed to entertain the many guests as minstrels sang songs of love to honor the newlywed couple.

Sabina sat beside her husband at the high table with a look of sheer amazement on her face. Never in her life had she attended such an extravagant affair!

Tommaso leaned over and whispered, "Are you enjoying yourself, my Tempesta?" She nodded and he smiled in satisfaction. "I did this all for you. I hope you are pleased, Sabina."

For a brief instant, Tommaso resembled a lovesick young man. Did this mean he could be easily swayed? She smiled at the possibility and said, "I'm very pleased. Thank you."

Later, after eating and drinking more than she should have, Sabina wandered away from her husband's side to a staircase located at the far corner of the main hall. Feeling excessively warm, she decided to get away from the revelry and cool off for a bit. Several of the florid-faced guests were already drunk and dancing merrily as she ascended the stairs. At the top was a spacious room with cream-painted walls and a red-tiled floor. There was a big window in the room, its green shutters thrown back to reveal the tiny orange grove in the courtyard below. The wide wooden bench beneath the window was piled high with soft cushions, and it beckoned invitingly.

Sabina sat down and pulled the heavy brocade skirt up past her knees, revealing a set of shapely bare legs. Teresa had tried to convince her to wear stockings for propriety's sake, but flaunting rules for the sake of comfort was nothing new for Sabina. She kicked off her shoes, relishing the deliciously cold tile beneath her toes. Resting her head against the windowsill, she closed her eyes and allowed the breeze to caress her clammy skin. The lazy hum of bumblebees in the courtyard almost lulled her to sleep. After several minutes, she felt a presence in the room and her eyes snapped open.

It was Marco, dressed in a black tunic and hose as if attending a funeral. "*Signora*, should you not be with your husband and your guests?" he inquired drily from the doorway.

She sat up straight, quickly slipping her feet into her shoes. "What are you doing here?"

"An old friend can't offer his congratulations on your wedding day?"

"I know you too well to believe this is your true intention."

His gaze swept over her bare legs, her cleavage, and finally rested on her full mouth. She let her skirt fall to the floor and adjusted her bodice as he sauntered into the room. "So, how does it feel to be the wife of such a wealthy man, *Signora*?"

"Stop calling me that!"

"You are now married, are you not?"

"Yes, but—"

"I'm merely giving a married woman the respect she is due."

He sat beside her on the bench and boldly traced the curve of her breast with his fingertip, compelling her to slap his hand away.

"Marco, I don't know how you got here—or even why you came—but you must leave right now." Ignoring her words, he leaned forward in an attempt to kiss her lips and she shoved him. "I'm serious. Go!"

"You know you'll always be mine," he whispered.

She stood and walked to the center of the room. "Leave now

or I shall be forced to summon my husband's guards."

"You wouldn't dare," he said menacingly.

Tommaso walked into the room and looked from Marco to Sabina. "Some of the guests have been wondering where you went off to, my dear."

Her face paled. "Forgive me, Signore Tommaso. It was sweltering downstairs…I came up here to cool off."

"First of all, you must stop calling me *Signore* Tommaso. I'm your husband now. Secondly, who is this man?"

"Signore—I mean, Tommaso, this is an old family friend," she replied. "He is Marco, son of Signore Niccolò Alfani."

The men nodded to each other without saying a word.

Tommaso offered his arm to Sabina. "If you will excuse us, Signore Marco, my wife and I must return to our guests."

Marco did not move as he silently watched them leave.

"I never want you to be alone with that man again," Tommaso whispered as they descended the stairs. To drive his point home, he gave her arm a painful squeeze. "Do you understand me?"

She winced. "Yes."

He released his vice-like grip. "Good. We shall get along fine if you do as I say."

Obviously, her husband was no lovesick fool, nor would he be easily influenced by feminine wiles.

"Sabina! Come and dance with me," Cecilia called out when she caught sight of her sister.

Sabina allowed herself to be pulled away from Tommaso and into the throng of dancing guests. The smell of sweet perfume, wine, and perspiration permeated the air, making her feel nauseous.

"What in God's name are you doing?" Cecilia demanded.

"What are you talking about?"

"I saw Marco follow you upstairs. Please tell me you haven't done anything dishonorable on your wedding day."

"I'm insulted that you would insinuate such a thing. I didn't even know Marco was here."

"Well, no one invited him. Two of Signore Tommaso's

guards just escorted him outside. What an embarrassment to our family."

"An embarrassment not caused by me, I assure you."

"Don't be stupid and ruin the wonderful opportunity you've been given. You could have married someone poor, like I did." Cecilia sighed. "If only I'd been blessed with your beauty, I would have fared better in life."

Sabina was tired of her sister's constant disparaging comments. "Enough, Cecilia!"

Some of the nearby guests tossed curious glances in their direction, causing Cecilia's cheeks to redden with shame. "How dare you speak to me in such a manner?"

"How dare you insult me on my wedding day! I've endured enough of your reproaches. Papa's too, for that matter."

Cecilia raised an eyebrow. "Now that you've married a man with prestige and wealth, you think you're better than me."

"That's not what I think at all—Cecilia, wait," Sabina protested, but her sister was already walking away.

First her father, then Tommaso, and now her sister. How many more people would she offend today?

Tommaso came to stand beside his wife. "Is anything amiss?"

"Not at all."

He knew harsh words were exchanged between the two sisters, and he was willing to bet they had to do with Marco Alfani. "May I have the pleasure of this dance?"

"Since when does a husband ask permission of his wife?"

"You have much to learn, my dear," he said as he slipped a hand around her slim waist.

Sabina was pleasantly surprised to learn that Tommaso was not only surefooted, but also physically fit for a man of his age.

"Are you feeling unwell?" Tommaso inquired.

"Why do you ask?"

"Your face is flushed."

"Perhaps it was the wine," she lied.

"Perhaps," he repeated. "Tell me, is Marco your lover?"

"Marco?"

"Yes, *Marco*, the man whom you were alone with upstairs during our wedding celebration. Do not bother lying to me, Sabina, I'll know when you do."

"How will you know if I lie?"

"Your lips lie, but your eyes do not. I have dealt with enough people in my life to know when someone is being dishonest, especially women."

She looked away before admitting, "Yes, he was my lover."

"And now?" he demanded, taking hold of her chin and forcing her to meet his gaze.

"Now I'm married and have no lovers."

"Did you invite him here today?"

"No. I didn't know he was here, I swear."

"Are you still in love with him?"

Sabina hesitated. It would be improper either way she responded. If she said "yes," it would threaten her marriage, but if she said "no," she would seem like a whore. She decided to be honest. "I was never in love with him."

"You're telling me the truth."

She nodded. "I was a stupid girl."

He found her honesty refreshing. Of all the women he had known, and he had known many, Sabina Rossi was the most peculiar. She was strong and rebellious but possessed a childlike quality that was almost endearing.

"Good," he said, pulling her against him. "I prefer a stupid girl over a woman who is in love with another man."

Don Antonio tapped Tommaso on his shoulder. "May I have a dance with my daughter on her wedding day?"

Tommaso handed his wife to his father-in-law. Don Antonio beamed with pride. "Signore Tommaso is a fine man, Sabina. I'm certain he will make your life very comfortable and offer you many niceties that I cannot."

"You've given me everything I need, Papa."

"Yes, but you deserve more and I know you want more. You are nothing like your sister, Cecilia, who was content to marry a simple man and now basks in motherhood. Such a dull existence would kill your spirit. Life would have been easier had you been born male, but Fate can be cruel." He paused. "I wouldn't have married you to Tommaso if I didn't think he could provide you with what you need in life."

"What is it that I need?"

"Excitement."

She could not deny it. "Thank you, Papa," she said, kissing his cheek.

Don Antonio narrowed his eyes. "You may think me a simple old man but pay heed to the counsel I'm about to give you. Do not let your heart or your headstrong ways lead you astray."

Sabina rolled her eyes in anticipation of another onslaught of admonitions when her father took both of her hands firmly in his own and pulled her forward. His face was serious, his eyes fearful.

She frowned. "Papa?"

"Listen carefully to what I'm about to say, my child. Be wary now that you are a member of Florentine society. You should know who your friends are but, more importantly, know your enemies. Watch that tongue of yours; be mindful of what you say and to whom you say it. Control your temper. Never reveal anything you do not want repeated—speak little and listen twofold." Don Antonio cast a furtive glance over his shoulder and whispered, "And for God's sake, do not concoct any of your silly potions! Being accused of witchcraft is no trivial matter here in Florence. Signore Tommaso deals with important and influential people, and you would not want to jeopardize your husband's position in society."

Don Antonio's wise words hit Sabina with great impact. As she scanned the room, she noticed several sets of eyes watching her carefully. For the first time since her arrival in Florence, she felt insecure of her new role. She had been afforded a good education and learned basic court manners but never had the opportunity to actually mingle in high society until now.

"Papa, take me home. I don't want to stay here in Florence," she said, gripping her father's hands tightly.

Don Antonio saw the panic in his daughter's eyes and found

her vulnerability disconcerting, especially since it was something she rarely, if ever, displayed. "Now, now, Sabina," he said soothingly. "There's no need for you to fear. You are a lovely young woman and you know how to behave properly. You'll be fine as long as you heed my counsel."

She immediately straightened her shoulders. "You're right, Papa," she said, glancing around the room and coolly meeting the eyes of those who stared in her direction. "I know what to do. I'll be fine."

Don Antonio embraced Sabina and walked away, leaving her alone in the center of the room. With her head held high and several eyes following her, she walked to where Tommaso stood and placed a hand upon his arm.

He gazed down at her and smiled. "Come, dearest, there is someone I want you to meet," he said, leading her through the throng of guests. "Giuliano de' Medici has arrived from Milan only a moment ago and is here to offer his congratulations."

Sabina was led to a group of well-dressed men. The most exquisitely dressed was an attractive young man in his mid-twenties with brown, shoulder-length hair and a serene face. He smiled at Tommaso before embracing him with great affection.

"Giuliano, I'm so happy you could come," Tommaso said.

"I wanted to arrive earlier, but we were delayed," Giuliano explained. Noticing the stunning woman at his friend's side, he added, "Is this bella donna your new bride?"

"Giuliano, may I present to you my wife, Sabina, daughter of Don Antonio Rossi."

The dark eyes that studied Sabina were alert and intelligent. Giuliano stepped forward and gallantly kissed her hand. "It's an honor to meet you, Signora. You are living proof of Tommaso's impeccable taste."

She smiled. "You are too kind, Signore Giuliano."

Giuliano turned to Tommaso. "I congratulate you on finding such a lovely treasure."

"Thank you, my friend. Where is Lorenzo?"

"Unfortunately, my brother was forced to remain in Milan and instructed me to convey his best wishes to you both. He regrets not being able to attend your wedding today."

"I know the business he tends to is urgent; there is no need for him to feel any regrets. I shall see him soon enough."

"You must present your wife at the palazzo when Lorenzo returns," Giuliano said, winking at Sabina. "He will be charmed."

"It will be an honor. Now, please, I want you and your men to eat, drink, and enjoy the festivities," Tommaso said before quickly summoning his servants and instructing them to pay special attention to the Medici entourage.

Giuliano mingled easily with the guests since he knew everyone.

Sabina was duly impressed that her husband was on such friendly terms with the wealthiest and most politically influential family in Tuscany. "How long have you known the Medici brothers?"

"I was a good friend of their father, so I've known them since birth. Before that, my father and their grandfather did business together."

"Oh? What kind of business?"

"Why, banking, of course."

"I see. Do you regularly attend court at their palazzo?"

Tommaso stepped closer to Sabina and lowered his voice. "You must never refer to the Palazzo Medici as a royal court, my dear. It's offensive."

"Forgive me."

He waved away her apology. "You must always keep in mind that Florence is a republic, not a monarchy."

Her brow creased in confusion. "Oh."

"You will be presented to Lorenzo, who, although not being a prince, assumes the role of one." He paused. "Do you understand?"

"So I should treat him like a prince but never call him that to his face."

Tommaso nodded in approval. "Correct."

"And the Palazzo Medici is not an official royal court but it operates as such, although everyone pretends it doesn't because

Florence is a republic."

"I think you'll learn how this city operates very quickly."

The wedding festivities lasted until nightfall. Don Antonio wished many blessings upon the marital union and kissed his daughter's cheek before retiring to his guest chamber. Cecilia also approached her sister and brother-in-law before retiring. She hugged her sister coolly, muttering a blessing on their marriage before heading off to bed.

Later that night, after the guests had gone home, Sabina sat at the dressing table in her bedchamber. Teresa had already helped her mistress out of the wedding gown and was now brushing her hair in the light of three flickering candles.

"You are very lucky, Signora Sabina."

"Why do you say that?"

"Signore Tommaso is a good man who gives with an open hand to those whom he loves. He is always helping people and never asks the cost, which is why God has blessed him with so much wealth."

"How do you know this?"

"My father was cousin to his first wife."

"Tell me about her."

"We're not allowed to speak of her because...Well, she fled with another man."

Sabina hid her surprise. "I see..."

"Signore Tommaso helped us very much after my mother died."

"I'm sorry for your loss, Teresa. My mother is dead, too."

"May her soul be blessed in Heaven," Teresa said before crossing herself and kissing the tiny gold crucifix that hung from a chain around her neck.

"How well do you know my husband?"

"Well enough to assure you that he loathes impropriety and does not tolerate disrespect," she replied candidly.

"I'll keep that in mind."

"He seems very fond of you, Signora Sabina. One of my cousins served as the lady's maid to his second wife, Signora Mariella." Teresa lowered her voice and added, "She and

Signore Tommaso were never in accord. She died in childbirth. The baby died, too."

"What happened to your cousin after her mistress died?"

"She was sent to another Florentine lady across the city."

How clever of her husband to get rid of the girl. It certainly prevented any gossip about the late Signora Mariella. "Anything else I should know?"

Teresa froze, her cheeks bright red in the reflection of the looking glass.

Tommaso stood in the doorway. "Leave us."

Teresa bowed her head. "Yes, Signore Tommaso." She laid down the brush, curtsied to her master and mistress, and started to walk out of the room when Mendi began to caw loudly from within his cage.

Tommaso frowned. "Take that damned bird with you. I know you love that wretched crow, Sabina, but there is room for only one male in your bedchamber tonight."

Teresa retraced her steps and picked up the cage. Mendi, unhappy at being moved, threatened to peck at the girl's hand, but Sabina's sharp reprimand kept him from doing so. Holding the cage as far away from her as she could, the maid hastily vacated the room.

"What do you think of Teresa?" Tommaso asked with feigned nonchalance.

"I like her," Sabina replied cautiously, wondering how much of the conversation he had heard before entering her room.

"Good. I want you to be happy." He stood behind her and placed his hands on her shoulders. "I don't expect you to love me." She stiffened at the unexpected statement and tried to turn around in order to face him, but his grip on her shoulders tightened. "I'm well aware your beauty and youth, Sabina. After seeing what your former lover looks like, I know you'll probably never love me."

"Tommaso, I—"

"Don't interrupt me again," he warned. "Unlike other men, I do not care that my bride is not a virgin. I'm no longer a young man prone to frivolous jealousies, nor do I wish to engage in any hot-tempered duels for the sake of your virtue. Time is precious to me."

He moved her hair aside to expose her nape and bent to kiss the soft skin. "Now that you're my wife, I expect your loyalty and respect. I want you to provide me with a son and not make a cuckold of me. In return, you will be afforded freedoms that are usually denied most women. You can read as many books as you wish, learn any subject you desire—with my approval, of course. I may even share political views with you, but only if you adhere to my conditions. If you refuse to abide by my rules and decide to take on a lover, or dishonor me in any way through improper conduct, you will be cast out of this house in shame. Your reputation will be ruined forever." His hands fell to his sides. "Do we have an agreement, Sabina?"

"Yes, Tommaso."

Without further words, he led her to the bed. Sabina was surprised by the unexpected finesse of his lovemaking. Marco had been lustful and clumsy in comparison with Tommaso's expertise. When they finished, she stared at the exposed timbers on the ceiling. The act itself had been pleasant enough, which was somewhat of a relief.

"You must be tired," he said, kissing her cheek before getting out of bed. "I will retire to my chamber now. Goodnight, Sabina."

"Goodnight, Tommaso, and thank you."

"For what?"

"For everything."

He cast a wry smile over his shoulder and left the room.

Do you want to keep reading? SABINA: A Novel Set in the Italian Renaissance is available on Amazon. Thank you.

Printed in Great Britain
by Amazon